It all began with young, patrician Henrietta—and a night of seduction. Now her descendant, Ariel, discovers what it is to be a Roundtree woman.

". . . you are awakening, Ariel. You will learn the difference between love and the fires of your body. It is in our blood, Roundtree blood. We are like swans. We cannot swim in an empty lake. We are women. We belong in the world. You will walk on coals of fire to be with one man. If you cannot have him, you will make of your days—and nights—what you can . . . with others."

The Roundtree Women

BOOK I
OF THE THRILLING SERIES

THE
Roundtree Women

Book I

Margaret Lewerth

A DELL BOOK

Published by
Dell Publishing Co., Inc.
1 Dag Hammarskjold Plaza
New York, New York 10017

Dell ® TM 681510, Dell Publishing Co., Inc.

ISBN: 0-440-17594-1

Printed in the United States of America

First printing—March 1979

O heaven, O earth, bear witness to this sound,
And crown what I profess with kind event
If I speak true! If hollowly, invert
What best is boded me to mischief! I,
Beyond all limit of what else i' th' world,
Do love, prize, honour you.

Shakespeare's The Tempest

Part One

New Orleans 1867
Maryland 1870

Chapter One

August heat lay heavy on the city. It steamed from the great river, bearing the stench of fetid wharves into narrow streets. It clung damply to the iron lacework of empty balconies and hung stifling in the enclosed courts of the gentry's houses. Not that the gentry minded. They had shuttered their town lives and fled to the coolness of plantation verandas.

They returned with reluctance for the funeral of Claudette Martin. As if Claudette could still care. She had died lingeringly and gracefully as everyone had expected. Phillip Martin, still handsome despite time and indulgence, would mourn his lovely wife convincingly. And for all they knew, honestly.

But it was the child, Henriette, on whom guarded glances fell, in the hot ennui of the cemetery. Slight as her mother, with a brilliance that only Claudette and Phillip could have produced, the girl stood in tight-waisted black, a sheer black veil over her face. Too young to marry (even in the early flowering of that languid and over-heated society), Henriette would have to go somewhere. It was unthinkable that at fourteen she should remain in her father's house uncared for, alone.

Glances slid to the large, black-clad woman beside the girl. That would be the aunt, wife of poor Claudette's brother, Joseph. One wondered that he had dared to come back but, of course, it had all happened so long ago. Joseph, once dashing and elegant like all the Beaulaires, had changed, his sunburned face re-

9

flected his days, as the stolid woman beside him reflected his taste. Plain Joe Boler now. Of interest to no one.

Glances stole again to the girl.

Young Henriette, aware of them, shifted.

"Stand still!" Mathilda Boler's breath was hot in her ear, and, as usual, cinnamon laden. It mingled with the odor of perspiration from the folds of her tightly packed flesh. Henriette closed her eyes to the threat of nausea and wondered if she could ever learn to call the woman 'Tante'.

It was Mathilda Boler's fault that she was encased in stifling black. Maman would have permitted white, or the pearl gray that had fluttered and enfolded her in mist as she lay on her chaise lounge. Henriette tried not to think of Maman now, lying inside that carved mahogany box, on fluted chiffon of a particularly hideous shade of violet. That had been Mathilda Boler's idea, too.

". . . *sanctificetur nomen tuam in terra sicut et in coelo* . . ." Father Benoit's voice came faint and interminable, robbed of its usual accusing tone by the dazzling air.

Henriette shifted again and concentrated on a single fly hovering over the coffin lid. To her dismay, she saw it alight, drawn by the decaying jasmine bloom she had tossed there in a small release of pain.

Flowers lay heaped against the miniature Greek temple that was to be Maman's cemetery home. But not a petal on the stark, polished box. "We come into this world with nothing, we take nothing out of it . . ." Someone in kindness had let the wilting blossom remain and now Henriette's transgression had been exposed. To her relief, the fly flew away.

She pushed at her black veil and felt Mathilda Boler's hand heavy on her shoulder. She stiffened, daring only to move her eyes around the circle of pallid figures. Faceless strangers. Behind them were her friends. She had heard her father say that with his losses this year he could not afford to put the servants in black. So they stood, nodding to custom in black bandanas and shawls; Darcy, the coachman, with black crepe tied around his hat and his arm. Their grief was told in tears too warm to hide. Everyone who knew Maman loved her. Except. . . . Henriette would go no further.

Rosilee was standing at the very outside of the circle beside Jubel, her own dear Jubel, the deep-bosomed terror of the kitchen whose rocking chair and warm lap had been a refuge to Henriette as long as she could remember. That was, until *it* had happened. Henriette had found reasons not to linger in the kitchen since then. Not with the secret knowledge that lay like a stone beneath her heart.

Henriette sought her father's face. He stood behind Father Benoit, slender as a sword, his face proud, expressionless, lined with long vigil-keeping. He did not meet her eyes.

Henriette wondered that Rosilee had dared come today. But Jubel never would have permitted her to stay behind. Unless of course she, too, knew the secret. But Henriette had told no one. You could not share a stone even when it was too heavy to carry.

Rosilee's head dropped in the heat. Maybe she really is sorry, Henriette thought. The round, darting, shoe-button eyes were lowered. Her cotton-clad body was beginning to thicken like Jubel's, and the sparkling olive-toned face was broadening. Henriette wondered if beneath her striped work skirt, she wore those savage pink and purple petticoats Henriette had glimpsed through the broken louver of a window.

Petticoats tossed nearly to her face, as her father lay writhing on top of them, his gray trousers in a heap on the floor. Henriette, on tiptoe at the drawn blind, had watched those petticoats begin to rise and fall in searching rhythm. Then to her astonishment, a cry had burst from her father in the thin voice of a boy. She saw his face flushed with youth and helplessness, and Rosilee taking his elegant head in her arms with a laugh of triumph.

Henriette had fled across the hot courtyard to the cloister of her own room, locked the door, and thought for a long time about what she had seen.

What she had not seen was Phillip Martin sitting at the edge of the tousled bed, his face in his hands. He had heard the rain of small footsteps. He had been caught, found out. He'd never had any luck. But one deep question that weighted the bottom of his mind had been answered. When Claudette on her chaise in her pale draperies finally succumbed, he had known what he would have to do.

"... *per omnia saecula saecularum* ... *dominus vobiscum* ..."

It was almost over. Henriette's young, dry gaze returned to the carved coffin. Her mother would soon be out of this blinding glare and inside the cool little marble temple. To her horror, Henriette saw the fly had returned. It was crawling downward, toward the brown petals. In another instant it would be over her mother's face.

"Go away!" Her scream cut through the droning heat and grief. Henriette felt herself pulled roughly back, through rows of shocked faces. In another minute she was in the curtained confines of a carriage being rapidly driven out past the cemetery gates.

Mathilda Boler was beside her.

"Poor child. It was too much for you. I know you didn't *mean* it. You loved your mother. But you've never been properly taught. You're to come North to live with me. I'll take care of you, as a child should be cared for."

Without tears Henriette locked the door of her room.

The great house lay quiet at last. Downstairs a single lamp had been lit against the graying twilight. The crowds flocking like blackbirds through the two parlors and the dining room, with its spread of silver and lace and funeral foods, had gone, their voices lifting in forgetfulness as they reached the street.

Rain had begun to fall, the gentle, steamy rain of a New Orleans summer, washing the dust from the black wreath on the door, plastering the stiff crepe streamers against the panels.

In the safety of her bedroom, Henriette listened to the new silence. No matter what anyone said, you could hear silence. It rustled in the halls, creaked in the corners, throbbed with the inner life of a house left to itself. She had torn off the stifling black dress for a floating peignoir nearly like her mother's. Her dark shining hair, freed from Mathilda Boler's braiding, rippled below her shoulders. She waited, as silence deepened, for a commanding knock on the door or her father's light signalling rap. But none came. Human sounds had ebbed away. Perhaps that was to be her punishment.

If it was, they didn't know her. She had never been afraid to be alone or in the dark. Her father had taught her that, as he had taught her to ride a horse, not a pony. "Ponies are for children," he had said. "You'll have all the horses you want some day, so that's what you'll learn to ride now." He had put her up on his own spirited bay gelding when her little legs could barely reach the saddle flaps. She had laid a baby hand against the arched neck and the gelding had dropped his fine head in response. "You have a way with them, Henriette. It's a gift of God."

Suddenly she found words for the unnamed longing. She would like to see her father now. But she would not unlock her door to seek him. She could guess. Her father would be in his study, the cut-glass decanter filled and on his desk. It would be empty by morning.

She opened the shutter to the rain. There was never anything to be seen out there except a dreary patch of side garden and a drearier iron-grilled fence. She wished again that her room looked onto the inner court, where she could watch Lavenia come from market with a basket on her head, proud as a panther. Or hear Jubel crooning. Or catch a glimpse of Juan, the saddler's boy—handsome, nimble, Spanish to the core. Juan had once tickled her stomach to make her laugh and run away. But it hadn't made her laugh. It had left curious tremors in her legs, new and exciting. Jubel had snatched her out of the hot courtyard. "Time enough for that, missy. You stay where you belong, and you leave him where he belongs." Jubel had half carried, half dragged her to the front of the house.

She shouldn't be remembering things like that now. But if they left her alone, was it her fault that she couldn't turn a lock on her mind as she had on the door?

She tried to think of her mother, as palely beautiful in death as in life, with the rain soft on her white marble temple. Her mother liked rain. She called it the singing of the clouds. Like everything about her mother, the words were lovely and mysterious and Henriette didn't understand them. But her mother's voice was sweet and clear and when it soared in church, Henriette had held her breath and looked up to the vaulted arch as if she could see the notes in crystal. She would never hear that voice again.

She latched the shutter with a bang and went to the wicker cage hanging beside her bed. As she opened the cage door, a tiny yellow bird hopped out on her hand.

"I wish I could cry, Jolie. But I can't. I can only feel hot and dry, like when I burned myself on Jubel's kettle."

The little bird sat motionless. From the folds of her peignor, Henriette drew out a dried remnant of Jubel's fruit cake and held it between her lips. The bird pecked at it until it was almost gone. She put the bird and the last crumbs into the cage.

"They were wrong this afternoon, Jolie," she whispered. "There was a fly. A dirty little old fly *you* could have swallowed in a gulp. It was crawling. I

14

didn't scream at any*body*. . . . Not Maman. Or Father Benoit. Or anybody." A solitary dimple flashed in Henriette's left cheek. "Though I'll tell you a secret. I could have screamed at Mrs. Boler. I'm to call her Tante, Papa says. How can I?" The dimple again. "Though I could call her double-Tante—she'd make two. I'm to go to Mary's Land with her. I don't know where that is. She says I don't know anything that I should. I'd like to go away though. And be beautiful. And grown up. And . . ."

The whisper pinched and died. Shadows were filling the room. Henriette went quickly to the door and unlocked it. At last she knew what she wanted to do.

Phillip Martin lifted his handsome head from the library table that served as his desk, and listened. The knock was repeated. "Who is it?"

"I want to talk to you, Phil." The heavy voice was firm.

"I'm busy."

"I must talk to you."

Phillip rose, lit a porcelain oil lamp, and stoppered the half-empty decanter on the desk. The last man on earth he wanted to see at that moment stood in the doorway.

"What the devil, Joe! Can't you wait until morning?"

Joseph Beaulaire, now Boler, his brother-in-law, sank his muscled frame into a leather chair. Phillip frowned at him with distaste. Once so like Claudette, in refinement of feature and style, the man had let himself grow into a raw-necked, blunt-fingered parody of a Yankee farmer. Judging by the way his black suit hung on Joe, Phillip imagined his Pennsylvania Dutch wife had run it up. His forehead was veined like old leather, his eyes squinted into the lamplight. Still, he was going to be useful.

"Brandy?"

15

"No, thanks. Not now." If the tone carried rebuke, Phillip ignored it. He refilled his own glass.

"A bad time, Joe."

"You knew it was coming."

Phillip set the glass down, sloshing the contents on the table. "Damn it, Joe, if you've come here to quarrel . . ."

"I've come to avoid a quarrel. Till and I have talked it over. We're leaving in the morning."

"They'll have the girl ready."

"We've decided not to take Henrietta with us." He gave the name the stolid Yankee *ah*.

"That's for me to decide." Phillip drained his glass. "I've settled it."

"It won't work, I tell you. I don't know how you and Claudette brought her up. Her head's filled with everything and nothing. Put her on a farm and what is she good for?"

"Anything you and Mathilda want to make of her."

"How old is she? Fourteen? She's her mother to the bone. A beauty maybe. But has she ever trimmed wicks, or swilled hogs, or plucked a goose?"

"She's as strong as a horse. She can learn." Phillip wiped beads of perspiration from his forehead, his long fingers itching to reach for the decanter. But he'd need his wits at this turn of events. "What are you saying to me, Joe? You don't want her?"

"She belongs here in New Orleans. Let her grow up, marry her own kind. No. We don't want her. She hasn't even had any schooling. Till doesn't like popery."

"Till can go to damnation. Did you marry a twelve-stone woman to hang her around your neck? I took Henriette from the Sisters to be with her mother. She didn't need to go to school. I taught her more than she'll ever learn with a slate. Look." He reached for a small, five-inch high book bound in amber-colored suede, on the bookshelf. It came from one of two rows of matching volumes. "The Bard. She's learned more

16

about life and the world and the knaves that fill it from him than she could from all the Sisters on their virgin knees." For an instant his face lightened, his voice deepened. " . . . To thine own self be true, thou canst not then . . ." He dropped the book on the table, the moment gone, the dream of playacting he had never achieved. "You can't be false to anybody then, Joe. Know any better advice? You'll take her, Joe. That's the end of it."

The other man rose. "You'll have to find some other way."

Phillip's thin lips tightened. He took a circle of keys from his pocket, pulled one free, and opened the lower left hand drawer of the desk. From a thick, elastic-bound bundle he pulled three $100 bills and dropped them in front of Joseph. "You'll get the same amount in three months, and every three months until it's gone." He snapped the elastic band. "Two nights' winnings. While I was still sleeping with Lady Luck."

Joseph's eyes lingered on the bills. Drought had seared his corn that season. "I don't take money for keeping my dead sister's child," he said stiffly.

"I'll put it in a Washington bank. You might need it someday. Henriette's a hot little filly." When Phillip laughed, his white teeth brought youth to his face. "She's already tried to seduce the Spanish saddler's son."

"Send her back to the Sisters." Joseph was at the door. "If we don't see you in the morning . . ."

"By God, Joe, you'll listen to me! The girl's your blood, not mine." Phillip bent quickly and drew from the drawer a long narrow box. He pushed it across the desk. "Open it. Go on, open it. You've seen it before."

Joseph came slowly back into the room.

"Open it, I said. Or I'll do it for you." He flipped open the lid. Against a faded green-velvet lining lay a long-muzzled pistol, its silver handle heavily enscrolled and newly polished. "I've kept it well. As you see."

17

Joseph sat down heavily. "How long have you had it?"

"Since the night you used it. It could have hung you."

Joseph licked his dry lips. "Somebody had to do it."

"Of course. Sister's honor. All that kind of thing. But society doesn't make such a fine point of honor these days." Phillip lifted the weapon and sighted down the shining muzzle. "And after all, I had reason to be grateful. So had Claudette. One shot and she was rid of a lover, gained me for a husband, and had a father for her bastard child."

"Henrietta is yours, Phillip. You've only to look at her."

"You always had a streak of chivalry, Joe. Which means you lie as easily as you shoot. Henriette is her mother to the smallest bone. God knows who her father is. I never thought Armand had it in him. He died a coward as he lived. Claudette had witchery but no judgment." He was talking beyond the lighted circle of the lamp, as if no man sat opposite. "Oh, I was mad for her, I admit. And Claudette was grateful to me. But a man gets tired of gratitude. And pretense. I think the child cares for me. In a way. Or did. But she'll know the truth some day if she stays here. She has too much of Claudette in her to bow to duty. She'll be ready in the morning, though. I'll see to it myself."

Joseph thought of the kindly woman upstairs, packing into suitcases the firm order she had brought to his shattered life. "It isn't right, Phil. Can't you see that?"

"What's right got to do with it?"

"I mean the girl's—different," he groped for words. "That scream today. Till said she never uttered a word or shed a tear all the way back in the carriage. Till's afraid . . ."

Phillip was on his feet, one hand grasping the fluted edge of the desk, the other waving the pistol unsteadily toward the man hunched in the chair. His words came thickly.

"Afraid? Afraid of what? You're the one who should be afraid. I'm not going to shoot you, Joseph. I don't give that much of a damn for any of you. And I doubt that this pistol could hang you now. The city's got its hands full, hanging Yankees or hanging rebels, depending which side you were on. But by God's blood, I've had my bellyful of you Beaulaires. It cost me $6000 to get the death certificate signed "accident," Armand properly buried, and you off on that ship. I'd sell the whole story, names and proof, for half that amount now."

He dropped the pistol into its green velvet box. "And I could, you know. The city's crawling with Yankee journalists sniffing out southern rot. Let Till get the stink of that up her nostrils. Then she'd have something to be afraid of, all right!"

The man opposite stared at him, expressionless.

"I'm tired, Joe. I need a drink. Tomorrow when you're in the carriage with Henriette, I'll make you a present." He cradled the narrow box in his long hands. "I've kept it well, Joe. Even the bullet. I had the devil of a time removing it from Armand's chest. Not a hair on that chest either. White as a girl's. What in hell was Claudette after?" He laughed and his face went boyish. "Tomorrow it's yours. When you leave with the girl."

Joseph rose without a word. Phillip watched the door close on the slumped shoulders. "Damn well-suited to a team of oxen," he thought. He set the tipped glass upright and reached for the decanter. Damn. He'd have to refill it. A man couldn't start drinking from a half-empty bottle. But he had something to do, and he'd do it first. He opened the door on the empty hall. Slowly, carefully, he began to climb the broad curve of the stairs to the upstairs silence.

Mathilda Boler, listening from the guest room, heard the uneven steps. She turned to her husband.

"He's drunk, Joseph. Is that why you gave in to him?"

Joseph pushed the muslin petticoats aside and sat numbly on the edge of the bed. "She's my sister's child, Till."

"You're not telling me the reason. The girl's as odd as blue butter. But my father said fight the Devil where you find him. Turn your back and he'll have you." She reached out to her husband. "I haven't given you children, Joe. God in his wisdom knows there isn't a night I haven't cried in my heart to hold a child in my arms. If this is His answer, I'll bear it. But Joe . . ." she pressed against him. "Help me to do what's right and teach her the way."

Because she was warm and good, and had given him all the sweetness and solace he had known in his life, Joseph put his arms around his wife and gently, gently urged her back on the brass bed. With a deep and releasing sigh he laid himself beside her and sought her softness.

Henriette's room was nearly dark. The tiny bird chirped sleepily as Phillip opened the door. The canopied bed was unmarked. The slender black dress spilled like ink over a chintz chair.

"Riette?" But even as he called, Phillip knew the room was empty.

In the hall he listened sharply. From somewhere came a tangle of voices, the servants' court, he guessed. A square of light fell into the hall below. A distant giggle was abruptly hushed. And the faint pungency of steaming okra feathered his nose. The house was coming to life. How quickly death loosened its grip. He wondered how long the black wreaths must remain. Jubel would attend to all that. Thank God, by tomorrow he would be rid of all that smothered this house. He had a moment of pity for Joseph Boler, grown calloused and thick, with his homespun conscience and his kitchen-bred wife. Joe had pursued honor to its emptiness. Had he ever known ecstasy with a desiring woman?

Phillip found himself moving half unconsciously toward the spacious corner room into which Claudette had retreated years ago. Had it been only this morning that he had stood in the numbing torpor of hot sunlight and worn litany, letting release flow through him, lifting at last the burden of those years? Then the scream, a knife-blade of reality. He should have talked to the girl before this. But it did not really matter. She was her mother. He had never understood either of them.

He pushed open the door of his late wife's room. And stared. The room glowed like a fishbowl of light. Every lamp was lit. A billowing of robes and dresses covered the bed, drifted over the chaise, and erupted on the chairs. Chiffons, silks, tulles, and satins, shimmering in colors warmed to the light. In front of the gilt-framed pier glass stood Henriette, in a cascade of ivory ruffles to the floor, her arms lifted as in a dance, the gauzy front of the dress falling so low on her skinny chest that the nipples showed like hard little brown buds. In the glass he saw her face, lips parted, skin flushed, eyes shining, hair loosened in a sheen of dark curls around her shoulders.

"Henriette!"

She spun and saw him. "Papa!" She stumbled over the ruffles and threw herself at him. "Oh, Papa!" He caught her and held her from him, his fingers biting into her arm.

"Take that dress off!"

"It's Maman's. She said I could have it. She said— she said I could have them all!"

"How dare you come into this room to play the slut? You did enough at your mother's coffin!"

She backed away but only as far as his steely grip would allow. "It was a fly . . . crawling . . . over . . ."

But brandy, the heat of the day, the frustrations of a

life deafened him. "Take it off or I'll . . ." His free hand reached for the ruffles on her shoulder. A savage rip brought them to her waist, another and the ruined dress lay in a heap around her feet. He released her. In the white mask of her face only her eyes showed life, a fire he had never seen, banked with contempt.

"I don't care. I didn't want it anyhow." She kicked away the heaped lace, her eyes levelled on him. "Give it to Rosilee."

For the first and only time, Phillip struck her. The blow flung her against the chaise lounge, the welts from his fingers a red fury on her cheek. "Be ready to leave in the morning."

He was at the door when Henriette crumpled like a child. Loss was greater than pain. He was all she had now.

"Papa!" She flung herself at him, clinging, grasping. "Papa, don't send me away! I'm sorry for everything. I'll do what you say. I'll go back to the Sisters! I won't play with Juan again! I'll never wear Maman's dresses again! I'll do anything! Anything!" Her voice rose to a thin wail. There was no more breath for the catalog of her sins. "Let me stay here! With you, Papa . . . with you!"

He turned in the doorway. "You will need one small trunk. Jubel will pack it. You will take only plain clothes, and shoes for walking. And for God's sake cover yourself. You're an ugly little wench, but some farmer may want you someday."

He hated the words as he uttered them, and the heavy brandy breath on which they flowed. But he could not have stopped, either. Something old and dark and long-buried was churning in unadmitted depths within him, a morass of lies and self-deception that had never borne the weight of daylight.

Tomorrow he could at last watch uninterrupted the young Spanish boy playing in the sun. This spindly, unclothed girl would no longer cast a shadow.

Without looking back Phillip Martin swayed unsteadily down the darkened stairs to the solitude of his study. As he locked the door and pulled the decanter to him, he faced the leaden certainty of truth. Here was his fate, to draw these walls inevitably and finally around him and to let the sunlight and its evils drain from him in peace.

Henriette pulled her peignoir close. The simple act lifted her from frozen humiliation. For the only time in her life she had poured out love and need. For it, she had felt her arms fling free, her father's fine face turn savage with indifference. She felt as if she had been caught naked on market day, in the square, to be jostled, stared at. There was no place she could turn. Not now. Humiliation burned deeper than the scarlet bruise on her cheek.

Never, never again as long as she lived would she beg any man for anything. There was another way. She wasn't quite sure of it yet. But she remembered that same handsomely arrogant face, pride gone from it, as her father lay pleading and helpless on the crest of pink and magenta petticoats, and Rosilee's laugh of triumph as she took him in her arms.

She could humble a man as the black girl had done.

Henriette Martin had learned the most useful lesson of her young life.

Chapter Two

Isaac Roundtree slackened the reins, letting his horse pick his own slow way through the dust of the Maryland turnpike. There had been no rain for more than two weeks. On either side of the rutted road parched fields of three-foot corn stood wilting. He had planned to reach Washington by July third, lay over the holiday, sell his rested horse, and take the train north the next day. He was still, by the milestone marker, seventeen miles from Washington.

He usually shunned a roadside tavern, the hard, suspicious eyes, the bawdy talk, the stench of raw whiskey and tobacco spit. But this time he would have to put up with it, if only for the sake of his tired animal.

The weather-beaten, slope-roofed building lay close to the road. Isaac was dismayed to see the number of wagons and two-wheelers drawn up in the sideyard. Four horses, still under saddle, were tied to the rail, heads drooping, tails relentlessly switching at the swarms of flies drawn by the dung beneath their feet.

"Take your horse, young sir?" The whine came from a gnomelike man with his hand already on the bridle. His left hand. The right arm ended at the elbow and his right leg was stiffened into a permanent limp. His eyes wore an empty glaze, but as Isaac looked into the stubbled, dirty face, he realized the hostler was young, probably not much older than himself, if you could call a man past twenty-seven young. He had been young once himself, how long ago? Nineteen, when he had stepped smartly out to the roll of drums, with the Sixth Connecticut, in new blue, rifle shouldered smartly, Old Glory ahead, and the Hartford crowds cheering themselves hoarse. He remembered pretty Hartford girls running alongside the men, throwing kisses. He hadn't time for them then, nor since. The Devil had a way of trapping a man with a woman. Same as he could with a full wallet.

Isaac had learned that, too. But that day he had been young with life wide as a river ahead. The $400 bounty paid him by Judge Nathaniel P. Thatcher to take his son's place in the Union Army, could remain safe in Thatcher's new bank. Well, the bank had gone broke in the flood that had swept half the village away, and young Phineas Thatcher had died of fever. So what had it all meant? He had done better staying on in Tennessee after the War, clearing logs. That is, until April 20 when the letter had come. It had taken a year and two months to reach him. He had thought about it for another month. Temptation took many shapes, the Bible said. He had gone into the forest, as he often did at night, to wrestle with the Tempter. A month later he had set out.

He slid now from the saddle and unhooked the dust-crusted saddle bag.

"A half pail of water," he said to the stooped little hostler.

"Yours'll have to take his turn. I got them others first."

Isaac drew a small deerskin pouch from the inner pocket of his jacket and took out a coin. It was enough to give the hostler a glint of more.

"Get me a pail. I'll tie him there under the tree and water him myself."

The hostler was back almost at once with a full pail and a dirt-stained remnant of woolen cloth. Isaac recognized the threadbare rag. Union Army blanket. "You were in the War?"

The hostler nodded. "Manassas. Antietam. Until there wasn't no more left of me."

Isaac might have answered. He might have said "Chancellorsville. The Wilderness." But a burst of startling rifle fire exploded from a nearby hill. The horses whinnied and stamped at their halter ties. His own horse reared.

"Whoa, there. Steady now," Isaac soothed. It had been five years since the War between the States. These horses were new-bred. Like the boys of today, they wouldn't know about rifle charges. But the young-old hostler had dropped his pail, spilling precious well water, his eyes wide, his mouth open in panic.

"That's only for the Fourth," said Isaac. "Beginning early, I reckon. They always shoot it up on the Fourth."

The hostler covered his face with his one hand. "I know, young sir. I know. It'll all go away in a minute.

I always shake when I first hear 'em. Like I'm looking right at 'em again—with the bullets spitting at *me*."

Isaac picked up the pail, saw where the well stood in the rear of the inn, and led his horse into the shade.

The public room was what he had expected. Thick with cigar smoke, loud with whiskey-sodden arguments, the floor slippery with brown tobacco spittle. A few men looked up as he stood in the doorway. One or two nudged each other and laughed. Isaac was conscious of his frontier breeches and jacket, but not ashamed. He was surprised at the fine linen and well-fitting coats of many of the travelers. Things had changed.

He turned away and bumped sharply against the serving girl, her hair tied in a soiled bandana, her face pocked, one tooth missing, and the others blackened with baccy-chewing. But she had measured with quick eyes his six-foot frame, his thinness. She was in no hurry to pass.

"I'm sorry," he said quickly. "Where's the innkeeper?"

"If you mean Mrs. Blodgett, she's in the butter room. If you'll take a seat I'll serve you."

"I'll wait in there." Isaac was blunt with women, though he felt compassion for this misbegotten wench.

"If you like . . . " The girl bobbed, flung her brown skirt from a good ankle, and turned. "I'll tell her."

The small parlor he entered was close and cluttered in a way he could not begin to sort. Mrs. Blodgett did not keep him waiting. A small, fussy woman moving with a rustle of unseen taffeta, her bleached hair piled high. Had Isaac known more about women, he would have known the artifices that produced that hair, and the purpling of beet juice on her heavy cheeks. Now all he could identify was the onslaught of a heavy scent. He felt outsized in the tiny parlor.

The innkeeper liked what she saw. "Oh, dear! You'll want a bed, I expect?"

"Just for two nights, ma'am. Rest my horse." He saw her dismay. "One night would do. I don't mind ridin' on the Fourth."

"The trouble is I haven't anything. Three to a room and not an inch more to spare. Four mattresses in the attic. The servants are crowded into the barn so there's scarcely room for hay and harness." She could have taken him into her own narrow bed if he'd shown a sign, but his eyes were chips of flint and she didn't like losing a customer. "It's as if everybody in the world's trying to get to Washington or get out of it. The election's coming, and everybody's wanting to see General Grant. Well, he's a good enough man, I guess. But I was born right over in West Virginia, and when you've got southern quality . . ."

She talked rapidly while she tried to think her way through the problem. It wasn't often a young man like this rode in, tall and straight, his hair all sun-washed, his face burned strong. But his eyes—cold as marbles. She sighed.

"I'll think of something. You just sit here and make yourself comfortable. I see you're looking at my souvenirs. My treasures." She put a plump hand on his arm. "The lace on that pincushion comes from the curtains of the White House when Mrs. Lincoln had her reception. Oh, it's hard to believe. But the lady I worked . . . I mean, a very dear friend of mine went to a levee there with her embroidery scissors in her reticule and just snipped it out. Fashionable ladies liked to . . ." she saw that he was getting impatient. Her mind was running like a mouse in a cage.

"And that little black button," she pointed to a plush-lined box. "I got that at the hanging."

His eyes turned back to her. It was a word he was too familiar with in the mountain-country. "What hanging was that?"

"*The* hanging. Leastwise, that's the way it's called around here. That woman and the three others who helped to murder Mr. Lincoln. Mind you, I don't think he was right but nobody should have murdered him. My, such excitement. We got up before dawn the day before to go. It was worth it, just standing outside the walls. I thought I was going to faint and I looked down and saw that black button on the ground. Like something *she* might have had on. So I picked it up. It's been there on the mantel ever since. And if I do say so, it's brought me luck. I'm a widow and it isn't easy running a place like this. Alone." The last word trembled nicely.

"If I could see to my horse, ma'am."

"Of course. I do rattle on, but . . ." she touched his arm again.

"Ma'am, if you've got a field where I can stake my horse, I'll sleep out there."

"In an open field?" Could she charge for that?

"It won't be the first time, ma'am. And it's a dry night."

In the end he had paid highly for a dinner of fried beef and turnips. When he refused a glass of spirits with his hostess, the bill was doubled. But at last he was at peace. A breeze had sprung up, the stars hung close and bright, the celebrating rifle fire had grown fitful. He drowsed in the stubbled pasture.

Suddenly his horse whinnied. He was aware of a shadow, darker than the trees, near him.

He sat bolt upright. He carried no weapon but he had not lost the army-camp habit of instant suspicion.

"You awake, young mister?" It was the hostler.

"What do you want?"

The little man squatted beside him in the bright darkness.

"I thought you might be leavin' before I could talk to you. You're a rich young mister . . ."

Rich. A pouch of coins and eighteen dollar bills in his wallet. All he could get for selling everything he owned. Until he got to Thatcher. In a panic he reached for his saddle bag. Had the Devil found his

Bible and the letter creased into it? But the bag was locked. He could feel the Bible solid within it.

"What are you after?" He had felt sorry for the man. Now he wanted riddance of this beery whispering that stank of conspiracy.

"I want to show you something." The hostler struck a match. In his dirty palm lay a woman's brooch of onyx, pearls, and diamonds, Isaac guessed, from the depth of their light.

"Where did you get that?"

"A lady gave it to me. A nice lady, a sweet lady. Lived by herself with her girls in a nice house. She gave it to me."

The match flared. Isaac saw by the look on the man's face and the sudden flick of his tongue on his lips, that the bribe hadn't spared the woman. He had seen women raped by soldiers. He had blotted out the images of sin and violence in the pages of his Bible, reading relentlessly into the dawn. He had grappled with desire and lust in Tennessee when the young wife of a homesteader passed, her skirts lifted over a spread of mud. . . .

The matched flared and went out. Isaac's arm flung into the darkness. He heard a yelp and a whine.

"What are you doing, young mister? I want to sell it to you. Anything you want to give me for it. So's I can leave here. Get me a bit of land out West the govmint's giving away. You got a wife? She'd like it. Or a sweetheart?" The hostler's voice grew wheedling, lascivious. "Or maybe a fancy woman?"

"Get out!" Isaac rolled over on the ground, drew his saddle bag closer, and buried his head in his arms. He heard the hostler's rustling limp fade into the dark. His forehead was hot with sweat. He would wrestle with his images of sin to forgetfulness.

Instead, he fell into a heavy sleep.

He was awakened by his horse's soft whinny. The pallor of the false dawn edged the sky. The air was sweet and cool. He felt purified and refreshed. In the semidarkness he watered his horse, doused his own lean naked body. He had paid his bill the night before. He had only to dress, saddle up, escape.

Dawn found him on the turnpike, riding slowly into the new day, already raucous with exploding firecrackers and rifle blasts. His horse began to go lame. The Lord's way of testing him, Isaac told himself.

He was down and on foot, leading his horse over the hard baked road when he heard the runaway, somewhere ahead. A moment later he saw the animal—black, lathered, reins dragging, eyes and nostrils wide with fear as it bolted toward him. Isaac halted his own horse, threw up his arms, and the frantic black mare slid to a stop. Expertly, he caught the reins, soothed the frightened animal, and led both horses. Somewhere he would find the owner and a barn. Rest for his own horse.

He soon came on the fallen rider. She was sitting in a spread of petticoats, on the side of the road. She had the dirtiest face he had ever seen on a woman. She jumped to her feet.

"Where are you going with my mare?"

She had an odd softness of speech, but her tone infuriated him.

"Haven't you sense enough not to ride a young horse on the Fourth of July?"

"If it doesn't scare Lady, why would it scare me? She—she saw a snake."

The girl could lie. He wouldn't argue. "Get back up on her. I'll lead you to where you belong."

"*Lead* me?" Henriette took the reins. "Lady doesn't lead easily, and neither do I!" She jumped up on the mare's bare back. Light as down, he might have said. If he had been an admiring man. She leaned over the mare's withers and smiled, her left cheek dimpling under its coat of dust. If she was hurt she didn't show it, and he wouldn't ask. She was a free kind of woman. He was uneasy.

"I live five miles down the turnpike, and a mile and a half left from the sycamore tree. I'll be glad to thank you properly for catching Lady, if you stop by."

"I don't need thanks. I'll be on my way."

He had barely turned to lead his horse over the wagon ruts again when she called.

"Where are you taking that horse?"

"Washington."

She rode up closer to him. "Why, the horse has gone lame!"

"That's why I'm walking."

"You can walk anywhere you want. But Lady and I are taking that horse home. What kind of man are you, letting a horse go on like that? A good-for-nothing Yankee who'd sooner eat a horse than take care of it!"

Free as he was with his right arm, Isaac had never struck a woman. Never would. Henriette had rubbed some of the dirt from her face and he saw she was nothing more than a child. Sixteen. Seventeen maybe.

"I'll pay your pa for a night's keep in the barn."

"A night? I'll take a week to bring that horse sound. Besides, it isn't my father's barn. It's my uncle's. Come on. Get up on Lady behind me. What's the matter? Haven't you ever ridden tandem with a girl?"

"I'll walk."

Mathilda Boler looked out her kitchen window anxiously. It was two hours since she had seen Henriette slip from the house and ride down the lane. She hadn't told Joseph. But then, in the three years she had coped with the child there were many things she hadn't told her husband.

The girl had bloomed. The plucked-chicken skinniness had rounded. But she was still so slender, so fine-boned that Mathilda despaired of ever plumping her into that sturdiness her world demanded of its women. Nor had she forgotten the first weeks. The girl's odd speech, fanciful with lapses into foreign-sounding words. "But Tante Till! I wore that yesterday. I must make a new toilette today!"

The "Tante Till" grated. Too Frenchified for a good Pennsylvania Dutch woman. But it was Henriette's dutiful compromise with their relationship, so she had not corrected it. Besides, the child's tearless silence when she was rebuked frightened Mathilda. Just as her lightning response to whatever was new moved her.

"Look what I found!" She had dragged the old, standing wool wheel from the storage room and spun it with rapture. *"Ne laissez-moi, mon amour . . ."* she sang, the little melody like thread on the whirling wheel. "Whatever is it for?"

"My mother spun all the wool for our clothes on that wheel."

"Clothes!" Henriette lost interest. "Maman's dresses came from Paris. That's where mine shall come from!"

She had run from the room and Mathilda saw her next in the yard, fondling a pigeon to her cheek, crooning the snatches of foreign-sounding songs that never seemed to be far from her lips. It was as if a small flame—bright, unquenchable, uncontainable—darted through the farmhouse.

Mathilda bided her time, did her duty, let kindness work like the pans of warm milk on the back of her stove, fearing lest the stolid flesh that had imprisoned her own somber girlhood would wall her forever from this quicksilver child who looked for beauty through every opening door. Mathilda would confess to no one how much she wanted Henriette's love.

It was early fall, time to think of warmer clothes, when she had gone to Henriette's room to look into the pathetic little trunk the girl guarded. Flat on the bottom, concealed by a large layer of tissue paper, Mathilda came upon a spill of ivory lace ruffles, a dress so fragile, so lacy that she had no way of guessing where any woman could wear it.

"Don't touch that!" Henriette had sprung at her from the door.

"But it's beautiful. . . ."

Henriette snatched the dress. "You've no right to. It's mine!"

Mathilda had remained placid. "But it's torn. How in the world did that happen? We must mend it. Someday you might wear it."

Henriette, her eyes dark with suspicion, would not yield the dress. "I'll mend it. Not you!"

In the days that followed, Henriette struggled for long, determined hours with a needle and thread. She learned from Mathilda how to hold it, how to make fine stitches, keeping to her task as if she were stitching her own young life into the lace. At last the dress hung whole and living. The next day, Mathilda had come on Henriette savagely cutting out every small stitch.

"It looks patched! Maman never wore anything patched in her life!"

Mathilda should have thought of it, of course. The white thread stretched a long wound on the old ivory lace. That evening Mathilda forewent her own mending to dip spools of white thread in light tea until every inch had turned matching parchment beige. When it was done, Henriette had flung her arms around her aunt, "Tante Till, *je t'adore*. Never, never will I leave you."

"She's not been taught anything," Mathilda sighed to her husband. "Waited on hand and foot, I expect. She doesn't know sums and she thinks Paris is nearer than Boston."

At the single-room country schoolhouse where Mathilda and Joseph conscientiously sent her, Henriette's oddities blazed into new light. She could read anything. She would recite endlessly, a torrent of words as unintelligible to her fellow students as they were startling to the school mistress. When a ruler at last stung her slim knuckles, Henriette had sprung hissing at the unfortunate teacher. "Hie thee to a nunnery," she had shrieked. "Thou cream-faced loon!"

Legally, a girl of fourteen did not have to attend school. At home, Henriette found excitement in everything that moved and changed. Cream coming to butter in the churn. Kneaded dough set to "prove" on the stove. In the fields, Joseph discovered she could bring along a strayed calf with a touch. In the barn, the most restless horse would grow quiet under her hand. The great farm creatures would lift any hoof she demanded.

"She'll make a farmer's wife," Joseph said.

Mathilda didn't answer. That afternoon when the first snow fell, Henriette had run into the kitchen, her sleeve coated with flakes. "I wonder who was cut into such tiny white stars," she cried, scattering them into Mathilda's lap. "Like Romeo."

Still, she would not learn sums, she would not relinquish her own ideas of geography, and she had no notion of a proper catechism. When the new schoolmaster came, Joseph decided she must return to school. She was fifteen, her slight figure had filled, and she had acquired a new gracefulness. Joseph noticed that men's heads turned when she drove to market with him.

The schoolmaster was not young. His face was sallow, his forehead high and shining. He wore silver-rimmed spectacles, a long black coat that emphasized his thinness, a high white collar, none too clean, and a flowing black tie. He had been to China and that gave him an air of mystery. He would go back some day as a missionary, he told his class.

One day in late November he asked Henriette to stay after school. He had put more wood into the iron stove and pulled up a chair close to his own desk. It grew very warm.

"You don't like sums, do you?"

"I think they're dull."

"Have you learned your catechism?"

She didn't answer.

"Who made you?"

What on earth did that mean? "My father and my mother."

"You shouldn't know that. God made you."

"Yes. I guess so."

He drew his chair closer. His hands had a dry bald look. "Where did you learn all those verses?"

Verses? Was that what he called them? "My father taught me."

"Why?"

"He said words were the most important things in the world. Especially beautiful words."

"Did you believe that?"

"Yes."

"And did you sit on his lap while he taught beautiful words to you?"

How did he know that? The room was growing too warm. She could only nod, mesmerized by his closeness and the dry insistence of his questions.

"Did he tell you other things?"

"Yes . . . no . . ." she broke off abruptly.

"Why do you hesitate, little one? Was there something you didn't like?"

She shook her head. She had worshiped her father until . . . but she would never tell anyone about Rosilee's pink and purple petticoats.

His eyes were small, the color of wet clay. He sat silent for a time. When he spoke his voice was hoarse.

"I would like to look at you."

She did not understand. She sat rigid beneath those damp, unblinking eyes. His fingers thrust at the neck of her dress, fumbled downward. Her breasts felt a pulsing warmth. Her head spun. As his bone-thin fingers touched her flesh, fury surged through her. She flung one hand into his face and with the other clutched the top of her dress as she sprang back from him.

His head dropped in his hands. "Go home!" The

words came from a choked distance. "You are stupid. *Stupid!*"

She snatched up her wraps and fled into the cold twilight.

Leafless trees laced the fading light with black. By the time she had walked the two miles to the farmstead, a few stars pricked the sky. A freshening wind whipped the pallor of fright and fury from her face and replaced it with an overbright flush.

"You're late," said Mathilda without looking up from her biscuit dough.

Henriette did not answer until she had hung up her cloak and scarf. "I will never go back to that school again," she said quietly and went upstairs. Mathilda heard the door close softly, too softly. Henriette never banged a door when she was angry. Any more than she let tears fall.

Next day she threw her slate and sumbooks into the stove fire. And she would never mention school again. She had her own world—small, suede-soft books, forty-eight of them in two layers at the bottom of her trunk. Hadn't her father said they would tell her everything she needed to know?

That night, Henriette lay in her bed, watching the sliver of a new moon hang in the window, remembering those skeletal fingers and the unexplained, yielding dizziness in her head. A shudder slid through her. Her face hot, her body icy, she burrowed into the sheltering dark of the feather bed. Never, never again as long as she lived would she let any man touch her unless she loved him madly. And she could—she knew that much about herself. Suddenly the bed became stifling. She sprang from its shelter, ran to the window, and pushed it open. Standing in her flannel nightgown, her young face radiant to the spangled night, Henriette felt longing race through her body like a flame. She drew a deep breath. She would love someday. She would feel strong hands, needing arms. Someone she could love was there beyond the rim of the night. She could wait. She wondered how long.

Joseph, in the door of the barn, looked up to see a strange procession coming down the lane. Henriette, supple-spined and graceful on the new black mare, beside her, a stranger—silent, stiff-necked, leading a horse. The man wore homespun and leather and he was stern-faced, a harsh-looking man. Not from these parts. Joseph couldn't judge his age. He noticed the stranger's horse limped. Henriette slid from the black mare's back with a flounce of skirts. Her small chin lifted defiantly as Joseph approached. He ignored her for the stranger.

"You've got a lame horse there, sir."

"You've got a fool girl. Keep her home on the Fourth of July."

Joseph straightened from his inspection of the horse. If he disliked the stranger's abruptness, he didn't show it. "He's pulled a tendon in the off foreleg. It'll be a week anyway before you can ride him."

The hard eyes looked troubled. They certainly didn't linger on Henriette, Joseph noticed.

"I hoped to be in Connecticut before then."

"That's a long way off."

"I was planning to sell my horse in Washington. Take the train. He's honest and he's strong."

"I don't need another horse," said Joseph mildly. "But you're welcome to stay until your horse is fit. I've got hay to get in before the weather changes. I'll need another pair of hands."

"I'll pay you for a night's board." Isaac started unsaddling his horse. "I'll give you a hand with the haying. I'll leave the horse with you. Use him if you can. But I'll have to be moving on."

Joseph went into the barn to ready a stall. The man knew his own mind. So be it. But Joseph didn't like coldness. He liked a man to shake your hand, show some friendliness.

Henriette took the bridle off her young mare and replaced it with a halter. She stood watching the stranger thoughtfully.

He wasn't looking at her. "Where's your water?" he said over his shoulder.

"I'll get you a pail."

"I'll do my own fetching."

"What makes you talk like that to me?"

"You need it, I'd say." He laid a worn saddle blanket on the ground beside the saddle. He was stroking the horse as he worked, soothing it with strong, gentle hands. The column of his neck rose powerful above his sweat-stained shirt. There was a loneness about him, she thought. Like the single oak on the crest of Gunner Hill. Something further back came into her mind. Her father, elegant and alone in the hot sun, beside her mother's coffin. No, not her father. This man was like no one she had ever seen. She watched his hands moving on the bay's flanks, down the injured leg.

"Where's Connecticut?"

"Where I come from. If you've got a rub-rag I'll rub him down. Or a handful of straw will do."

Joseph was coming out of the barn. "I'll take the mare, Henrietta." He spoke sharply. It still annoyed Henriette that he refused to pronounce her name properly. "You go in and help your aunt."

"In a minute." She took a couple of rags from a nail and handed one to Isaac. "I'll rub down this side."

He snatched them both from her. "No woman does my work."

She flushed, turned on her heel, then glanced back. "There's going to be a Fourth of July picnic at the Pavilion this afternoon. And dancing after." The dimple flashed. "Not that I care if you come."

"Well, who is it?" Mathilda was setting cold ham and corn bread on the table as Joseph entered the kitchen.

"Name is Roundtree. Isaac Roundtree."

"Looking for work?" She tried to keep the concern from her voice.

"No. Where's Henrietta?"

"Gone to her room." She had seen the guarded brightness in the girl's face, and was relieved that the stranger was moving on. She had known his like among her own people. Close-mouthed, unsmiling, working the land. Not easy for a woman to live with. She lifted warm bread from the oven and sighed.

"Tell him he's welcome at table if he wants to come in."

That afternoon the rains broke with pent-up violence. Henriette at the window saw her uncle and the stranger running in from the field, small rain-whipped figures against the pursuing blackness of the sky. She saw that almost all the mowed hay had been cocked and brought in. The farther field, still standing in deep grass, would be cut later and saved.

The men were soaked. The stranger would have to come into the house now. She would wear her sprigged dress with the green sash to supper. A small smile played at her mouth. She wondered how far away Connecticut was.

She opened the lid of her trunk on her treasures, her real world. The ivory lace dress spread carefully between its layers of tissue. She could wear it. When the time came. She had also secreted a dog-eared copy of *Lady's Magazine* she had found on the train from New Orleans, so long ago. Whenever she could, she pored over the pages ". . . Miss K. in pink tulle and rosebuds draped charmingly . . . Mrs. V. in looped purple satin with gold flounces . . . Mrs. N. in pale green Grecian silk, wearing her full necklace of emeralds . . . a ball in honor of Duc and Duchesse . . . fifty rose trees against the gilded walls . . . ices and champagne as the guests waltzed . . ." she knew the words by heart but she would read them over and over until they blended in a whirl of colors and fantasy.

"Henrietta!"

She closed the trunk quickly.

"Henrietta!" Mathilda was at the foot of the stairs. Henriette opened her door.

"Mr. Roundtree's coming to change in the spare room and taking supper with us. You be sure you're proper."

"Yes, Tante Till." Henriette closed the door, leaned against it, and wondered if you wore looped satin or draped tulle in Connecticut.

Supper was uncomfortable and silent. Henriette's sprigged dress earned a frown from her aunt and a glance of solemn puzzlement from her uncle. Isaac Roundtree ate steadily and politely of cold pickled pork and squash pudding, molasses bread and green tomato relish, shoofly pie and strawberry dowdy. When Joseph at last took his pipe down, Mathilda, somewhat mollified, gestured them to the parlor.

The storm had given way to steady rain. Isaac rose to help clear the table. Henriette confronted him, her small breasts rising and falling rapidly beneath the light cotton.

"That's woman's work."

"So it is." He followed Joseph into the parlor.

By the time the kitchen was tidied and Henriette could escape to the parlor, Joseph and their guest were in sober conversation.

"I reckon there's a stage going through to Washington. So I'll be off in the morning. I figure to pick it up back at the tavern."

Joseph nodded.

"It'll be early so I'd like to pay for my supper and my horse's keep."

"You've paid for that, Mr. Roundtree. A day's work in the field saved my hay."

"What's to be done must be done. But you could

oblige me by taking my horse. He'll serve you well enough. And it'll be a satisfaction to me to know that he's in good hands."

For the first time, Isaac Roundtree seemed to notice Henriette. His glance was so direct that in another man she would have thought it bold. She flushed and looked down.

"Your niece has a real kind way with horses."

Henriette concealed a smile, but the dimple flashed. "Even to taking one out on the Fourth of July?"

"I said kind, not sensible." It was his turn to redden.

An invisible spark seemed to leap across the room. Isaac rose restlessly and felt inside the inner pocket of his deerskin jacket. "I'd like to pay you now, sir. And turn in."

"We don't take money for hospitality." Mathilda was standing in the doorway, relieved that he was going.

Isaac didn't seem to hear her. He felt again for the leather coin pouch. He couldn't have lost it. The pocket was fashioned tight to hold it. He rummaged in a second pocket.

They watched his expression change to bewilderment. His hand came from his pocket tightly clenched. He opened it. In his palm glittered a woman's brooch, an exquisite pattern of black onyx, pearls, and diamonds.

Henriette gasped. Joseph was on his feet.

"Where did you get that?"

"I don't know." He did, of course. The hostler must have dropped it into his coat while he was washing himself before dawn. For it, the man had taken his coin pouch and his wallet. Everything in the world he possessed except the letter folded into his small, stained Bible. Or had he taken that too?

Forgetting his hosts, Isaac dashed into the spare room beyond the kitchen. He tore open his saddle bag. The Bible was there, the letter within it, creased and fragile with rereading.

Joseph had followed him. "I think we'd better have a talk, Mr. Roundtree. Away from the women."

"No." Mathilda loomed large behind her husband. "This man has sat at my table. I have a right to know what he's done."

Henriette crowded behind, her eyes bright as the diamonds she had seen.

In the end Joseph appeared satisfied. They would go back to the tavern in the morning to find the hostler, though they both guessed the man would have put mud-deep miles between himself and his employers by this time.

"Here!" Isaac thrust the brooch into Joseph's hand. "It's not mine. I don't want it."

As final proof of himself, he took the letter from between the pages of the little Bible and reluctantly handed it to Joseph.

Joseph turned up the oil lamp, sat down at the kitchen table, and began to read. For long minutes the only sound was the hiss of flames inside the stove. Mathilda sat motionless in her rocking chair. Three times Henriette's eyes strayed to Isaac but he stood as if carved into a corner of the low room, his gaze fixed beyond the walls, at some distant point she could not guess.

At last, Joseph put down the letter. "Who is Nathaniel Phineas Thatcher?"

"He lived in the village I come from, Thatcher. He paid me bounty to take his son's place in the army."

"A relative of yours?"

"No."

"It says here he wrote a will leaving you 5000 acres of land."

Mathilda opened her mouth, thought better of it, and closed it. Henriette struggled silently with the numbers. 5000. That was more than her father had ever had. Thatcher. . . . Joseph's voice plummeted her back to the kitchen.

"*Are* you Isaac Roundtree?"

"I am."

"You're going to have to prove it."

"To you?"

Joseph folded the letter and handed it back. "Are you a deserter?"

"I have a discharge for shrapnel wounds."

"You'll have to prove that, too."

"Why does he have to prove it?" Henriette's voice rose, her face hot with startling beauty. "He said so. Isn't that enough? Why don't you believe him?"

If Isaac Roundtree was grateful for the outburst, he did not show it. Without a glance at her, he creased the letter back into the Bible, picked up his saddle bag, and crossed to the door.

"I have a lame horse and no money. I'll be obliged if you'll let me sleep in his stall and work your fields for his keep. I don't want the brooch and I won't sell it for labor. It isn't mine." For a bare instant his eyes flickered to Henriette, then hardened on Joseph. He nodded to Mathilda. "I thank you, ma'am, for the food."

The door closed quietly behind him.

Henriette mounted the narrow stairs to her room. Landless or not, nameless liar, deserter, thief or man of honor, she would not get this plain-spoken, grim-faced man out of her mind for a long time. If ever. The aura of his masculinity swept over her. She lay wide-eyed, listening to a shutter creak out syllables in the dying wind. Thatcher. What was Thatcher like?

In the week that followed, Isaac Roundtree worked from dawn to after sundown. Sometimes alone, sometimes in silence beside Joseph. He knew the working of land. He needed to be told nothing. He never went to the house. He ate the fresh bread and meat pies Mathilda carried to the barn but tried to avoid her when she brought them.

His horse was better and the turnpike soft now but not mired. Tomorrow he would leave and get work where he could find it until he could afford the rail fare north. Once in Hartford he'd find work enough to take him the forty-five miles northwest to Thatcher.

On this last night he sat with his back against a locust tree on the far side of the barn. The leaves filtered a spray of moonlight across him and his lantern and mottled the Book in his hands. Beyond him the fields rose and fell, a sea of whitened mist. Isaac lowered his eyes against the loveliness, as he had against the girl who hovered like a moth on the horizon of his long workdays.

The Lord, thy God, is a just God . . . terrible *in His might.* . . . *Vengeance is Mine saith the Lord . . . whosoever sinneth . . .*

He did not need to read the words. They had been branded in his mind long ago. He blew out the lantern and dropped the book beside him. The stain on the cover bore living testimony to his sins. The faded brown blood of the boy who had dropped soundlessly from his powerful bayonet thrust. A boy, not more than fifteen, who neither knew him, nor bore him malice. His eyes had stared, his young mouth gaped open in the surprise of death. He, Isaac, was alive now to the shimmering peace of this summer night, as that boy might have been.

If Isaac had been able to temper the principles of justice with intent, he might have walked into the innocence of the moonlight and known himself for a good man. But he could only sit with the weight of God's hand on his soul, and with an unsaid vow to walk in the paths of righteousness, as he knew them.

He did not see the wraith of a figure in rippling lace, a flash of light at the throat, at the edge of the tree's shadow.

"Mr. Roundtree!" The whisper came soft as a sigh. Isaac started to his feet.

"No. Don't get up. Please." Henriette dropped beside him, her hand a small pale wing on his coat sleeve.

"You shouldn't be out here, miss."

"I know." A half giggle. "Do you like my dress? It was Maman's. And the brooch . . . you must take it, Mr. Roundtree. It's yours. It does not belong to my uncle." She settled herself closer. "You're leaving tomorrow."

"How did you know that?"

"I counted the days. You said you would stay a week. I believed you." She gave a little a sigh of contentment as if purpose tasted sweet. "That's what I came to tell you, Mr. Roundtree. I do believe you. Everything you said. Even about the land in—in Thatcher."

He glanced at her, then away. Her face was blanched of all expression, her large eyes shining, her lips curved in a half smile. So young.

"Not that it matters about the land. But it does matter that when you say what is true, somebody believes you. And you see, I do. With all my heart."

She was a creature of mist and radiance, so beautiful that Isaac turned abruptly from her, his hand fallen on the book beside him.

"Go back in. There's been trouble enough."

She moved closer to him. "You've been reading! How funny! Can you really read by moonlight?" She saw the dark lantern. "Oh, that's it. You bring a lantern with you! What are you reading? Let me see!"

He would have risen but she stretched an arm across his chest and snatched the book.

"It's the Holy Book. Leave it alone."

His voice was so rough she would have left him. If she could.

"I don't want it." She dropped the book against him. "The Bible's dull. All queer-sounding names and begats and sins. I don't believe in sins, anyway!"

Her voice was light as a flute, the words bewitched of their meaning. She laughed softly. " 'But shall I go mourn for that, my dear? The pale moon shines by night; and when I wander here and there, I then do most go right.' That's nicer than the Bible, isn't it? It's in one of my little books. It's Shakespeare. I'll read him to you someday." She drew a quick breath. "If you'll let me."

He sat rigid beside her. She saw a pulse throb above his temple.

"You're not listening, are you? You don't even look at me!" She reached for the brooch at her throat. It came away easily from the old lace. "Here, take it. Give it to somebody you—you want to have it. There!" The open pin drew a scratch across her palm. She thrust it at him. Suddenly, with the abandon of a child, she pushed her body against his, shaking with dry sobs. "Let me go with you tomorrow. To—to Thatcher. I promise you . . . I promise you . . ." words and breath tumbled together. "I can do so many things . . . you'll see!" Her lips were against his ear. "Take me with you!"

The lace had fallen from her throat and shoulders, her skin was silver and silk.

His arms went around her and closed. "Oh, my God!"

In a moment she gave one small cry of unexpected pain. It faded into the night breeze as he sought her again. At long last he lay still and she saw his face in the moon's scattered light. Innocently handsome, washed of anger, and at peace. A small laugh of triumph bubbled in her throat. But there was a headier beat inside her. Whoever this man, no longer a stranger, might be, she would follow him all her life. The intensity of her love burned like a wound.

She did not hear the steps on the dry pebbles of the barn yard. Isaac had left her side and was standing beyond the tree, looking away from her and across the moon-washed fields. She straightened her dress and smoothed her tangled hair. She longed to go to him but something unfathomable, brooding, held her back.

"Henrietta!" Mathilda's cry came from the darkness beyond the fence. Then a lantern illumined her broad worried face. Joseph was beside her.

"Find the man! Maybe he'll know!" Henriette heard her uncle's angry voice. She saw a glint in his hand. He was carrying a pistol.

Isaac stepped quietly from the shadows, his shoulders flung back. He walked boldly toward the fence.

"Miss Henrietta is with me, Mr. Boler."

She heard Mathilda's frightened gasp and Joseph's furious "Why?"

"I have asked her to be my wife. And she has consented."

Henriette walked slowly from the tree. She wanted Isaac to look at her, to take her hand, but he did not turn. She came to him, stood beside him, and nodded.

A future, inexpressible and unknown, had arisen from the night's magic.

In the heavy, brass-latched Bible that Mathilda had bought for a wedding present, Joseph wrote in his careful hand.

Henrietta Martin and Isaac Roundtree, married this day, July 12, 1870. Elmswood, Maryland.

The next entry was written by Isaac.

To Henrietta and Isaac Roundtree, a son. Born April 7, 1871. Died April 8, 1871. Thatcher, Connecticut.

Plowing his stubborn acres in the cold spring winds, Isaac made his vow. His marriage had been cursed by God. But for the price of his seduction, he would demand heirs, living, strong progeny who would help him make the land fertile and found his house. For this, and only this, would he yield to the temptations of the beautiful, sin-loving woman who was his wife.

Nine more entries of births and two deaths followed before Isaac felt his sin lifted.

Henriette, her small head high against empty horizons, knew her betrayal.

On November 8, 1887, the *Thatcher Standard* announced that Justice of the Peace Isaac Roundtree had acquired the former homestead of Nathaniel P. Thatcher on West Street. "The fine old house has stood empty since the tragic death of young Orville Thatcher, four years ago."

January 2, 1894, the *Thatcher Standard* reported that Mrs. Isaac Roundtree gave her annual New Year's Day reception at the Roundtree residence on West Street. "The large gracious home was brilliantly lit and overflowing with distinguished guests. Despite her recent accident, Mrs. Roundtree looked ravishing, in pleated ruby silk said to come from Paris, and a splendid brooch of jet, diamonds, and pearls."

On November 7, 1902, a stark inscription was entered in the brass-bound Bible in Isaac Roundtree's blunt hand. "My wife, Henrietta, gone this day."

The town marveled at the granite monolith that rose, then, draped and urned, above the lowlier headstones of Thatcher's nearly three-centuries-old cemetery. It shadowed an iron-railed plot and bore a single name: ROUNDTREE.

On the gray and wind-lashed day of March 17, 1928, the mortal remains of Isaac Roundtree were carried up the graveyard slope. The *Thatcher Standard* reported: "A large crowd followed the coffin, the honorary pall bearers and the dignitaries to pay their last respects to Thatcher's first citizen."

The summer sun glinted on the monolith's new lettering.

"Isaac Roundtree 1843-1928. All men shall call him righteous."

The town assumed that Henriette lay in final peace beside him.

Part Two

Thatcher, Connecticut
1970

Chapter One

September again came sweetly to the land. The earth had turned, the seasons rolled, and once more the hills that cupped Thatcher flaunted the brilliance of autumn.

In the trim streets, windows were opened in farewell to summer. The voices that flowed through them were heightened by a new excitement, as if Time, which flowed as quietly as the river beyond the town, had suddenly rediscovered Thatcher.

A simple impetus had brought Thatcher to this pitch of agitation. Lowell Roundtree, daughter of Martin Roundtree, of the town's most prominent family, was to be married. Everybody knew the curious history of the founding Roundtrees. There had been Isaac (such a fine man); there had been the darkly tempestuous Henrietta and the final silence surrounding her.

There had been other things, too, as the years had passed. Hadn't Martin Roundtree's eldest son walked out of his father's house never to return? And Willard Roundtree, the patriarchal and benign senior member of the family, who had inexplicably refused the judgeship he so well deserved. Some of Henrietta's unpredictability undoubtedly lingered in the blood.

But Thatcher had been quite willing to let respectability drift like the leaves of autumn over the past.

Now, with the invitations out and the wedding a week away, snippets of old gossip scurried like mice through front rooms and back kitchens. The more fair-minded assured themselves that, whatever the past had been, it had nothing to do with Lowell, quiet-eyed and gentle. There was none of Henrietta's nonsense about her. Or about the man she was to marry, Duncan Phelps, strapping and handsome and soon to be a minister. The town had watched the two young people grow up. It had watched Lowell wait while Duncan went off to Vietnam. Now with a sigh of relief like a postponed heartbeat, all of Thatcher was to see them married.

Martin Roundtree had shown his sense of fitness. *Noblesse oblige* would crowd the little square-towered stone church next Saturday, and the oversize tent that would canopy the lawn behind the fine old Roundtree house. Thatcher relished every happy detail.

Nor was there doubt in anyone's mind that Duncan would make a splendid young successor in that same church when old Dr. Wilcox retired. In the euphoria of anticipation, the town saw its own youth rekindled. Men talked of the railroad that had long ago abandoned Thatcher and the state's new superhighway that should be persuaded to send a branch across Birch River. There would be no need then to sell off their beautiful hills to grasping newcomers like the Orlinis.

How Duncan and Lowell were to be a part of all this was not clear. But a wedding was a beginning for everybody who witnessed it. The two young people had infused the town with romance. More than one Thatcher matron would see to it that her best handkerchief was within easy reach at the wedding.

In the mellowness of September, emotions quickened like new wine at Thatcher's tables and in Thatcher's beds.

Edythe Roundtree gazed past her husband to the white wainscoting of the old fashioned dining room. It needed painting. But then so did the entire house. And new carpets on the stairs. And living room furniture reupholstered. But there was nothing she could do now, or for that matter, if she had a year.

She wished again that Martin had not insisted on a large wedding. But she knew the reason. The gathering of the clan, the triumph of pride over decline.

"Where's Lowell?" Martin Roundtree's voice had grown petulant of late.

"Why, you know she went to Bollington to meet the Hartford train. I can't get over that girl coming all the way from Paris to see Lowell married."

"We invited her, didn't we? And she's Lowell's first cousin. Why shouldn't she come?"

Edythe did not mention expense. It was a subject Martin usually chose to ignore. Instead, she gave him a warm smile.

"I hope we won't be too countrified for her."

"For whom?"

"Ariel. She was brought up in Europe."

"And she probably has as little common sense as her mother. Alice, or Alicia as she calls herself now, may be my sister but the way she's raised that child is a disgrace. Heaven knows what we'll see."

But Edythe knew that Martin was pleased. He wanted as many Roundtrees on hand as possible. We're old family, he liked to say. We stand for something. On very thin ice, Edythe would add silently.

Claude, their second daughter, a worrisome silver-blond sprite, skipped into the room. "Lowell's not going to make that train on time."

"Why not?" Martin peered over his glasses.

"Because she stopped at the library to see Mrs. Haskell about the music." Mrs. Haskell was the church organist when she was not serving as town librarian. "Mrs. Haskell will talk right on to the last semidemi quiver."

"Quaver," said Edythe. "An eighth note."

"Quaver. The only one Mrs. Haskell lets talk in the library is Mrs. Haskell."

"She's a good woman," Martin regarded his fifteen-year-old.

"You know something, Dad?" Claude slid an arm around her father's neck. "The one thing I never want to be known as is a good woman."

"I wouldn't worry about it," said Martin mildly.

There were times when the love Edythe felt for her proud husband filled her throat. This was one of them.

"I'm off, people!" Claude was at the door.

"So soon?" But Martin Roundtree didn't say it aloud. His children came and went so fast these days, through the house and out again, that it made him feel older than he saw himself. Fifty-six. Not so old. One minor heart attack. He preferred not to think of it or the night it had happened. All the Roundtrees had gone to their appointed destinies without hand-holding. Sometimes it seemed to Martin that the old house stood stronger and wiser than any of them.

"I'll be back by the time she gets here."

Martin returned to this fourth child. He suspected Claude's silvery brightness would bring him no peace. Not like Lowell, who understood silence and could sit long enough to hear a complete sentence. Now he was losing Lowell. But not yet. And not entirely, thank God.

Claude was still chattering. "I told Mrs. Poole that my cousin was coming from Paris so my maid of honor dress had to be perfect. That's where I'm going now. For a fitting."

Martin glanced at his wife. "Why Hannah Poole?"

"Because she's a good seamstress, dear."

"I don't like her either, Dad. She's a terrible tattle-tale. Tell her anything and it's all over town. But she tells marvelous fortunes. She says I'm going to meet a handsome, mysterious stranger." Claude giggled. "Then I meet Dunkie who's going to be my brother-in-law. Though he's certainly handsome. And mysterious."

54

"I find nothing mysterious, Claude, about a man who has chosen to go into God's service."

"When he's as sexy as Dunkie?"

"Claude!" Edythe was watching Martin.

"But he is, Mom. He's really got it. Oh, when he came back from Vietnam he was sort of cool and remote. But when he starts preaching I'll bet that church will be filled to the brim. Not like it is now. They won't be listening, they'll be looking at him. I don't think Lowell even realizes it. That's why she'll be perfect for him. She doesn't flap at anything. If it was me I wouldn't live in that old rectory house for anything! It would be like having sex in a gold fish bowl. See you!"

They heard the front door slam.

The hall clock struck. Martin took out his watch, as if taking the pulse of the aged sentinel in the hall.

"That third note rattles. I must see to it." He rose stiffly. "I'm going down to the office."

"This afternoon?" Edythe knew she should have held her tongue. Martin crossed to where she stood.

"Say it or don't say it, Edythe. I'm a burden and I know it. But for God's sake, treat me as a burden or treat me as a whole man. What I can't stand is half talk, hints. That look of guilt or panic or whatever you're thinking. I'm living. I'm going to live for a long time. So let's both forget it."

A woman doesn't forget it, Edythe thought. But her arms went around his neck. For an instant he stood rigid, then one arm closed around her. Habit or love, or did it matter? She was his, the frame of his life, whatever warmth it still held.

He kissed her cheek gently and walked slowly out into the afternoon light, made golden by the great yellowing maples that sheltered the house.

The telephone was ringing.

Edythe remembered that she was the mother of the bride.

Once out of her sight, Martin quickened his pace.

55

He was not finished yet, not by a damn sight. This town was his responsibility. If nobody else had the guts to fight Ben Orlini's marauding, he had. There was a town meeting next week on the newest Orlini variance. He intended to be ready for it.

At the corner, he waved to slow an oncoming car and crossed the street at his own gait.

The Hartford local was ten minutes late.

As the warning bell jangled and the red crossing lights blinked, a rakish white sports car slid to a stop, its low pitched nose within six inches of striking the descending gate.

A police whistle blew. Officer Schiller sauntered from his post and looked into the car. "You, again."

"Hi, Schiller." The driver grinned. "I didn't quite make it today."

The officer did not return the smile.

"I warned you if you tried that trick once more—"

"You can't pinch me for stopping. That's the law." The younger man's grin faded. "Besides, I don't think you want to try. The name's Orlini, remember. My old man . . ."

The train, pounding into the station, drowned out his words. The police officer gestured angrily, and Nick Orlini backed his car.

"Thanks, chum." He reached out his hand toward the officer. It held a folded bill, the figure 20 showing.

"What do you think you're doing with that?"

Nick Orlini laughed. "Just testing your character, Schiller. It's funny money." He opened the twenty-dollar bill. The center picture was Mickey Mouse. "I passed a fifty the other day. Oh, don't worry. I sent the poor guy a check. One of nature's little fun-makers. That's me." The good-looking face went slack. "If you don't make your own laughs these days, where in hell do you get them?"

The train discharged a youngish woman with a

small girl. Officer Schiller touched the visor of his cap. "How was the city, Mrs. Elton?" An elderly man followed. Officer Schiller knew what those weekly trips were for, so he simply smiled and waved.

The fourth passenger was a girl. Beautiful seemed an inadequate word. Different? Officer Schiller settled for class.

She carried a large, brown-patterned suitcase and a matching shoulder tote. The police officer did not recognize expensive French luggage. But she did not look burdened and she did not look helpless. Her dark hair swung freely as she looked up and down the platform.

Officer Schiller released an explosive sigh. He might have known.

Nick Orlini was crossing the platform toward her, wearing his most engaging smile.

"Looking for someone?"

"Yes. But I suppose they are not here. Is there a taxi?" Her voice had an odd rhythm.

"There's the stand. But the train's late and both taxis are out. You might have quite a wait."

"Is there a bus?"

"Depends where you're going."

"Thatcher."

He glanced at her sharply, then his easy grin returned. "Every hour on the hour. You missed one by five minutes." His grin widened. "It just so happens . . ."

She turned a cool smile on him. ". . . that you live in Thatcher?"

"No, I don't. I wouldn't live there if they gave me the place." He would enjoy cutting this ravishing charmer down to size. "I live eleven miles beyond. But I'm going through Thatcher and if you want a lift, be my guest."

His thin face had a satyr's dark good looks. His narrow lips had the sardonic twist of self-indulgence. His black straight hair, his too-flashing smile, his easy assumptions—she had seen them all in Paris bars and bistros. He could not surprise her.

"Do you know the Roundtrees?"

He laughed. "Everybody in Thatcher knows the Roundtrees. They *are* Thatcher. Or they expect you to think so."

"Do you know where they live?"

"9 West Street. Do I pass?"

"Thank you." She got into the car. She knew her mind. That, to Nick Orlini, was a change. She sank back in the bucket seat as if she'd been born to it, and tied a scarf over her hair.

"Doesn't the top come down on a day like this?"

"Not on this car."

He gunned across the now-empty tracks, narrowly missing an oncoming truck, and side-slipped onto a narrow road. He picked up speed and glanced at the girl beside him. She had a contained air, an elegance, an aloofness. A loner, he thought.

"Just what Uncle Henri says," she said suddenly.

"Who's Uncle Henri?"

"Monsieur le Baron. A friend—of my mother's. He makes these cars and he says he is sorry for every one of them that goes to America. All an American driver can do is—what's the word?—jackrabbit."

"Well, that's two points for you." But he relaxed his speed.

"Oh!" she gasped.

"What's wrong?"

"Nothing's wrong. Everything is quite right. Look at those trees! The yellows! The reds! And golds! Incredible!"

"You've never been here before?"

"Once. When I was five. But it was winter and there was snow. Oh, my mother talked about Thatcher. But she never told me about the trees in autumn." Her mother. And the airless, scented apartment on the Boulevarde St. Germaine. Her mother knew a great deal about flowers in silver bowls, and table-settings for twenty, damask walls, and slender-legged furniture, but nothing about trees.

He was studying her. "Isn't it time we gave out with names?"

"I'm Ariel Roundtree." She said it so simply that it became important.

His smile faded, but only for a moment. "I began to think so."

She was silent.

"Sorry if I offended you."

"Not at all. It's rather interesting. Uncle Henri says you can tell more about people from their enemies than their friends."

"I didn't say the Roundtrees were enemies."

"They wouldn't stand for much if they didn't have a few."

It wasn't the usual talk he heard from girls in Thatcher, and he was unsure of himself. She was obviously very different. Besides, she hadn't even asked his name.

"I'm Nick Orlini."

"How do you do?"

"I thought we'd gotten past that. But if you care, I'm very well, thank you."

She laughed but he sensed indifference.

"I must say you don't look as if you belong around here, Miss Ariel Roundtree."

"I've lived abroad all my life. Paris, Athens, Vienna. Wherever my mother took me."

"My, my."

"You're being rather rude."

"That's my thing. I'm told I do it very well."

"I suppose it is a kind of accomplishment." She wasn't bothering to look at him. "Why don't you like the Roundtrees?"

"If you want it in a word, they're uptight."

"Isn't everybody? My cousin Lowell's being married."

"So that's why you're here?"

59

"I'm to stay with them."

He noticed that she had a dimple on her left cheek. It reminded him of something, someone. He could not place it. But it would prove amusing to break through that airy indifference. He could wait. She threw back her head and breathed deeply.

"Marvelous!"

"What?"

"The fresh air."

"We have lots of it, if you go for it."

"I do." She sank back into the seat, content to watch the rolling, open land, the hills sweeping to the horizon, the swatches of forest, marked with alternating stands of dark firs. Through the trees, she caught glimpses of water, lakes holding the blue of the golden afternoon. They crossed a bridge, and the river below showed bright and placid. Beyond she saw a church steeple.

"Thatcher," he pointed. "Over that hill. Four churches, a library, two streets of stores, a cemetery larger than the town, a shopping area with a liquor store and a travel agency, God knows what for. Oh— and a gift shop, not your type."

She felt the town reach toward her. She was coming at last to a place where she might belong. She could never explain that to Alicia (who had long ago banished the word 'mother'). Or to this uncomfortable young man beside her. She had won.

It had not been easy.

For an instant she saw Alicia again, opening the square, cream-colored envelope from America, with that little crystal laugh her admirers so enjoyed.

"Darling! Your country cousin's getting married. 'Mr. and Mrs. Martin Isaac Roundtree . . .' Will they ever drop those dreary Biblical names? 'Mr. and Mrs. Martin Roundtree request the honor of your company . . .'—yours and mine, darling. One envelope, two names outside! Never economize, Ariel, where it shows. '. . . at the marriage of their daughter Lowell . . .'—she was the plain one, remember? '. . . to the Reverend . . .'—oh my God, a minister, wouldn't you know? '. . . Duncan Phelps.' Why, he must be the son of Martin's former law partner, Harlan Phelps. I remember Harlan, shrewd as a weasel and no principles. Which you need in Thatcher. So his son's a minister. You never can tell, can you? Such a handsome little boy. Well, I'm sure it's very nice for them all. Just what Edythe would like. We'll send a piece of silver—Henri will get it for me at a discount."

Alicia had dropped the invitation into the waste basket. Ariel had swooped after it.

"Couldn't we go, Alicia?"

"To Thatcher? You can't be serious!"

"I haven't been there since—"

"You were a child. And that was a mistake."

"I loved it."

"You can't possibly remember anything about it. Of course we're not going. Think of the cost! For a wedding? Whom could you possibly meet in Thatcher? Besides, Henri has arranged for us to go to Milan in September for the Exhibition. After that we'll all go on to Rapallo for a little holiday. Now throw that silly thing away!"

Ariel had quietly slid the invitation back into its envelope. "I have some money. Saved from Christmas and from my job."

"Your job!" Contempt sharpened the false youth in Alicia's fine features. A little silence tightened into a tug of wills, one of the pointed little silences which Ariel had come to dread.

"I've done the best I could, Ariel, for you and your future. You're old enough to make your own mistakes. If you want to waste your money going all the way to Thatcher on the cheap for that dreary little wedding, I can't stop you. But don't expect me to go with you." Alicia glanced in the gilt-framed Venetian mirror and smiled at the delicate blond beauty she saw reflected. The enamelled brightness returned.

"Henri has promised to bring a Spanish count to Rapallo. Not yet thirty, darling. And drowning in Libyan oil money. Well, there will be plenty of other pretty girls to amuse him."

Ariel had written her acceptance that night. Since then the most important thing in her fragmented young life had been Thatcher. And Lowell Roundtree's wedding. But she wished someone had been at the station to meet her. Driving beside this unlikely stranger made her arrival seem more like an intrusion.

Ariel was suddenly aware that the road had narrowed and roughened. The white church steeple she had remembered like a beacon from childhood no longer rose ahead but lifted distantly on her right. The river lay below and behind them. They had left the main road.

"Is this the way into town?"

"The long way. Why?" He grinned at her and his eyes returned to the road. He was older than she had first thought. When he was not engaged in mocking banter, the slackness went from his face, leaving a stamp of self-indulgence, self-absorption that had its own strength. She had seen it often in the rich and idle young men who crowded her mother's drawing room, handsome in casual, faultless tailoring, their eyes searching, their hands restless, their talk shallow, sex-laden. Nick Orlini could well be one of them, except for the hooded intelligence in his eyes. This man could be cruel, she thought.

"I'd prefer the shorter way."

"Aren't you enjoying yourself?" He slid the car around a turn. They were now climbing steadily on a road that was dirt and gravel. Tall pines lined either side, blocking out the sun. She shivered.

Nick brought the car to a stop. Ariel gasped. As far as she could see, the hills unrolled a billowing tapestry of reds and yellows. Below, the river curved its silver thread around one edge of Thatcher, holding the town in its embrace. But it was not the open beauty of autumn that made Ariel gasp. It was the scene at the top of the ridge.

It looked like a battlefield. Great boulders lay pushed from their moorings. Felled trees lay in a tangle of branches. One giant, straight enough for a mast, lay with its shattered crown, still green, hanging over the cliff, its stump three feet in diameter, jagged as an angry wound. Ariel felt its invisible bleeding.

"What happened?"

"Nothing happened. Let's get out. Look around."

But the desolation had moved her. Bred to old cities as she was, she saw in the slaughter of the trees something savage, a wanton cruelty.

"Who did it?"

Nick was steadying her elbow as he led her through the tangle. She moved slightly away from him.

"What are you talking about? I brought you up here to show you the site of my family's new home. Welcome to Montioro. Locally known as Bluestone."

"All this—for one house?"

"I admit it's a mess now. But when we get the rest of the trees down, that's where the swimming pool will be. Three tennis courts over there. The house will be native rock—strictly modern, two wings—the garage and parking place where those tulip trees stand. They'll go next week. It's been the devil of a job, but when it's finished, we can spit straight down on Thatcher."

"Lovely." She said it without irony, without expression.

"I thought you'd be impressed."

"I am. Very. Now may we go, please."

She started alone across the ravaged clearing when a new sound reached her, a soft purring. Unmistakably, a car was coming up the ridge. She looked back at Nick. The sun had dropped into a cloud bank, leaving the area shadowed and chilled. Nick was standing, rigid, his eyes fixed on the road. Was it her imagination that produced the sense of menace that seemed to rise in the graying afternoon?

The car came into view and stopped. Low and black, a hood absurdly long for the small interior that could hold only two passengers and now held but one. The familiar chaste silver grilling told her it was a Rolls, but nothing about the man who stepped from it identified him. He was short and heavy, with a thickly handsome face and the smallest hands and feet she had ever seen on a man. He was looking directly, unblinkingly, at her.

"Hello, Dad." Nick approached his father slowly, formally, it seemed to Ariel.

"I wouldn't say we were ready for visitors, Nick."

"I was giving Ariel a lift into Thatcher from the train. She's a stranger here. I thought I'd show her the view." Nick's face had gone slack again with small-boy petulance. "Ariel, this is my father. Dad, Miss Ariel Roundtree. She's here for the Roundtree bash."

"Very nice, I'm sure." Ben Orlini neither shook hands nor changed his expression. "I regret, Miss Roundtree, we are not ready for guests. In fact," he turned to his son, "I've decided to put a chain across the road just above the second curve. People who come up here will find it rather difficult to turn around and go back. I don't imagine they'll try it more than once." He smiled for the first time. "Bluestone Ridge was a picnic ground once for the locals, Miss Roundtree. They can't seem to realize they no longer own it."

It seemed to Ariel nearly an hour before Nick Orlini drew up in front of a rambling white clapboard house on West Street. Actually, it was barely twenty minutes.

Nick ran an arm along the back of the bucket seat. "Now tell me something. Where have I seen your face before?"

"I don't think you have." Ariel opened the door on her side quickly.

"It will come to me. Next question. When do I see you again?"

"I'm going to be very busy. But I do thank you for the lift."

Ariel slid out of the car, reached for her luggage behind the seat, and straightened. He had made no move to help her.

"Like doing for yourself?"

"Yes. I guess I do."

"Good. I like girls who aren't helpless. Be seeing you."

The front door of the house had opened. A pretty girl with short, dark, curly hair stood in the doorway. She smiled as Ariel started up the walk.

"Ariel . . . I'm Lowell. I'm so sorry—" She held out her hand. Ariel impulsively leaned forward to kiss her. Then she realized Lowell's serious gray eyes were not looking at her. They were following the small white car as it picked up speed down the street.

Chapter Two

Martin Roundtree opened the street door and climbed the narrow staircase slowly. The block of buildings had been prestigious once, with their Victorian cupolas and scalloped-roof fronts. They were still neatly painted and the narrow alleyways swept clean. Martin had ceased to care that the bookstore on the ground floor had given way to a split barber shop and shoe cobbler establishment, both run by Leo. Martin approved of individual enterprise, and at Christmastime he and Leo shared a bottle of ouzo wine, a plate of bitter olives, and a few earthy jokes that Leo's Greek peasant heritage nurtured.

Now as he climbed the stairs to his office, Martin was reminded as usual of his friend Leo, by the pervasiveness of leather and bay rum. Yet it was part of all that he loved in Thatcher. The large, clean window looking down on Main Street, with the shining gilt letters, "Martin Roundtree, Attorney at Law," reading backwards in the room. The flat carved-oak desk, the black-framed diplomas, the gilt-framed pictures his grandfather had painted—Indian scenes in the Berkshires—and the rows of solid, leather-bound volumes of the law, weighting the shaded room with dignity. Here was the world he commanded. Within it Martin believed he could hold time and the frailty of the flesh at bay.

"Mr. Roundtree!" His secretary, Betsy Muller, was round and rosy as a young russett apple—and six-months pregnant. But Betsy was the new generation. She had assured him that she was coming back as soon as the baby arrived. Martin wondered what on earth young women today thought happened after a baby was born to them. Well, he had learned to live with bay rum and leather. He could no doubt adapt to a play pen in the back room. Though Edythe had insisted to him with some finality that play pens were a thing of the past. Babies today crawled where they pleased. He would deal with that when it happened.

"Mr. Roundtree, you should have told me you were coming in. Mr. Phelps called and said he'd be late and I told him he must have the wrong day because you never came in in the afternoon and . . ."

"My fault, Betsy, I neglected to tell you. He will be here. Don't worry."

And late. There was a time when Harlan Phelps would have been waiting in the office when Martin arrived. There was a time before that when the reversed letters on the window had spelled out "Roundtree and Phelps, Attorneys." In those days Harlan had shown deference amounting to obsequiousness. But Thatcher had become smaller and the Roundtree office less and less busy. So five years ago Harlan Phelps had moved his practice to Bollington, where he had contacts in Hartford and lately even in Washington. It was rumored he'd soon receive a political appointment. Martin could guess what brought Harlan here today.

Harlan Phelps was exactly thirty-eight minutes late. He sank his heavy frame into one of the red leather chairs, crossed his legs, and lit a cigar with a "Bother you?"

"Not at all. I don't smoke any more myself but it does me good to smell it once in a while. Reminds me I still live in the world." Martin noted a new jowliness in Harlan's fleshy face, the florid forehead rising toward a receding hairline, a bulging torso straining the lower button of the expensive gray-striped suit. Prosperity shows more than does adversity, and less becomingly. It was difficult to remember that Harlan Phelps would soon be his favorite daughter's father-in-law. Not that that would change anything very much. Lowell had made her choice. Duncan was a fine young man and their future belonged only to them. Besides, he thought, she's still my daughter. No man can take her completely away.

"How's the bride?"

"Fine. Though I only catch a glimpse of her through the clutter. Boxes, tissue paper, phone calls. . . . You're lucky, Harlan, being father of the groom."

"Maybe. Maybe not." The easy pleasantries were over. "Well, Martin, let's have it. What will the decision be, on my client's variance?"

Martin shook his head, with an untroubled smile. "Not a chance, Harlan. If Mr. Orlini wants to build a filling station, he'll have to go farther out of town than Twin Elms Corners."

"By whose say-so? Yours?"

"I'm not the law—"

"Damn it, Martin. You try to be. Everybody knows you're trying to block Orlini at every turn he makes."

"Not at all. He's got Bluestone Ridge, and he's free to chop down every tree on it. Which he's doing."

"Thatcher needs him. And his money."

"That's a matter of opinion. At all events, I'm sorry I couldn't do more for you." Martin suddenly wanted to go home. He was tired.

"You can show me the law that stops the building of a filling station."

"Gladly. It's been on the books one hundred and fifty years. I dug it out yesterday.

"And I'll bet it took some digging."

"Here we are. No building shall be erected for commercial purpose nearer than five hundred yards to the First Congregational Church. Elms Corners is four hundred yards."

"I never heard of that law."

"There it is."

"Going to pull it on Tom Brady and his crummy little saloon?"

"Tom's eight hundred and thirty-five yards from the church and on the other side of the road, around the curve."

Harlan rose. His face was flushed with anger. "You're wrong, Martin. You can't fight progress forever. This town needs a man with Orlini's money."

"You mean you need him, Harlan."

"God damn it!" The heavy fist struck the desk. The crystal ashtray jumped and the double-faced clock shook. Betsy Muller's round little form filled the doorway. "I'm your friend, Martin. Our kids are going to be married. If it wasn't for me Ben Orlini wouldn't still be waiting with his offer of $100 an acre for Will Roundtree's land. $100 an acre for land that isn't good for anything."

"The land isn't for sale, Harlan."

"Okay, but Willard's past seventy. Orlini's willing to hold on."

"The land isn't for sale."

"You can afford to turn down $80,000?"

"Willard has turned it down."

A flash of understanding lifted Harlan's heavy features. "Martin, you haven't got some idea in that twisted brain of yours that Michael's coming back, and the land will be his?"

Martin leaned back in his chair. His face had gone gray. He closed his eyes. Harlan stared at him, then quickly poured a glass of water from the carafe. Martin opened his eyes and brushed it away.

"I'd better be getting home. We have a family dinner tonight." Martin rose from the desk. But Harlan had been frightened. He had seen in Martin's pinched features something more than the refinement he had always envied, the probing intelligence he could never match. He had seen the bony structure over which the thin skin stretched. Had he been given to imagery, he might have thought he had seen—death.

"Martin, I'm sorry. Forget that crack about Michael. I don't know what happened to our kids. Michael walked out—what is it, four years ago?"

Four years, ten months, three days. But Martin said it only to himself. The pain had come back, blind and terrible.

"And he never came back. To this day you don't know where he is. Well, let me tell you something. I'd rather be in your shoes, I'd rather have had Duncan walk out of my life forever, than have him come back from Vietnam the way he did—throwing a whole future away with a lot of Jesus talk. Settling in this rotting town for the rest of his life. With nothing. Except Lowell. You ought to feel the same way. He could have given your girl everything in the world. I had it all staked out. Run for the state legislature this year, where he'd meet the right people. Maybe Congress in two years, the Senate. Duncan could have done everything John Kennedy did. And with the right girl beside him . . . ? God Almighty, how could he have done this to me? Martin, you have four children left. Duncan's all I've got."

The late sun, reflected in the windows across the street, filled the office with cold revealing light. Martin looked at the big man he knew too well, and thanked God again that his son-in-law-to-be had taken a different path. Martin himself would see that Lowell would never be hurt. Or wanting. $80,000 . . . but the land was to be Michael's some day. As long as he had breath left to fight for it.

Harlan had gone. Martin called a good night to a frightened Betsy and went down the stairs. He walked as briskly as he was able past Leo's window. He had no wish to talk to anyone for a little while, not even a good friend.

Ariel sat on the edge of the four-poster, canopied bed, patted the thick hand-crocheted coverlet, and gave a sigh of contentment. It was all as she remembered it. The white ruffles over the bed, the white ruffled window curtains, the garden-flowered wallpaper, the bentwood rocker with chintz tiebacks. And the milk-glass lamp on the small cherrywood writing desk.

Her red dress for dinner hung on the door, her delicate sandals stood beside the chair, and fresh, new pantyhose lay folded on the bureau. All with the French neatness Mam'selle had engendered in her years ago. *Toujours la politesse.*

Even now, Ariel could smile to herself, remembering the rigid schooling by her beloved, starched governess. Politeness meant more than good manners toward other people, she said. It meant good manners to yourself, to everything you touched and did. And Mam'selle's pale cheeks had colored faintly: *"La politesse pour l'amour."* Ariel had never been sure whether that meant politeness to the one you loved, or politeness *in* love, or politeness *to* love. She could not quite imagine how politeness could be a part of passion that swept you off your feet and gave you no time to breathe, much less think. But when she had asked Mam'selle, the good nun-like woman had turned quickly to the multiplication table of seven (always a trouble to Ariel) and that ended the discussion of *la politesse* and *la passion.* To Ariel, it seemed that one would definitely interfere with the other. "Seven times six, *ma petite?*" "Fifty-one." "*Non! Attendez . . .*" How could one stop for courtesy when the one man you'd found at last took you in his arms, his lips on yours . . . "*De nouveau*—seven times six, Ariel?"

Fifty-three! Ariel jumped from the bed, whirled around the room, Fifty-three, darling Mam'selle! She wished Mam'selle could see her at this moment. In this lovely flowery room, in this white, green-shuttered house that had enfolded her the moment she had entered it with—what? Happiness? No, that was too strong. When happiness came she would know it. She imagined happiness as a great flooding tide that poured through one. This was contentment. She would like Mam'selle to know that here there was quiet, here was *politesse.* After Mam'selle had left them there had been the endless traveling, the restless search for distraction, the men with whom her mother sought to pursue youth. All behind her now. Ariel had been invited to stay in this house as long as she wished. Perhaps forever, she thought.

Yet, there was a disquieting note. Behind the warmth of Edythe Roundtree's welcoming smile and the sparkle of those china-blue eyes, Ariel had sensed a faint anxiety. "Would you like tea, dear? No tea bags. We know how to warm the teapot first." Lowell had spoken quietly.

"Mother, that's British, not French."

"So it is." Edythe's little laugh belied the apologetic flutter of her hands.

"I've never been abroad, Ariel. You'll have to tell us all about the big world." Ariel had declined tea, and Lowell had picked up her luggage and brought her to this room. "You'll have plenty of time to rest before dinner." Lowell had turned at the door. "We're all *so* glad you're here, Ariel." And Ariel was alone.

The sense of difference. They had shown it lovingly but unmistakably. She would have to bridge it, somehow. She would have to show them that all she wanted was to jump into a sweater and jeans like Lowell's, to run out into this glorious but fading sunlight. Or maybe sit on the floor and play rock records and laugh with Lowell over the impossible Nick Orlini who had driven her to Thatcher. Well, it would take time. She began brushing her dark hair, a nervous habit she had acquired in strange hotels, while Alicia was napping. She would have to make them understand she was not different. She would try to explain this overpowering sense of *coming home.* And that, Mam'selle, Ariel said to herself, would take more than *la politesse.*

There was a knock at the door. Ariel opened it eagerly. "May I?" Lowell entered carrying a china-glass tray with a glass of what looked like lemonade and three fat sugar cookies.

"Mother thought you'd like some refreshment if you didn't want tea."

"I'd adore it if . . . if you'll stay." Ariel spotted a daisy imprinted mug next to a matching water carafe. She poured half the contents of the glass into it. "There. And a cookie for each of us. We'll split the third one."

Lowell hesitated, then took it. "I'll clear the desk."

"Can't we sit on the floor?"

Again the slight hesitation. Lowell dropped to the floor. Ariel followed and kicked off her shoes. Lemonade sloshed from the mug.

"It's my fault." Ariel took an elegantly laced handkerchief from her pocket and mopped. "I'm impulsive, that's the trouble. Mam'selle always said . . ." She stopped. It sounded foreign. "It won't hurt the rug, will it?"

Lowell laughed for the first time. "We've all spilled everything on that rag rug from hot chocolate to sloppy joes. This used to be the playroom."

"The room wasn't always like this?"

"Long ago. Then we needed a playroom. When the

room outlived that purpose, Mother moved my great-grandmother's bed and desk back in here." Lowell stopped. "I guess she's your great-grandmother too, isn't she? She must be. You'll have to ask Uncle Willard about Henrietta. He's got all the family history down pat."

Ariel had little regard for history. It was like seven times six, all numbers and dullness. But if it brought her into this magic circle she would learn anything.

"What a lovely dress!" Lowell's eyes were on the silky red folds hanging against the door. "Is that from Paris?"

"Off the peg. The Galleries Lafayette."

"Oh." Lowell looked away.

"It's just a big department store. I bought it off a rack where there were a dozen just like it." Ariel checked the rush of words. Why couldn't she have told the truth—that her mother had the dress made of real silk from Italy by a little seamstress who worked for one of the couturier houses. Was it part of wanting so desperately to be like them? But to lie! She hadn't been in the house two hours. *La politesse.* Had Mam-'selle never realized that if you lived by *la politesse,* you had to lie a great deal?

Lowell had risen. "Don't be polite about the cookies. They're not very good. Kim makes them."

"Kim?"

"She's nine. The youngest. She makes sugar cookies and keeps animals and wants to be a fireman. Mom moved her to the third floor so she couldn't bother you."

"I love animals. And I'd love to meet Kim."

"You will." Lowell had collected the tray and glass.

"Lowell, don't go yet. Tell me about everything!" Ariel felt that if Lowell left now the visit would be a failure. "I mean—well, you're a bride, you're going to be married in a week. You must be terribly happy. What's he like?"

73

"I am happy. Duncan's a wonderful man." Ariel marveled that she could say it so steadily.

"You've known him a long time?"

"We were in school together."

"How marvelous." Privately Ariel wondered if it *would* be marvelous to know a man you were going to marry that well. "And he's a minister?"

"He left college to go to Vietnam. When he came back he said being a minister was one thing he wanted to do because there was nothing else left. He never talked about what happened to him in the war. But I could understand how he felt."

Ariel thought this gentle-voiced, capable girl could understand anything. "You didn't mind? I mean his becoming a minister."

"Mind? Of course not. I knew Duncan had to do what he most wanted. And we're going to live right here. Dr. Wilcox wants Duncan to take his church. He'll retire soon. No, I didn't mind. It's worked out very well. You'll meet him tonight. He's coming to dinner."

"I'm looking forward to it." But she wasn't. Something that Nick Orlini had said lingered in her mind. "The Roundtrees. They're uptight." But he was wrong. Lowell was anything but uptight. She was calm and pretty and—and adjusted. But the radiance, the pounding excitement that would have throbbed through Ariel a week before her wedding wasn't there. Or didn't show.

And then it was as if Lowell read her mind. "I—I do want to say something, Ariel. And I hope you don't mind. I'm terribly sorry about missing your train this afternoon. Mrs. Haskell talked a lot and then . . ."

"Don't think about it."

". . . and I'm so glad you got here—so easily. But . . ."

Ariel waited. She disliked hints and circumlocutions. It was her mother's way when she had been at fault.

"Well, it's Nick Orlini—who brought you home."

"I certainly didn't like him very much."

Lowell appeared relieved. "Neither do a great many other people. It's not really Nick himself. He's what he is. Always on the make. A lot of girls find him fascinating. Maybe you do too. That's okay. But it's his father."

"I . . ." Ariel stopped. It would be better not to discuss her afternoon with Nick.

"Mr. Orlini . . . well, nobody knows exactly what he's after. They had a summer home on Birch Lake for a few seasons. Now they just seem to have moved into Thatcher. Buying land, spending money. Nobody knows what for. Dad can't abide them. That's what I wanted to say. Dad isn't well, these days. And we try to keep everything calm and pleasant. . . ."

Ariel understood. She went to Lowell and gave her the kiss she had failed to give at the door. "Lowell, I'm so happy to be here. I've already forgotten Nick Orlini. He is not my cup of tea, and I don't have any wish to see him again."

"Date him if you want," Lowell spoke so quickly Ariel couldn't believe she meant it. "Only don't talk about it here, in front of Dad." Her intensity brought a flush to her face, more than had anything she had said about her coming wedding or the man she was to marry.

The flush faded. Lowell smiled, and Ariel saw warmth and friendship. She will make a good wife for a minister, Ariel thought. Understanding. Gentle. Patient, probably. All the qualities that Mam'selle considered virtues, little as she had found them in young Ariel. Well, she, Ariel, wasn't marrying any minister. It would be like undressing in front of pale, mild-eyed Father Duclerc at St. Agathe where Mam'selle had taken her to Mass when Alicia was away. But she deeply wished Lowell happiness even if it was not her kind of happiness.

"Dinner's at seven," said Lowell. "But do come

down earlier. Dad wants to celebrate your being here. He's having cocktails. And wine."

"How nice!" Ariel hoped she had struck the right balance of enthusiasm and restraint.

"The Roundtrees are living it up this week!" For an instant excitement flickered like a small flame across Lowell's soft features. "So wear the red dress." Lowell almost giggled. "Because if you don't, I will!"

She was gone, leaving Ariel to wonder how she would pass the next hour, and why, suddenly, her drive home with the rather obvious Nick Orlini had become a secret.

But Ariel never brooded long on the complexities of human nature. She had been too entrapped by them. "Circumstances beyond her control." The story of her life. She went to the window and flung it wide open to the deepening dusk. There was the land as she remembered it, rolling from the rear of the house, down an incline and up a distant hill. There was a sprinkling of houses she could not remember, and across the hill a march of telegraph poles, the new power line, she would learn later.

The air had a sweet tartness so different from the night dusk of Paris, and the twilight carried a scent of wood burning in a fireplace. She drew a deep breath of contentment. She was free at long last, free to belong. Would anyone ever understand that? Probably not. But she knew it and felt the room enfolding her.

Lowell might say this had been a playroom, but it was the room Ariel remembered back over all those years. Even to the chest of drawers with its scrolled maple veneer, and the keyhole in the top drawer. She knew when she opened it she would find the key neatly placed in the left corner of the three compartments, painted white inside. One to hold her ribbons, one her socks and pantyhose, and the third—secrets, that is, anything she wanted to hide under handkerchiefs. She pulled the drawer open, ready to laugh with relief at its mute testimony. There was no key.

There were no compartments. Only a deep empty drawer lined with sprigged shelf paper.

Somewhere below a bronze-throated clock struck.

Ariel turned on a lamp and reached for the red silk dress.

Duncan would be late. Lowell returned from the telephone with a serene face. It was Claude, in an unaccustomed dress, who pouted.

"Probably old Mrs. Plummer wanting to talk about her rheumatism and he'll have to listen because she gave the church the new organ." She turned an impish grin on her father. "Lowell won't admit it but it's worse than marrying a doctor. Because poor Duncan has to hang around and listen when it isn't even important. Right, Dad?"

"Wrong," said Martin. "But I think we'll go ahead and have drinks. Ariel has already put up with us too patiently."

She had come downstairs too early. Martin had gone upstairs to rest. Edythe, in a sweater pushed to her elbows, was tending violets in a living room bay window. Lowell was nowhere to be seen. And Ariel had had one disquieting little experience in the upper hall. She had just left her room, absorbing the graciousness of the old house, the wide hall, the white woodwork, the doors with their oak-leaf scalloped lintels, the staircase with its white balustrade and polished mahogany handrail. She wondered if the rounded newel post at the bottom still had one loose spoke.

Down from the third floor had bounced a chubby little girl, with brown braids, carrying a ventilated tin box.

"You're Kim!" Recognition had been easy.

The little girl had smiled brightly but shyly.

"I'm Ariel."

"I know." Then the smile had gone and Ariel was aware the child was staring at her. Suddenly she had darted past her down the hall and knocked on a door. "Claude! Claude! Can I come in?" The door had opened and closed. Ariel heard nothing, then an outburst of high voices, and Kim, who must have been near the door, saying, "Well, you just see for yourself!"

Ariel had gone downstairs with a sense of another small failure. But there had been no children where she had grown up, and except for fleeting acquaintances in the many schools she had passed briefly through, she hadn't known children. She supposed she would have to win this child over with the others. Ariel had begun to be thankful she had come to Thatcher only for a visit. Too much was different and too much surprisingly the same. The wedding, though, would carry her unthinkingly in its tide of events.

Sitting in the living room, with its deep chairs showing wear, large shelves of books on either side of the fireplace, and the old rosewood grand piano with its yellowing keys, Ariel felt less than at ease. Perhaps it was because young Claude had hardly taken her eyes from Ariel's face in the long half hour since they had gathered.

"What'll it be, Ariel?" Martin was smiling down at her.

"I'll get the drinks, Dad."

"Not a chance, Lowell. Not when I have a young lady as charming as this one to serve." There was something old-fashioned and rather sweet about him, Ariel told herself. But also something she could not fathom, an inner tightness, a shadow.

In the end, Edythe, surprisingly, had a dry martini, Martin a small Scotch, Ariel a sherry, and Lowell would wait for Duncan.

"What about me?" said Claude. "And don't say a Shirley Temple, Dad, or I'll—"

"You can have anything you want, Claude, when you're old enough to vote and pay your own taxes."

Martin said with finality. Ariel realized he could be severe.

"I'll bet they drink real things at my age in France. Don't they, Ariel?" It was the first time Claude had addressed her directly. But for Ariel the question seemed to weigh her in the balance.

"Well, not spirits."

"Spirits?"

"I mean whiskey and things like that. But yes, they give little children wine and water."

"I think wine and water would be all right, Martin." Edythe spoke with a sense of mischief.

"Thanks a bunch, Mom. But no thanks." Claude settled back in her chair. Ariel wished the coffee-brown eyes would look somewhere else.

Conversation was politely brisk. Ariel learned that the little girl Kim had gone to stay overnight at a friend's. "Debbie Haynes, her best friend, has a new pony. You can't compete with that, my dear." Martin patted her hand.

There would be four bridesmaids, and two maids of honor, Claude and Kim. The youngest Roundtree had flatly refused to be called a flower girl.

Ariel also learned that Duncan's parents had invited them all to dinner after the rehearsal, the night before the wedding. She saw Lowell's mouth tighten. "I wish they wouldn't. I mean, I wish they hadn't offered. Duncan's father hardly speaks to him, and it will be miserable." Ariel saw Edythe flash a warning glance. "But that's what you do, Ariel, in a small town," Lowell finished lightly. "And I'm used to it."

The doorbell rang.

Claude leaped from her chair. "It's Dunkie. I'll go!"

"That young man doesn't realize how many of the Roundtree girls he's marrying," Martin observed dryly. "And for heaven's sake, somebody stop her calling my son-in-law Dunkie."

"*You* try, darling." Edythe rose.

79

Duncan Phelps entered with Claude clinging to his hand. He was above average height, and his broad shoulders fitted easily into a tweed jacket. He wore good brogues and a turtle neck sweater. His hair was crisp, rumpled and straw-colored and his eyes a narrow, amused, steely blue that did not miss anything.

"So sorry, Edythe." He stopped to kiss her cheek. "Martin." He shook hands with his future father-in-law, and Ariel felt a flow of strength between the two men.

"Darling." He kissed Lowell on the lips. Ariel saw her color faintly, whether from emotion or embarrassment it was hard to tell. "And the French cousin."

Without introduction Duncan crossed to her, took both her hands, and kissed her lightly, brushingly, on the cheek.

It was then Ariel said something she was to regret. But she was helpless as the words came out. "In France, we kiss on both cheeks."

For a moment, his steel-blue eyes caught hers. Ariel felt an odd weakness.

"Gladly." He brushed her left cheek, then crossed the room and sat on the divan beside Lowell.

Edythe broke the small silence with a laugh. "I think I like that. Ariel's teaching us all kinds of new manners." She had not sat down again. "Duncan, have a drink if you wish and bring it with you to the table. We'll have dinner now if you don't mind humoring my lamb roast."

On the way to the dining room, Duncan's eyes met Ariel's once more. This time Ariel turned her head away. But she knew it was too late. He was not smiling. Something had passed between them—a spark, a flash of hidden lightning, a—recognition.

"Will you say grace, Duncan?"

"I'm at *your* table, sir."

Martin bowed his head. It was a small gesture toward his dignity, his position, and he appreciated it. Ariel closed her eyes, thankful for a few seconds in which to quiet the pounding within her. She must have had a moment of madness. She would be all right.

". . . and for these gifts we thank You. Amen."

Chatter broke like a welling spring. "You'll have to say it at Thanksgiving and Christmas, Dunkie."

"Why, Silvertop?"

"You have more authority."

"We're going to have you all for our Christmas Eve, aren't we, Duncan?" Lowell said.

"Anything you want, darling."

"You're going to make a perfectly terrible husband, Dunkie. Lowell won't have a thing to be liberated about."

"I hope so." His eyes slid to Ariel and as quickly slid away.

"Ariel, I hope you like lamb with garlic."

"Oh, yes, we always have it that way." It was the first time she had spoken. Her voice in her own ears sounded small and distant. And her cheeks still felt hot with the imprint of those two light kisses. She must make an effort. She was aware that Claude was looking at her again with that odd intensity and then beyond her. She wanted to say something light, amusing. The kind of thing that had always come so easily at home. What could she say?

"John's coming home from law school Thursday. Do you remember him, Ariel?"

"Oh yes, yes I do. He built a snowman for me."

She must chatter now, casually, as if a member of the family. That was safest.

"And Michael? He was older, of course, and sort of distant, but I remember he was terribly good looking. He told me he had signed up to go to the moon on the first spaceship. Did he get there?"

There was a silence. She caught glances, and then everybody began to talk at once. It was Martin who answered.

"Michael's away just now. We—we hope he'll be home for the wedding. We don't know."

"I've made salad," said Edythe rising. "Lowell, will you toss?"

"Let me." Ariel pushed back her chair.

"Not tonight, dear. You're our guest of honor. Tomorrow you'll be family. Everybody else sit still."

Ariel found herself with Duncan's eyes compassionate and direct on her. She had made a gaffe of some kind. He was trying to reassure her.

Suddenly the whole scene became for Ariel, overbright. The candles, the talk, the obviously best china, the second bottle of unaccustomed wine, all of it *déjà vu*, already seen, already lived through. Tomorrow she would be back in the stuffy little rear room of Mme. Voisine's boutique, slipping into still another Voisine creation to model before Argentinian and Brazilian ladies with their piled and lacquered black hair and too much money, or Arabian men with thick fingers unrolling cash, and moist eyes that roved lustfully over her. She had hated it but now it seemed a refuge from this web of emotions she could not understand, this warm, close room that seemed to hold only one presence, a man she did not dare look at.

"*Can't anybody see?*" The young voice had knifed through the chatter.

"See what, Claude?" Edythe noted uneasily the hectic red patches on Claude's cheekbones. But Claude had not had wine.

"Well, just look, everybody. Kim saw it, and I was just waiting for somebody else to."

She was staring over her father's head at the oval framed painting that hung behind him. The others followed her eyes. Ariel saw the portrait of a dark-haired young woman, her curls caught up in heavy masses, her white throat and face reflecting the glow of a ruby silk dress pleated over full, firm breasts. Her beauty had a startling intensity.

"Don't you *see*?" Claude repeated. "It's Ariel. It looks exactly like her. It could be Ariel up there!"

Ariel herself could see it. The short tilted nose, the high cheek bones and forehead. Most devastating of all was a dimple on the left cheek.

"See, even the devil's kiss. It's you, Ariel!"

There was general laughter. Martin patted her hand.

"I'm glad someone in this family has inherited Henrietta's spirit. Your great-great-grandmother, my dear. You have as much right to her as we have."

"I wouldn't wish Ariel all that, Dad." Lowell's hand lay on the table, secure in Duncan's.

"Why not, darling? She was an interesting woman." Duncan released the small, capable hand to fold his napkin.

"Well, if you like scandal. She was a remarkable woman, Ariel, in a lot of ways. But the town never forgave her."

Ariel hesitated. But if Henrietta was her ancestor too . . . "Forgave her for what?"

"Oh, it was juicy!" Claude's face shone. "She had a lover, and when her husband Isaac found him out at the farm he was never seen again."

"That's quite unworthy of you, Claude." Martin's rebuke was short.

"Why? She even rode to the witches' sabbath, they said."

"Claude, that's nonsense. I think we've heard quite enough." Edythe rose and blew out the candles, forgetting in her irritation that everyone else was still seated.

Lowell spoke suddenly. "Ariel, if you want all the family history, I'll drive you around town and up on Cemetery Hill. The view's gorgeous, and we haven't anything planned tomorrow morning."

"Tomorrow . . . ?" Claude's voice rose. "Oh *no*, Lowell. I promised Mrs. Poole you'd come with me and see the way she's fitted my dress. She won't let me bring it home until you do!"

"Claude, you haven't had it changed!" Edythe spoke more sharply than she knew. The dinner table conversation had somehow twisted out of hand. She had been aware of currents she could not define, and there was Ariel's odd silence. Was the girl going to be unhappy with them? It was certainly true that this young cousin bore an uncanny resemblance to the portrait of Henrietta Roundtree. Appearances could bridge generations. So could temperaments.

"Claude, I'll go with you tomorrow. Don't worry. And whatever Mrs. Poole has done, I'm sure it will be lovely," Lowell said.

"Good girl."

Ariel heard Duncan's whisper and saw him squeeze Lowell's hand. She was outside this close circle. She must remain outside.

"Duncan, why don't *you* drive Ariel around tomorrow? You're not busy in the morning, are you?" Lowell turned a warm face to Ariel. "Duncan knows Thatcher as well as I do. Better, I guess. He gets around more places. And he's a very good guide. Would you, Duncan?"

"If our French cousin will take me as a substitute." He spoke lightly, almost mockingly.

She intended to refuse. She would not . . . she . . . he looked at her gravely. She knew she would go.

Chapter Three

Ariel awoke with that start that comes to a sleeper in a strange room. Her eyes traveled over the old-fashioned mahogany furniture, the chintz-covered chairs, the deep quilt, the ruffled canopy above her. Then she remembered—remembered a new rush of feeling, a man who had looked across a strange dinner table at her. For a moment she turned a flushed face into the pillow.

She was here in this place for a wedding, welcomed into the happiness of this family. Last night a man had walked into her life and changed it forever. He was to marry her cousin Lowell on Saturday.

The enormity of it was as stifling as her pillow. Could you pass between two continents, slip between two halves of the globe, and become in a single glance someone you could hardly recognize—a new self that left behind everything you knew and believed in, like an empty skin?

She sat up, reached for her robe, and jumped out of bed. The effect was dizzying. Jet lag? Well, you could be thrown off your time schedule by the speed of your flight. Unsettled, shaken from the familiar. It had never happened to her before. Yesterday she had not known Duncan Phelps. This morning her head was spinning like a schoolgirl's. He was coming to take her out.

Ariel had known infatuation before. Sometimes out of boredom, sometimes in revolt. But always there had been Alicia to sort out the values, to add up a doomsday forecast of profit and loss.

This morning there were no values, no forecast. She was in love. At first, surprised sight. And if her womanhood told her anything, he had known.

Perhaps they had all known at that tight, bright dinner table. But she would not admit that. Any more than she could admit to herself what had happened. Intensity like this could only be a mirage born of strangeness and new freedom. She did not yet belong in this family, except by blood ties thinned by neglect. She had come as a stranger. Only her startling resemblance to an old portrait linked her to them. She wanted to tell herself that what had happened could not matter, if she hurt no one, if no one knew. She would do nothing except snatch a few hours of this brief morning that no one would miss. Not Lowell, not even Duncan, in the end.

Her thoughts skipped perversely to the oval portrait downstairs. That earlier woman, Henrietta, her ancestor as well as theirs. Henrietta flaunting her beauty in the lift of her head, the half smile. Whatever she had done, she had lived on her own terms. It took courage for any woman to live on her own terms. Then. Now. Perhaps that was the scandal—that she had succeeded. Ariel wondered if she had married the man she truly loved. Or had met him too soon or too late.

She dressed quickly, slacks, a sweater, a scarf, then added the light scent Alicia told her was essential to every woman's toilette. She felt as new and tremulous as a child.

The big, rambling house was so quiet that she wondered with a pang whether last night's plans had changed. The living room was empty. In the silent dining room, Henrietta looked even younger in her oval frame. The large painted eyes in an uncanny way met her own. Are we really alike, Ariel thought? Did *you* ever face a morning when you could think only of one man, the man you could never have? Or—the buried thought surfaced—did you take what you wanted when you found it?

"Ariel, my dear, I didn't hear you come down. How sweet you look." Edythe Roundtree had pushed open the pantry door.

"Good morning, Aunt Edythe."

"What would you like for breakfast?"

Ariel kissed her aunt on the cheek and remembered her little joke to Duncan about both cheeks. "Don't worry about me. I never eat much breakfast and, and, this morning I'm not really hungry."

"You must have something before Duncan arrives. Coffee's hot in the percolator on the sideboard. There's orange juice. . . ."

"No thanks, really. But I'll help myself if I want

86

anything." How much Ariel would have liked to slip out of the house with only Henrietta's understanding, ". . . thank you."

"There's toast. And blueberry muffins. If you like them. Very New England, dear. Just remember this is your home as long as you choose. We want you to do just as you please." Edythe Roundtree's bubbling prettiness was at its best in the morning. She had long ago learned to melt dissent and round sharp corners with a smile.

"Help yourself to whatever you find in the kitchen. Lowell and Claude left at eight. Martin's gone to his office, and I have two dozen things to do and can only remember ten. Martin says I don't make enough lists. When I do, I just have one more thing to remember. Where I put them." Her face grew serious. "Ariel, my dear, it's so good to have you here. And you've made Martin so happy by coming all this distance. He's set such store on bringing all the family together for Lowell's wedding."

"All the family?" It was the first time Ariel realized that she would be on public display.

"Not quite all of them. Some of them live too far away and we haven't heard from them in years." Edythe's smile carried a hint of mischief. "Cousin Lili will be here from New York. But Martin was simply adamant about not inviting her gentleman friend, though he's a very important man. Kitty and Douglas are coming from Westchester. I'm not at all sure what shape that marriage is in. And Susan, their daughter—I just don't know." She sighed.

"And of course we could hardly expect Simon to come from California. But we did rather hope that Alice—oh, dear, I can't seem to learn to call your mother Alicia after all these years. Alicia is such a traveler. Anyhow, we're all grateful that she sent you."

Edythe was enjoying herself. There was something about this vibrant, charming, and courteous girl that lifted the household out of its humdrum, a hint of something faraway that reminded Edythe of her own youth, her own vanished horizons. Ariel would help to fill the void for them all after the wedding.

"The truth of the matter, Ariel," Edythe's laugh was girlish, "is that the Roundtrees have never learned to rally as a family. I tell Martin if they had, they would have conquered the world. It's probably just as well they aren't all coming. Too many Roundtrees would simply make waves and tip the boat."

She glanced out the window to the still-empty street. "Of course I don't say that to Martin. He thinks of himself as the head of the clan. But the Roundtrees aren't docile enough to fit the pattern. Anyhow you're here and you've made us all happy."

Ariel warmed to this serenely capable, bright-spirited woman. She knew no one like her and she wanted her as a friend. But her overcharged emotions made her stiffly self-conscious.

"Do you think I'd ever fit the pattern, Aunt Edythe?"

Edythe took one of Ariel's hands. It was cold but Edythe did not seem to notice.

"I don't think you're a bit docile, my dear. I don't think you'd want to fit any pattern but your own. But you are a Roundtree and there's no doubt you look like *her*." She nodded toward Henrietta's portrait. "Don't be surprised if a lot of people notice it at the wedding."

The doorbell rang.

"Duncan! I should have warned you. He's always prompt. It's his only flaw. But it doesn't bother Lowell and she's the one who has to live with it. You open the door. I must make at least one list. Just to please Martin. We'll see you at lunch. Enjoy the day, dear. It's a lovely one."

Duncan drove a dull-green rattle box of a car that showed its age. He held the door open with the seeming indifference of a tour conductor and settled in wordlessly. If he was eager to see her or aware of her appearance, he gave no sign. He wore a sweater. The jacket over it, like his tweed last night, showed a good cut but overlong wear and made no pretense of matching his trousers. A good scarf would help. Ariel let the thought die. Duncan Phelps this morning was a preoccupied man with a great many things to do beside the chore he had undertaken at his fiancée's request. Ariel silently wished herself in Paris.

"What would you like to see first?"

"Oh, anything. I know you must be very busy."

"I wish I were. But the assistant cleric of a small-town church with a dwindling congregation isn't exactly under pressure. So—at your service."

His coolness made her uncomfortable. She had carried to her room last night the sudden electricity when he had touched her arm. Had it been only in her mind?

"Seat belt, please."

"What on earth for?" It was a short reply but at least it drew a glance from him.

"Rule of the management."

She obediently hooked the belt into place and saw him conceal a smile. He was going to be superior, she decided—a little above it all and especially above this flirtatious—what had he called her?—French cousin. By now, Ariel was telling herself furiously that she had openly flirted last night. That was all. She would get through this morning somehow, she would look at his dull little town, ask polite questions about his dull little church, and when it was over she would attach herself to Lowell and smother in a welter of wedding gifts, gowns, flowers, and sentiment that had nothing to do with her. She could almost hear Alicia's brittle little laugh. ". . . all the way to Thatcher for a wedding!"

"We'll do the cemetery first."

"What? Oh, yes." In another man she would have

thought it a poor joke. But Duncan, his eyes fixed on the road ahead, was serious.

"I think you'll find it of historical interest, as well as informative. If you like cemeteries."

She was determined not to look at him so she did not see the corners of his mouth twitch. Nor could she guess that Duncan Phelps was fighting an inner battle as intense as hers. One that he must not lose.

"I don't. Do you? Or do you have to? I mean in your business. Profession, I guess I should say." He was a minister of the church. If she could just remember that she would get through the drive.

But Duncan burst into a laugh.

"I hate 'em. I see no reason for them. Land should be used for the living, not the dead. But you're right. I can't say so. They are undoubtedly part of my chosen—business."

It was not as if ice had been broken. There had been no ice, only a thin wall of artificiality. As their eyes met it vanished.

She turned her head quickly, to watch, without seeing, the passing storefronts. Benson's Hardware, Higgins Pharmacy and Soda, Slater's Stationers, Pop's Delicatessen, Pizza and Hamburgers . . .

"The only Dutchman I ever knew who could make a pizza." He gestured suddenly, boyishly. "But for hamburgers I'll take you down to Juno's Landing. My friend Big Moon's Diner. Lowell says." He stopped. "They're better than the Grist Mill. That's another of our eateries. I—we'll take you there sometime, too." His eyes were on the road again.

They had left the shopping area behind and were passing houses with smooth lawns and trim hedges, Cape Cod roofs, Victorian cupolas, widows' walks, and Federal doorways. It was a town, she thought, where everyone knew exactly who everyone was and joined invisible hands to keep it that way. A yellow sprinkling of leaves on the grass added to the timelessness.

She wondered if anything had ever shaken or changed this settled little world.

A white church, its tall windows reflecting the morning light, rose ahead. Its steeple must have been the one she had seen yesterday from Nick Orlini's speeding car. How eager, how sure, how young she had felt. She had lived a decade since yesterday. Or had it been only the duration of a heartbeat?

"Is that your church, Duncan?"

"I have no church of my own yet."

She wondered if you could talk to a minister about his work as you talked to other men.

"I never really belonged to any church," he went on after a pause. "My mother went to the Presbyterian, the one we just passed. My father never went. Neither did I until—well, Vietnam. Sometimes."

He was looking into a distance of his own.

"When I made up my mind what I wanted to do, Dr. Wilcox of St. Mark's—that's the Episcopal church, you'll see it—gave me some encouragement, so that's the way I went. He's retiring the first of January. I'm lucky to be able to take over in his place."

It was more than he had ever said to her, and like a prism it threw shifting lights across him.

They were out of the town now. The land had begun to rise and the air to freshen. He swung right at a fork, took a left turn into a narrow dirt road leading through a birch grove, and came out on a grassy plateau. He stopped the car. There was no sign of a cemetery.

"I thought you'd like this better. It's one of our nicer views. It's called Preacher Hill. A century ago it was the hottest spot in Thatcher to fight the Devil. Lord, those itinerant hell-and-thunder boys used to pack 'em in up here. Rolling and wailing, torch-light, and damnation. Hard cider and local mule. And everybody felt fine the next morning. Like to look around?"

She walked beside him up the grassy slope to where the hill dropped away. A flat rock made a natural back rest, sun-warmed in the morning light. It was not the magnificent view she had seen from Bluestone Ridge yesterday with Nick Orlini, as intimidating in its vast spread as the Ridge itself was awesome in its ruin.

A gentle, inviting country stretched below her, rectangled into tilled fields that edged up to a gray farmhouse, a red silo, and a red barn. Beyond, clumps of trees caught the shadows of passing clouds. In the distance the land lost itself in a blueness of hazy horizon.

At her feet the hill fell away in a barrier of scrub brush, reddening sumac, and cat briar, though she would not have known their names.

He dropped on the ground beside her.

"It's heavenly," she said. "Didn't anyone come here but the preachers?"

"They've gone a long time ago. There was an old dance pavilion after that. They used to call it Preacher's Rest. I guess the Devil was back staking his claim. But that didn't last long either. Now the kids come up here for picnics and cookouts. The only place left since the Ridge went."

She wondered whether she should mention her visit there with Nick Orlini. Why not? But then again, why?

Duncan was pointing to the sky and a long V of large flying birds, evenly spaced, their wings beating in a rhythm of majestic power, their cries a raucous triumph.

"What are they?"

"Canadian wild geese, flying South. I never get over that sight. Sometimes when I was in Vietnam I'd wake up hearing them. But it was always something else."

"What made you become a minister?"

He gave her a wry grin. "I wondered how soon you'd ask. Everybody does."

"Sorry."

"Not at all. I'd like to tell you. If I could. I'm not sure it even adds up to a story. But it would take more time than we have now." He gazed out across the valley and the farm below. "Take a last look. It's Roundtree property."

"Roundtree?"

"Didn't you know?"

"How would I?" Then she remembered her single childhood visit. "Uncle Willard's farm!"

"Yep, the old autocrat himself. That was the original Roundtree holding. Eight hundred acres still left. He farms about ten of 'em now. With the help of Charlie Redwing."

"Who's Charlie Redwing?"

"A full-blooded Algonquin Indian, grandson of a chief and the last man of his people in this part of the state."

"I have a lot to learn."

He looked at her. "You'll make it."

Silence. A light wind. Dancing particles of September light all blending into a new intensity. Suddenly he shook his head like a big dog coming out of water. Or a man emerging from a dream. He jumped to his feet.

"Time's a-wasting," he said, and reaching out his hand, pulled her to her feet. For an instant they stood together. Then imperceptibly his hand tightened.

All pretense, all denial slid away. There had been no mistake. The outer world vanished. An inner, invisible secret wrapped itself about them. It was all that she had guessed last night, all that her pulsing body had told her was true. It was forever. And it was never.

"I'll race you to the car," she said unsteadily.

He released her hand.

But she did not run. Nor did he. Instead they walked slowly, wordlessly to the car.

He opened the door. "I'll buy you a cup of coffee," he said, "before I drive you home."

* * *

Juno's Landing, two miles downriver from Thatcher, had an unsavory reputation. It was named, more than two centuries ago, for the ferry *Juno*, the stubby, reliable carrier of man, horse, wagon, and cargo across the Birch River. Juno's Landing had then been the center of bustling prosperity, the wharf piled high with sacks of flour, potatoes, produce, crates of poultry, bawling calves, frightened lambs, crowded with shrewd-eyed farmers and bargaining Yankees. Together, they almost, but not quite, obliterated the shouts of the captain, a man dedicated to the practical notion that time was money. The *Juno* crossed on time.

A bridge doomed the *Juno*.

When the textile factory was built, rows of identical clapboard houses replaced the farmers' sheds and stretched gray and monotonous as the factory belts themselves.

And then time passed Juno's Landing by. The Yankees had long since gone west to land that was kinder to the plow. The spools and bobbins of the old factory slowed, then stopped. The men who had tended them took their work-worn wives and pale children eastward to the cities. The rickety gray houses succumbed to neglect and decay.

Yet Juno's Landing lived in its own unconquerable way. On cheap land a car wash did a thriving business. Next to it, an auto repair shop displayed a yard full of twisted wrecks, like broken teeth, mute relics of human fallibility. Further down the single street, a pizza parlor advertised quality and twenty-four hour service. Across the road, a weathered house with a sagging porch bore a flowing neon sign, "Pete's Rock." A new rear wing troubled the curiosity of Thatcher and tempted its young.

Backing to the river, behind all this, the grime-streaked brick shell of Juno's textile factory rose, a mournful reminder against the sky. In answer to its silence, a radio loudspeaker from a tobacco and paper store blared rock-and-roll into the street.

Juno's Landing still throbbed with a seedy vitality.

At its heart, next door to the car wash, stood Big Moon's diner, an oasis of polished chrome and spotless stainless steel. Big Moon, a large man with a handsome mustache and a soft voice, wielded his counter rag like a gavel. The commanding sharpness of his eyes tolerated weakness, understood pain, and presided over his kingdom with the assurance of a man who respected himself. His wife, a dark, angular woman, worked at his side with a flare that equaled his dignity. She wore golden hoops in her ears and a red-orange bandana that unabashedly matched the red-orange curtains and red plastic stools of the diner. Against the center mirror behind the counter hung a pair of pink baby shoes.

This September morning, a single customer sat at the counter. He emptied his cup and pushed it away.

"Your coffee gets worse all the time, Moon."

The big man turned to his wife. "Princess, Mr. Orlini doesn't like your coffee."

"I heard. You tell Mr. Orlini that anytime he wants to come around this counter and make it himself, he's welcome." The golden hoops bobbed vigorously.

Nick looked out of the window. His car had not yet come through the wash and he was irritated.

"Ira, how come a beautiful gypsy like you married a big rascal like Moon?"

"Something you wouldn't understand, Mr. Orlini." She flashed a brilliant smile at her husband but there was no need to lay a cautioning hand on his sleeve. Moon knew Nick Orlini.

Nick flipped a couple of coins on the counter, walked to the door and stopped short. "Well, well, well." He returned and sat down. "Moon, you're having company. Think I'll take another cup of that lousy coffee."

The door opened. Ariel and Duncan walked in. Nick rose and bowed low.

"If it isn't the bridegroom himself. Morning, Deacon. And Miss Ariel Roundtree. A pleasure to see you again, honey." He held out his hand.

Ariel saw the sudden tightening of Duncan's jaw, the curt nod. To her dismay she felt her face flush. She automatically extended her hand which Nick held longer than courtesy required. He seated himself beside her.

"You know, Deacon, I had the pleasure of driving this lovely girl home from the train yesterday."

"I didn't know." Duncan reached for the plastic-covered menu.

"Ariel, be warned. Everything gets around Thatcher. Everything. Ultimately." He grinned at Duncan. "How's Lowell?"

"Fine." Duncan studied the menu.

"She's a sweet girl. Nice. Old-fashioned. She'll make a great minister's wife. You're a lucky man, Deacon. A very lucky man."

"Your car's come through the wash, Mr. Orlini." Big Moon picked up the untouched second cup of coffee and emptied it behind the counter. "No charge for this."

Nick dropped a hand on Ariel's shoulder. "Just when we were getting to know each other again." He gave Ariel's shoulder a squeeze. "Lots of luck, Deacon."

"Thanks."

"Be seeing you, honey." Nick turned at the door and winked. "Just get to the church on time, Deacon."

Big Moon sluiced his rag across the counter.

"Don't let that guy tighten you up, Duncan."

"I don't."

"Well, I do. He makes me so polite I could punch somebody."

Duncan laughed and Ariel saw some of the tension go out of his face. Some. But not all. The morning's sheen had been flawed. Nick Orlini's behavior had been outrageous. But the fault was hers. She had accepted a ride with him. She had allowed him to assume that she was friendly, at least. And the moment when she might have mentioned him to Duncan, told him how it had been, she had let pass. Now, suddenly, the small omission had ballooned. Yet she had no right to tell herself even that. She had no rights at all. *Well, get to the church on time, Duncan.*

"Ariel, this is one of my best friends, Moon Wright." Ariel held out her hand. "Moon, this is Lowell's cousin, Ariel Roundtree, just arrived from Paris. I brought her down here to taste a real cup of coffee."

The big man smiled and wiped his hand. His grip was strong. "You'll get it, Miss Roundtree."

"Ariel's one of the family, Moon."

Ira emerged from the rear, drying her hands. Duncan's smile warmed. "And here's the real boss . . ."

"Oh, no, Mr. Duncan."

"They call her Princess around here . . ."

"I can believe it." Ariel liked the striking, dark woman.

". . . and if you'll let her, she'll read your palm."

"No, Mr. Duncan." The words came so sharply, Ariel glanced at her in surprise. "You've got vibes, Miss Roundtree. I felt 'em as soon as you walked through that door."

"Vibes? What are vibes?"

Duncan grinned, but not at Ariel. "The lady's been brought up under primitive conditions, Princess. You have to explain."

The dark woman busied herself with cups. "It doesn't mean much of anything, love. But I'm just not telling fortunes with all I have to do. What'll it be, Mr. Duncan?"

"Two coffees. Anything else, Ariel?"

"No thanks. Just coffee." Ariel's discomfort increased. She would like to be through with this morning. Through with the week ahead. Through and forgetting. She was aware Duncan was talking to her.

". . . and Moon and I have known each other, how long?"

"February 23, 1966, Company D, Platoon K, Mud Hell Swamp . . ."

"Wait a minute, Moon. We knew each other before that . . . and the rest is history, chum."

Big Moon's smile faded. "When a man saves your life, Miss Ariel—"

"I said cool it." Duncan drained his cup, and his easy manner returned. "How are things around here, Moon?"

"Pretty good, since the summer's over. But they could be better. Young Billy Haskell was down hanging around Pete's last night."

"Give me a chance, Moon. Big Moon is unofficial mayor of Juno's Landing, Ariel."

"Not unofficial, official, your Reverence."

"No kidding!"

"They voted me in at the Lodge last week."

"Moon, that's great. That makes me feel good. Between us we'll get things moving. Aren't you proud of him, Princess?"

"I didn't need that to make me proud, Mr. Duncan. It's not good around here and . . ." she stopped. The big man had flashed her a look. "But Moon knows what he's doing."

"I think he does, Princess."

Ariel wished some of that tenderness would turn on her.

They finished their coffee quickly.

Duncan said nothing on the drive back until they stopped at the traffic light. Then he spoke stiffly.

"I've kept you out too long, I guess."

"Duncan, don't." Time was running out. It must not end like this. "I've had a beautiful morning. Don't be angry with me now."

"Angry? What right have I . . ."

But she was not listening to him. "It's Nick Orlini, isn't it? He gave me a lift home yesterday and drove up to that Ridge."

"You must have enjoyed it."

"I didn't mention it because—because why should I? It was nothing. I thought it was nothing, until he made it sound . . . I mean, I knew you were furious."

"I was not furious. Except he's hardly the type I would have thought you . . ."

"What right had you to think anything?"

They were quarreling like lovers.

He turned the car away from West Street and onto a road that climbed toward the hills and the river, sparkling in the sunlight. And then, as if he had changed his mind, he silently swung the car into a circling road and back into town.

Edythe Roundtree was standing in the doorway when they stopped in front of the Martin house.

"I thought it was Lowell," she called. "She isn't home yet."

Chapter Four

Lowell shifted restlessly on Hannah Poole's sofa and saw the enormous ginger-striped cat stretch a malevolent paw toward the tissue paper.

"Oh, no!" There was a rip.

"Naughty Nero!" Mrs. Poole swooped the cat from her work table and dropped it on the floor. "Naughty, naughty Nero!"

"It's all right, Mrs. Poole. He only got the paper." She tried to keep impatience from her voice. She had had enough of this overheated little sitting room with its clutter of plants, bird cages, pillows, and cat. Enough of Mrs. Poole's endless and Claude's mindless chatter. She longed to escape into silence and the brilliance of the day. She wondered, crossly, why. Other times she had easily tolerated Mrs. Poole's running commentary of opinions and misinformation, letting it flow away and fade. Today she was nervous. She had even let the thought cross her mind that she would like to see wedding, gifts, gowns, cards, cakes, and tissue paper disappear into thin air so she could run out into the light. With Duncan, of course. Nerves.

"It's okay." Claude was folding the tissue paper back over the moss-green velvet. "He didn't reach the dress. You *do* like it on me, Lowell?"

"You'll look lovely, Claude."

As she suspected, the neckline had been lowered and a layer of discreet padding filled out what Claude considered her woeful deficiencies.

"And Phyllis Elton will look sick, she'll be so jealous," rattled Claude happily. "She thinks I'm just a kid. Oh, Sis, I'm so glad you're having a big wedding. Bonnie Smith's sister ran off in blue jeans and . . ."

Mrs. Poole had pounced on the box and was lifting the dress.

"Don't bother, Mrs. Poole. It's all right. Please. We've looked."

"Lowell, my dear, *I* must know it's all right." She shook out the folds and held them up to the window. She was not at all annoyed with the big cat. It gave her the excuse she wanted to delay the Roundtree girls. She did not often have them both in her net at the same time. And the week before the Roundtree wedding. She would have every detail before she was through.

Hannah Poole had stitched her curiosity into the lives of Thatcher and more than once drawn blood. A tall, gaunt woman, she was made thinner by the protuberance of a large, well-propped bosom. Deserted twenty years ago by long-suffering, bespectacled Clement Poole, who had run off with an ingénue from the Thatcher Summer Theatre Group, Hannah Poole had promptly announced her widowhood and taken her revenge on life by becoming indispensable. Her wig of streaked gray curls was as familiar to Thatcher as the big hats she wore to all public events. The rumor ran that gray curls were stitched into every hat.

She turned the unscarred dress slowly to the light. "And you say her name is Ariel? How charming. And she looks exactly like . . ."

Claude ignored Lowell's warning glance. "The spitting image."

"Your great-grandmother was a very beautiful woman, judging from her picture." Mrs. Poole turned the dress once more.

"Mrs. Poole, the dress is fine." Lowell had risen.

But Claude was enjoying herself. "Mrs. Poole, do you believe that people can come back again—I mean, in other people's bodies?"

"Claude, for heaven's sake!"

Mrs. Poole reluctantly began to fold the dress back into the box. Her eyes brightened. "I certainly do, Claude. I have no doubt whatsoever that dear Clement's spirit is often right here in this room, protecting me."

"I didn't mean that, Mrs. Poole. I mean someone living all over again. Like Henrietta in Ariel."

"Why not? Stranger things have happened." Hannah Poole gave an arch, knowing little laugh. "But I wouldn't think about it, dear. I'm quite sure that sweet girl from Paris could never cause the trouble that Henrietta Roundtree brought to this town. Begging your pardon of course, but it's no secret. Anyway it was long before your time, and you young people have no interest in the past. Which is the way it should be, I'm sure. There!"

Lowell reached for the box. "Thank you, Mrs. Poole. Let's go, Claude. You're late for school already."

"Just a minute, dear. I have a little something for you, for your wedding day."

"How kind." Lowell managed to produce a smile.

Mrs. Poole opened the drop front of a vintage desk

and rummaged in a clutter of spools, buttons, and patterns. At last she produced a gray envelope.

"Your horoscope, Lowell. I wrote it up the minute I heard the news. It's for your next ten years."

"Ugh," murmured Claude.

Mrs. Poole ignored Claude. "And it's so interesting, dear. It says a big change is coming. As we all know." She simpered. "But don't make any hasty decision during the gibbous moon."

They were finally at the door.

"And if that charming French cousin needs something stitched before the big day, I can match any Paris seamstress."

"I'll tell her, Mrs. Poole. And thank you."

The door closed. Hannah Poole went to the telephone. She had a great deal to tell her friend Gladys Beemer this morning.

Lowell started the car with a jerk and knew she was taking the corner too fast.

"What's a gibbous moon, Sis?"

"I don't know and I don't care."

"What's wrong?"

"That idiot woman. How could you go on jabbering all that nonsense, Claude! Everything you said will be all over town before lunch."

"What did I say?"

Lowell glanced at her sister's startled face. "Oh, nothing, I guess. It's that woman. She gets sillier all the time."

"You can't say things like that when you're the minister's wife."

"I can think them."

Lowell accelerated down Cedar Street, passed a school-crossing sign without stopping, and swung recklessly into the deserted school yard.

Claude opened the door. "You won't tell Dad about the padding?"

"Why should I?"

"Will you let me see your horoscope?"

"I'll give it to you."

"It won't do *me* any good. But I hope it's juicy."

At last Lowell was alone in the car. For a long moment she sat very still and let the golden September light warm her through the windshield. For no reason at all she felt an impulse to cry. She wouldn't, of course. She had everything any girl could want. A devoted family. A beautiful wedding. With the man she loved. She wondered where he was at this moment. She thrust Ariel at him, as if he had nothing else to do. She must remember that this was as difficult a time for him as for her. He would not take his church before Dr. Wilcox's retirement in January. Meanwhile he would continue to study. Perhaps he would go back to the Seminary. It would depend on Dr. Wilcox's health. More details. She would not think about them now.

Distant chimes struck the hour. Duncan's church. The church she would enter in a few days as a bride. Some day those chimes would regulate her life. But today they told her only that it was ten o'clock, barely midpoint of this gilded morning.

At the intersection she stopped. The right turn would take her into Main Street and the list of nibbling duties on a scrap of paper in her purse. She sat through one light. Then very deliberately she turned the car to the left. Ahead lay silence and solitude. No chatter. No demands. An hour suspended in sunlit emptiness. An hour of her own.

She headed the car up Preacher Hill.

She scarcely noticed the white sports car, slowing opposite at the intersection. She made no gesture. Nick Orlini was nothing to her. Nothing whatsoever.

The noon whistle blew.

Its familiar whine split Thatcher's day, keened up the valley, and dwindled into the distant hills before it was over.

Once it had been the factory whistle at Juno's

Landing. "Lunch whistle" it was called then, in the leisurely pattern of Victorian life. Except that anyone having to meet or depart by train knew that two minutes after the lunch whistle, the great Berkshire Express would dignify Thatcher with its single stop, spewing steam vapor, setting the horses snorting, and bringing small boys on the run from wherever they happened to be eluding school.

In the First World War, the noon whistle marked the end of the "milk shift," releasing red-eyed and blinking workers into the midday light.

In the Second World War, the old whistle, commandeered by the patriots of the Air Warning System, had more than once shattered Thatcher's peace of mind and sent the inhabitants to their cellars. If the alert was later traced to a solitary hawk or a trio of crows mistaken for enemy aircraft, no one held the watchers to account. Their vigil brought Thatcher nearer to an understanding of the bewildering and numbing Gold Stars that began to appear again in Thatcher's windows.

Those Gold Stars had long ago been transmuted to granite, as the Heroes' Honor Roll on the Village Green. Flanked by two Civil War cannon and four neat pyramids of cannon balls, the Monument stood at Thatcher's heart. Over them the Flag would be flown proudly, in fair weather. Noon now shrilled from Volunteer Hose and Engine Company No. 1.

Edythe Roundtree in her kitchen debated whether or not she should knock on her young guest's door. Ariel had come in with quiet courtesy and gone straight upstairs. Should she call her for lunch or wait until Lowell came home? Lowell was already late, obviously trying to do too much. It would have been so much simpler to have a small wedding. Edythe sighed and returned to polishing the huge scrolled silver punch bowl. A Roundtree heirloom, it would indeed grace the wedding. No one in Thatcher possessed a handsomer one.

* * *

In his church study, Dr. Wilcox flipped shut the church budget. It was slow work, and he had twice caught Duncan, in the chair opposite, gazing with somber eyes on the brilliance outside. Dr. Wilcox could not blame him. The young man was to be married within the week. Samuel Wilcox let his memory slip for a moment to that forgotten glow. He had been young once. So had Cora. The whistle jolted him to reality.

"Time for lunch, Duncan."

"Already?" Duncan peered at the copy beneath his hand. "I find this very interesting, sir."

"Poppycock." The old minister pushed the papers from him. "Dullest job you'll have to face, Duncan. Two columns of figures and a paragraph on the reasons for the three deliveries of fuel it took to heat the church. I can give it to 'em in three words. It was cold." He rose with a grunt. "Go find Lowell and take her out for a picnic. I would, if I were your age."

"She wouldn't thank me for it." Duncan straightened the desk. The old man liked it neat.

"Why not?"

"Too busy. Why, I wouldn't even know where to find her to ask her."

"Big weddings." Dr. Wilcox walked to the window. "I've seen fifty years of 'em. Young people coming to the sacrament of marriage not in a state of grace but a state of exhaustion. But maybe that's better than not coming at all." He turned a shrewd but fond look on his young cleric. "You're coming into the church at a difficult time, Duncan."

"I wouldn't like it so much if it were easy."

"I know, I know. But you may have made it even harder for yourself, coming back to your home town."

"I made my decision. If they can't accept me here, they won't accept me anywhere else."

It was old ground and Dr. Wilcox had no intention of retraveling it. Duncan was not himself this morning, and Sam Wilcox thought he knew why. Marriage was a sobering responsibility. And Duncan was bringing more than the usual uncertainties to his. No one in Thatcher knew what had happened in Vietnam. Harlan Phelps' popular, indulged son came back transformed into this suddenly matured, contained man with boyishness still in his face and purpose hard in his eyes. But everyone knew of Harry Phelps' open contempt for that purpose and Duncan's defiant resolution. Sam and Cora Wilcox had taken him in and Harry Phelps had promptly ended his tax-deductible contribution to the church. Duncan knew what he wanted, and Dr. Wilcox had found rich satisfaction in guiding him. When Duncan finished at the Seminary, Dr. Wilcox had been astonished and secretly gratified to learn Thatcher was where he wanted to serve. He would do well. He had youth and dedication and soon he would have a wife to match him in every respect. Only good could come from it when these two fine young people were at last left to themselves. And, thought Sam Wilcox wryly, when he took himself out of the way. A young man about to be married wanted his future settled. The old man was uncomfortably aware on this bright day that his portly shadow would lie for some months directly across Duncan and Lowell's new life.

Duncan had tidied the desk and now stood waiting. Dr. Wilcox was apt to get lost in reveries. The old man brushed his bald head with his hand.

"Mrs. Higgins is failing, Duncan. I promised to stop in this afternoon. But I have a few things to do. Would you call on her for me?"

Dr. Wilcox caught the slight hesitation.

"Certainly, sir." Duncan smiled, and Dr. Wilcox decided the morning's tension had lifted. "Aunt Nettie Higgins once told me I wasted too much time. I'd do better mowing lawns than kicking a football around. She was right, of course. I'd like to tell her."

"If she remembers."

"She'll remember."

Duncan is lashing himself, thought the old man. Too much wedding. Too much excitement. Too many plans. Too many people.

"Would you mind a little advice, Duncan?"

"Anytime from you, sir."

"Take Lowell out for dinner. The two of you, before the wedding, just the two of you." He rose heavily. He had done his best. The whistle had blown. "Coming to lunch, Duncan?"

"If you don't mind, sir, I'd like to finish with these figures."

Dr. Wilcox nodded, privately doubting that Duncan would finish what he had obviously had so little heart to begin. He felt an uneasiness he could not name. It was unlike Duncan to be so inattentive.

"Take her out to dinner, Duncan. Do you both good."

As he had every day for thirty-five years, Sam Wilcox followed the flagstone path across to the rectory where Cora would be waiting lunch. He would spend a little time with his dahlias. They always restored him. But he couldn't help wondering why these young people should make the morning of life so difficult when it was the evening of life that was always unresolved.

The sun spread a summer warmth in the shelter of the rock. Lowell opened her eyes, closed them to its glitter, and opened them again, dizzyingly unsure what had happened or where she was.

She sat up sharply. She had driven up here to Preacher Hill, sat down in the shelter of the rock. Yes, she had let herself daydream. She had let people, faces, events, Duncan's proposal, her father's kindness, her wedding veil fill her mind until she had fallen asleep. Now she jumped to her feet and sat down as quickly, giddy from her abruptness.

She steadied herself and held her watch away from

the sharp light to read its face. Noon. The whistle must have awakened her. She had let nearly two hours drop out of her life, she who never took a daytime nap, and everything remained to be done. Worse, she had promised to be home early. Her father would expect it. This was her last week at home.

She leaned against the warm, veined rock to steady herself. She was Lowell Roundtree, to be married Saturday at four o'clock in St. Mark's Church, reception to follow at Willow House, West Street, at the home of Mr. and Mrs. Martin Isaac Roundtree. Or was she?

Could one ever step out of one's own flesh and look down from the far end of the telescope at what one's body would do next? It must be the giddiness because that was precisely what she was feeling at this moment, as if time had slipped from her and she was looking at herself from far away. Late as she was, the curious sensation imprisoned her.

She saw herself beside Duncan on this very hill. Two nights before he left for Vietnam. They were engaged as they had always understood they would be. He had grasped her with a sudden cry, terrible in its physical intensity. In the darkness he was a hardening of muscle and power, a stranger in his new need. He had swept her to the ground, kissing her breasts, tugging at her skirt. She had felt the cold March air, like a barrier, a voice. Clutching at her sweater she had struggled to her feet. He had released her in bewilderment. She could not explain. She could only cry against him. "I love you, Duncan. I do love you. I always will." His tenderness had hurt her more deeply than her own sense of failure.

"It's all right, Lowell. Don't worry. It will be different when I come home."

They had driven silently away.

It was indeed different when he came back. He was changed. Not two years older, but perhaps ten, with a weight of inner experience she could not share. She knew better than to try. She could only support him in his new goal, defend him against all scoffers, and wait for him to test himself in three years of study at the Seminary. She would be here when he was ready.

It had been the right way, Lowell told herself now. They had not made a small coin, easily spent, of their love. It had grown deeper, richer, and on their wedding day it would reach fulfillment.

So Lowell told herself again as she walked to the gray family sedan parked on the slope. She loved Duncan and he loved her. On Saturday she would walk radiantly up the aisle to him. Forever.

She drew a deep breath and turned the ignition key. There was no response. Only the clicking of the starter. She tried again. The starting motor turned emptily. And the morning's spell vanished.

She should have stopped for gas. She should not have parked on the incline. Her father had warned her about the choke with a near-empty tank. She would have to walk down to the farm and Uncle Will. It would take time, even if she took the short cut, the path straight down from Preacher Hill, and once she got there she would have to explain. Then she saw that there *was* no path, only a tangle of wild blackberry vines and thorny catbriars, waist-high golden rod, and purple aster clumps. She had forgotten how long it was since Uncle Will had cut that path for their childhood picnics. Now it was overgrown and impassable.

There was nothing for it but to take the road down to a wagon lane through the old orchard and into the farm. Willard had opened the lane to higher ground in case of flood. It would take fifteen minutes to walk.

She had nearly reached the turnoff when she heard the horn behind her. She jumped to the side of the road as Nick Orlini stopped his car.

"Anything wrong, Miss Roundtree?"

How she resented his mocking deference.

"No. I'm just going down to Uncle Will's."

"Out of gas?"

"Yes."

"I saw your car parked up there. I could guess. Get in."

"I can get some from Uncle Will."

"Sure. You can get some three miles ahead, too. But why? I've got a full tank. And a siphon." He pushed the car door open.

Everything had gone wrong. Lowell told herself she would rather burn than get into Nick Orlini's car. But every minute was making her later. There would be the concern, the questions, ahead.

"Come on, Lowell. It's the only way that makes sense."

She sat stiffly in the bucket seat. At the top of the hill Nick Orlini worked quickly.

"There you are. Nearly half a tank. Take you anywhere your little heart wants to go."

"I'll see that you get it back."

"You do that. Shall I call for it in person?"

There would of course be no way to return it. Or his help. She was obligated and if they met again he would mockingly remind her. Nick Orlini could embarrass her anytime he chose. It was all the result of her morning's self-indulgence.

"I tell you what. When they fill up my tank again, I'll charge it to the Deacon." He laughed though his eyes were sharply on her. "I saw the happy groom this morning. Down at Big Moon's." He seemed to wait for an answer. She made none.

"With your gorgeous French cousin."

"I asked him to show Ariel around. I had too much to do."

"So I see." He grinned.

"Thank you for the gas." She opened the door of the gray sedan.

"You don't forgive, do you, Lowell?"

"There's nothing to forgive."

"Good. In that case you won't mind if I give the French cousin a ring."

"Why should I?"

"You shouldn't, honey. I'll be happy to take her off your hands anytime Duncan is busy."

He grinned. As she had always known, Nick Orlini was capable of cruelty. "I'll call her tonight."

"We're going to Uncle Will's tonight. . . ." she stopped. Why did she go on answering, as if he could always draw her into talking to him? Let Ariel make her own excuses—or see Nick, if that was what she wanted. It made no difference to Lowell. She turned the ignition key and the motor started.

He listened for a moment. "See how simple it was? When you relaxed." With a little laugh, he reached in the car, squeezed her arm. "See you, honey."

Lowell waited until the white sports car was out of sight. Then slowly, she drove down the hill.

The day had turned treacherous. Ahead she would find Duncan's solid reassurance. But deep within her, the morning's truancy had succumbed to a more troubled image, a dream. In that sun-warmed, unresisting sleep, she had yielded, joyously, unafraid, to a man who had come to her. She no longer remembered her sensations. Nor even any shock. Only the acceptance, the abandon. It was escape from everything she had lived by. She had awakened, still dreamlike, in his arms. Yet she had not seen his face. He had no name. He was a stranger. Or was he?

Duncan looked up in surprise at the light knock. He had finally managed to immerse himself in the dreary job. Now, like getting a second wind on a long march, he was plodding ahead. He opened the door.

He thought when Lowell walked in that she had been crying. But she smiled and color returned to her face. She had never, he thought, looked prettier.

"I know I promised never to bother you here, Duncan . . ."

"Oh, come on. I'm delighted." Oddly enough, he was.

111

"But I've just wasted the whole morning and I—I wondered if you were still here."

To his surprise she went into his arms and clung to him. He kissed her hair lightly and she broke free.

"I guess not here, Duncan."

"Why not?"

"Well, after all—it's a church."

The surprise and pleasure of seeing her began to fade. He loved her, he told himself. He would cherish and honor her all his life, and on Saturday he would endow her with all he had, body and mind. But he sensed that the reality of their life together had not yet begun.

He picked up a handful of papers from the now-cluttered desk. "Would you like to know how I feel about this church?"

"Tell me, Duncan." Her world was safe again. She was so late at home that it no longer mattered. What did matter was that he had been truly glad to see her and they were together within these snug, arched windows that would frame their future life.

"I wish it had no walls."

"Whatever are you saying?"

"I don't believe in buildings with labels. If we're going to find decency and goodness anywhere, we're going to find it out there, in people. I believe there's a spark in every being—call it good, call it divine, call it God. Bring them all together, anywhere you can, and maybe you'll come nearer to what God or goodness really is. It isn't hidden inside buildings like this one. It's out there inside a lot of people who don't know they have it. When they do, we can set a lot of things right in this world."

"Is that your first sermon?"

He knew she didn't understand and it irritated him. The whole day had irritated him.

"I don't want to disappoint you, Lowell, but I may not even preach a sermon. Or heat the church or burn candles or keep up an expensive organ to play music most of this town never hears. I'll ask anybody who wants to, to talk for me. If the church is too cold, we'll go to the school gym or your Uncle Will's barn. If it's good weather we'll go out of doors. And we'll get Big Moon's trumpet and young Billy Haskell's drums and we'll invite God and just maybe He'll show up."

She was laughing. "Duncan, you don't mean a word of that."

But he was not ready to soothe her. "What do *you* want of me?"

"I want you to be the best minister this town ever had. And fill this lovely old church every Sunday . . ."

"And not shout the devil down on Preacher Hill?"

"Oh Duncan! Honestly. If the Board of Elders heard you . . ."

"Maybe there's a spark of goodness in them, too. If we just dig deep enough. Come on, I'll take you to lunch."

"I've got to go home, Duncan. I promised Dad. And it's my last week."

"Sure. I'll walk you to the car. Lowell . . ." She stopped and turned, her face soft with hope. "Lowell, let's have dinner together tonight, just the two of us. What do you say? The Grist Mill, maybe, or Redcoat Inn?"

"Oh, Duncan, I'd love it. But tonight we're all going to Uncle Will's, don't you remember?"

He should have, of course.

"And Thursday Phyllis is giving a supper for the bridal party. She's including Ariel, thank goodness. Friday night is the rehearsal."

"Sure. It was just a thought."

"We could go tomorrow night, Duncan. It would be all right to leave Ariel, I guess. Besides . . ." She felt a surge of relief in talking. ". . . I happened to run into Nick Orlini today. He wants to ask her for a date. I think he's poisonous, Duncan. But maybe she doesn't. She knows a lot more different people than I ever knew. She's beautiful but I hardly know what she's really like. I keep thinking of Henrietta's picture, and what Henrietta was like. And that really isn't fair, is it?"

"What time shall I pick you up tonight?"

"Duncan, would you do something for me?"

"Anything."

"You know what this means to Uncle Willard. And he always insists on cooking everything himself when he has us all to dinner. He's good, of course, but Mom always likes to make sure with an extra ham and a casserole. So she and I are taking it over early. Claude too. Will you stop by about six-thirty and pick up Ariel?" She wasn't sure he was listening. "You don't mind, Duncan?"

"Of course not."

She was gone. Duncan did not return to his papers. Instead, he thrust them untidily into the desk drawer and walked slowly into the dim and empty church he had elected to make his life.

Chapter Five

Julia Orlini was a woman who knew what to do with the hour of four in the afternoon. She came alive.

Now, as she stretched lean and graceful as a panther against the long beige velvet divan in her living room, she was aware of her own repressed energy. Faultless in black-and-white tweed slacks, a close-fitting, black turtle-neck cashmere top, and heavy silver chain and plaque, emphasizing her still-firm breasts, Julia was enjoying her caller. She ran a thin capable hand bearing a large marquise diamond through her shoulder-length hair. Its blackness was streaked with just enough gray, and the rumpling gave it a freedom that she knew suited her.

Harlan Phelps, sitting across the coffee table, watched her appreciatively.

She poured herself another cup of tea from the elaborate silver service and offered him another scotch. He took it. Julia Orlini neither smoked nor drank. She didn't need to, he thought. Whatever she did, she had kept a superb figure in athletic trim. She was the only woman he had ever known over thirty who could wear pants. His own wife, plump little Emily, in her turquoise pantsuit was a disaster. But he would not think of Emily now. He liked where he was.

He would like to sleep with Julia Orlini.

"Ben is a fool," said Julia lightly. Half a head taller than her husband, she threaded that slight margin of superiority through everything she did. It gave her some solace.

"I wouldn't say so, Julia." Harlan knew she disliked being agreed with.

"He might have known he would be turned down on the variance to build a filling station. Why antagonize the town, anyhow? For peanuts."

She drank her tea with plenty of lemon and no sugar. It set Harlan's teeth on edge. But he watched her movements. He would like a tall woman like that. They were well matched. He could use her brains and her vitality as well as her body in the career he saw ahead.

"And you, Harlan, are to blame!"

"Julia . . ."

"Ben wants the Roundtree land. *I* want the Roundtree land. You, Harlan, assured us it would be no trouble. You said the old man would jump at Ben's offer."

"And he should. He has no use for the land. But there's more sentiment than sense in all the Roundtrees. And I suspect Martin's at the bottom of it."

"He's a sick man. What can he do with it?"

Harlan had no wish to quarrel with Julia Orlini. Nor to spend the brief intimacy of this hour talking about Martin Roundtree and his worn-out illusions. He sipped his drink and looked boldly at her. It was a boldness that had brought him success before.

"Why would a woman like you care? You have everything you could want. And everything any man could want." His eyes lingered on her.

She set her cup down with a rattle and shifted her body with its catlike grace. "You're a lawyer, Harlan. That's what Ben is paying you for. Why I want the land isn't the question. I want it. That's all."

He sensed that she would have no further use for a man she could vanquish so easily.

"Then there's no doubt you'll get it, as you get whatever you want. And you'll live in that mausoleum Ben is building up on the Ridge and look down on 800 acres of scrub and swamp and pine wilderness and call it your own. Then what? Happiness?"

"I'm not asking for happiness."

"You should have it. Just as you should have the whole world. You belong to it. You belong among the doers. People as smart and chic, as brilliant and vital as yourself."

She smiled and stretched languidly again, knowing that it became her. "Are you offering to put me there, Harlan?"

"I'd like to try."

"Then you're as much of a fool as Ben. I know those 'doers.' I've followed Ben among them for twenty years. All the life I've known. Ben, the funny little Italian who could turn anything into money anywhere he went. Buying, selling, building, destroying, and when he had another million, we'd move on. Belonging nowhere, hated when he got through." She coiled like a spring, jumped up, and paced to the floor-length window. She did not glance out at the well-tended green lawn, banked in a sunset blaze of marigolds and zinnias, nor beyond to the cluster of silver birches masking the blueness of the lake. Julia Orlini was not a woman to dwell on the passionless repetitions of nature.

"Shall I tell you why I want Ben to buy that land?"

"Yes . . . ?" his smile was indulgent. Women like

Julia should not concern themselves with the nitty-gritty of money-making. It was enough that they brought grace, intelligence, and desire into the world, qualities not readily available in the marketplace.

She laughed and to his surprise Harlan found it chilling.

"Because he's promised to give it to me."

"In God's name what for?"

"I have my own plans. Perhaps I want something of my own. Something to—bargain with." She turned back to him. "Harlan, you're being tiresome. I want the land. I'm determined to have it. Don't come to me asking stupid, masculine questions. Accept me as I am. If you can do that, you might take me out to dinner. Ben's gone to Boston."

He heard the front door open and knew he would not hold her attention much longer. He spoke softly and quickly. "Julia, I want to. But we've got the damned wedding on Saturday."

She laughed brightly. "Of course. And you're father of the groom. I'm so happy for you all. Lowell is a charming girl."

"I'll see you there?"

"No."

"Why not?"

"Don't be silly." She was listening for footsteps. For some reason there were none. "It's all so small-town. So Roundtree. And so dull. It would bore me to death. Even if it is your son who's getting married." She rose and her smile was brilliant. "Besides, we haven't been invited."

"But you were. I told Emily. In fact, I insisted."

"Thank you. For whatever that implies. . . ."

Nick Orlini stood in the doorway. With a half leap, he cleared the two steps down into the living room with his mother's grace. He had her height and her black hair, though her vitality had become nervousness in her son and her dark liquid eyes had narrowed to distrustfulness. Harlan had seen all these differences before but never so vididly as this afternoon when Julia had so unexpectedly revealed—what? He privately damned young Nick for the interruption.

"Hello, Mother." Nick kissed her.

"Darling." Her hand cupped his face.

"Afternoon, Mr. Phelps."

"How are you, Nick?" He was not comfortable with this arrogant young man.

"Never better. Saw Duncan this morning. Must say, for a guy who's giving up the flesh and fighting the devil, he doesn't lose much time."

"Whatever does that mean, Nick?" Julia's face, to Harlan's astonishment, was soft with pride.

My God, thought Harlan, she's fatuous about him. Weakness number two in the indomitable lady. Emily had nibbled away at their own son with her doting "understanding." God help this young man. If she had a mind to, Julia could be a piranha. Nick moved from her side.

"I mean that at ten o'clock this morning he was having coffee at Moon's Diner with the new girl in town."

"Maybe there's hope for him yet." Harlan had no wish to intrude domestic matters into this fading afternoon.

"You mean Ariel Roundtree, don't you, darling? Nick drove her from Bollington to Thatcher yesterday and according to Nick she's quite a—what was your word, darling? Swinger?" Julia's tones were honey.

"The word was 'interesting,' Mother." Nick showed a faint irritation. "I haven't followed up."

"But you will, dear, I know. Well, give it a whirl, I always say." Julia, the understanding mother, quite sure her son would never really disturb her by settling on one girl. Harlan turned toward the door; the mood of the afternoon had gone.

"Duncan seemed to be there ahead of me." Nick lit a cigarette.

"Nonsense, darling. He's going to be married this week. Harlan, must you go?"

"Don't let me interrupt, Mr. Phelps," Nick said.

"I have one more client to see before I get home."

Julia saw the rebuff at once. "In that case, we mustn't detain you. Let me know your progress. Remember, I won't change my mind." She did not let her hand linger in his, nor did she walk with him to the door.

The car's tires clawed on the gravel of the driveway. He was unaccountably annoyed with the afternoon, with Nick and with his own son. It had been hell enough when he had come home to announce he was going into the ministry. What the devil was he up to, now? And with a "swinger," too, if that's what she was.

But most of all, as he left the luxurious house and grounds behind, Harlan was annoyed with himself. The afternoon had made him feel useless. And a little older. The whole day had led nowhere. And it was almost over. He tilted the sunshade against the slanting brilliance of the light and suddenly remembered the evening ahead. Willard Roundtree's. The family. The parents of the bride and groom. And the masquerade he had allowed Emily to push him into. No, by God, not tonight. He didn't owe Duncan a week of this. The shoe was on the other foot. Duncan owed him not a week but a lifetime. Twenty years of hopes and plans, all a man could offer his son, then the world when he was ready for it. But he no longer had a son. He had a milk-and-water Jesus talker. Well, let him walk on the water until he fell in. He'd come home with his wet tail between his legs.

Harlan slowed to let a State Trooper pass and waved genially. But there was no use pushing his influence until he needed it.

He swung left up to the pump island of Thatcher's only gas station. He would call Julia. By this time she might have changed her mind. A tough woman. But Harlan liked a challenge. He knew how to meet it.

* * *

Standing in her living room, beside Nick, Julia slipped an arm through his.

"What is she like, Nick? Ariel Roundtree?"

"Paris. Breedy. Nothing that Thatcher could hold onto long."

Julia glanced up at her son, a little taller than herself, the way she liked men.

"Bring her to dinner, dear. I'd like to meet her."

"She already turned me down."

Julia patted his cheek, wavering between relief that her son was still safely hers and resentment that any girl would not find him irresistible.

"Then you didn't choose the right moment."

Somewhere in the big silent house a telephone rang. Duncan, tying his shoe, lifted his head, then went on dressing.

It surprised him how little the events in this, his own home, any longer touched or included him. He was staying here with his mother the last week before the wedding because it was the decent thing to do. He would have liked to say his "parents," but he no longer used that word. He and his father were strangers now. Fortunately, the house, ugly and gloomy as it was with its stucco walls and dark arched doorways, could roof two people who no longer communicated. It would have hurt his mother deeply if he had not come home this week.

It was expected of him. Conformity. "The name of the game" in Thatcher. Would that after all become the name of *his* game? Not if he could help it. He knotted the tie he knew Lowell would like him to wear tonight. If Thatcher expected conformity in his ministry, it was in for a surprise. He had tried to say that to Lowell this afternoon and had seen the smiling indulgence in her eyes. He believed passionately in the uniqueness of the human spirit, call it imagination, courage, the individual spark that made every human being different. "Let *your* light so shine. . . ." He had found it out for himself. He could lead others. Yet, was not every gesture he was making this week a nod to conformity?

All but one. There was no place in the fixed pattern now for that one.

He tried to think of his goals. He let his mind drift again to this house. Why had his parents ever settled in it? It had happened while he was in Vietnam. He had left the pleasant white clapboard house on Willow Street, with his room under a sloping ceiling, and the single window looking out on the backyard where he had punted a football to his school triumph. He had returned to this outlandish mixture of dark beams, mullioned windows, ersatz Renaissance and neo-Tudor. A bootlegger's dream in the twenties. Four miles out of Thatcher. His mother could no longer walk to her beloved stores.

"Your father's moving up in the world," Emily Phelps had smiled. He had listened to her scurrying through the wide halls like a small, brave chipmunk seeking some tiny corner of winter solace.

He wondered what Ariel would think. Ariel. For a moment, looking out on the twisting alien hedgerows beyond his window, he surrendered to the images he could not prevent. Ariel's first smile had banished everyone else in the room. On Preacher Hill—the very drive there had been a treachery—he had tried to talk, then fallen helplessly silent. He had touched her hand, then released it because it was a touch he must never know again. Whether she looked like Henrietta of that portrait, which indeed she did, or whether she was some demonic blend of sorcery and light come as test of his resolve, he did not know. She filled his mind. Not as an ephemeral, beckoning mischief but with the hard reality of the bullet that had surprisingly and impersonally spilled his guts in that distant, steaming swamp. Ariel . . . but something like this did not happen to a man who had made his decision and set his course. It would not happen to him. He would pick her up this evening as Lowell had asked him to do but . . .

The light from the opening door spun him around.

"Your father just phoned, Duncan. He's been delayed with a client. He doesn't think he'll be back in time for Willard's party." Emily's voice was gently cheerful.

"Then come with me. Dad can show up when he's free."

She shook her head. "Your place is beside Lowell. Besides, I'd rather stay home. Your father might be quite late. I like to be here when he gets in. It's such a big empty house for a man to come home to, alone." Emily smiled her soft, knowing smile. "You see, he doesn't know it but he expects it of me."

"Lowell's gone ahead. I . . ."

She didn't wait for him to finish.

"Duncan, we haven't had much time to talk. Maybe it's just as well. 'A son you lose when he takes a wife. A daughter you have for the rest of your life.' "

Duncan smiled at her platitude. His mother's entire life was a platitude.

"I'm getting a daughter, Duncan. A very lovely daughter and I'm deeply grateful to you for her. But this week belongs to her. Nothing must distress her. If I stay and wait for Harlan . . ."

"Who probably isn't coming . . ." He had not meant it so harshly, but she smiled.

"I'm sure he's not coming. But Lowell can accept the absence of both of us better than if I came alone. Don't you see?"

Duncan knew his mother was right.

"And Duncan," she laid a round, little, capable hand on his sleeve. "You must stay very close to Lowell these days. She needs you. Martin Roundtree will do everything he can to remind her she is leaving him. Oh, yes, he will. Without even realizing it. Ever since Michael disappeared, ran away or whatever he did,

Martin has made the whole family feel they must make it up. This big wedding is part of that. But we're all going through it for Martin's sake. Then you'll take Lowell out of that house. You're strong enough to do it. My, I've said a lot, haven't I?"

"In the vernacular, a mouthful, Mom."

"Oh, Duncan, I wish you so well." Her voice trembled slightly. She laughed over it. "I'm really being a perfectly terrible groom's mother."

"The worst kind." He stooped and kissed her. "Willard will miss you. I think he has a secret lust for you."

"Oh, I do hope so!" She twinkled. "It would take his mind off his trees. I don't think anybody in this town will ever forgive that Mr. Orlini for cutting down the old white ash. You could see it from every road into Thatcher." Her face clouded. "Your father was quite irate—he said so just now—because the Orlinis haven't been invited. He said he had wanted them there. I told him he was the only one who did."

His mother would make out all right. She had the inner steel. But he could never tell her or anyone what he found himself thinking now.

"You don't mind, do you, Ariel?" Lowell was standing in the doorway, looking lovelier than Ariel had yet seen her, in a long pale dress of unbleached linen with a brown velvet sash. Pinned to her shoulder was a corsage of yellow daisies and tea roses. Ariel hadn't realized that men still sent shoulder corsages of daisies and roses. Maybe in Thatcher . . .

Lowell caught her glance.

"Duncan's sent me a corsage for every party we've gone to. I tell him it's much too extravagant for a poor minister but he says . . ." she laughed and abruptly broke off. "Ariel, I've neglected you shamefully since you got here. There are so many things I want to show you—my wedding dress, and—oh, I want to hear about Paris. It just seems the whole week's tearing by."

"That's the way it should be." Ariel had long ago learned how to smile and answer. "You look beautiful, Lowell."

"Do I?" She was radiant. "Do I really? That's a lot from you, Ariel. I don't know why Duncan would look at me twice with you here." But the innocence of her small joke told in her eyes. "I just wish John were home. He could at least take you around, even if he is your cousin."

"Where is he?" It was a polite question.

"Out at the University of Colorado. He wanted to study forestry, but after Michael—went away—he changed to law. To sort of take Michael's place, I guess. We all try to."

Ariel was silent. Michael was a specter that walked this house. Yesterday she had been curious; today she wanted only to withdraw.

"You remember Michael, don't you?"

"A little. He was a dark, stocky boy who jumped out at us from the snow fort."

"You do remember. But he was never unkind or mean. He did wild things sometimes but never . . ." she hesitated. "Your mother must have told you what happened. I mean, as much as anybody knew."

Ariel shook her head. Family confidences were not part of her childhood. Even now she seemed to be listening through a veil. Soon they would all be gone and Duncan would be coming for her, and nothing seemed to turn the tide of inevitability. She longed to see him, yet she would gladly have fled from this house forever.

"Nobody really knows. Michael had just gotten moodier and moodier, and one night he had a row with Dad. It wasn't much but when we all got up in the morning, Michael was gone. He never sent us a single word again."

"Not even where he was?"

"Nothing. Nothing at all." Her voice trembled. "If

only he would come back . . . for the wedding . . . or even, someday . . ."

Claude spun into the room.

"They're waiting for you, Sis."

The glow returned to Lowell's face. "I'm ready. Claude, you're not wearing jeans tonight?"

"I have plenty of time to dress. I'll drive over with Ariel and Dunkie. Okay, Ariel?"

"Of course. That would be lovely." She had not yet learned the bright, young shortcuts of American speech.

"Well, you can't, Claude. You promised Uncle Willard you'd turn the ice-cream freezer for him. Ariel, he makes the most fabulous ice creams."

"He won't care."

"A promise is a promise. Come on. Bring your dress with you. I asked Duncan to pick you up at six-thirty, Ariel. You have lots of time."

Ariel listened to the flurry of voices downstairs, the closing of the front door, the car's engine fading down the street. Then silence. They had left her in a kindly innocence of unwitting conspiracy. Now the very quiet of the old house welling up the stairs seemed a threat, a prelude to the unknown. Somewhere a shutter creaked. She heard small scamperings. Inside or out?

Duncan was coming to her. It was a kind of madness. She walked to the closet and chose her most becoming dress.

It was dark when Duncan reached West Street. The old house loomed like a ship at sea in the dusk. It was lighted from top to bottom, part of Martin's extravagant vision of the week. He rang, waited, and rang again. He heard a light step.

Ariel opened the door. Backlighted by the hall lamp, she looked even more beautiful than he had anticipated. The color she was wearing—a blue-green or was it jade?—the aura of light behind her, the whiteness of her skin. She was not a classic beauty. She was one of those rare women who create an aura of beauty, whatever they wear.

She smiled and the single dimple flashed.

"Hi," she said. "Come in. I'm all ready. In fact, my coat's on the chair there."

"Good. I was afraid I'd come too early."

The nervousness in her voice echoed the unsteadiness in himself. He felt awkward, too large for the hallway. She was everywhere around him, like light. He knew if he touched her the fragile barrier between them would shatter.

She moved quickly to the coat on the chair.

"Here, let me," he said.

"That's all right. I have it. Everyone's gone so we'd better lock up, I guess."

"Nobody locks their doors in Thatcher." He knew he was looking at her too steadily.

"I'm just a city girl, I guess. I kept hearing things in this big house while I was dressing."

"All old houses speak to you if you listen to them." At least they were talking. She was holding her coat. She had not yet slipped into it. They were standing in a closeness as if the entire house had melted away. Another step and he would have her in his arms. Another step and she would come to him.

"You look lovely."

"Oh, do you think so? Thank you." Her small laugh was high-pitched. "Alicia, my mother, had this skirt made from, you'll never guess, the draperies in her bedroom. She changes her room all the time. That is, whenever she can afford it. She said this water-silk was too good to waste and, besides, she was economizing. But she nearly had a fit when I matched it with a cheap little blouse off the peg at the Galeries. She said you don't put good things with cheap things. But I don't think it always matters what things cost. I mean as long as . . ." her voice trailed in her intense awareness of him. "I'm glad you like it."

"I like it very much."

"We'd better go, don't you think?"

"Yes."

Neither of them moved. Suddenly she stepped toward him. "Duncan, there it is!"

"What?"

"That sound I heard. And I hear water running."

"It comes from the basement. It may be a leak. There's a lot of water under the land around here. I'll go down and see."

"He crossed into the dining room toward the kitchen. She followed him.

"You wait here," he said quietly.

"Of course I won't. If there's anything down in that cellar I want to know."

"I'm sure you do. And I'll be glad to tell you."

"Duncan, that's ridiculous. I want to go with you. Or do you think I'm so helpless?"

"I think you're too damned beautiful for your own good. Or mine." He left her. She heard his firm steps descending into the basement and found herself looking into the portrait of her ancestress at the far end of the room. She noticed the artist had painted an old-fashioned trick into Henrietta's dark, lively eyes. They seemed to follow one around the room. Ariel gazed at the knowing, secretive face.

"What did *you* do?" She asked silently. "Did you do whatever he told you—because you loved him? Whoever he was."

A sudden splash came from the basement and abruptly Duncan's deep laugh.

She ran to the kitchen where the cellar door stood open. At the bottom of the stairs in the glare of a bare light bulb she saw Duncan. Behind him stood Kim, her blue-and-white striped party dress splattered with water. She was holding a small frog.

"I've found your spook, Ariel!"

"I was just giving Treadwell his bath and Dunkie frightened him. And it isn't funny."

"Of course it isn't." Ariel stared at the indignant child. "Kim, have you been here all along?"

"I'm supposed to go to Uncle Willard's with you and Dunkie. Didn't Lowell tell you?"

Did Lowell tell her? Or had she been so bemused with her own feelings she had only half listened. They might have left the child here.

"You don't mind, do you, Dunkie?"

"You're supposed to come with us, Kimmie. We were just surprised to find you down here." His little lie covered Ariel as his eyes met hers. He too was aware of the brink. "You're soaked, honey."

"Oh, I'll dry off. Besides, this is my best dress. I'll put Treadwell back and get Freddie. He always goes to Uncle Willard's with me." She hesitated, her eyes fixed on Ariel. "You could have come down with me if you wanted."

"Next time, Kim."

"You're not a witch, are you?"

"That's silly, Kim." Duncan spoke sharply.

Willard Roundtree stood on the porch of his farmhouse reading the brilliance of the night. The planet Venus was low in the west. She had been pursued across the summer heavens by the thunderer, Jupiter, and now had become the Evening Star. She would come with the morning again when Spring returned.

His own springtime had gone forever, as the chatter of women's voices from the kitchen told him.

But there were compensations. One was the wisdom to know what was important. It was important to let the women take over preparations he preferred to do himself. It was important to round up the members of his family under this roof. Willard had long made it a practice to bring the Roundtrees together on every occasion he could justify. Christmastime, Thanksgiving week, births, funerals, and now Lowell's wedding. They needed it, he told himself. They needed to be reminded. After he was gone, they could scatter as they would and be the poorer for it. But this farmhouse was where they had started. This was where Isaac Roundtree had brought his young bride. Now, a century later, the house with 800 acres of valley land was still theirs. Willard considered it his personal triumph. He hoped Martin would have the sense not to bring up the Orlini offer again.

He felt deep affection for Martin and a compassion he was careful not to show. Martin's pride was as intense as his own but in frail soil it was withering to petulance. Lowell's coming marriage was right for all of them. Duncan would be the missing son, the missing brother, the missing strength. Perhaps then the shadow of Michael . . .

Willard did not let himself dwell on Michael. He knew his own guilt in the matter and, helpless to change it, had let the years carry it from him. Another compensation of age. It gave a man perspective, helped him toward that balance between innocence and guilt which every man has at last to find for himself.

Yes, this wedding would be a good thing for everyone. It couldn't happen soon enough. Lowell was beginning to show strain. She looked thin. She was too docile with her family. Martin insisted on too much fuss. Why couldn't the two young people be brought together in tribal simplicity? He recalled the primitive rites he had once read about. The young man exercised and muscled to stallion strength, the girl secluded and rested, her body rubbed with warm oil until it was pliant and eager. Ushered to each other by young followers and left to the mighty fulfillment of nature.

A shadow moved on the grass. Willard jolted his mind to the present. Fine thoughts for a man of his age, they'd say, if any of them guessed. Well, he had a lot more like them. He had loved two women in his life. Each had brought him brief but transcendent happiness. The rest was makeshift and dreams. When a man stopped dreaming he stopped living.

The shadow took shape. It was Charlie Redwing,

his farm-helper and friend. Charlie had returned from his personal war with the Nazis to find his skills no longer needed in Thatcher. He had come to work for Willard for two reasons. He respected age and the common bond they shared with the land. Charlie had his own cabin, his own way of life, and one disconcerting talent. He was a full-blooded Algonquin Indian, and he walked with the silent tread and the night vision of his people.

"All is good, Mr. Will."

"Sure you won't look in on the party, Charlie?"

"The land is still awake."

An old formality between them. Willard always included Charlie in social occasions and Charlie always refused with one or another unanswerable reason.

Willard saw the stocky man blend with the darkness and at the same time heard the distant sound of a car. At last. Duncan and the new girl, Ariel. Ariel Roundtree. Another one. They had already told him about her, her resemblance. But he put little stock in that. There had been a deceptive strength in Henrietta. She had stood and endured, as Willard himself did. Without endurance, without standing firm against indulgence, temptation, all the distractions that destroyed the soundness of living, where would any of them have been? There was more to Henrietta than the giddy passions gossip had kept alive. This girl, Ariel, might have strength and passion, either or none, whatever her face. He wondered idly why Lowell had not brought her.

"They're coming!" Claude had pounced from nowhere to take his arm. She was his favorite. He would live to see her settled too. Though less predictably. "I wonder what kept them. Wait'll you meet Ariel!"

"So you warned me."

"It wasn't a warning. It's just that she's so . . . she just makes everybody here look like a frump."

"I doubt that, my dear. Not you."

"I do love you, Uncle Will. If you were only younger . . ."

"I share your regret."

The lights of the car showed now around the hill. Claude had wriggled from him and was looking up at the sky.

"Uncle Willard, what's a gibbous moon?"

"It's a moon that isn't new and isn't full. It's either waxing or waning. That's a gibbous moon up there."

"It is? That sort of bulging half?"

"You might say so."

"Mrs. Poole told Lowell this morning that she should not make any decision under a gibbous moon."

"Lowell's got more sense than to listen to that."

"Anyhow, she's made her big decision. Unless she says 'I don't' instead of 'I do' on Saturday. There they are!"

The car stopped. Willard watched the girl get out. For an instant, in the night's brightness, he saw her turn her incredible face to Duncan.

Dinner was a noisy success from the start. Lowell and Duncan sat together at one end of the table. Ariel sat at Willard's right, and found that she could not talk to Martin on her other side without looking directly at the end of the table. Once or twice she had caught Duncan looking at her gravely, then shifting quickly into the light, easy chatter that filled the table.

She wondered how long they would allow her to remain silent.

Not that she couldn't chatter. How often had her mother drawn her aside in that crowded little damask-walled drawing room to whisper: "Ariel, be clever. Learn to listen. Once you're married, you can say what you please but now you must listen. It is what a man wants." Instead, she had run back into the throng with a trill of quick phrases and an even quicker dimple.

131

Now she sat self-conscious as a provincial. Nor was she listening. She had walked into the low-ceilinged farmhouse parlor with an overwhelming sense of having known it for a long time. The large hooked rugs, the stiff little chairs, the Victorian love seat, and, in the corner, a solid wooden stand holding a brass-bound Bible. The only strangeness was the slight gray-haired man whose eyes were both kindly and sharp. She had never seen Willard Roundtree before.

"I hear Duncan drove you up to see the rest of us this morning." He caught her unaware. "The cemetery, I mean. Family plot."

"No, we didn't quite get there, Mr. Roundtree."

"I didn't think it was the liveliest place to show a visitor her first day in Thatcher." Duncan spoke quickly from the end of the table. There was a small silence.

"Quite right, Duncan. But you're a Roundtree, Ariel. You ought to see it. As many of us up there as down here and the same mixture of sinners, scalawags, and saints. So if you're interested I'll give myself the pleasure of escorting you."

"I would like to see it. Thank you." Had she somehow betrayed Duncan? She would avoid his eyes.

"I'll show you a bit of my own stonework up there."

Ariel flashed her dimple. "Stonework. You are a real Renaissance man, Mr. Roundtree."

"In that case, you may call me Uncle Will." His eyes twinkled.

"I mean, well, a Renaissance man could do everything."

"Around here we call that being a Yankee." He leaned toward her, holding her attention. "When this town was started, Ariel, a man had to do everything or he wouldn't survive. Your Renaissance man had his cities built for him." He was teasing her. He knew more about the world than she ever would. He passed her a plate of biscuits. "Squash bread, a specialty of mine."

"You made these, too?"

"I do all my own cooking. That doesn't quite come up to lute playing but it keeps me busy. I like cooking, when no one gets in my way. Cooking is chemistry. I like to see what happens when you put different elements together. Like people. Mix 'em up in different ways and you get different results."

The dinner somehow continued. Roast goose, glazed cranberries. The—what in the world—parsnips baked in beer. But delicious. A dark, ambrosial pudding Willard called honeycomb. The climax, a delicate ice cream unlike anything she had ever tasted.

"Rosewater." Willard seemed to be concentrating his full attention on her. "Rosewater ice cream was a favorite of your great-grandmother's. She practiced elegance whether she could afford it or not. Genuine rosewater is hard to come by now. Henrietta made her own. So do I."

Ariel was beginning to find his watchful glance disconcerting.

"I must agree with them, my dear. You might be her double."

At last it was over. Willard rose from the table, a glass of champagne in his hand.

"My dear friends and dearer family, one and the same as we are, at this table. We all know where our hearts are tonight. On Saturday all of Thatcher will wish them happiness. Tonight I rise to thank them for the happiness they are giving us, for the enrichment their love and their union will bring to our lives. May we live to see it grow in strength as this table will grow through the years in length."

A scattering of small laughs. Tears in Edythe's eyes. Duncan rose, holding Lowell's hand. His face had gone pale beneath its summer bronze.

"Thank you, sir. Lowell and I can only hope that we will never prove false to that trust and those thanks."

It was an odd little speech but Duncan sat down to applause.

The evening took a surprising turn. In the parlor Willard went to the dark, old-fashioned piano, lifted the lid on its ivory-yellow keys and bowed to Edythe. She blushed like a girl.

"But I must have my accompanist," she said.

To Ariel's greater surprise, Duncan rose. How little she knew about him. How much a part of this family he already was. How often must he have done this before.

"I'm not much of a pianist, Ariel." He had stopped where she sat primly and alone on the Victorian love seat.

Denials. Claude's voice cutting through. "Don't you believe him, Ariel. Dunkie's fantastic. Why, at all our parties . . ."

He was looking down on her. "I can't read a note of music. But once I hear something it seems I never forget it."

Edythe began to sing. Old songs, ballads, favorites the family knew and called for. Ariel watched his big capable hands flow over the keyboard, confident, possessive, a side of his life she had not even guessed. He would be happy with this family. The converted oil lamp on the piano netted them in its glow and left her where she had been since the moment she had stepped off the train. Outside. If she could only leave now, forget her name was Roundtree, return to the safe cocoon of exile her mother had woven around them both, and leave Duncan and Lowell. Lowell and Duncan.

"You're not enjoying yourself, my dear."

Willard Roundtree had seated himself beside her.

"Oh, but I am. I didn't realize Aunt Edythe sang so well."

"She might have been famous. She gave it up to marry Martin. Now, what can we do to entertain you?"

"But I am . . ."

"Nonsense. A young and beautiful girl sitting here alone. John should have come home sooner. On the other hand, he's a bit too earnest these days. We'll try to do better." He patted her hand. "But I'm glad you've come for Lowell's wedding. It will make it that much prettier for all of us."

He had somehow changed toward her. As if, after watching her so closely at dinner, he had reached a decision.

"You can't monopolize Ariel, Will." Edythe called across the room. "I'm going to sing one last song. In French. And I wouldn't dare do it without Ariel beside me. Come along."

She found herself standing mechanically at Duncan's tweed shoulder. He smelled faintly of shaving lotion and wood smoke.

"Plaisir d'amour . . ." Edythe began in her rich, silvery soprano. Ariel knew the song. She had known it since her school days in Paris. It was old and sweet and eternal. The pleasure of love. Suddenly the words came from her, the French-bred huskiness of her voice rising in a tide of feeling. Edythe's trailed into silence. Ariel sang as if she and Duncan were imprisoned in the pale globe of light.

She finished to a breath of silence, somewhere a sigh, then a burst of hand clapping. Had Ariel been a performer, she would have recognized the tribute. She felt instead exposed, embarrassed. Duncan's hands had dropped from the keyboard. She could see a muscle working in his jaw.

Claude was hugging her. Lowell looked radiant. Edythe was applauding. "It was lovely!" "Ariel, my dear." "I wish I could sing in French like that."

She was in the midst of sudden activity, Willard was setting out liqueur bottles. Lowell was arranging cordial glasses on a slender, pie-crust table. Kim was coming toward Ariel holding a small wire cage. Duncan had not looked at her.

"Ariel, I'm sorry about what I said, about being a witch."

"I didn't mind, Kimmie."

"That was the most beautiful song I ever heard. I have to go into the kitchen to help Mrs. Beemer. Can I leave Freddie with you?"

Ariel heard only dimly. Duncan was approaching her. He carried a small crystal glass of dark liquid. He looked strained but he smiled. "Lowell says you must try Uncle Willard's black raspberry cordial. Nothing like it in Paris. Will you?"

The room had become stifling. He was too near. There were too many people. "No, thank you. Please. I don't care for anything more. Please excuse me. I—I'd like to get some air."

"Are you all right?"

She wanted to cry out: "No. I'm not all right. The world has gone mad and I want to run out of it. With you." Instead, she said quite steadily. "Of course I'm all right. I want to go out and look at the sky. There's so much of it."

He had not moved and yet she felt he had stepped toward her.

"Please, Duncan."

She slipped by him, opened the front door, and shut it quickly behind her.

From where he was standing beside Martin, Willard Roundtree followed her with thoughtful eyes.

Outside in the tingling darkness, Ariel stood at the railing of the narrow porch and drew deep, soothing breaths. He would not follow her. He would understand that she needed these few cool minutes to put the disordered night straight again. The first spark, the tenuous current that had flowed between them—was it only at last night's dinner table?—had surged into tonight's reality, as visible as light to anyone who saw them together in that room. It was up to her to escape the enchantment, to fix the barriers, to throw herself at any distraction that did not include him.

But she had not thought this all out yet. It was enough to lean against the pillar of the porch railing and let the silver-sheened night speak to her. As her eyes opened to the darkness, Ariel saw that a path led from the steps, down a slope, bordered open pasture land, and twisted into a copse of slender trees.

Some deep pulsing of the blood, some long-buried response to the overcharged brilliance above her, stirred in Ariel. As it had stirred long ago in the dark-haired girl they saw in her. With a small unburdening sigh, Ariel gave herself to its magnetism. Like a leaf she drifted down the path. And felt the hot moisture behind her eyes, the tears she never shed, dissipate.

Willard emptied his pipe into the battered pewter porringer that served him as an ashtray and waited. He had reluctantly seated himself on the abandoned love seat. He knew in another moment Martin would join him with a good deal on his mind. None of which Willard wanted to hear. But he knew when to bow with grace to inevitability.

"Mind if I join you, Will?"

"I was expecting you would. Sit down." He looked quizzically at his nephew. Martin must be over fifty now. Will no longer troubled himself with the artificial markings of time. He recognized that he and Martin shared the same slight frame and the same pride of family. But Martin had dwindled. There was no other word for it. His hair, his face, his voice had gone gray. Too gray, Will thought, for a man his age. The gray of trauma, not to his body nor to his mind but to something deeper still, his belief in himself.

A burst of feminine voices came from the kitchen. Through the open door, he could see Lowell laughing, her face shiny with exertion. She was tying an apron around Duncan's muscular girth. For an instant Will watched the little byplay. Duncan untied the strings and caught her up in them. She wriggled free.

Puppy play, he thought. No heat. Not yet. Aloud he said, "Martin, you should be a very happy man tonight."

"I am." The studied heartiness of the father-of-the-bride, Willard thought. "I'm getting a fine son-in-law."

"And Lowell's getting a fine husband." But he knew Martin was not thinking of his daughter. "That's about as much as any man can expect from a wedding."

Martin did not answer. The older man understood the dark pain that lay coiled and brooding inside him. Willard would do nothing to spring its release. Not now.

"Damn it, Will! I thought the wedding would bring him home. He and Lowell were so close. I put it in every paper."

"You can't blanket the world."

For some reason this obvious little reply seemed to reassure Martin. As if some one beside himself believed that Michael, rebellious, willful, exasperating, was still *alive*.

"Let's forget it. If he walked in now it would only spoil things for Lowell." Martin made the effort and won. "I want her to be the happiest girl in the world. And I think she is."

Willard glanced through the kitchen door. He could see Lowell, stretching on tiptoe to put dishes on the top shelves. A slender girl, too slender for his taste, the apron strings spanned her waist twice around. Her short brown hair tousled now, her face drawn into a small studied frown of concentration. Suddenly he could see her in ten years. A little fuller in the figure (or did thin girls grow thinner?), the children in bed, Duncan, heavier, at work on his sermon. Lowell, still pretty, still competent, the admired wife of the Reverend Duncan Phelps of St. Mark's Episcopal Church, Thatcher.

For a reason he could not define, Willard Roundtree sighed.

"Harry Phelps came in to see me today." Martin was at last getting to the point. "I thought he and Em would be here tonight."

Will busied himself filling his pipe.

"Just as well," Martin added. "He makes it pretty miserable for Duncan. My God, when he has a boy like that right here—"

Will held a match to his pipe and sucked noisily.

"But that's his business." Martin's voice turned dry. "He came in with another offer from Orlini."

"What's he up to now?"

"One-fifty an acre. That's a lot of money, Will."

"Is it? I haven't counted."

"Maybe you should. You could be comfortable the rest of your life on money like that."

"I'm comfortable enough now." But he knew that Martin was not thinking of a man soon inching toward eighty. He was thinking of—what? Himself. Martin was a hard man to reach now. He had turned inward in shock, though outwardly he still bore—what was the word for it? Will searched his mind. Courtliness. That was it. The grace of inheritance, of knowing who he was, the respect of a town that saw him before they saw the flaking paint, the faded upholstery. Martin commanded it still.

"It's your land, Will. Your decision."

The older man shook his head. "You know better than that, Martin. The land was here before us, it will be here when we're gone. What happens to it is up to all of us. But while it's in my custody, I'll keep it as it was meant to be."

It was the answer he knew Martin wanted, without the responsibility for making it himself.

"I don't think Orlini's ready to take 'no,' Will. He's a tough man."

Willard leaned back. "You know what I saw down near the gorge last Thursday? The first snow owl in this area in nine years. And I found traces of a family of bobcats up near Big Rock. I thought they'd gone forever." He let a puff of smoke drift lazily toward the ceiling. Ben Orlini's small patent image dissipated with it.

The sharp-eyed little foreigner had nothing to do with him or his. The land was deeper in him than he would admit to any man. Roundtree land for a hundred years. Bequeathed to a self-taught Roundtree for taking another man's place in war. A legacy of honor not greed, courage not opportunism. The legacy was never far from Will's mind. It had kept his back straight, his head high, his eyes clear against the long encroachments of time.

"You know what I've been thinking about, Martin? Those 800 acres are the last of the 5000 old Isaac inherited. I'm wondering about a perpetual trust, a kind of conservancy. The Roundtree Conservancy."

"That's rich man's talk, Will. You'd have to sell half the land off to support it."

The older man found it easy to draw on his pipe. He knew where the money might come from. Soon after Lowell and Duncan's engagement he had been summoned to the lonely sixty-room barony of Eagle Hill, home of Mrs. Curtis Plummer. An aloof woman, coldly gracious, chillingly distrustful, imprisoned in a wealthy widowhood, she had made distant and often anonymous gifts when it pleased her. With surprising bluntness she had told Will that she liked this coming marriage, lovely young Lowell so unlike the modern girl. And dedicated young Duncan. She would like to do something for the town which this fine young couple would serve. Had he any ideas? Will had met her bluntness. He said he couldn't speak for the town but he could speak for a new family of bobcats. Mrs. Plummer had thrown back her carefully coifed gray head, laughed with unexpected earthiness, and offered him some excellent bourbon.

Willard smiled at the memory but he wouldn't share it with Martin. Not yet.

The rattle of dishes in the kitchen had ceased. Martin had begun to look anxiously toward the door, a habit he had acquired whenever Edythe remained away too long.

Willard rose. "Well, it was just an idea, Martin. But I'll say this, and you can tell it to Harry Phelps. If the time ever comes when for any reason we have to sell the land, it won't be to Ben Orlini. I'm writing that into my will."

For an instant, in a trick time played on him more frequently these days, he saw Ann, his young bride of so long ago, at the window of this same room. She stood looking up toward the Ridge, at the towering white ash carved into the sky above it. Her tree, she had claimed at once. And it was. For their brief two years, it had lifted to wind and sun, bending, never breaking, eternal to her as the love she saw ahead for them. She was gone. And now the old giant, beacon of their happiness, had been felled.

Willard tapped his dead pipe on the pewter bowl. "I'll see Orlini in hell first."

Ariel followed the path until it branched at a copse of woods. The pupils of her eyes were wide now to the luminous dark. She welcomed the strangeness. Instead of entering the copse she chose the path that led around it. Her face, her body had cooled. If she could only walk on and on through this sheltering night and not return. Not ever, she thought.

The path carried her to the other side of the copse, toward a fenced field. It ended at a cabin with a single lighted window. She could go no further.

As if to confirm it, a huge dog rose from the grass and came toward her. Ariel had never surrendered to fear. Not even when one of her mother's young men had put her up on a two-year-old colt fresh from the race track. The young horse had promptly bolted. She had clung to his back and the horse had gradually come down to her hands, as if recognizing in her that awareness beyond humanity that an animal can trust.

It stamped her mind in a single flash of memory. The young animal as frightened as herself.

The massive dog came steadily toward her. The darkness was no shield. He made no sound. Speak to him. Stand still and speak. Where had she learned that?

The words came in quick French. "Hallo, mon ami . . . bon chien . . ."

"He won't hurt you." A man detached himself from the darkness, squat, broad shouldered, unsmiling. "But I see you know that."

She felt the dog's cold muzzle in her hand and saw the great plumed tail slowly wag.

"I'm very sorry if I've trespassed."

"You do not trespass. What is that?" He looked at her sharply. "You are not a stranger."

"I'm Ariel Roundtree. I left the party back there to—to take a little walk. I must have come too far. You're . . . ?"

"My name is Charles Redwing."

"How do you do?" She held out her hand. He took it solemnly. "The dog is yours?"

"He is Mr. Willard's. But when the little girl comes with her pets he is sent down to me. He would never touch the little creatures. They speak to him of the child. But she does not know that. It is better for everyone that he comes here."

"He's so big."

"He's powerful and wise. He has taught me many things."

The man fell silent. She did not move. She wanted another moment to be caught up in the vastness of the night. To be not herself but a bodiless being, part of the dark innocence of sky and hills. She felt the dog's head beneath her hand, silken and still. And the unspoken kindness of this man carved out of darkness and as silently rooted to the earth as the trees behind her.

In the crowded streets, the lighted boulevards of her life she had known nothing like it. She felt small and remote yet oddly at peace.

"It's so still," she said at last.

"You have come to the land. It has accepted you."

"I'm only staying a few days."

"You will come back."

She drew a breath. "What smells so sweet?"

"It is the time of the Harvest Moon. Next will come the Hunter's Moon. The nights are colder then."

"What's the Hunter's Moon?"

"That harvest is finished. Then man must kill to live."

"Kill?" He had made the word primeval.

"To eat and clothe himself. But when hunter among my people kills, he must apologize to the animal for taking its life for his own food and warmth."

Absurdly she saw her mother's closet, the beautiful furs, wrapped and stored. The skins of dead animals. For her vanity. Suddenly the gap between herself and this primitive night widened hopelessly. She was only herself, Ariel Roundtree, a stranger in this place where everything that touched her had bruised her. She need not stay. She had no ties. She would escape as the woman in the portrait had not. She had broken free of the stifling Paris apartment. She would not be trapped here in a web of her own making. She would leave tomorrow.

"Ariel."

It was Duncan. In another moment he was beside her, his voice dark with anger. The dog leaped up on him joyously, then dropped as if sensing his mood. "Charlie, if I had known she was down here with you I wouldn't have worried. Ariel, for God's sake, running off in the dark without telling anyone where you're going!"

"It was better than staying." Fury and relief mingled in her. She pushed past him.

"Did you know that old stone wall you passed is full of copperheads? Poisonous snakes."

"They've been cleared out, Mr. Duncan."

"She didn't know that."

It was marvelous illogic and Charlie Redwing concealed a smile. "She will be safe on this land," he said gently. Man and dog walked slowly into the dark.

"Please let me pass, Duncan."

"I'm going to see that you get back."

"I'm not a child."

"Then don't act like one."

She pushed up the path ahead of him, his long stride catching up with hers. At the fork, she hesitated, turned uncertainly into the trees. Or was she drawn there by a force she could no longer resist?

Suddenly he was beside her. His arms went around her, his mouth hungry, his body bruising hard against hers.

"Ariel!"

"Duncan! Oh, Duncan."

The release was so complete, the knowledge so deep, they stood there, shielded by the trees, locked in time and the earthy fragrance of the night. It was enough to feel their hearts pound, to know that against all separation, for this moment they were one.

His hands began to move. She pressed deeper toward him. She would give herself to this man and live forever in the fullness of this single night. It was not too much to ask, one night. She wanted this man as she had never wanted anything or anyone in her life. It was in her blood to take what she must have. The passion, the fire, the heritage denied so long leaped through her eager body to meet his.

Suddenly, and inexplicably to her, his arms loosened.

"No, Duncan, no! Don't let me go!"

"Do you think I want to?"

She felt a tree at her back and leaned away from him, against it.

"My God, Ariel, what can I do? What can *we* do? I want you as I've never wanted a woman. I love you. I didn't think it ever happened like this to anyone. But it has."

"Yes." She wasn't sure she had even spoken. Words had no meaning now. "Duncan, take me!"

"Is that the way you want it? Here? Now? Maybe tomorrow we can sneak off once more."

"Don't say that!"

"That's what it would be, wouldn't it?" He was talking to himself, anger bursting at the incongruity of this absurd fate that had shattered his careful plan. And substituted a glory, a need so overpowering. . . . "That's all. A last romp in the hay for a phoney priest with an obliging French cousin."

"Duncan, don't. Don't hurt us. Don't say anything. We have so little time."

He caught her to him and she crumpled. She felt the tree harsh against her back, his head burrowing deep in her shoulder, her throat. "Ariel, Ariel, if I take you now, it will be forever. You know that?"

"Yes. I know."

They heard the sound. It was as small as a bird's call. But no birds called at this hour. It was a half sob, and through the slender trees, in the clearing beyond they saw her.

"Ariel. . . ." Kim's distant cry belonged to the patchwork of the night.

What she saw, what she did not see, they had no way of knowing. Duncan pushed Ariel deeper into the trees and went out to the path.

Kim's small mouth opened in surprise. Without a word, she turned and ran, away from him and up the path.

"Kim!" He called harshly.

Then silence. From beneath the trees, Ariel heard the whine of a jet far overhead. Incongruously, from the distance, the wobbling beat of a siren. She walked slowly through the shattered night to where she knew that nothing would ever be the same for her again.

Chapter Six

Julia Orlini stretched like a cat and opened her eyes, then buried her head immediately. The morning sun slanted through the drawn chiffon drapes directly on her face. She was past the age when the sun could do anything for her untouched face. Although she had her own bedroom which she never shared into the morning, her self-image did not permit this cruel probing of early light. In the new house her bedroom would be on the west side.

She moved languidly out of the sun's rays and glanced up. Her husband was standing in the doorway, in his immaculate tailoring, his face freshly shaved, his small feet encased in the two-tone shoes she deplored. She had told him in a moment of contempt she liked men with big feet. In answer he had embellished the small pointed feet of which he was seemingly proud. Today, the shoes were black patent and pale tan. They made her wince.

"Good morning, Ben."

"Good morning, my darling. I'm afraid I woke you up."

"Which was exactly what you intended." Amusement was her best weapon in the give-and-take of this thinning marriage. "How was Boston?"

"I finished business earlier than I expected so I came home. About midnight. You were asleep."

"Did you call Tess?"

"No." Ben Orlini took Italian pride in his children. Savvy as he was to the world which gave him such success, he could not accept his only daughter's easy, slovenly living with the faceless young man who might some day choose to become his son-in-law.

His wife slid from bed and wrapped a flame-colored velvet dressing gown around her supple figure. He was proud of her ways. She was a magnificent woman, taller than himself. She had used his success to ornament his life and his home. A long way from the shy skinny girl he had met on the Atlantic City boardwalk at the first builders' convention he had attended as head of his own company.

She had smiled at him and they had walked out on the Steel Pier together. Her father was a school teacher, she had told him. No money. He could see that at once. But class. And class was something Ben Orlini wanted with all his five feet, six inches. He could provide money.

He had done so. And Julia had seemed reasonably content with two sons, a daughter, and a background of which most women dream. Sometimes, looking at her chic, remote beauty, he had misgivings. She could have graced a foreign embassy or a ducal court. She could lead a cause or entice and enchant the great. Yet here she was, by her own choice, looking forward to a preposterously large house overlooking a faded town.

She came to him with a scent of a new musky perfume and kissed him.

"Harlan Phelps took me to dinner last night."

He rarely gratified her hopes of jealously. He had not yet met the man he felt could replace him in any woman's bed. Moreover, for all her flare, her beauty, her endowments, he had early on discovered his wife's limited appetite. Sex not only bored her, it left her untidy. They had reached a mutual understanding (separate bedrooms) and a candor that was probably the true staple of their marriage.

Julia was brushing her mane of dark, streaked hair. "He wants to sleep with me."

"I am not surprised. Many men do, my darling."

"Would you mind?"

"Not if you wouldn't." He usually enjoyed this game but this morning he had many things on his mind.

"He's a dull and, I think, stupid man, Ben. I wonder that you could put your affairs in this town in his hands."

"For that reason."

"What reason?" Ben's cryptic speech often irritated her. But he was shrewd and he was smart. He had learned easily everything she had taught him. Except the shoes, of course. His aptness, his intelligence continued to fascinate her.

"Harlan Phelps knows this town and the people in it like the back of his hand. When money won't work, he knows where the pressure points are."

"Well, money didn't work this time." She spoke sharply. Ben was so sure of himself. So sure he could not make a mistake.

"What does that mean, my darling?"

"It means that you're not getting the variance for the gas station."

"Pennies, Julia. A warm-up. Testing the water. What in hell would I do with a gas station?"

"They don't want the elm trees cut down."

"Trees. My God, Julia, these people are mad. What are trees? You know what they say? Before white men came to this country, the trees were so thick that a squirrel could travel from Newark to Ohio without once coming down to the ground. Are we squirrels? My father was born in Perugia. It's on a hill. Like a lot of other towns in Italy. There is not one tree on those hills. Only sun and rain. And maybe little olive trees that are useful. Beautiful. Beautiful. Who needs trees?"

"Maybe you don't but they do. You shouldn't have cut them all down on the Ridge. Not the big one, Harlan said."

"Do you want a house or a jungle to live in?"

She rose and went to him. Her dressing gown had fallen away from her breasts. They were thin and the breastbone rose between them. Julia paid heavily for her style, he thought, and for a second his thoughts strayed to the full-bodied, soft women who had surrounded his youth.

"You know what I want, Ben. You know why we came here to Thatcher. You promised me . . ."

"I know."

"In blood, if you remember." She smiled. "In blood, Ben."

That had been one time when the savagery he had discovered in her repelled him. She had been dressing for the evening when she told him she wanted him to buy the Roundtree land. He had agreed lightly. She had taken his hand and asked for his word. Suddenly she had stabbed the end of his finger with a pin. "You've promised, Ben," she had said with a little laugh. "In blood."

He did not need to be reminded now. He was no wild-eyed Sicilian. He was a successful American businessman and someday he would be beyond even his wife's maneuverings.

Something of his thoughts must have reached her. She knew him too well.

"You need me, Ben, you've always needed me. I've done what you wanted and I've taught you what you know. Now I want to be paid."

"My darling Julia . . ."

Her irritation built. "Not in clothes. Not in all this!" She kicked a feathered mule at him. "Ben, I've gone with you wherever you chose. I've seen you move into a town, buy up land, eat up the land. Destroy, build, make more money until people hated you. Then we'd move on. And on."

He wished she would stop. He had heard all this. It did not become her to rant. She looked old, her skin gray. Ben Orlini did not want an aging woman for a wife. He made the mistake of glancing at his watch.

"Don't push me off, Ben. Not again. I want to live where I'm respected. Where I'm somebody. Where I have something of my own. Not something you've handed to me like a servant. Which is all I have been;

at your beck and call. I'm a Thatcher, Ben. I'm proud of that. As proud as the Roundtrees. That land was Thatcher land once. We were cheated out of it. My father told me that."

"Julia, Julia."

"You won't believe it, will you?"

"I don't believe anything that can't be proved."

"I haven't tried to prove it. I've gone along with you. You can afford to buy it. But Harlan Phelps isn't getting it for you. If he can't, I'll get it my own way."

"I'm making Willard Roundtree another offer."

His complacency stung her. "There are ways beside money."

"Don't interfere, Julia." She usually respected that warning. But this morning, for reasons she would not admit, she was at odds with herself. Nick and his talk about the girl, Ariel. A Roundtree, but a different kind. She could lose him to a girl like that. She might find a use for her.

Julia let her irritation cool. She rubbed her cheek against her husband's face.

"Pressure points, Ben. There are all kinds."

Ariel had lain awake until nearly dawn, slept briefly, and awakened again to pallor at her window and the sounds of sleep-heavy birds. She had no desire to stir from this cocoon of sleep and safety, not even to grope for her wrist watch on the table beside her.

Images of the night flowed through her mind and returned again and again. The splendor, the utter completeness of Duncan's arms around her. How long had they stayed there? There was no measurement of time. Only the sympathetic dark and the wordless, ecstatic completeness of being with him. All her previous life had telescoped to a fragment.

Had there been glances on her return to the farmhouse? She would think of that later. She would face the day when it came. But now she would drift a little longer on the night's tide, lulled by an odd and irreversible security. Hopeless as it was, she had revealed her love. It had been returned. She turned restlessly in her bed. She wanted fulfillment now with all her body. Duncan. . . .

She yielded to another image, a subterranean pool that had lain deep and incomprehensible in her mind. Her mother. She had gone with her mother one distant spring to Lake Como. There her mother had surprised her.

"You're nearly fifteen, my pet. You should have a room of your own."

It was a famous hotel, once the castle of the self-exiled English queen, Caroline. Ariel had heard all the legends. The Queen was fat and ugly. She had built the castle for her lovers; she preferred them in the dress of court ladies, as she preferred her court ladies in the dress of lovers. Her husband despised her and she finally went mad. The Queen was no more mad, declared her mother, than any woman married to a man whose weapon was humiliation. She had chosen to live exactly as she wished.

Although it was April, rain had fallen steadily. Clouds descended almost to the surface of Lake Como, masking the villages, concealing the mountains and turning the water iron-gray. The hours of day held the mystery of twilight. No excursion boats plied the lake, the black Venetian poles that moored small pleasure craft along the hotel dock stood solitary and forlorn in the lapping waters.

Ariel discovered, as she had many times before, that such weather did not depress her. She could find beauty wherever she found freedom, wherever there were no walls, no damask walls. She had walked the shore, her face lifted to the blowing mist. She had climbed the hill up which the mad queen elected to lay out her elaborate cyprus gardens. At the top was a waterfall. In the somber green overcast stood a young Italian gardener, with hot eyes and soiled hands, watching her.

"Bellissimo!" she had called.

He misunderstood and came toward her.

She had learned to distrust only the men who closed in on her in her mother's drawing room.

"Isn't it beautiful! Tell me, does the mad queen's ghost walk up here?" She laughed, enjoying her freedom as much as her fantasy. In the moist, gray-green light her face showed pale and startlingly lovely. "Will you show me the way up the falls?"

He misunderstood again. Or perhaps not. Without a word, his arm gripped her, his hand was searching her flat chest, his mouth, large, wet, and fleshy, was forcing hers open. She struck him. He pushed closer on her. She brought her thin hard kneecap upwards in sharp fury. With a gasping cry he let her go. Mam'selle had taught her that lesson. She fled down the hill, through the dark cypresses and up to her room. Her mother had gone for a drive, so she would not have to answer shrewd questions. Thankfully, she was alone with the strange tingling those ugly hands had left.

But it was not the end of this Italian interlude. She might have forgotten the stupid gardener's boy but for what lay deeper in her consciousness.

The following day her mother went driving again and left word she would not return for dinner. Ariel had finished her own dinner in the half-empty dining room and, bored with television she could not understand, she had obtained a key from the desk and let herself into Alicia's sitting room. The room was in chilled darkness, the drapes drawn against the mist. Ariel shivered, more in loneliness than cold. As she reached for the lamp, she heard voices. Her mother's unmistakable ripple of laughter, a deeper voice, then sounds she could only guess about. Ariel fled from the room, letting the door bang shut.

The next morning Alicia summoned her to breakfast in the little suite. She looked lovely, her blond hair tied in yellow velvet ribbon, her pale apricot dressing gown clinging in chiffon folds to her slender figure. Alicia was direct.

"I'm sorry you came into my room last night, without knocking, my pet. I'm even sorrier you chose to slam the door behind you.

"As you discovered, I was not alone. With me was the young Polish diplomat who joined us here two days ago. He left this morning, regrettably."

"Mother, I don't care."

"But you do, my pet. Very much. I found him diverting and he suits me. You are too young to understand that. Just as you are too young to judge."

"I'm not judging you!"

"Whether you are or not does not matter. I care most that you should understand."

"Maybe I do!" Ariel might not have said it with such intensity the day before, but her encounter with the gardener's boy had left her bewildered.

"How could you? How could you know anything at your age? I've done everything I could for you but I cannot tell you what is inside your own body. You have to find that out for yourself. But I will tell you this. Some women are given the capacity for a great and passionate love."

Ariel shifted uneasily. She wanted to escape this room, the clinging sweetness of her mother's morning scent, the relentless scratching of the words she had no wish to hear. She wanted to flee into that imprisoning mist that made everything inaccessible and remote. "Alicia, I do understand."

"You understand nothing. You feel I've disgraced you. You're embarrassed. Not for me but for yourself. Your image of me is soiled. You feel soiled by it."

It was not the first time Ariel had suspected that her mother had a lover. But the gaiety, the immaculate chic with which Alicia surrounded herself turned suspicion into fantasy. Now the ugly word brought back to her the gardener boy's hands. She flushed.

"I was with Alex . . ." Alicia began again.

"Alicia, please!" Ariel's hands were at her ears. Her mother jerked them down.

"You shall hear this, Ariel, because you must. You are of the same blood as I am. Yet you have judged me. I see it in your face. You have a transparent face, my pet. Never try to lie. You'll make a botch of it."

"Alicia, may I go now?"

"I was with Alex," Alicia continued evenly, "because I find him intelligent, civilized, a charming companion, diverting. And necessary."

"Alicia, I do understand!"

"But I am not in love with him."

Something in the expression of her mother's face caught at Ariel.

"Ariel, have you been touched by a man?"

"No."

Alicia glanced at her sharply. "I do not believe you. I do not expect you to tell me. Unless you wish to. But you are awakening. You will learn the difference between love and the fires of your body. When they are one . . ." Alicia was looking at something beyond the walls, through the trailing mists. "I was once truly in love, Ariel. With one man. I would have walked on my knees to be with him. Of course, he wouldn't have looked at me twice if I had. Oh, we must play these little games, my pet. He was the only man I have ever loved. I still do."

Ariel could not read her face. Only a sudden softening hinted how she might have looked in her youth.

"One man. I could not have him. Yet I've always had him. Because he loved me.

"It's in our blood, Ariel. Roundtree blood. We are like swans. We love only once. It is complete and forever. But we are not swans. We can't swim in an empty lake for the rest of our lives. We are human. We belong in the world. I loved him, I could not have him. I made of my days what I could. You may be luckier."

The little drawing room had become an oasis of

quiet. Far away a motor sounded. The lifting mist revealed the shape of the mountain across the lake.

Alicia carried the breakfast tray to the table beside the door. She liked neatness.

"Go pack, my pet, won't you? We're leaving for Paris at two."

Paris. And safety. Her own blue-and-mauve room. Images blurred like reflections in water. The Thatcher dawn whitened the window. Ariel fell into heavy sleep.

"Ariel, we've neglected you shamefully!"

Lowell turned from the sink in the old-fashioned kitchen. She was washing pieces of silver as Edythe polished them, when Ariel entered. The accusing hands of the hall clock had told Ariel it was past eleven. She could postpone the day no longer.

"Did you sleep well, dear?"

"Yes, thank you, Aunt Edythe."

"Help yourself to coffee. And then take a towel. We need you."

Nothing had happened. Everything had happened. Three days ago this was all she wanted. To be included, to be assured she was part of the circle. Now, it had closed around her to become a trap. She felt betrayal on her forehead like a brand. Did they know? Had Kim blurted out what she had seen? Or had she seen anything?

"You gave us a little scare last night, Ariel." Edythe was as bland as morning. She handed Lowell a dented candlestick.

"I don't know why we bother to polish that one, Mom."

"Neither do I, but we can't put just one on the mantel."

"If it's nice weather nobody will come inside the house anyhow." Ariel looked pretty and refreshed.

"Don't you believe it, Ariel. If I know this town, there isn't a tent big enough to keep them outside. Everybody will come poking through, telling you how they remember the house, and how different it looks. But I've stopped worrying about that. We've lived here all our married life, Martin and I, and raised a family. If it shows, it shows." She laughed and took off the rubber gloves. Edythe was as careful of her hands as she was of her neat clothes and her short, well-kept hair. Pride, Ariel thought. The Roundtree pride. Her own mother had mocked it, but it was their shield. She wondered if it was now their shield against her.

"Anyhow, Ariel," Lowell turned off the tap. "When I asked Duncan to go find you and he didn't come back, we were sure you'd gotten lost. Then he told us you'd met Charlie Redwing."

"You're to be congratulated, my dear." Edythe took the dish towel from Ariel's hand. "Anybody who can get more than two words in fifteen minutes out of Charlie is special. He's the grandson of an Indian chief. He would never tell you that but if you know it you never forget it. Ancestral pride. It's a man's backbone, Martin says. Now run along and enjoy the day. Oh dear, I hope the weather isn't changing."

Lowell put her arm through Ariel's. "We really have neglected you. And it's my fault. I realized that last night. Uncle Willard means it when he says he's coming to take you out, you know. You'll enjoy him. He's the most ageless person I've ever known."

Nothing had happened, except that she was still left with the unknown. But beneath that lay a curious steadying sense of relief.

Last night, unfulfilled though it was, had told her one thing. She had revealed her love to the one man she would never forget and could never have. And he returned it. There was a splendor about it now, that no one could take from her and that was worth anything she might have to go through in the next three days. Last night she had resolved to leave at once. This morning she knew that would be impossible. But she would avoid him as much as she could. She had done nothing false. They had shared for one blinding, broken moment the deepest emotion she could know. She would live a lifetime on that. Her secret reassurance. Her own kind of pride.

Lowell was leading the way into the dining room, beneath Henrietta's half smile. She turned impulsively.

"Ariel, you will come to Mrs. Wilcox's with me this afternoon, won't you? She's been a minister's wife for forty years and she has some awful ideas. She's going to tell me every one of them. At tea, Could you bear it?"

Ariel had a sudden wrenching glimpse of herself. It was a trick that often happened, a basic honesty that had made a shambles of her resolutions.

"Of course I can bear it, Lowell. I'd love to go."

But beneath her warmth, she knew that beyond anything she ached to see Duncan again.

Cora Wilcox was a dried-apple-cheeked little woman who turned out to be livelier than Ariel had anticipated. She poured tea into fragile cups, chirped like a bird, and fixed an examining eye on Ariel.

"Ariel? How interesting. A French name?"

"No. English, I think, Mrs. Wilcox."

"Your father was English?"

"Yes, I think so." Ariel was looking out the mullioned windows across the grass to the church study.

"You think so? Didn't you know him?"

"I lost him when I was six months old."

"Dear, dear. An accident? Or was it the war? I've always held that war was the outward and visible sign of inward and invisible sin. I have thought that idea was rather good and hoped Dr. Wilcox would use it in his sermon. But he hasn't yet. He's so full of ideas himself. Ariel. Of course it's English! It's in Shakespeare! One of all those fairies in Midsummer Night's Dream. Bean Pod, Pepper Corn . . . I never did see why the man chose names like that."

It seemed needless to correct her. Ariel thought she caught a glimpse of Duncan's head through the study window.

"Ariel. Well, it's a very pretty name, I'm sure, even if it is foreign. You mother lives alone in Paris?"

"I live with her, Mrs. Wilcox."

"But you're only a girl."

"We're lucky to have Ariel with us," Edythe said hastily.

"Yes, of course. Indeed you are. Now, Lowell, your wedding presents. I didn't send them because I believe they should stay right here. I'm sure you'll make some changes. It's your privilege. But I find that most things fit best just where they are. Change doesn't always improve things." Her button eyes followed Ariel's out the window. "We won't wait for Dr. Wilcox and Duncan because I haven't invited them. I'm old-fashioned but I do believe in a separation of the sexes on a great many occasions. I also find it a relief." She set down her cup and pointed to a dim corner. "There, my dear. Turn up the lamp."

A small cabinet of black ebony inlaid with a Chinese pattern of gilt stood on four slender legs.

"It belonged to Dr. Wilcox's father, the bishop. It was given him by a very wealthy parishoner. For a humidor. But of course neither the bishop nor Dr. Wilcox ever smoked. So the Doctor had it made over for me into—well, open it."

Lowell lifted the lid on an awesome array of spools, scissors, needles, thimble, tape measure, and objects too numerous to identify. Their rigid order forecast hours of duty as clearly as the ticking of a clock.

"I made all the altar cloths, Lowell. I'm sure you will want to."

"It's beautiful, Mrs. Wilcox. I know I'll have so much use for it."

"If you don't sew, it will make a gorgeous jewel box." French mischief caught up with Ariel. Lowell flashed her a smile but Cora Wilcox's birdlike voice thinned.

"Perhaps in Paris, Ariel. But not in Thatcher. Now, Lowell, if you'll just open that closet."

Under a sheet was a small cradle of dark, polished wood.

"It's been in our family nearly a hundred years, Lowell. Our son used it. He was in Vietnam with Duncan, Ariel. One of those who didn't come back. That's why Duncan is so dear to us. He is carrying on as our son. When you and Duncan have your children, Lowell . . ."

Ariel felt something slide from her. Assurance. Resolutions of nobility, sacrifice, and a secret love that would sustain her. Despite what she had done, what she had allowed to happen, wanted to happen, Duncan was no more hers than he would ever be. Last night. Was it a last fling, raw malehood responding to her intensity as men always did?

She heard the front door open.

"Duncan!" Lowell flew into the hall. No one could miss the relief in her voice.

He wore a dark suit. Ariel had never seen him look quite so formal. Or quite so handsome. He kissed Lowell, greeted her with a flash of surprise but nothing more. Dr. Wilcox followed him into the room.

"Cora, my dear. I think you should all know that Mrs. Higgins died at three o'clock this afternoon." There were murmurs, a small sob from Cora. "She suffered a stroke last night. She was taken to the hospital, but she did not suffer. She had earned her rest. Thatcher has lost a fine and good woman. We are thankful for the beauty of her life."

Dr. Wilcox leaned down, kissed his wife, and patted her shoulder.

Would Duncan sound like that some day, Ariel wondered, always seeming to be talking to a congregation and thus in the unending pattern of deaths, marriages, and births that lay ahead? He was standing with his arm around Lowell.

"It leaves us with a problem," the Reverend Wilcox went on. "The funeral will be held at three on Friday."

"Oh, no, Duncan!"

"Honey, it can't be helped."

Cora and Dr. Wilcox were staring at Lowell uneasily.

Lowell seemed to lose control. "But our wedding rehearsal is at five. Duncan, I don't want it held right after a funeral. Why, that's awful!"

"Lowell!" Cora's voice was possessively sharp.

Dr. Wilcox took her hand. "I know how you feel, my dear. You are young, happy, and life is ahead. You cannot think of it in any other terms. Especially now. But death has come. It is the great finality to this mortal life and it must be served first."

"I'm sure, sir, if Mrs. Higgins . . ." Duncan stopped and Ariel saw defeat in his eyes. Whatever had driven him to this career, he pays a price, she thought.

"I was going to suggest that you and Lowell set your rehearsal earlier in the day. I am quite free at eleven in the morning. That may be an unusual hour but these are unusual circumstances."

Lowell was standing rigid beside Duncan, as if a silent quarrel had not yet spent itself. Ariel found herself looking directly at him. Whatever she might tell herself, nothing had changed.

Then Lowell was at the door. "I'll tell Phyllis that we can't come to her party tonight."

Dr. Wilcox put down his teacup which had restored him to cheerful normalcy. "Nonsense, my dear. Of course you shall have your party. Nettie Higgins would not want a bride denied that. Not Nettie."

"I'm sure of it, Lowell. I would go if I were you." Cora Wilcox had the apple-cheeked satisfaction of setting the day to rights.

Ariel went with Lowell out the door. She carried

Duncan's look with her. But more than that, Lowell's sudden outburst.

They reached home in silence. From upstairs they could hear the faint throb of Claude's radio. Otherwise the house was still. So still that Ariel felt as she had before, that it was held in a web of time. When this week, this endless, painful, speeding week was over, they would all return into frames, like Henrietta, and live in the past. She wondered again how soon after the wedding she could leave. She should begin to think about plane schedules and taxis and trains and escape.

The door to Martin's study at the rear of the hall opened. He came toward them holding a slip of paper. He looked drawn, his fine features pinched and gray. But his eyes lighted when he saw Lowell, in a way that Ariel envied.

"Where's your mother?"

"She left a note to say she'd go over to the Higgins'. Dad . . ." Lowell went to him as if to shield him. "Mr. Higgins' mother died this afternoon."

"Oh, I am sorry. She was a good woman. She stood for something in this town. Decency. Principles."

"The funeral is Friday at three. We're changing the wedding rehearsal to eleven in the morning."

"Of course. That's proper."

Lowell kissed her father, willingness sweet on her face. Ariel wondered that this could be the same girl who had flung out that single tight 'No' into Mrs. Wilcox's dark living room. There were two sides to Lowell. She wondered if anyone had ever seen more than a glimpse of the other.

Martin was holding the slip of paper out to her. "A telephone message Claude took for you, Ariel."

"For me?"

Martin turned back to his study.

In Claude's careful block letters, Ariel read "Phone call for you, Ariel. Nick Orlini. He said he would call again. Wow."

She showed the note to Lowell.

"I thought he'd call you. If you want to see him, go ahead." There was a tremor in Lowell's voice. "It can't be much fun for you here."

She went up the stairs. Ariel tore the paper into shreds and followed silently.

Chapter Seven

Ben Orlini looked across the desk at his caller and calculated. He was not used to losing. He did not like losers. At this moment Harlan Phelps seemed to embody losing.

He wished he were back in his opulent office on the forty-sixth floor of one of New York's newest glass skyscrapers. He could operate there. The city spread below him gave him a sense of power and there he could taste success. But he had kept a low profile in Thatcher. His office in Bollington was small and bare. On one wall hung a large-scale map of the township of Thatcher. Opposite, he had yielded to his love of display with a Caneletto print.

"Have you made up your mind to run for Congress next year, Harry?"

"Not yet. I'm pretty busy. I don't know that I'm ready to leave the state just yet."

"Sure. Sure."

It was a chess game. Ben knew that Harlan Phelps was as hungry for the House seat as Julia was for the Roundtree land. He should be able to maneuver as he always had. But he would have to move warily this time. Harlan Phelps was not clever but he had tenacity. And Ben Orlini had not forgotten that it was blunt, dogged Harry who got him the contract for the dam he had built above Upper Birch Lake. Ben wished he had never taken on this new acquisition. He should have kept Julia out of Thatcher. But it was too late now.

He put the tips of his small fingers together and blew through them. "All right. I'll raise the ante. How much does the old man want?"

"It's no use, Ben."

"God damn it, Harry. Every man has his price."

"But not to you, Ben."

"What do you mean not to me?"

"Martin told me the old man has written into his will that if the land is ever sold, it must not go to you."

Ben was on his feet. Then he sat down. He looked taller behind his desk than standing.

"It would never stand up in court."

"I don't know about that."

"Harry, you're not dealing from both sides of the deck, are you?"

"I don't know what that means."

"Sure you know what it means. Your son is marrying the Roundtree girl next Saturday. When the old man dies—"

"You can forget that, Ben. I have no son. If the land goes anywhere, it will go to Martin."

"Martin! Martin! I'm sick of Martin. That's your trouble, Harry. You walked out on his small-town office but you're still afraid of him. You know why, too. Because he has class. You haven't. How do you know Martin will get it?

"Ben, that land is going to stay in the family. You're not going to get it. Look, there are thousands of acres to the north, to the west. There isn't so much money around that somebody wouldn't be glad to take yours."

Ben Orlini could laugh when he had to. "Maybe you're right."

"Why, way back at the turn of the century somebody tried to get that land, every way he could."

"Who?"

"Name of Colin Thatcher. Nephew of old Nathaniel P. Thatcher's sister. Thatcher left the land, you know, to Isaac Roundtree, after the Civil War. Colin came back with the notion he could break the will. He couldn't. Nathaniel Thatcher was the biggest man around here in his day. The town was named after his family. He was no fool. He was a lawyer himself. Judge. Ran for governor of the state once."

"What happened to Colin?" Impatience danced in Ben Orlini's narrowed eyes.

"That's the funny party of the story. He got mixed up with Isaac's fancy wife, Henrietta. There was a scandal. Nothing more was heard of him. She died a year or so later."

"The man must have had some reason for thinking he could break Nathaniel Thatcher's will."

"Sure."

"Have you looked at that will?"

"What do you take me for? I've been over every comma in Nathaniel Thatcher's old will. And over every deal and claim and survey relating to it. You couldn't get a ray of light through one of 'em. It's Roundtree land now. Solid."

"Colin Thatcher must have had some reason for thinking he could get it."

"If he had, it's gone with him. If you ask me, he just liked to play footsies with Henrietta. I understand it wasn't unusual."

Ben rose. "I intend to have that land. Whatever it takes."

Harlan Phelps hoisted himself out of his chair. "You're crazy, Ben. It isn't worth all that."

"You're going to get it for me, Harry. Or someone else is. Or . . ." Harlan heard that undercurrent that made Ben Orlini so successful. ". . . I might just have to do it myself."

"Okay. Okay. But would you tell me one thing? *Why*, for Christ's sweet sake?"

Ben's smile was as sweet as it was chilling. "I like to

sleep with my wife, Harry. You ought to understand that."

Lowell hung the glistening white gown back in its cellophane sack. "Do you really like it, Ariel?"

"It's beautiful, Lowell. Just beautiful! Madame Voisine would say *parfait!*"

"Who's Madame Voisine?"

Lowell's mood had changed. She had dressed early for the evening's party. She had urged Ariel to hurry and now, with time on their hands, she had almost shyly brought out her wedding gown. "The train can be taken off and the sleeves removed so I can wear it as a dinner dress next winter. But heaven knows where I'd go to such a formal dinner in Thatcher. Besides, it would always look to me like my wedding dress."

"You can save it for your own daughter. Isn't that what they do?"

Ariel had come to grips with herself. To her relief, Nick Orlini had not called again. Events had brushed past her, isolating her. She had no right to fantasy or even to pain. Oddly, Lowell seemed to need her.

"I suppose you've been to a lot of fashionable weddings in Paris."

"Not many." She would not explain why her life had given her little time to make friends of her own. Her mother's friends were not the type to have big family weddings, or even families. "But I remember one," she went on gaily. "At the Madeleine. The bride wore lace embroided with diamantes. Sequins. With a candle on her head she would have made a very chic Christmas tree."

Lowell laughed. She had shown strain after her near-quarrel with Duncan and the long, pale blue dress she was wearing for the evening did not help. But now a little color returned to her face.

"What is the Madeleine?"

"It's a lovely church in the middle of Paris. It looks

like a Greek temple. You and Duncan will come to Paris some day and see it."

"We'll never get that far."

"There's no reason why not, Lowell. Duncan likes to travel, doesn't he?"

"Since the war, I—I don't know. Oh Ariel, I haven't had time to ask you half the questions I wanted. Do you have a job in Paris?"

"Yes, of course. But I can never stay with one job very long. Alicia, my mother, is always traveling. She likes me along, sometimes. But I model some, too."

"I should think so."

"But I don't like it. Many of the buyers are men and they think they can do what they like. Ugh. I did get one job I adored. On the Paris *Herald*, the American newspaper in Europe." Ariel smiled wryly. The disappointment still stung. "But they wanted a reporter who would stay around. I told them they were absolutely right."

Lowell zipped up the bag on her wedding dress. "I went to college for a year, then I came home and worked at Mr. Bixler's insurance agency. Until two weeks ago. It wasn't very glamorous."

"Anything's glamorous if it's what you want."

"It was dull. But it was steady."

"You have a very full life ahead, I should think."

"Yes, but of course I can't work. Not as a minister's wife."

"You'd never have time."

"Oh, I'll be busy all right. With volunteer work and everything. I'm going to make Duncan a good wife." She grew serious. Ariel saw for the first time that duty was a formidable part of Lowell's idea of marriage. "It won't be easy for him, Ariel. They don't have much confidence in young people in Thatcher."

"You'll make it, Lowell. You and Duncan will do just fine." Impulsively Ariel put her arm around Lowell. "Oh, I wish you so much happiness. Now, when do we leave for the party?"

"As soon as Claude's ready. She's always late. Duncan will be coming later. He went over to have supper with the Higgins family. They adore him."

"Then we three girls will go alone. The three Furies."

Lowell giggled. "And hex the party. I'd love to. Oh, Ariel, I have to tell you, I can't take my eyes off that dress you're wearing. Nothing to it. Spaghetti straps. You'd never find anything like that little black silk around here. Is it an original? I mean, Paris?"

"Oh, come on. It's strictly M.L.S."

"What's that?"

"Mother's little seamstress. She goes to the showings, takes one look, and copies. For practically nothing."

"I adore it. But then I just fade away in black."

"Nobody fades away in black if they use the right makeup."

"Honestly?" Lowell's face lighted for an instant. "Oh, well, Duncan likes blue. And he likes this dress. He's seen it before. But I want to keep my new things for my honeymoon."

"Lowell!" Ariel hesitated. If only she knew this pretty—Nick Orlini's word flashed through her mind: "uptight"—cousin better. She had wanted to until it all turned so unreal. Well, she was facing reality now. "Lowell, would you do me a favor?"

"Of course."

"Would you try on my dress? I think you'd look absolutely wonderful. Nobody's seen it. If you like it, wear it tonight!"

"Oh, Ariel!"

"I'll help you make up. I know it will fit you. We're about the same size and it just wraps around." She was already getting out of the sleek black silk.

"I don't know what to say."

"Don't say anything. Come on. We have time."

The black dress not only fitted but Lowell saw herself as she had never looked before. Bare ivory shoulders accentuated with the thin black straps, her breasts round and free, the black silk rising only to the cleavage. Her legs not exactly thin but looking slender and good.

"Have you black slippers?"

"Not for this."

Ariel kicked off her sandals. "Wear mine. They're so light they won't hurt. And oh, black hose. I have another pair." Ariel darted from the room, returned with stockings and a plastic case. "You're right about black, Lowell. You do need makeup. And blush. And pale lipstick. And eyes. You have marvelous eyes, chérie, but you have to make them *look* marvelous. Now sit down. And let me fix you." She worked swiftly, expertly. "Great skin. It must be all this fresh air."

In five minutes she was finished. "There. Look."

Lowell looked. Even under the skillful makeup she had gone pale. But her eyes glowed, large and luminous. She saw for the first time in her life what every woman sees once. She was radiantly young and beautiful.

"I don't know what to say, Ariel. I don't know what Duncan will say."

Ariel's eyes were warm. She swallowed the sudden knot in her throat. "Tell him you're one of the Furies. And this is your night to roar." She gathered up her makeup kit. "Well?"

"But what will you wear, Ariel?"

"Oh don't worry about me. I'll pick out something else."

"Lowell!" Claude stood in the doorway, her mouth gaping. "Lowell!"

Lowell turned, her smile gone.

"Wait'll they see that in church!"

Ariel brushed past Lowell and clutched Claude's arm.

"Come and help me dress, Claude!"

In the hall, she put her face against the younger

girl's. "If you say one word more to Lowell," she hesitated, "I'll haunt you forever!"

They were a little late. The semicircle of bungalow-type houses lay on the outskirts of Thatcher, like an outpost. Behind them, in the last rim of fading light, Ariel could see the hogback of Bluestone Ridge where the lights of the town surrendered abruptly to dark countryside.

"A lot of young marrieds are moving here to Bluestone Terrace," said Lowell. They were walking past a line of parked cars, to the third of the identical houses. "But when I see it I'm glad Duncan and I will be living in the old Rectory. Even if it is dark as a pocket!"

"You can always paint it white inside," Ariel answered.

"And get a water bed, Duncan says." Lowell laughed nervously, pressing Ariel's arm. "Now stay by me, Ariel. I don't feel like myself."

"You look marvelous!"

Phyllis Simpson, plump and friendly as a puppy, opened the door. Voices, charged laughter, and the rattle of ice cubes met them.

"Here comes the bride, everyone!"

Craig, her husband, thin, stooped, and already balding, pushed past her.

"Where's Duncan the Deak or Deacon the Dunk?"

"He's coming later." Lowell's eyes were over bright. She clutched her tweed coat.

"You look great, honey. Just great." He kissed her. "Looks like marriage is going to agree with you. Great institution if you like institutions." He kissed her again. "Hi, Claude." He turned to Ariel. "This is the French cousin . . ."

"Ariel—" began Lowell.

"No introductions needed," shouted Craig. "I'd know you anywhere, Ariel." He kissed Ariel soundly, took her coat, and, with his arm around her, led her into the room. It was filled with faceless people whose names she would never get. "Jim, Hank, Peggy, Rick, Lisa . . ."

Phyllis giggled. "He always finds somebody to love up at a party, Lowell." She wore the authority of two years of marriage. "No matter what he does, I always remember I'm the girl who gets to go home with him. No key parties on my list. But then you're marrying Duncan and he's the minister and . . ." She broke off. "She is stunning, isn't she? Your cousin."

"She's great."

Phyllis looked across the room and saw Craig, his arm still around Ariel. "How long is she staying?"

"Mom says she hopes until Thanksgiving."

"I'll take your coat, Sis." Claude was subdued.

"Do that, Claude." Suddenly Phyllis gasped: "Lowell! You look absolutely terrific! Fabulous. What a dress! I could never get into anything like that! Where did you get it?"

"It's Ariel's. She wanted me to wear it. So I did. I wanted to surprise Duncan."

"You sure will."

"I don't know whether it's too much. I mean, with Mrs. Higgins dying today."

"Look, you're not the minister's wife yet. Live it up! The whole gang's here. Everybody you and Duncan knew in high school." Her eyes followed her husband again. Ariel had shaken free but Craig now had her elbow. "Just the same . . ." she smiled as archly as her plump soft face permitted. Phyllis Simpson had long ago guessed she could never have an extra-marital lover and was lucky to have caught Craig. "Just the same, I'm glad you're wearing it and not Ariel. She isn't married, is she? Not that it would matter, I guess." Her voice rose piercingly. "Here comes the bride, everybody! Here—comes—the—BRIDE!"

Suddenly there were wolf whistles, good-natured cheers, shouts, squeezes, hugs. "Who needs Duncan?" "Lowell, I wouldn't know you!"

From across the room, Ariel saw Lowell begin to glow.

"How about a drink, honey? Bar's right over there."

"No, thank you." Craig was still beside her but at least she had twisted free of his dry, hot hand. She felt a little sorry for him but she could handle small and unnecessary men. Her mother had taught her how.

Phyllis was bearing down on her. She had in tow a thin girl with long, black, lanky hair, gold-rimmed glasses, clunky shoes, jeans, and a tight-fitting top. "Lowell tells me you work on a newspaper in Paris. You ought to know our local celebrity, Louise Vale. Everybody calls her Vivi. She works on the *Thatcher Standard* with Craig. She's our famous girl reporter, aren't you, Vivi? She was in high school with Lowell and me and all of us. Remember, Vivi?" Phyllis suddenly flung her arms out wide. "Chickalack boom, Chicalacka rah . . . chickalack sis boom rah rah rah!" To Ariel's astonishment, she crouched to the floor, hissed like a snake, and toppled. There were guffaws, applause. With a wiry arm, Louise pulled her to her feet.

"Guess I'm getting too fat for that, Vivi," Phyllis laughed good-naturedly.

"You always were," said Vivi Vale coldly. Craig rambled over to his wife's rescue. "Hi, Pussycat," said Vivi. "I'd have gotten to this party a lot sooner, if that louse Frank hadn't put me on the Orlini call. Wasn't even a story there. I'd have liked that. He just wanted a little information. You had gone, lover boy."

"I'm sorry, Vivi, honestly."

Ariel saw something flicker between them.

"Don't let it happen again, Pussycat. No tickee, no shirtee."

Phyllis had moved on. Craig followed in her safe wake. Louise turned a coldly curious gaze on Ariel.

"So you're Ariel Roundtree. Last of the tribe."

"Oh, no. I'm not even one of the tribe."

"Good for you."

Ariel smiled. "Not as yet. I grew up abroad. But I didn't work on the Paris *Herald*. I had a job with them for a little while but I couldn't stay with it."

"Your type generally doesn't. Anyhow, it's a bourgeois paper. It can't last much longer." The music had begun again. Vivi glanced with contempt at the dancers. "Whatever got into Lowell, getting herself up like that? That's going all the way all right—from square to square root."

"Don't you approve of dressing up?"

"Oh, come on. Like a sex symbol? I settled all that a long time ago. But the guys around here aren't much good. Except—and this will rock you—little old Craig, maybe. If you could get him started." Vivi ran nervous fingers through her waist-long hair. "Don't tell me you came all the way from Europe for a wedding? That's really being rotten rich."

Ariel sensed an enemy. Yet she felt a compassion for this girl, with her bad skin, her hostile eyes, and her need to talk. She wondered what had frightened Louise Vale. Then she laughed. "Well, I'm not. If you knew what I did to get enough clothes together—"

"Why? Weddings are decadent. I wouldn't be caught dead at one if I didn't have to cover it for the paper. The boss—that's Phyllis's father, he owns it—says I have to wear a skirt. I said if I did the paper could pay for it. Oh, well, it's the Roundtrees' last hurrah."

"What is that, the last hurrah?"

"It means the last gasp. Oh, come on, don't tell me you don't know Ben Orlini's buying up all that land."

"Oh, I don't think so."

"You'll find out. They deserve to lose it. Men are oppressors, but those Roundtrees . . ."

Ariel no longer found the girl amusing. She moved away but Vivi followed her. "You don't believe that either, do you? I could tell you a few things. Just ask any of them why Hester Brady isn't going to be at the

Roundtree wedding. She was about Lowell's best friend in school."

Somebody put on a rock record. A fat boy was approaching. "Like to dance, Vivi?"

"I don't go in for mating rites, Rick," she said coldly.

Somebody called out. "Eats are on, everybody. When you get the urge!" Vivi marched toward the table. Phyllis caught up with Ariel.

"Don't mind Vivi. She always says what she thinks. She's terribly bright and good at her job, Craig says. I think she talks like that because she's afraid of not being noticed. She doesn't mean half of it."

Ariel wondered.

But her own annoyance was real. She went quickly to where the fat boy was standing. "Would you get me something to eat, Rick?"

He looked at her in awe. "Why sure, Ariel."

"We could sit over there." She indicated two chairs in the six-foot dining area.

"I'll be right back. You want a drink?"

"No, thank you."

"Me either." His face glowed with gratitude.

Ariel wanted desperately to go home, when Duncan walked in. If he had rung no one heard him. Suddenly he was there, at the edge of the crowd. As if in pantomime Ariel saw Lowell run to him, throw her arms around his neck, and watched as Duncan held her away and looked at her. She saw him throw back his head and laugh and follow Lowell into the room.

But now none of it mattered—whether he danced with Lowell or not, whether Lowell wore the black dress or, for that matter, whether Lowell or anyone else was in the room. She had met Duncan's eyes, as she had done the first night. Nothing had changed.

She started dancing listlessly with the gentle fat boy.

"Gee, you're great, Ariel."

"I have a good partner. Rick, would you get me a glass of ginger ale?"

"Sure. You tired?"

"Oh no, just thirsty."

They sat down. He returned quickly.

"You know, I never met a girl like you, Ariel."

"I never met a boy like you, Rick. You're so kind."

Then she held her breath. She knew without looking up that Duncan was coming toward her. He was standing in front of her, looking down with that half-smile.

"Mind if I cut in, Rick?"

"Sure, sure, Dunk. Go ahead."

"Would you like to dance, Ariel?"

She rose. "Yes. Yes, all right." The room had begun to flow. "Thank you, Rick." She flashed a smile. "Don't go away."

The music slid into a slow dance. She saw Lowell dance by in Craig's loose embrace. She thought, if Duncan touches me!

She had to say something. She felt that everyone in the room was watching them. "Well, what do you think of your bride, Duncan?"

"She looks great."

His arm went around her. She trembled, felt the arm tighten.

"Duncan, not so close. Please."

His voice was in her ear. "I want to see you. Just once more."

"No."

"My God, Ariel!"

She did not try to answer. She felt his body stiffen. The room faded. She was aware only of the dreamlike music and his arm.

"I can't pick you up at the house. But I could see you downtown."

"Duncan, we can't."

"I'll be in Slater's Stationery Store tomorrow at two-fifteen. It's next to the Deli on Main Street. You can walk to it from the house."

The music had switched to rock. He had to release her.

"Two-fifteen, Ariel. I'll wait for you."

Chapter Eight

Willard Roundtree pushed back his wide-brimmed straw hat and watched the car come around the bend from Preacher's Hill. He did not recognize it.

"Looks like we're about to have company, Charlie."

Charlie Redwing lifted the last of a row of pumpkins into the pick-up truck and squinted at the sky. "Weather's changing, Mr. Will." Conversation with Charlie was usually off on some tangent. He might mean something or nothing.

"See that it's clear on Saturday. We want Lowell married in sunshine."

"The gods know. I'll take the truck down to the shed now."

Which meant he had seen the car and, like Willard, did not recognize it. Charlie Redwing was as cautious of strangers as he was of friends. And he liked no one to look directly at him.

Willard nodded and started across the field to the driveway. If any man could be said to value another, he valued the stocky Charlie. He was more than a brother. Without him, the earth itself would be the poorer. He gave Willard part of his strength in holding back the enemy.

The car was extravagantly long, a deep blue with whitewall tires. It gleamed with expensive care. As the lone occupant stepped out, it occurred to Willard that Charlie Redwing had read more in the shifting wind than the coming of rain.

Julia Orlini held out a gloved hand. "Good morning, Mr. Roundtree. I'm Julia Orlini."

Willard bowed. "Of course. Good morning, madam."

"I didn't think you'd remember. We met only once, at the ceremonies opening the dam."

"I doubt that any man who had met you once could forget you."

Julia's laugh was sudden and girlish. "Mr. Roundtree! It's no wonder everybody's in awe of you."

"I don't see that it follows."

"Oh yes, you do. You're a very clever man. You take people by surprise and off guard."

"How very Machiavellian of me. Will you come in, Mrs. Orlini?"

"No, really, I can't. I'm intruding now. But I've just come down from the Ridge. I want to tell you how sorry I am for what Ben has done up there. All those trees . . ."

"He has a different set of values."

"I hoped you'd understand that. And Ben—well, other things are more important. So he makes mistakes. I'm going to do what I can to repair the damage.

"In that case you would be mightier than God."

"I would only try to replant there. New trees," she answered shortly.

Willard knew that he was looking at the face of the enemy. Julia Orlini in no way deceived him. Yet there was something in her, uncertain, afraid. He had seen it in the eyes of a cornered mountain lion. Dangerous, yet in need. Charlie Redwing would sense it. Perhaps he had.

"It's very kind of you to come here."

She looked at him directly. "No, it isn't. I had a purpose. You know, Mr. Roundtree, you're not the only one who wants this land to stay as it is. I will live up on the Ridge some day. I want to look down on this whole valley, without any change."

Willard inclined his head. He knew when to be courtly.

"I was sure we would have something in common. And that is a great deal." There was nothing more to say, yet she hesitated. "I do wish your family great happiness at the wedding on Saturday."

"Thank you. Could you include a little sunshine in that?"

"What's weather when you're in love?" She was at ease now and her charm was evident.

"I'd have to admit I've forgotten."

"A man like you never forgets, Mr. Roundtree." She laughed girlishly again. Julia Orlini had never met the man she could not charm. Willard Roundtree presented a challenge but she was at her best with challenges.

"Lowell's a lovely girl. I had hoped once that Nick, my son. . . . Oh, he was interested, but Lowell had eyes only for the handsome young minister—what is his name . . . ?"

Willard saw no need to answer.

"Well, Nick tells me there is another beautiful Roundtree girl in town. Quite different. With the enchanting name of Ariel. From Shakespeare, isn't it? The magic spirit in *The Tempest*. I looked it up. I told him he must bring her to dinner. Perhaps you'd join us some evening?"

"You're very kind, madam."

Her smile was honest. "You don't like me, Mr. Roundtree. You don't trust me. You think I am what my husband is. I assure you I came here much more as a friend." She opened the car door, then held out her hand. He took it.

"Goodbye, Mr. Roundtree."

He bowed again. This time with a reluctant respect for Julia Orlini.

As he went up the steps of his farmhouse, Willard remembered he had promised to show young Ariel some of her heritage. This would be as good a time as any. But he would have lunch first.

❖   ❖   ❖

For the third time Ariel crossed the hall to look at the hands of the tall clock. She had her own watch, but of course it could be wrong or she might have forgotten to wind it.

She would not meet Duncan. It was more of the week's madness. They had escaped narrowly the night in the woods. She was not yet sure that they had not been seen. Little Kim had avoided her. It almost seemed on purpose. And Lowell's warmth—was it gratitude for the borrowed dress or reflection of her innocent happiness? Or, worst of all, her confidence as if she knew what had happened and was showing Ariel how little it could matter?

But here at nearly one o'clock in the afternoon, Ariel found herself unable to sit in one place or continue a conversation. Duncan wanted to see her and she had not refused. She had silently consented.

There would be no harm in a chance meeting in the stationer's store. He would drive her home. They would not be gone long. A few shared moments in the car, a reaffirmation, the passion of love she would carry forever.

Yet when she ceased her fantasies, a reality remained. Why had he asked her to meet him? Why? Was he mad enough to think they could run away? Leave everything and everyone? Make a life somewhere together? The image was as dizzying as it was frightening. How could she make such a decision? How could she agree? How could she refuse?

A burst of laughter came from the sunporch. Claude and Lowell were unwrapping gifts.

"Ariel!" Lowell called. "Come and see this!"

One-thirty-five. She would have to leave before two. She had no idea how far it was.

She went out into the sun porch.

"It's from Aunt Millicent in Houston." Claude giggled. "She must have had it for forty years."

Ariel found herself looking at a bronze log, four feet

178

long, with six small, brown bears climbing over it. "What is it?"

"Well, it looks like bears but we'd call it a white elephant. It's probably worth an oil well. What am I going to do with it?" Lowell looked glowing.

"Put it in some dim old corner of the rectory where nobody will see it," offered Claude.

"The rectory isn't going to have any dim old corners when Duncan and I get through with it."

"Think they're going to let you change it?" Claude fired a tissue-paper ball into a waste basket. "Ariel, you should have heard some of the comments because Lowell really looked like something last night."

"I didn't hear them, Claude. Besides, I don't care. I was going to ask you, Ariel, if you'd mind if I took your black dress to Hannah Poole and had her copy it. I mean, we wouldn't be wearing it the same places. It wouldn't be identical. Yours is so smart. Duncan adored it."

"Take it, Lowell."

"I'll ask her to rush it, and you won't be leaving for a while."

"No, no, Lowell. I mean take it. Keep it. I want you to have it. You looked so beautiful!"

"I couldn't!"

"Please. It would make me so happy. Please."

Somewhere the phone rang. Ariel glanced at her own watch. One-forty-five. Was it fast?

Lowell threw her arms around her. "I will take it, Ariel, if you really mean it. I adore it. I'll think of last night every time I wear it. I had such a good time. And I know what I'll do with the bears." She giggled. "Duncan and I will send them to you when you get married. If we can afford the freight."

"Ariel, dear." Edythe stood in the doorway. "That was Willard. He's on his way to pick you up and take you for a drive. I told him he couldn't have picked a better time. You'll find him fascinating. He knows more about this area, about everything!"

Ariel's mind worked, as it so often did in panic, with clarity. She found the little lie she needed.

"I'd love it, Aunt Edythe. How kind of him. But I'd like to run down to the stationer's store first, if there is one . . ."

"Sure. Slater's," Claude broke in.

"I need a box of writing paper. I haven't written Alicia a word."

"I have plenty, dear."

"Use mine. It's neat! Yellow with a green and orange rim."

"I'd like the walk. I need exercise. I walk a lot in Paris." Ariel was backing toward the hall. As usual, when she told a little lie, she talked too much. If she could just get out.

"If it begins to rain, we'll send Willard down for you."

"It isn't going to rain, now or for the rest of the week!"

"Oh, for heaven's sake, let her go." Lowell was picking up tissue paper. "Ariel, you must be so bored with wedding talk by this time."

"Are you, Ariel?"

For an instant she thought Claude was coming with her.

"Slater's is next to the Deli. Bring us home some dill pickles, will you?"

The voices crossed, tangled and lost meaning. Ariel snatched up her coat, which hung beside the others in the hall closet, and escaped. She had enmeshed herself in another lie. They were tightening around her. If she had only refused to meet Duncan. But she was drawn as directly on this course as a bird flying south to the sun. Let them think what they would. Duncan was waiting.

The sky had grown sullen. A drop of rain fell. She began to run.

Hannah Poole was standing at the revolving paperback-book stand, reading one of the more lurid covers when she saw Duncan enter. She liked to keep her taste in literature to herself so she stepped quickly behind the stand. She was excited to think that she had run into him this way. She could make a lot of the incident when she talked to Gladys Beemer again. Duncan looked so handsome when he was serious. And he certainly looked serious now. Almost distraught. The wedding, no doubt. She slipped the book back into the rack, watched as Duncan bought his paper. To her surprise, he did not leave. He stood riffling through the magazines. He glanced at his watch. Curiosity kept Hannah Poole where she was. She would know soon enough.

The rain, falling steadily, now blurred the windows, as Ariel entered the narrow store. To her relief it was empty. There was no one behind the long counter that ran to the back.

"Duncan."

He came to her and took both her hands. His look, his touch told her again all she wanted to know.

"Duncan, I couldn't get away sooner. I can't stay. Uncle Willard is picking me up." It was a whisper.

He held her hands an instant longer, before he let them go. His voice was so low she barely heard it. "You're here. That's all that matters."

"He's coming for me here . . . I can't explain it all."

He nodded. "Ariel, it's all right. No one will be hurt."

"Except us."

"We can't be. After what we've found . . ."

"Guess the rain caught up with you, Duncan." Mr. Slater was returning to his counter. "Want anything else?"

"Nothing thanks, Mr. Slater. But maybe Miss Roundtree . . . this is Miss Ariel Roundtree, Lowell's cousin."

Mr. Slater settled his spectacles. "Here for the wedding, eh? Well, I'm mighty pleased to meet you."

"So am I, thank you." A pick-up truck stopped at the curb. Through the rain she could just make out the driver, lowering the cab window.

"There's Uncle Willard now, Duncan!" She started for the door and remembered. "Oh, I need a box of stationery, Mr. Slater."

"What kind, Miss Roundtree?"

"Oh, any kind. I mean, it's for me. Is this it over here?" She was aware of sounding rattled.

"Help yourself."

She picked up a box, saw the price, put two dollar bills on the counter. "Bye, Duncan. I'll give your love to Lowell!"

Mr. Slater picked them up with a smile. "Guess Lowell's cousin is kinda new to these parts. Doesn't know about the tax."

Duncan reached in his pocket. "She's here from Paris, Mr. Slater."

"Might've guessed that from her looks. Reminded me of someone. Sixteen cents, Duncan."

Hannah Poole came slowly out from behind the bookstand, her smile a triumph of suppressed anticipation.

"The Reverend Phelps! How delightful! But of course I'll still call you Duncan until you take the pulpit, may I? The happy groom, Mr. Slater. How is dear Lowell?"

Willard drove the pickup truck through the gates of the cemetery, followed the winding road to the summit, and stopped there. Ariel had said almost nothing on the drive. Nor did he expect her to.

"There, just near those oak trees, you can see the granite shaft, Roundtree!"

Ariel opened the truck door.

"It's too wet to get out. Get your feet soaked. You girls today have no sense about wearing overshoes."

"I'd like to see it all, Uncle Willard." The rain was dwindling to a fine mist curtaining the hills, drifting among the headstones, cooling her face. Veiling it, she would like to think. She would like to lose herself in it. Forever. Instead, she would lose herself in Roundtrees. Drink up their names and their past until she could believe she was no longer an outsider. Only then would she feel free to take Duncan's love with her where she could never hurt them or they her.

She followed Willard over the low iron railing and into the large plot. The headstones were all cut in the same precise, stark pattern, the large and the small ones. There were more than a few small ones. " 'Nathaniel Isaac, 1871. Died by God's will at birth.' 'Jonathan, 1879. Died aged 12 by God's swift hand. Vengeance is mine saith the Lord.' 'Susannah, 1893–1896. Blessed are the pure. They shall not behold evil.' "

"These are just children."

"Henrietta and Isaac had ten. In those days to lose three was not out of proportion."

"But the words are so grim."

"Isaac Roundtree was a grim man. He may have been a demented one before he died."

She walked among the stones as if in a surrealist landscape. The intensity of her encounter with Duncan, the emotional meetings and renunciation in the last three days had drained her sense of reality. These were not gravestones. They were men and women, human beings who in an odd imagery of mist and mind were not turning from her but to her.

She tripped and Willard caught her arm.

"Oh, how stupid. I didn't see it." A corner of granite nearly sunken into the trim wet grass had caught her foot.

"Nobody does. Did you hurt yourself?"

Her ankle ached but it would pass. "I don't bruise easily."

"I hope not."

"Someday," Willard grunted, "somebody will take a real fall over that thing and it will be removed. I hope it won't happen when they're putting me up here."

"That will be a long time from now." She smiled warmly. She liked this shrewd-eyed old gentleman. She felt comfortable with him. That is, she could feel comfortable if she were less uncertain. Every incident with Duncan seemed etched in light, visible to anyone who saw them together. How long had he been outside the store?

"Why don't they straighten up that little stone?"

"Old Isaac wrote in his will that nothing in the plot was to be moved or touched. He laid the whole place out himself."

"It's a footstone, isn't it?"

"To what? Come along, my dear. The rain's beginning again. I must be reaching my dotage to bring a lovely young lady up here on a day like this."

"I'm very grateful, Uncle Willard. I've never known anything about them all. I like knowing." She moved on among the headstones. " 'Rachel Roundtree, 1872–1951. Spinster.' "

"Henrietta and Isaac's second child."

"And Mary Patience. 'Thou shalt cleave to thy husband.' What on earth does that mean?"

"Mary Patience married a school teacher, a dismal man who took her to Chicago and abandoned her. She obtained a divorce. She didn't dare come back. Except to die." He saw no reason to tell her that Mary Patience was his mother.

"And Chastity? What a name! Only 22."

"Lovely and wild as a gypsy. But they discovered that too late. I have pictures of her."

She saw that he was restless. And yet. And yet she would never see this place again. She had begun to sense that he had brought her here for a reason. What reason, she could not guess but if she stayed long enough she might know. She walked more quickly among the gravestones. "Peter Martin. Your father?"

"No. Martin's grandfather. And your great-grandfather."

"Mine?"

A figure rose from the headstone, in her mind, beyond Alicia, beyond all the silly, transient people of her life. Dignified, upright, important. She wondered how he had lived, what he had done in the flesh and blood that was now hers. Peter Martin Roundtree, 1884–1931. So she did belong, she thought wryly, if not to the living then to the dead.

"Had enough, child?"

"Not nearly. But I'll come in a minute."

She had reached the granite shaft that commanded the plot from the upper end. The ten-inch, block letters ROUNDTREE looked larger and more forbidding close up. On the shaft she now could read the smaller letters. "Isaac Roundtree, 1843–1928. And wife." *And wife* . . .

"Uncle Willard!"

He had started down the slope. He retraced his steps. He was beginning to regret this undertaking. Her face was glowing with discovery.

"Yes, my dear."

"Isaac Roundtree. And wife. Is that Henrietta?"

"Yes."

"But that's dreadful. He doesn't even mention her name."

"He didn't, for many years."

She sensed that she was near the heart of this little journey.

"Why not?"

"Well, there's a story—legendary, I believe. There's even some doubt that Henrietta lies there. Come along. We'll go back to the farm and a good fire. Have you ever tasted mulled cider made from new apples?"

She sat on a low hassock, her arms around her knees, watching the flames. Beside her lay the big red dog, Clancy, content to have her hand on his silky back.

Willard found this all more difficult than he had foreseen. How long had it been since a woman, lovely and young, had sat like this at his fireside? Ariel, for all the suppressed passion he recognized in her, had the talent of quiet grace. She could sit motionless as if there were no other place she would rather be. He prayed inwardly, fervently, that the man she would someday find would understand and value that grace.

"But what did she do, Uncle Willard?"

He handed her a second mug of the sweet hot cider. She took it to warm the numbing chill that was spreading inside her.

"Henrietta? It was not what she did, it was what they thought she did."

"Who?"

"The town. In those days a small town the size of Thatcher fed on itself."

And still does, she thought. That's what he's trying to tell me.

"What did they think she did?"

He went to a plain wooden chest in the recess beside the fireplace, "They didn't think. They didn't know. They could only talk. And gossip is more deadly than fire. It preys on its victim long after it has destroyed her." He lifted the lid. "All that we actually know of Henrietta is here. A few newspaper clippings about her parties. Some letters from an aunt. A lace dress. A complete set of Shakespeare in small volumes. They're crumbling now. She must have read them often. Many of the lines are underscored." He let the lid down gently. "You are so like her, Ariel, you must look into this chest some day."

"Now." She set down the mug. The cider was headier than she thought or perhaps she was more vulnerable. "There was a man, I suppose."

"There were always men in the town's mind. Henrietta was New Orleans born. She didn't transplant well. But the man who made the trouble was one Colin Thatcher, a no-account relative of the Nathaniel who had willed the land to Isaac. Colin set out to prove that Isaac Roundtree was an impostor. When he couldn't do that, he tried blackmail. None of that

186

would have mattered but Colin was rather dashing. And Henrietta was Henrietta. The town put the story together."

"And her husband believed it?"

"Isaac believed what he thought God told him to believe. That made him a very uncomfortable adversary. But Henrietta lived it down, as she lived everything else down."

"She loved her husband."

"She never left a word to explain or deny anything. But she held fast. That's the point, my dear. She knew what was important. More important than herself or what others said. Passions die. Blood ties, stability, family, they shape a society. They have shaped Thatcher."

A log crashed, sending a shower of sparks upward and breaking the silence.

"As I should know it, Uncle Willard?"

"My dear, I am answering questions you have asked."

"Oh no, you're not! You're telling me something, something I haven't asked. Something I should know. Why don't you say it directly? Why don't you say what you think? What they all think . . ." She jumped to her feet. "If I told you that I would leave Thatcher today, tonight, tomorrow, if I could, would you believe me? I've done nothing . . ."

He had not expected this. He was alarmed at the blaze of anger and pain in her face.

". . . and maybe Henrietta did nothing either. But you're judging me. And you're afraid. When you have nothing to be afraid of. I'm not one of you. And I don't ever want to be. I'm different. I know it every time I walk into that house. But it's not fair."

"Sit down, Ariel. Please."

She hesitated, then sat stiffly on the edge of the Victorian seat where she had sat two nights ago. Then she was blind with enchantment. Now, she was saying too much. If she could have wept she would not have spent her anger in words. But she had never learned to shed tears, only words in a hot, dry flood.

He waited for her breathing to steady.

"You are her," he said at last. "If I were a superstitious man, I would believe she had returned in you. I would respect and love you for it."

"I don't ask that from you. Or any of them."

"Instead, I respect you for yourself, Ariel. I have lived a long time. I have learned in my own life that whatever the pain, the larger purpose comes first. There lies the only ultimate peace." His eyes were kind, his voice as gentle as she had ever heard in a man. A father might have talked like this. Or a brother. She had neither. And Willard Roundtree had become the enemy.

He paused. Then he rose and poked the fire. "Kim went looking for you the other night because she had lost her hamster. Or thought she had. I found her sitting outside on the porch step."

Ariel sat rigid. Only the fire and the big dog stirred.

"She wouldn't talk to me. So I sat down beside her. When you came up the path with Duncan she ran to the kitchen. I don't need a child to tell me how to read human faces."

So he knew.

"Kim loves you, Ariel. We all do."

"Will you drive me back to the house now?"

He put a hand on her shoulder. She drew away.

"The hurt can be very deep. But the goal, the larger purpose must come first. Anything else could shatter us all."

She barely heard him. He knew. Perhaps they all knew. She felt an odd kind of relief. No more decisions to be made. No more fears. She tied her scarf over her head and followed him out to the car in silence.

In silence they drove back. In silence she entered the old house. The lamps had not yet been lighted. The dim emptiness suited her. Two more days and she could leave forever. At the foot of the stairs she heard voices. The door to Martin's study at the end of the hall stood slightly ajar, letting a ray of light slice the shadows. Martin's voice came through sharply.

"No, I didn't like it, Lowell. It's not you."

"Must I always be me, Dad?"

"I hope you'll never change."

"Is that really what you want for me?"

"I couldn't wish anything better."

To Ariel's surprise she heard something near a tremor in Lowell's voice.

"That's what everybody wants, isn't it? Steady, dependable Lowell. Always the same."

"My dear girl . . ."

Her voice rose. "If you saw that dress on Ariel you'd like it. But on me . . ."

"Lowell! You must be overtired. I would not like vulgarity on anyone. Ariel is not like us. She is our guest and we will show her every courtesy. But she doesn't belong here. Her whole life has been oriented to something else."

Ariel fled upstairs. On her bed lay the black silk dress. On the desk lay a written message.

As had happened before in her life, hurt at last gave way to outrage. She had come among them wanting only to belong. They had taken her in, not because of herself but because of some remote family code. Now, without knowing her, they had judged her. Well, let them!

Lowell's wedding was safe. She would see to that. She might have run away with Duncan. She had sensed long ago her attraction for men. It lay in the power of her body. It had shown in early adolescent stirrings. She knew by instinct that when the day came when she gave way to those stirrings, she could have what she wanted. But not Duncan. That was over. That had been moonlight and madness and an old man telling her that purpose came before love. What did he know? What did any of them know?

They had judged her. She would give them something to judge. Nor would she stay around this town and be brought to heel like the earlier passionate woman whose hot blood surged through her own body.

She twisted the black dress in a ball and hurled it into the closet. She snatched up the note she was sure was from Lowell. Then she read it.

"Mr. Nick Orlini telephoned you. He asks that you call him back before five." The number followed. She did not recognize the handwriting. It might be Martin's.

It was three minutes to five. She stopped only long enough to pull the black dress from its crumpled heap. She ran to the telephone in the upstairs hall and dialed rapidly.

"Hello, Nick? This is Ariel."

"You see, Nick. A little time, a little distance, and you have her."

Julia Orlini drew the last of the long silk bedroom curtains against the dusk. Fog had settled on the lake, making phantoms of the trees, walling the house. Driving rain, high wind—they were a challenge she could meet. But this nothingness diminished her. Julia Orlini had struggled against smallness all her life.

"I don't propose to 'have' her, Mother. Unless she shows interest." He had stopped at Julia's room on his way out, a habit he heartily wished he could break.

"Whether she shows interest or not, don't be a fool this time, Nick. You rushed your fences with Lowell."

"Lowell! Mother, for sweet Jesus's sake, will you give up on that? I was bored that summer. I must have been."

"You haven't met the girl to match you, Nick." She kissed him lightly. "Just the same, this girl Ariel . . ."

"I'm taking her to dinner. That's it."

"Except for the fact that she called you back. As I told you she would. That shows promise."

"Mother, will you get off my back?"

"The day I think you can manage your own affairs, I will be most happy to. You're not your father, Nick. But you could be."

"If I married the right woman?"

"Yes. Bluntly."

"And you've decided without even meeting her that Ariel Roundtree is the right woman?"

"She could be very useful."

"To me or to you?"

"How well you understand me, darling. If you'd stop spending yourself. To live is to plan. You won't plan for yourself, and heaven knows your father won't. So it's left to me."

"And how much you enjoy it."

"I'm having my last dinner party next Friday, before everyone has left the lake. Why not bring Ariel?"

"Because she's leaving Sunday. Right after the wedding."

"Did she say that?"

"Yes."

"Why?"

"Because I asked her."

"Then you could just as easily persuade her to change her mind."

"Good night, Mother."

"Good night, dear. If my light is on when you get home come in and say hello. You know, Nick . . ."

He turned at the door.

". . . you're quite right. I do meddle, I'm afraid. I will try not to, I promise you. I think of you as a boy. You are very much a man. Very much, my darling. Good night."

Nick understood his mother. Or told himself he did. If she decided Ariel would be useful, her promises would be as empty as air.

As for himself, his only interest in the exasperating Ariel Roundtree was to find out why she had so suddenly changed her mind. Blood will tell. Hot blood, he sensed.

Ariel was waiting under the porch light when the white sports car drove up. She ran down the steps, noticing only that he pushed the door open for her. He did not get out, as Duncan would.

Duncan. As far behind her as childhood now. She had dressed quickly, avoiding all of them. She had passed Lowell's room and learned that Lowell and Duncan were having an evening to themselves. Lowell in her long blue dress. She had passed Claude on the stairs and had caught only a glimpse of Kim disappearing down the hall.

She felt an odd kind of release. She settled into the car, a pale coat over the black silk that moved so sensuously on her body. She was almost free. The rehearsal tomorrow at the ridiculous hour of eleven. The wedding on Saturday. She could even be generous enough to hope the weather would clear.

Yes, she was free, except for the sodden weight of a pain at the pit of her stomach which she could neither subdue nor banish. Had Alicia once lived with this? Had Henrietta?

How long would it last? *Is this forever?*

As the car passed a street light, she turned a lively smile to Nick. "Where are we going?"

"A surprise." He put his hand over hers. "I knew you'd have enough of them. I didn't guess how soon."

The night had turned raw. In the rushing darkness she found a coziness in the small car, a sense of adventure in which she could lose herself, without thought. She did not want to think. She did not want to feel. She wanted movement, escape. Nick Orlini had offered it. She guessed by his little play of mystery, by his self-confidence, he had offered it before. Perhaps that was all he had ever needed to offer.

In the close darkness, his face eerily lit by the dashboard glow, he was not the young man who had picked up her bag with such presumption on the sunny railroad platform. He was a stranger. Darkly handsome, with a brooding profile, a casual elegance, an air of indifference. She had seen the burnt-out apathy of the young-old men in Europe, but Nick Orlini was not burnt-out. He was masculine, a man who would show lust before love. Women would come to him easily, to be hurt.

She could not care less, she told herself. It would be a long time before any man would stir her again. *The Roundtree women are like swans. One mate for life. The rest—to pass the days.*

She would stop thinking. She settled deeper into the seat. The headlights cut into the night only so far. Beyond and around her spread a vast darkness without shape, without identity. She had no idea how far they had come.

"Where are we going?"

"Worried?"

"Of course not. Just excited." Provocative, she knew, but also surgical. She would exorcise this pain. Duncan. And Lowell. Together tonight. Having dinner, holding hands, talking about—what? Later, in his arms. *No!*

"What's wrong, honey?"

"I just shivered."

"Also from excitement?"

"Of course."

"I couldn't ask anything better." He covered her unresponsive hand with his. "You're cold. I'll turn up the heat."

"No. I'm all right. I'm always cold when I'm hungry."

"I'll make a note of that." He grinned and she smiled back. A game she could understand, harmless and without meaning. Her mother would call it by an old-fashioned word, flirting. *"It is all right, chérie, but you must know your man."*

"Here we are." He swung into an even darker winding drive. There were no lights.

"Where are we?"

193

"You'll see in a minute. Bluebeard's Castle."

"Bluebeard's? A restaurant?"

"The best. If we'd gone up the road further and turned in, it would be called Alexander's. The house was built nearly a century ago right across the state border. One half in New York, the other in Connecticut. Old Schuyler Beard, who built it, must have had his reasons. But he went broke gambling, then tried to recoup by running the place as a speakeasy during Prohibition. It was on the Montreal-New York run. The entrance on either side of the state line came in handy but not handy enough. They found old man Beard in the river one day with a bullet in his head. About eight years ago, a guy named Alec bought it. The two entrances still come in handy."

They came out of the wooded drive into a clearing. A huge, gray Victorian house, as many turreted as a castle, rose against the trees. There were no floodlights, but from every heavily curtained window came a rose-warm glow. Two carriage lamps framed the bulky oak door.

The doorman saluted Nick.

"Twenty-eight rooms and every one of them part of the restaurant," said Nick. "I'll show you around after dinner."

The mâitre d'hôtel also saluted Nick and glanced twice at Ariel. The mist-laden wind had tousled her rich, dark hair. The sudden warmth brought a flush to her fine skin. In the narrow black silk dress, she walked with a grace that only Mam'selle's early book-on-head training could bestow.

Classy, thought Nick. By God, she's classy. She fits this background as if she'd been born into it. Probably like all the Roundtrees, not two sous to her name. But she's a woman to show off anywhere.

"Your table, Mr. Nick."

She noticed the 'Mr. Nick.' He was better known than she had guessed.

They were seated on a curved banquette in a quiet

corner. Ariel looked around. The room was nothing more or less than a red velvet jewel box. Red velvet covered the walls, banquettes, and chairs. Red velvet hung in heavy draperies across the French windows. Folds of it festooned the ceiling. Three glittering crystal chandeliers completed the illusion.

"No woman should wear jewelry in this room."

"Very clever of you, Ariel. My mother would agree."

"You have a father and mother?"

"It's usual, isn't it? Also a twin brother and one sister. Not, thank God, all under the same roof."

"Don't you like them?"

"No, frankly. The Lord sends you your relatives. But you can choose your own friends. Not original, honey. But I didn't bring you out here to talk about the Orlinis."

"I think families are beautiful."

"I wouldn't know. I avoid mine as much as possible. Now, what would you like to drink?"

"Now? Nothing, thank you. Just a little wine with dinner."

Nick and the waiter exchanged glances. "In that case, two champagne cocktails, Moet et Chandon. If the lady doesn't like hers, I'll manage both."

Ariel smiled inwardly. So the evening was to be a tug of wills. She needed a challenge to restore her identity and banish the numbness of the past three days. A numbness that had robbed her of self and replaced it with empty longing. That numbness had nothing to do with this night.

The menu was also covered in red velvet. You could smother in a room like this. The languid softness of the air, the tantalizing, faint, and sensuous music, the studied voluptuousness. She had seen the same effect with less effort in a Parisian *café intime*. She wondered again where she was and how the great spread of Thatcher's clean forests and hills, which she had loved on sight, had yielded such a bubble of bad taste.

The menu she was handed listed no prices. How

that would annoy Alicia, who liked to know what value she received for every centime spent, hers or anyone's else.

"See anything you like?"

The waiter hovered. "I would recommend the canape de Fois Gras, madame, and the Aiguillettes de Caneton Roti Duxelles . . . that's duck with mushroom sauce."

Ariel's eyes were all innocence. "Ah, yes." She turned to Nick. It was a trick her mother had taught her. *Never give your order to the waiter, chérie; tell your escort what you would like. Just a little flattery. Giving a touch of importance. The male ego needs it.*

To Nick she said, "Clear consommé, filet rare, and a little salad with just oil and lemon."

"The same but hold it back." This time he did not exchange glances with the waiter. His first impression of Ariel rushed back on him. This was a girl who knew her own mind, who could humiliate if she chose. She would take some taming. He had never had patience for that.

The champagne cocktails arrived. He lifted his glass. "To you, my love. The girl who has seen the light."

She left her glass untouched. "I am not your love." The dimple flashed and robbed the words of sting but not of meaning.

"Hope—the champagne of life."

"What light do you think I've seen?"

"Thatcher. You could no more stay in Thatcher than I can. We're two of a kind, Ariel. I've waited for you to find it out." He drained his glass.

"Why do you stay in Thatcher, then?"

"Because my father pays me well, and my mother wants nothing more than to live above the town and sneer at it."

"But why?"

"Do you know what happens to the little girl who asks why?" He tipped her chin. She tried not to draw back.

"No. What?"

"She gets kissed."

"Nick, don't!"

"Afraid someone will see us? This whole place was planned for privacy. I'll show you the private dining room upstairs. And The Gilded Cage, where men don't take their wives. That doesn't surprise you, I'm sure."

"I don't really want to be kissed like that in such a playboy *milieu*."

"Very well. You tell me how you want to be kissed and I'll oblige."

"I won't put you to that trouble. Too much would have to be changed, I'm afraid." She blamed herself for being in this place, with its arty vulgarity, its banal little games, the French dishes she knew too well, the wines she had grown up with. A sudden surge of childhood loneliness returned for a fleeting instant.

She had rather disliked Nick Orlini on sight. Now his handsome, spoiled face was growing puffy and weak with the wine. He began to lose his air of obvious yet awkward anticipation.

"We are two of a kind, Ariel. We both know it."

"I take it that is some kind of compliment to a Roundtree woman?"

During the rest of the dinner, Nick Orlini made himself distantly charming, reminding her of certain French males she had had occasion to cut down with a word. Like them, he would conceal his self-pity in elaborate casualness.

"Have you ever seen a New England country fair? There's one in Bollington next week. I'll take you to it. But that means you can't leave us on Sunday. Anyway, why would you go to a wedding rehearsal that isn't your own? If you do, I'll be outside the church to pick you up."

There was no resisting him, nor did she try. She let her thoughts wander. Duncan, across the dinner table three nights ago. Duncan and a moonlit patch of woods. Duncan holding her hands in a shabby little store. Then the hard-edged image of a stone fireplace, mulled cider, and a hurt deeper than flame.

"I'll give you the guided tour now."

Dinner was over. She had said almost nothing. He must have been aware. She must do better, if only for courtesy's sake.

"I'd love it."

He escorted her through the rooms, each one more outrageously ornate than the last.

"It was old Beard's idea to give each room some fancy name from the turn of the century. The Bird and Bottle, where we had dinner. The Diamond Horseshoe, that's the bar. Dark as a pocket until you've had your first drink, then you see the bar is studded with little lights. The upstairs private dining rooms are the Crib Section. That mean anything?"

"No."

"New Orleans' old time street of whores. There's a gambling room called Canfield's. It's closed tonight. And another in the west wing called Five Points."

"What are Five Points?"

"Once the roughest area in New York City. A stabbing a night, three on Saturday night. Here at Bluebeard, it's gambling. Mostly for out-of-state high rollers. The police leave it alone, too."

They were in a corridor heavy with potted ferns, dimly shaded lamps, and dark divans widely spaced.

"Peacock Alley. It leads to the West wing. That's the part across the state line. You need a key to get through."

"You are a high roller?"

"No, but Dad is. I go along for the small change."

He unlocked the door at the end. The corridor, with its ferns, lamps, and divans, continued as if there had been no barrier.

"But there's nobody around," she said.

"Oh, yes."

"Who would come so far into the country?"

"There's a small landing field two miles north."

She began to understand. She was curious now. Ben Orlini, it appeared, was not merely a man who cut down trees to build houses that would annoy Thatcher.

A solidly built, gold-toothed man appeared and whispered into Nick's ear. Nick nodded and dismissed him with a ten dollar bill.

"Artie. He's the soul of discretion. He's also a pretty efficient bouncer. He told me Dad's in the dining room. This one's called the Gilded Cage. From the old song, "A Bird in a Gilded Cage," and the birds come pretty fancy. Like to see it?"

"Yes, I would." She was more than curious now. "Your father comes here?"

Nick took her arm cosily. His mood had grown mellow. "Baby, Dad *owns* half this place."

The room was dome-shaped and ribbed in long strips of brass-colored metal. Behind the ribbing the walls glowed with iridescent bluish light. Opaque glass walled the banquettes. The floor was mirrored. From the top of the dome hung two large perches and a small cage. In each swung a nearly naked sequinned girl.

"It all comes off at midnight," Nick grinned.

The room was nearly full. The girls, Ariel noticed, were young, chic, and unvaryingly beautiful. The men looked older.

"There's Dad."

Ariel saw Ben Orlini's small sleek head and opposite him, his back to her, a bulky man. Did she know him? What was familiar about the shape of his head, the crisp hair curling at the base of his neck?

"Dad, you remember Ariel Roundtree?"

For an instant she caught an icy flicker in the little man's face, something menacing in the hooded eyes. Then he was on his feet at once. "A pleasure. A most delightful surprise, Miss Roundtree!" He kissed her hand.

"And Ariel, have you met the father of the groom? Not that he likes the title but he's stuck with it."

Harlan Phelps did not rise. His face was flushed and his girth pressed against the small table. The two girls seated between the men were as uniformly lovely, superbly dressed as the other girls in the room. And hard-eyed with suspicion. Ben nodded to them. They slipped from the table.

"This calls for champagne."

"We've had some, Dad."

Ben snapped his fingers. "Piper Heidsieck, Max. Miss Roundtree, sit down. You have demonstrated at last that my son Nick is capable of good judgment." He patted her hand. "One Roundtree you can talk to. Sit down, dear."

"Thank you, Mr. Orlini. But I'd really prefer to go home."

"Nick been boring you?"

"No, of course not. That's not what I mean." She was dismayed that Nick sat there so silently, toying with an emptied glass.

"Then he's doing better. He'd do a lot better still if he'd listen to his old man more often. Harry, how come your boy couldn't pick himself a Roundtree like this?"

Harlan Phelps eyed her blearily. "If he had, he'd be out of his Jesus shoes by now."

"God damn it, Harry, Miss Roundtree is a lady."

"They're all ladies, Ben. All the Roundtrees. Except the ones who are old women. Martin. And old Willard. Met the old son of a bitch today driving that old pick-up truck because he can't afford a car. I told him I knew how he could get a real car. Cash on the barrel head."

"Miss Roundtree isn't interested, Harry."

"She ought to be. She's one of 'em. You know what old Will said?"

"I said, skip it!"

"He told me he'd see you and me in hell before you

200

got a square foot of that land of his. I told him the first thing I'm going to do when I get to Washington is push a six-lane highway right down the middle of it. And I will, Ben. I sure will." Harlan Phelps slumped against the table.

Ben stood up. "I apologize, Miss Roundtree, for Mr. Phelps. But I promise myself the pleasure of seeing you again. How long are you staying in Thatcher?"

"I'm leaving Sunday." If she had wavered before, she was sure now. Duncan's father. Why had Duncan come back to this? Why had he chosen to stay in Thatcher? Was this the cause of that steely restraint she had found in him? How much had she added to his anguish?

"Only two more days," she repeated firmly.

"Well, Nick, then it's up to us to find enough entertainment to persuade Miss Roundtree to stay."

"Yes, Dad."

Ben Orlini dismissed them with a nod, sat down, and with surprising strength shoved the big crumpled man upright. "You damn fool, Harry!"

"Me? Me, Ben? Why the hell do you let that kid have a key to this side of the house?"

"Because he's useful. You've got loose brains, Harry. You spread 'em all over the place for anybody to pick."

"What'd I say? What'd I say? Everybody knows you've got the hots for Willard Roundtree's land. And everybody knows you ain't going to get it. No way."

Ben took the fresh bottle of champagne from the cooler and opened it expertly. Harry pushed his glass forward. Ben smiled at him and poured the wine steadily into the open cooler until it fizzed to the floor. Then he set the empty bottle into the ice, upside down.

"You're a snake, Ben."

"And don't forget it, Harry."

Ben Orlini wished with all his soul he was rid of Harry Phelps. But he had gone as far as he could without Washington. He needed his own man there. Bought, paid for, and in his pocket. Harlan Phelps was the likeliest candidate. He himself had made too many enemies elsewhere.

But first he had to get Julia her bauble. She could make his private life heaven or hell. She alone. And all the girls in the Gilded Cage couldn't change that, not for any pay.

Eight-hundred lousy acres of scrub and pine and swamp and he'd be off the hook. Miss Ariel Roundtree might just have her uses. To be paid for, of course. Money. The root of evil, maybe. But as Ben proved to himself, money was the root of *money*.

"We're getting out of here, Harry. Come on."

Ariel found the drive back mercifully short. Nick made no effort to break the silence until the lights of Thatcher showed between two dark hills.

"Harry Phelps is a fool," he said abruptly. "I don't know why Dad bothers with him."

"What did he mean about Uncle Willard's land?"

"Oh, come on. You know the answer to that. Dad wants to buy it. It's no good to old man Roundtree but he won't give in."

"Why should he?"

"Look, do you care? You made a hit with Dad tonight. When he likes somebody he'll do anything for them. Next thing he'll invite you on that private plane of his. Not a bad idea. We could skip down to Halcyon for a week."

"What's Halcyon?" Her mind was turning slowly from outrage to curious, unbidden loyalty.

"An island Dad owns off the coast of Florida. It's pretty plush."

"Does he really think he could steal Uncle Willard's land from him?"

"Now, wait a minute!"

"I just asked."

"Dad always gets what he wants. Ultimately." He laughed. "You might remember that."

They were approaching the town. "I'll buy you a nightcap at Thatcher's hot spot. The Grist Mill. Stays open until eleven for the late parchesi players."

She found she could laugh. Confidence was beginning to seep back into her because she could never stay depressed for long and because indifference had been, from childhood, her most successful weapon.

"And don't worry your beautiful head about the Roundtree land, baby. You're not one of them, thank God."

"Maybe I'm an imposter, too."

"What does that mean?"

"Uncle Willard told me that somebody had tried to get the land once by proving that the Roundtrees were all imposters. That didn't work either. Tell me about Halcyon, Nick."

The evening had not been the anesthetic Duncan had hoped for. Lowell had been quiet. At this late hour she looked strained. Maybe it was the color blue. Maybe it was the grayish lighting of the Grist Mill that lent shadows to her face.

"Ready to go, darling?"

"Pretty soon. I haven't been very good company tonight."

He held her hand on the table. "The best any man could want. It's been a big week and the worst is yet to come. I mean the best."

"I should think so." She gave a very small laugh. "Getting married should be the very best. If we'd only done it the way we wanted. Like Judy Smith, in a field full of daisies."

"You'd have regretted it all your life, Lowell. You know why we're doing it this way."

"I know. There's going to be a lot more of the same. Christmas, Thanksgiving . . . it'll be wonderful, I guess, but oh, Duncan!"

"What?"

"I wish we hadn't taken that cottage Phyllis's family offered on Nantucket. I mean, for our honeymoon."

"I thought you liked the idea."

"I did then. Besides, you hate the tropics. You love the sea."

"My darling, let's get this straight. Now. You don't tell me what I like and I don't tell you what you like. Where do *you* want to go?"

"We can't change at this late date."

"Oh, yes, we can. I have all tomorrow."

"How can we afford anything else?"

"We'll just try to, Lowell. You can make us Texas hash for the next three months."

"I don't know. But you are sweet."

"Hope you'll continue to think so, Mrs. Phelps."

"Mrs. Phelps. It sounds so funny. But don't say it yet."

"No, not yet."

They fell silent. The music began. Lowell murmured the words to the thin melody. " . . . I learned to love you . . ."

"Like to dance?"

"Not right away. Oh, Duncan . . ." she broke off, her eyes bright. "Could we go some place exciting, exotic, maybe for a shorter time? Some place like . . ."

"Like where?" He must be gentle with her. She trusted him, and he would give her all that he could of his life and his affection. That was the least he could do. "Like where, darling? You name it."

"Well, Paris is out. That would be ridiculous for us. But maybe some place nearer, like . . ." she broke off, staring at the entrance to the dining room. "Look! Look who's coming in!"

Ariel and Nick stood in the doorway. Ariel, rigid, her eyes on Duncan as if there were no one else in the room.

"Well, well, well—the bride and groom. Shall we

join them?" Nick, too, had spotted Duncan and Lowell immediately.

"No."

But Lowell was darting toward them. "Ariel! Nick! Over here in the corner. Come join us, won't you? Duncan was trying to get me to go home. But now it's a real party!" She turned a flushed, excited face to Nick. "Please."

Duncan had risen but Ariel knew as she approached the table that they had made a mistake. She looked helplessly at him but she might as well not have been there.

"Can't refuse the bride, Deacon," said Nick.

"Neither can I, Nick. Sit down, won't you?"

"Let's have champagne, Duncan. Or something exciting!"

"I'll buy the drinks, Deacon."

"I think Lowell and I have had enough. But you and Ariel . . ." How could he couple their names?

"Duncan, you're being stuffy!"

"I'm afraid so, darling." The music had begun. Duncan put his arm around her. "Care to dance?"

"We must dance with our guests first. Come on, Nick, we'll show them." Lowell giggled, as if the wine she had drunk at dinner was only now intoxicating her. She tugged at Nick's sleeve.

They were alone. Ariel sat small and chilled. Duncan had gone pale. In the closeness of the small table beneath its checked cloth, their knees touched for an instant.

"Ariel—"

"Don't talk."

"Not Nick Orlini."

She did not answer.

"Not Orlini, Ariel!"

"What am I going to do?"

"I wish I could take you a thousand miles from here."

They said nothing more.

Their knees touched again and this time held as if rivetted. Until the music stopped.

Edythe Roundtree lay in the dark beside her husband, listening to the spattering of drops on the leaves, the rain she had wished for. "Ask not too much of the gods lest they grant it." How true she had found that; when you wished for something patently wrong, you so often got it. And got the remorse that followed. Now she wished more than anything else for a sunny golden day for her daughter's wedding. She would never complain about weather again. Edythe was fond of making bargains with her world. They made her days more manageable. She thought of her own wedding twenty-six years ago. What mother of the bride doesn't? She had made a bargain for that. If she could marry Martin Roundtree she would never ask anything more. Two days before the wedding she had made her last visit to her singing teacher, the dark intense maestro in his cluttered studio in New York.

"You are a fine singer, Edythe. You could be a great one. But greatness takes total dedication. Total. You have made another choice. Where is Thatcher?"

That night she had lain awake listening to the snow blowing against her city window. Edythe Templeton. Famous. In headlines. In lights. But dedication, without Martin? Fame, without Martin?

The gods had granted all she had asked. She had walked, radiantly happy, down the aisle of a crowded church, to Martin. And resolutely buried the lingering regret in the fullness of her days. Five children, a husband she loved and who loved her, a world of prevailing natural beauty. For Edythe Roundtree could find glory even in the savage storms that blackened her skies. All these were hers. And now her daughter, like herself, was marrying in happiness.

If only the rain would stop before it lashed all the color from the trees. It was lessening now. What she heard was only dripping, she told herself.

She heard something else. A quiet mouselike opening of the bedroom door. She sighed. Martin's even raspy breathing had stopped and she knew he was lying awake too. He would not get back to sleep now.

"Mommie?"

"Yes, Kim."

"I had a bad dream. Can I come into your bed?"

"Of course, darling. What was it?"

"The witch was chasing me through the woods."

"That's the second night, Kimmie. Too much pizza at Beth's?"

"We had lamb chops."

"Pretty expensive dreams you have," Martin grunted from the darkness.

"I can't help it, Daddy. Where's Lowell?"

"She went out to dinner with Duncan. If you're going to talk you can't stay here. We all must get some sleep." Edythe cradled the tense little body. It was unlike Kim to have nightmares. Kim was the steadiest of them all.

"What do we do at rehearsal tomorrow?"

"We go through the wedding ceremony. How we march down the aisle, where we all stand or sit."

"Will Dunkie be there?"

"Oh, yes, of course."

"And Ariel?"

"Only if she wants to come. She isn't in the wedding party."

"When is she going home?"

"What a question, Kim! I hope she'll stay with us a long time. We need her to fill Lowell's place."

"She can't fill Lowell's place. When Lowell and Dunkie come home I'm going to bike over there every day to see them. I'm so glad they're going to be here in Thatcher forever."

"We all are. Now go to sleep."

But the little body remained rigid.

"Mommie, are you awake?"

"Oh-h, Kim!"

."Can I bring Freddie to the rehearsal tomorrow?"

"You cannot!" Martin sat upright in bed.

"Martin, please. She'll go to sleep."

But Kim was wide awake now. "He's better than a silly old basket of flowers. Why can't I, Daddy?"

"Because a wedding is no place for a hamster. Damn it, Edythe. I can still hear that loose shutter."

"It isn't the shutter, it's the witch!" Kim clung to her mother. "I want to bring Freddie tomorrow. Please, can I?"

"And lose him the way you did at Uncle Will's party?"

"I didn't lose him! I didn't!" Her voice rose to a shrill pitch. "Mrs. Beemer put him up on a shelf. Freddie hates shelves. That's why I couldn't find him and I had to go out . . ." She hung passionately on Edythe as the tears came. "Please Mommie, let me bring Freddie!"

"I'm sure it will be all right, darling. Don't you think, Martin? Just at the rehearsal."

Martin was out of bed and on his feet. "I'll find that shutter."

"Not tonight, Martin, go back to bed. I'll take Kim down for some hot cocoa and sleep in her bed. Martin, we have the rehearsal tomorrow. And Emily's dinner party tomorrow night."

"Why, in God's name?"

"Because it's what happens when you have a big wedding. Come along, Kimmie. Oh dear, the rain's begun again."

In the darkness, the stairs showed faintly in the light of a single hall lamp. The front door opened.

"That you, Lowell?"

"It's Ariel, Aunt Edythe."

Edythe felt Kim push closer to her. She watched Ariel come up the stairs, quickly and lightly, more phantom than girl.

"Did you have a nice evening, dear?" She asked that question of every one of her children. It came naturally, too naturally to her now. She had not told Martin of Nick Orlini's car outside the house.

"Thank you, Aunt Edythe. Goodnight." Ariel turned and ran to her room. She had said neither yes or no. But then, as Edythe had reflected before, Ariel was different.

"I don't want any cocoa. I want to go to bed."

Kim was trembling.

"You're chilled, dear. We'll both go to bed."

Lying beside Kim in the narrow bed, Edythe knew that sleep would not come again for her either, that night. "Ask not too much of the gods . . ." Yet what she asked was for Lowell, for this youngest, for Michael, for all her children. Yet where in her heart did a woman separate her children and herself? Wishes for them were wishes for herself. The threads of living were so tangled that, not for the first time, Edythe saw herself living in a maze too knotted for one woman to unravel.

Kim fell asleep at last within her mother's stiffened arm. Whatever was the matter with the child would have to wait, as all crises must, until the new day. Edythe Roundtree lay, waiting for the dawn, listening to the whispers of the old house.

Chapter Nine

The rain fell relentlessly, stripping the trees of their leaves, weighing down the straggly yews, and running like an open faucet down the mullioned windows of the pompous dining room.

Duncan poured himself another cup of coffee. He would have liked a quick pick-up in the kitchen and an even quicker departure. But his mother had set his place on the heavy oak dining table, with the percolator ready beside it. Friday, his last full day in his parents' house. He would do it her way.

But the rain. It plucked at his nerves like bird claws.

Dry and sheltered as he was now, rain could always being memories to sweep him back. The tropical rain, the endless steaming rain, bringing the mud with its blood-sucking leeches to his knees and higher, beating a brittle tattoo on palm and bamboo. Worse, the hissing rush of it in the jungle walled out every hostile shape and warning sound.

He reached in his pocket for a non-existent cigarette and remembered. The Reverend Duncan Harlan Phelps was dedicated to leading an exemplary life before God. His God would understand a man's need. But this morning he had deeper reasons than a craving for a cigarette to call on God's understanding. He was not about to push his luck for small indulgences.

He had grown up lucky. He realized that now. Life had been easy and pleasant in Thatcher. His father had been too busy to take an interest in him until it served some self-interest. His mother had brought him up to believe in God, country, and self-reliance, in that order. He was an effortless athlete, and his golden good looks had brought him rewards far beyond what he might have otherwise earned. The college of his choice had apparently been waiting for him with arms outstretched. The only flaw in his idyllic maturing was that in the end he had turned down Yale and opted, in an inexplicable decision, for the University of Chicago.

"You'll regret it, son. Take my advice . . ." Harlan Phelps had struggled through law in a southwestern Panhandle college. The ivy of the east had offered, as he saw it, the first tangible reward of fatherhood.

"Thanks, Dad, but I really want Chicago."

Duncan had seen his father's face turn angry and then ugly. Physically gross and harsh, as if a mask had slid from it. But only for an instant.

"I'm paying your tuition. You'll go where I say."

"Then I'll have to find a way to make it myself. I've made up my mind."

"What do you want to do, spend your time with a lot of pinks, commies, and niggers?"

"Maybe I do."

Harlan had struck him, flat-handed across the face, with a blow that sent him against a chair. He recovered to find his hands clenched, his shoulders taut. His father's heavy forehead was wet with perspiration.

"Don't ever try that again, Dad."

Their eyes met. Their confrontation was deep and final. The older man had grunted and left the room.

Duncan had been in Chicago for six months, wrenching a living from his student laundry business, when the draft found him. He sat through the hot nights of student rapping. His mind told them they were right; there was no morality, no reason, no excuse for this bloodbath of the innocent. But Duncan could no more think of refusing his country than of tearing down the flag on Thatcher's Flagpole Green. The Honor Roll was long and illustrious. The names went back to Thatcher's beginning.

Duncan went home, asked Lowell to marry him, and was paraded to the bus stop by his former teammates, with his father in step beside him. He still flushed at the memory.

If he could have gone on from there, as he foresaw it, into surging battle with proud and dedicated men, to live or to die in the rightness of victory, or the nobility of defeat . . .

In the raw suddenness of the event when it came, he had lost all sense of time in the crawling mud. He lay for how long? For the last hours a sudden maddening sun had glazed him in hot slime. He lifted his head only enough to breathe and buried it again from the onslaught of the monstrous flies and mosquitoes. He cradled his rifle in his poncho against the mud. For his rifle was his life, closer to him than his own skin.

He was alone except for his pal, Rod. Rod lay beside him, his head and both arms blown off. He would think about that later. All that Rod could offer him now was the stink that made him want to retch. And there was nothing new in that. Rod would have been the first to agree. "There's got to be something more to a guy than 97% water, 3% chemicals and 100% stink." How long ago had he said that? Duncan took a breath and saw the butt of Rod's rifle above the ooze. If he looked further he might see . . . he buried his face. Rod did not have to be in this place, in this condition. He had been company chaplain, but one night, after a missing patrol had been found mutilated beyond identity, he had torn the cross from his lapel and picked up a rifle. How long ago? Time had copped out.

Was he condemned, like so many veterans of so many wars, always to remember—no, not remember, so much as see again actual scene after scene, scenes he could never talk about to anyone who had not shared those days?

There was that one time . . .

It had been quiet a long, long while. The sun was becoming a brass hammer and the silence deafening. He would have to move out or lose the fringe sanity he clung to.

He lifted his head, coming slowly to awareness. He was unwounded but badly concussed. Nothing moved but the insects and a cloud of carrion birds. Through the waves of heat he thought he saw a figure. A man running, beckoning others with a sweep of raised arm. They were attacking again? Hadn't they cleared the monkeys out once? He pulled himself from the swamp's mud and struggled to firmer ground. There was no running figure, no attack, only iron sun and silence. In the distance a few mangled trees offered shade. There should be a village. He gripped his automatic.

The cluster of huts seemed deserted. Only one showed a smoke plume of life. Cautiously, he pushed open the door. Three Cong were inside. One, with a rifle, held an older man and woman at bay. The other two had a girl on the earthen floor. Some of her clothes had been ripped off; her breasts and belly showed bleeding slashes. She lay crumpled like a small, bleeding animal.

He shot the man holding the rifle. He fired at the other two as they leaped through the door. Whether he hit them or not he did not know. He picked up what might once have been a brightly flowered bed cover and put it over the girl.

She whimpered.

The mother crouched, huddled, her hands pinned to her face.

The father came slowly out of his dark corner.

"American?"

Duncan nodded.

"I learn English once. When war start." He did not look at the girl on the floor. His tight-skinned face was stoic with sudden aging. "She should die now."

The girl, Duncan guessed, could not be more than fourteen. She showed the drained beauty of ultimate terror and martyrdom. He thought her abusers not more than seventeen.

"I sell her to man from Saigon. To save her. She no use now." He gestured toward the slashes.

"How much do you want?"

"What you give. Ten dollar American."

He had stayed in the hut until the girl could leave. The mother never spoke. The father found cold rice and some beans. Duncan waited for the Cong to return. They never did. Time again copped out until one day a motorized Australian unit came through. Duncan was able to take the girl to a village in a northern tree-covered valley, and, with $25, leave her in a female schoolteacher's care.

At the last moment she clung to him, slight and timid as a wounded bird. He learned her name was Pi-Liu. He promised to send American dollars that would take care of her. He would come back.

When he at last caught up with his wearied company,

they were in unexplained retreat. As unexplained as their advance through the same valley three months later. But this time the tanks, the flame throwers, the high explosives, and the mop-up squads had done their work. There were no trees, there was no village, and even the sheltered end of the valley had vanished in churned-up, violated soil. Only death lived there now.

Then once again, the season's heavy rains had come. Duncan recalled sitting bare-headed in the rows of G.I.s while a visiting Senator, dry and neat, accompanied by two three-star generals, also dry, told the men of their country's pride. And assured them they were to be reinforced with 10,000 more troops and another 100 fighter planes.

After a year, Duncan came home. To a changed man, Thatcher was changed even more.

"Why in hell the ministry, Duncan?"

"If that's what you really want, Duncan, I'll wait."

"Do what you think best, son."

"You're crazy, Dunk. With your father's contacts you could clean up."

He had no answers for any of them. And the only explanation he would never share. But he found some measure of peace in the quiet hours of the Seminary. Peace and purpose.

Now, as abruptly as the coming of this rain on the day before his wedding, his peace had been shattered, his purpose tainted with doubt, with self-doubt.

He had met a woman whose one full glance had banished the artificialties of his life, clearing the glass through which he had seen so darkly. Ariel. Should he exorcise his demon now? If he could. On his knees before the God he felt called to serve.

He poured himself another cup of coffee and stared out at the rain. It was playing tricks. It was snipping at his nerve ends. It was recreating mirages of the past. It was veiling reality. And Lowell. Lowell counted on sunshine. "Happy the bride the sun . . ." he had heard that, too, among the burden of clichés of the past week.

In fact, it had surprised him to discover how many things Lowell counted on, how much intensity lay beneath that quiet surface. Her outburst at the rectory when Mrs. Higgins' funeral was announced. Dr. Wilcox had chided Duncan later; he must explain to his young wife-to-be that the work of a minister was the work of life itself and of death and of birth. But he hadn't explained. There would be time enough for that, a very long time. But there was the matter of the honeymoon, too. Some "exotic" place, she had pleaded. He would do what he could. But intensity was a new side of her. She had gone through the petty demands of her days with such compliance, such grace. The word fitted her. She had grace. She would grace any man's life. He would try to make her happy. He would count on time to heal.

Ariel.

He cursed the rain and the demon he could not exorcise. To exorcise meant to call on God. But this was no evil. His God would surely understand a man caught in a fire of mind and flesh that had begun without warning and would have no end. Nor did he want it to end. If he could not have her, as he knew he could not, he wanted to keep the radiance, the excitement, the beauty of her in some deep, closed corner of himself, as long as he lived.

But he would ask, not of his God but of himself, that the next two days pass numbly and quickly at a distance from her. That too was a sham because all he wanted at this moment was to see her. And touch her. Sweep her into his arms and take her, as he had so nearly done in the moonlit woods that night a thousand years ago.

Ariel.

God help him, he would take his bride to the other side of the moon to escape her.

"Down so early, Duncan?"

Emily had come in with her small, quiet steps.

"Oh, good morning, Mother." He pushed the half-empty cup from him and rose.

"Only coffee, Duncan? And it's cold."

"The first cup wasn't. Are you coming to the rehearsal?"

"Edythe asked me. But your father can't come."

"I didn't expect him. See you later." He kissed her. She put a restraining hand on his arm. It looked older than he remembered. It was true that women's hands aged first.

"Duncan, your father's up. Could you wait to see him?"

"What for?"

"It's your last day with us. I'd like it to be nice—the way—the way it might have been."

He hesitated. He had no wish to see his father now. Or ever. But he realized with misgiving that for the past half hour he had thought of nothing but himself.

"I'll wait."

"And I'll make you a hot breakfast."

"No. No, please, Mom. Sit and talk to me."

She smiled like a girl. It was the nicest thing he could have said. For a few brief minutes he had stitched over the open wound of her latter days.

"Are you going to wear your clerical collar at your wedding?"

"No ideas like that, Mother."

"But you look so . . ."

"So different. I'll put the damn thing on when I can't avoid it. Otherwise this town will have to take me as it always has. I didn't come back to make an oddball of myself. And I don't think the Lord cares."

"Such modern ideas, Duncan."

"I have a lot more but I'll make you a promise, Mom. I'll try 'em out on you, first. If you react badly I'll know they're good." He grinned and some of the gloom of the morning lifted for Emily Phelps. This only child, this strong-willed, perplexing son, had come back to her a stranger. What had happened in Vietnam she might never know. But Emily was born with Scottish doggedness. She always enjoyed getting to know people. Why not her own son, if there was still love? She believed there would be.

She cocked her head toward the stairs and listened. The dim vast house was quiet.

"Duncan, I want to say something to you about your father. He came home very late last night."

"I heard him."

"You did?"

"He tripped on the stairs."

"It's not the first time, Duncan."

"I didn't think so."

"Duncan, I know that he is becoming an important man. He works hard, he knows a lot of people I've never met. I know busy men must go to late meetings and . . . I know all those things and I've accepted them. But lately . . ."

"Are you sure you want to talk about this now?"

"I've got to. Lately he's come home that way you heard last night. Duncan, he didn't used to drink like this." Her eyes filled.

She can't still love him, he thought. But love, love was a clown with a thousand faces. It would take him a lifetime to sort them out. Even God's love—whatever that was—to which he had dedicated himself.

He was gentle with her. "What do you want me to do? I'll do it."

"I want you to know. That's all, Duncan. This is the happiest time of your life. Your father's conduct must not burden you. But it must not surprise or hurt you and Lowell."

"Why haven't you talked to me before?"

"This has been coming on a long time. All the while you were away. It's in his blood. He had an uncle . . . and his grandfather on his father's side died . . ." She put her hand to her mouth.

Steps fell heavily on the stairs. Emily fled to the kitchen.

Harlan Phelps sat down to his breakfast, groomed, tailored, fresh-shaven, and pink as a baby. Only his red-rimmed, red-veined eyes, and the slight palsy of his hand on the coffee cup gave away the night's excesses. He had been very drunk but what he couldn't tell his sharp-eyed, fawning little wife was that it was easier to come home that way. Sober, he could hardly bear to walk into the house. Especially since she had prevailed upon Duncan to come home.

Duncan, sitting there in silent judgment. He hadn't deserved a son like this. It was Emily's mollycoddling.

"So it's the happy day, eh?"

"Tomorrow's the wedding, Dad. Today's the rehearsal."

"Oh. Not much difference, eh? Not these days."

"There's a difference. Tonight's the dinner you and mother wanted to give."

"I never wanted to give it. A lot of damned nonsense. Your mother's idea."

"It makes her happy."

"Everything makes her happy that I don't want."

Emily set fruit and toast in front of her husband.

"Doesn't it, sweetheart?"

"Doesn't what, Harlan?"

"Doesn't everything that I don't like make you happy?"

"I hope not." She smiled at him. "That would be quite a dreadful way to live, wouldn't it?" She let the kitchen door swing shut behind her.

"I'll be going along, sir."

"What's your hurry? A hot bride?" Harlan had an annoying habit of gulping his coffee, using it as a mouth wash before he finally swallowed it. "Take it easy. I saw the new girl from Paris last night. What's her name? Fancy name. Ariel. That's it. Light and airy Ariel. Nick brought her up to Alec's last night."

The muscles in Duncan's fist tightened. Honor thy

218

father . . . love thy neighbor. Inherent in his vows. But had he taken vows to cease to feel? Or was this loutish, mocking parent part of the testing? As Ariel was part of the testing. He had assumed a living purpose the day he had made his decision. To reject the old corruptions. He had seen what they could do to men. Men still young enough to dream, systematically lowered to brute level. Knowledge, the ultimate hope, channeled to the uses of destruction. There was no place for him in the old system. He would start afresh and unfettered.

Now here he stood with hands clenched, entangled in man's oldest passions, hatred and desire.

" . . . she's what I call a real wench. She'd give a man what he wants, son." Harlan drained his cup. "If you'd latched on to a girl like that I could even forgive that non-stop collar. Prove you had some manhood left. Nick Orlini hasn't got what she takes. But the old man . . ." he laughed. " . . . my God, Ben couldn't keep his eyes off her. Be his hands next. Where you going?"

"I have things to do."

Harlan pushed back his coffee cup. "You're under my roof and you owe me something for it. So you'll listen. You won't have the opportunity much longer. You're going to marry Lowell. You've been long enough getting to it, boy, but that's your business. I haven't got anything against Lowell. She's all Roundtree and Thatcher. Some class, no style. And less money."

"Is that all, Dad?"

"No, it isn't. Lowell's bright enough. And she's pretty close to her Uncle Willard, isn't she?"

"What are you getting at?"

"Sure, she's close to old Willard. And she's bright enough to know what that land of his is worth. At least to Orlini. It would put the whole family, including you and your god-damned church, on Easy Street."

"You can cool it right now. If you think that Lowell or I . . ."

"Not you, son. Not with the milk and water that runs in your veins now. But Lowell—as I say, she's bright."

He could see by the slight crack in the kitchen door that Emily was behind it, listening. He would get through this day and tomorrow. It was part of the testing.

Suddenly Harlan laughed. "Forget it, boy. You can't see your hand in front of your face. Why should I ram it at you? So that's all. Except for one little thing."

He drew an envelope from his inside pocket. "I don't want you and the bride to think that I'd forget your wedding." He dropped the envelope on the table and rose. "But not a cent for your church."

Father and son looked steadily at each other. The older man walked out of the room. Duncan turned to follow. Then his mother caught up with him. She was holding the envelope.

"Please take it, Duncan. Don't make things worse. He can't help the way he is."

"I think he can. I don't want anything from him."

"You're just as stubborn as he is. Neither of you can see anything but the black and white of things. Maybe you've hurt him too, never heeding him, despising everything he wanted for you. Maybe the Lord should teach you a little tolerance about other people's weaknesses—especially when one of them is your own father."

He stared at her. She was defending this man like an angry wren. He opened the envelope. The check was made out to Duncan Phelps and Lowell Roundtree. It was for $1000.

"Please, Duncan, don't throw it back at him. It's the only way he knows."

It was Lowell's. It would buy her the honeymoon she wanted. It would cost him his pride but that might be his penance.

He put the check in his wallet. And touched his mother's cheek. "Don't worry, Mom." He left her smiling.

Eleven o'clock. The rain was still falling.

The great maples, weighted by water, drooped over the slate roof and gothic entrance to St. Mark's small stone church. It had stood on the same site for more than two hundred years, lifting its square belfry in blunt Episcopalian defiance of the soaring white Presbyterian steeple higher on the hill.

Inside the church two electric lights served only to deepen the late-morning gloom and emphasize the chill.

Ariel sat alone in the last pew wondering why she had come, yet knowing she could not have avoided it.

Behind her, Dr. Wilcox was marshaling the small assemblage with the gentle authority of a man at home in his own house. Only two bridesmaids had appeared. Mrs. Haskell, the organist, had arrived breathless and with a cold. Between sneezes she was coaxing a repetitious Bach out of a reluctant organ.

Across the aisle from Ariel and at the far end of the pew sat Kim, holding the shoe-box-size metal cage, and looking neither right nor left.

Ariel was aware that someone slid into the pew beside her. It was Cora Wilcox, her apple cheeks pink with excitement. "I really shouldn't be here. Goodness knows I never interfere with Dr. Wilcox's work. But Edythe insisted, and I just couldn't bear to miss any part of it. Isn't this rain awful? But it's the Lord's will and Willard said it would stop by night. That Indian of his knows more than anybody else; how, I don't know. I brought Lowell my recipe for Scripture cake. You probably don't know what that is. So few young women do today. You have to know your Bible to figure it out. My grandmother gave it to me and it's delicious. My, there's the groom. Isn't he handsome?"

Duncan was sitting motionless in the front pew.

Ariel had longed for him to turn and look at her. Just once. But Cora Wilcox had brought the cold air of reality with her. Ariel could only sit and hope that it would all be over soon. Soon. Soon.

Last night she had left the Grist Mill as soon as Lowell and Nick returned to the table. Lowell oddly overexcited and Nick sulkily resistant. She had left without meeting Duncan's eyes again. Through the night her whole body burned with an unutterable longing. Lowell came to her room apologizing for what she called her silliness at the Grist Mill and begging Ariel to come to the rehearsal.

"You don't have to do a thing, Ariel. And it will probably bore you. But please come. I do so want it to be a real rehearsal even at this awful hour."

Lowell had not explained how or why but in the end Ariel had agreed.

So she sat in the last pew, her ears closed to sound, her mind to sensation. She would have liked to disappear into the damp twilight. She felt unsteady, almost ill. But she could at least look at the back of Duncan's head. No one could deny her that. Until Cora Wilcox sat down beside her.

Emily Phelps arrived late. Ariel thought she had been crying. But she beamed on everybody. Willard took a commanding post and announced that if Sam Wilcox couldn't get 'em down the aisle properly, he himself had once drilled troops and he could do it again.

There was a flurry of voices and a ripple of laughter. The music turned sweet.

Edythe moved sedately down the aisle, her arm through Willard's, her face so expressive, so tender that Ariel marveled. Edythe must be past forty-five, yet she looked as if she loved every year of it.

Dr. Wilcox stood in his place before the altar. Duncan appeared at his left, his jaw rigid, his eyes on the rear of the church. On Lowell? In the vaulted ceiling? Certainly not on her.

The *Lohengrin* began.

Kim was pushed into the aisle, holding tightly to the little cage. Claude followed, head high, sensing every nonexistent eye. Plump Phyllis followed unsteadily. The girl called Judy whom Ariel did not know, too thin, angular, and unsmiling, marched confidently out of her step in wet loafers. Lowell took her father's arm.

The music rose. "Here comes the . . ." Suddenly Lowell stopped short, bolted from the procession. "I mustn't! I can't! Wait, Mrs. Haskell!"

"What on earth, Lowell!" It was Edythe's voice above the rest with a hint of panic.

"I can't walk down the aisle at my own rehearsal. It's bad luck. Oh, yes, it is. Besides, I can't listen to the marriage service with Duncan or I'll be married before I'm married. Honestly! That's the way it goes."

"I'll take your place, Lowell. You can take mine."

"No. I mustn't be in it at all, Phyllis. We need you where you are. Oh, I knew something would go wrong.

"Ariel!" Lowell was beside her in the pew. "You could take my place. For the rehearsal. Please. You're just the one. You have nothing to do with it—and there has to be a bride or there's no rehearsal. Will you, Ariel?"

In the waiting silence, Ariel heard the rain on the roof like the thudding of her own heart.

"I do think that's the solution, my dear." Cora Wilcox nudged her gently. "Of course it is just an old wives' tale but it is traditional and I think it's nice to keep the old ways."

Ariel found herself on her feet, her arm linked in Martin's. Mrs. Haskell sneezed. Fortissimo, the great theme began. "Here comes the . . ."

Mechanically, as in a trance, Ariel moved down the aisle. She saw no figures ahead, no faces near. Not even Dr. Wilcox. Nothing but a mist that seemed to have sprung from the stone floor and stretched endlessly before her. At the end of it stood Duncan, his eyes gravely on her.

The supporting music vanished. Duncan stepped toward her. Dr. Wilcox loomed close.

"Claude, you will take the bride's bouquet now."

Claude stepped toward her, then back again. Ariel got only a fleeting glimpse of the young face that looked past her without expression. A face in a dream that came and went with her breathing.

"Can I sit down, please?"

It was Kim. Without waiting for an answer she had gone to Edythe standing in the first pew.

"Kim," Dr. Wilcox showed a frayed edge of impatience. He had his Sunday sermon to finish and the church had to be emptied, swept and made ready for a funeral. "You're the flower girl, aren't you? You must stand right here near the bride."

"I will tomorrow. With Lowell. Please. Mom?"

"I think she'll do very well, Dr. Wilcox. Let her stay with me."

Ariel did not dare look at the child. She would see in her eyes all that everybody in the group must see by this time. She had always been able to hide her emotions. With a little laugh, a polite smile, she could lose herself in the crowd or behind her mother's brittle bravura and conceal the intensity of her hurts and her longings until she reached the mauve and white sanctuary of her own bed. But there was no retreat now, no escape. This child accused her, innocently. She fluttered for an instant like a bird against the bars of her own sense of guilt. Then, as quickly, the fleeting impasse was over.

Dr. Wilcox cleared his throat. Duncan stepped beside her. All else vanished into blurred nothingness except the altar, cold and unadorned, the lofty burnished cross and above it the blue stained-glass window rising like the finger of judgment. Mam'selle and the convent nuns, God help her, were watching her take false vows. Yet they were not false. What she said in this place, beside this man she loved, she would hold to the rest of her life, when all the rest of the sham had blown to dust. Had Duncan beside her any idea or did he too know they had come to the moment of truth? Dear God, forgive what I am doing but help me to do it.

Dr. Wilcox glanced down at her. He was a short man and he used the three steps to the altar to ordained authority. He was startled by the raptness of her expression and the wide, dark eyes fixed beyond him. On what? There was certainly something about her unlike any Roundtree he had ever known. Though he too had heard the gossip, the wildness that ran in the family.

He caught Cora's eyes at the back of the church and began with a fullness of voice he had not intended.

"Dearly beloved, we are gathered together in the sight of God, and in the face of this company . . ." if he remembered at all, it was too late. To the good man, the words were a hymn he knew only one way to render. " . . . to join together this man and this woman in holy matrimony which is an honorable estate."

"Do I take the bouquet now, Dr. Wilcox?" Dr. Wilcox came back to earth. Claude was stretching out her hand. Ariel looked down quickly. She knew Duncan had not taken his eyes off her.

"No, my dear. Not until the vows are exchanged. I'll tell you when we come to it. Now there's no reason to go through all this. We come to the end of the first part. 'If any man can show just cause, why these two may not lawfully be joined together, let him now speak.' And then I directly address the bride and groom. Duncan, you will bring your bride up one step to me. It works very well in this church."

The pounding within Ariel's ribs had settled to a steady throb and with it a kind of dizziness. She might have stumbled without Duncan's steadying hand at her elbow. For the first and only time she looked directly at him. The light played false. His face bore the lines and pallor of age. She saw him as she had once seen herself. She knew how he would look as an old man, his life slipped away like water and she no part of it.

"I require and charge you both, as you will answer at the dreadful day of judgment . . ."

Dr. Wilcox loomed closer, but his words came from far away. Suddenly they became a thunder in her ears.

"Duncan, wilt thou have this woman to thy wedded wife, to live together after God's ordinance . . ."

"I will."

She heard, or did she imagine it.

"You don't have to answer, Duncan. You know that part. Ariel—Lowell, wilt thou have this man . . ."

Forever. Forever, Duncan. The silent vow lay so large within her that she heard nothing else. The chill, the mist, the harsh lights, the cross behind Dr. Wilcox's head began to whirl. His voice rose and fell.

"At this point, Duncan," Dr. Wilcox's sonority slid into everyday dryness. "You will give Lowell her ring and plight her your troth. Lowell will give you your ring and . . ."

Someone must have opened a door. Ariel felt fresh air. But the waves of dizziness did not subside. Duncan's eyes had not left her face.

"Those whom God hath joined together, let no man put asunder . . ." Dr. Wilcox's resonance reached for the rearmost pews.

A triumphant peal of Mendelssohn swept her down the aisle beside Duncan. Her hand on his coatsleeve was trembling so noticeably he covered it. At the last pew, he released it and she sank on the bench.

"You were wonderful, Ariel!" Lowell kissed her. "I hope I can do as well. Thanks a million!"

She would sit until the gothic arches overhead stopped wheeling. Voices rose and broke around her. Groups formed and dissolved.

"Are you all right, Ariel?"

"Yes, I'm fine, thank you, Aunt Edythe."

"You'll make a beautiful bride yourself someday. Can we take you home with us now?"

The church doors were swung open. The rain seemed to be lessening. Through it she caught a glimpse of a white sports car, parked in front of the church. The sight steadied her. She had told Nick not to come. She had said she would not see him again. She rose.

Knots of people were moving toward the door. Someone called her name. She brushed past them. Nick was standing bare-headed on the sidewalk with a grin. "You made a beautiful stand-in, baby."

"You were inside?"

"Wouldn't have missed it! The bride was pale and miserable. I'm going to Hartford. Want to come? I'll see to it you miss that dull dinner tonight."

She glanced back. Duncan and Lowell were framed together in the gothic arch of the door. Behind them the others.

"I'd love to," Ariel said.

The fast little car swung onto the glistening road.

"Stick with me, baby." He patted her knee. "You won't be wearing diamonds. You'll be using 'em for checkers."

She laughed at the corny line, drew her coat close, and let the wind-driven rain shut out all vision.

Duncan and Lowell watched them out of sight. The others crowding behind must have seen them, too. But no one commented. Except Emily Phelps.

"Oh, dear, I hope that pretty girl hasn't taken up with Nick Orlini. He's as wild as mustard, they say. One girl after another. But I didn't think a Roundtree . . . maybe she's got a little of Henrietta in her. Well, it takes all kinds. Lowell dear, you do look pale. Take her home, Duncan, so she can get some rest."

They scuttled to their cars. Duncan put his arm around the girl he was going to marry. "How about some lunch first?"

"Oh, Duncan, I have so many things to do."

"Will it always be this way, Lowell?"

"Of course it won't. I don't know how you could ask that. It's just that time is running short now."

"Time always runs short. As a minister's wife, my darling, you'll have to manage time or it will run you into the ground. Come on, I'll buy you a steak special at the Redcoat Inn and get you back in plenty of time to iron your dress or wash your hair or whatever girls do the day before they get married."

She did not smile. And he knew he was being heavy-handed. He was painfully aware of the scene in the church, the walk down the aisle with Ariel clinging to his arm. It must have been obvious to everyone.

But it was over, he told himself angrily. Gone, as surely as that white car was gone, down the road. He had learned to cut dead tissue from living. Now at least she had given him an excuse. He would scrape the wound clean. Nick Orlini. The man even had the impudence to come into the church to wait for her. She had gone to him without a glance back, without a moment's hesitation. He could exorcise his demon now. He had only to think of her with Nick.

He picked up his raincoat and stopped lying to himself. He was being tested again.

"Come on, darling."

"I'd really rather not, Duncan." He did not miss the quaver in her voice.

"Let's have it out, Lowell. What's wrong?"

"Nothing. Except I—oh, Duncan, why did we take on so much?"

"You mean like getting married?"

"No. I mean . . . I guess it's too late for any regrets now about the big wedding."

"It certainly is. All you have to do is stand still and let it unroll. And a good lunch will help. I want to talk to you, Lowell."

"About what?"

"A couple of things that don't concern Dr. Wilcox or Mrs. Wilcox and they're coming out now."

A good wine and the light salad she had insisted on brought some color into Lowell's face. He decided the time was right. She helped him.

"You haven't yet told me about those two things you wanted to talk about."

"All right. The first let's get over with. I'm sorry the rehearsal upset you but I don't blame you one bit."

"What are you talking about, Duncan?"

"Well, I think it was a pretty poor idea to ask another girl to take your place at rehearsal."

"Duncan, I knew that would annoy you. You hate any kind of superstition, and it *is* silly. But that's the way it's done. Even Mrs. Wilcox said so. And if we're going to do the whole bit, that's part of it. I didn't think you'd mind Ariel. In fact I thought you rather liked her. Don't you?"

"Of course I like her. Everyone does."

She could not be putting him on. Lowell had the clarity of spring water. Was it possible that she had seen nothing, guessed nothing? He wondered what kind of world she really lived in. He began to think he didn't know her as well as he thought.

"She is different. And she certainly is Henrietta in the flesh. I was expecting her to burst out and do something wild. Instead she's been so quiet I've thought she must be having a really dull time. And spending all that money to come so far. Duncan, I'm sorry you were annoyed at the rehearsal. Tomorrow you'll get the real thing." She smiled and then her voice tightened. "But I really think it was a little much of her to ask Nick Orlini to the rehearsal."

"Did she?"

"Why else would he have been there? I can't bear him, Duncan! He's so—so smug!"

The quaver again. Only last night she had flung herself excitedly into dancing with Orlini. This overblown intensity was the price, he supposed, that one paid for the whole hectic ritual.

"Let's forget it, shall we?"

"Oh, yes. Yes." She slid her hand under his. It was cold. "Now what else, Dunkie?" She giggled. "That's a perfectly awful name but I'm afraid you're stuck with it from Claude and Kim, at least. You're going to have two adoring, annoying sisters-in-law."

"I'll take 'em just as they are. This is topic two." He drew from his pocket the long envelope Harlan Phelps had given him. "Dad's wedding present. For you."

"For us, Duncan."

"For you. He was very plain on the subject."

She opened it and gasped. "Duncan, do you know what it is?"

"Yes."

"But Duncan! Why? I mean—what a gift. I never saw that much money on a check—I mean, a check to me—in my life! $1000! We can really fix up the rectory. Or we can take a real honeymoon."

"We're going to take a real honeymoon. I've arranged for that."

"Where?"

"A surprise. No reason why the bride shouldn't be surprised, is there? I'll tell you tonight."

But she hardly seemed to hear. "Will you keep this for me, Duncan?"

"No, it's yours. I have nothing to do with it. Put it in the bank or cash it and spend it. For anything you want."

"I don't want it for myself."

"Because you don't know how to want for yourself. You've always done what someone else asked of you. Dad wants *you* to have the check. I'll take care of us without my father's help."

She put it into her purse and said no more. He had no idea what she was thinking. If they could have shared any kind of life beforehand. If they could have gone away, on a hidden weekend or two, and discovered what had happened to each of them during the long wait, they would be happier now.

It was he who had seen the breadth of the world, its greed, its cruelty, its places of heart-stopping beauty, its moments of soaring splendor. He knew the small chance, the long odds, against enduring human happiness. She had been bound within the rigid confines of hope and stifling devotion.

He promised himself again that he would make it up to her. They would not be the first man and wife to learn after the marriage ceremony the good and solid reasons for their coming together. It was another kind of love but it would stay the course.

They drove home in near silence. He stopped the car outside the house and caught her to him with a tenderness that he could not have put into words. He kissed her and to his surprise she parted her lips to his kiss and pressed her body against him.

"Thank you, Duncan, for being—you."

Martin Roundtree was standing in the open doorway.

"I'll pick you up at seven."

She slipped from the car.

One more day, and the life they had so carefully planned would begin. As had been intended. As had for so long been intended.

The six-lane highway that was Connecticut's great artery to the east and the south ribboned over the wet hills as if no towns existed. Thatcher had been left far behind. To Ariel, the ghostly whistle of the tires on wet highway, the occasional car that passed them, and the lengthening miles themselves were a surgery. The highway was the knife cutting away the trauma of the last hour and restoring her somehow to the health of indifference, which was her only refuge.

Nick seemed content to drive in silence. Once he had asked her if she would like to stop for lunch. That would have meant talk and confrontation and food she could not eat. He made no other suggestion. As the miles sped by, she saw Nick as a remote and necessary figure, a kind of *deus ex machina* descended out of the storm to untie the knot of her dilemma. That is, she would have liked to see him that way. But self-honesty gave it the lie. Nick had deliberately come to the church rehearsal. She had as deliberately walked to his car to show them all that they were wrong, whatever they thought.

Two big overhead signs loomed out of the rain. Left to Hartford. Ahead to New York. To her surprise Nick kept the car on a straight course.

"What about Hartford?"

"Glad you found your tongue. What about Hartford?"

"Isn't that where we're going?"

"I thought you'd like to put more miles between you and your recent—uh, 'wedding.' "

"What does that mean?"

"It means, my little witch, that if ever I saw a cat beside a saucer of cream she was about to lose, it was you in that church this morning."

"That is a rotten remark."

"Agreed. But like so many rotten remarks, it happens to be true. You've got a thing for the Deacon. I saw it the first day, down at Big Moon's diner. And he has the hots for you. Warmed up that church like one of his own hell fires." Nick laughed. Once again she saw in him not the self-indulgent slackness of Ben Orlini's spoiled son but a man who had found nothing in life to satisfy him. Yet his arrogance was matched by his shrewdness. There was little purpose in denying what he had seen.

"How far is it to New York?"

"Three to three-and-a-half hours. Nervous?"

"Why should I be?"

"Because you're a very clever little girl who can play Miss Wide Eyes anytime she wants. But you can't handle me the way you handled the Deacon. I don't twist easily around a pretty finger."

"I have no desire to try."

"That's more like it. We'll be in New York in plenty of time to freshen up at my place. Have a good dinner, see a few lights, and get back to Thatcher in plenty of time to miss everything."

"Sounds marvelous." If he had expected her to react to the mention of his apartment, she knew better. She disliked Nick Orlini. But his type was no stranger. She was more at home with it than with this overwhelming flood of raw feeling that Duncan had brought to her.

She was unabashedly using Nick. And there would be a price. She would handle that when she came to it. There was no way to rationalize or even justify this long rain-enwrapped drive. All she asked was to put whatever was possible between her and Duncan's voice, his touch, his very being. And his arm lightly around Lowell as they stood together in the Gothic doorway. She stirred restlessly in the leather-lined bucket seat.

"We're making good time," Nick said.

"Do you always kidnap your girls like this?"

"Oh, come on. You can do better than that. I've never invited any girl to my flat who had the least unwillingness to go." He took his eyes from the road to glance at her. "I don't have to." She was getting used to that mocking mood, that wry half grin. She wondered what kind of man he might be without those obvious defenses. Whatever he was, it would not be easy to know Nick Orlini. Nor would she try.

The needle slid to eighty-eight. The road was slick. She felt a tightening in her stomach muscles. Speed could exhilarate her. But not this kind of speed, purposeless, taunting, with a man she now realized she hardly knew. For Nick Orlini's thin, saturnine face with its brooding good looks seemed to wear a different mask each time she saw him. And there had only been three times. Three times. And Duncan. Every day

233

and yet never. Never alone. Never themselves. Minutes snatched in the sunlight on Preacher Hill, in the moonlight in Willard Roundtree's woods. Moments like cobwebs, guilt like a steady rain. A week and her life had been fragmented and drained, leaving a shell of herself to sit in this madly speeding car beside a stranger. As if she cared what could happen.

The needle touched ninety. Nick laughed.

"You've got guts, baby."

"I've driven in faster cars."

"Is that a challenge?"

"It's up to you."

But he slowed. "We're picking up more traffic. But I'll show you what she can do someday."

"I know what she can do." She opened the ventilator window. The cool, wet air tasted good.

"How do you know what she can do?"

"Uncle Henri lets me take them around the testing grounds. She will do one hundred twenty-five easily. Uncle Henri says any fool who takes the car over eighty deserves to be a statistic."

"Tell me about your Uncle Henri."

"He is not my uncle. He is short and round with a small mustache and he wears a diamond stickpin that he can reverse to emeralds with a touch. It's fascinating until you know the trick."

"And he is a friend of your mother's?"

"My mother has many friends," she said coldly.

"I can believe it. Now tell me about Ariel." He was weaving skillfully through increased traffic. They were approaching the city.

"I lead a very dull life in Paris. I work when I can get a job. Otherwise I travel with my mother."

"Don't you have a flat of your own?"

"That would be considered quite inappropriate under the circumstances."

"I see." He didn't, and Ariel was relieved to drop the subject. It had been a pleasantly mysterious way to cover what was a matter of simple arithmetic.

Soon the rain stopped. The heavy clouds were lifting. They were following the shoreline and occasionally she caught a glimpse of water and the unmistakable smell of salt water.

"Long Island Sound. Take you sailing on it some day. Unless you've already won the America's cup."

"I love the salt water. But I don't know much about sailing on it."

"Good. We can start there."

His possessiveness irritated her as he knew it would. But more disturbing was the subtle way he aligned her with himself, with the Orlinis. It made this very trip an act of betrayal. Ariel did not permit herself easy regrets. A thing done was a thing done. From there you went on, made up for your mistake, or lived with it and tried to be wiser next time. Partly Mam'selle's teaching, and partly her own discovery that it made life much simpler. Ariel had steered her life at school, at home with Alicia, at her job, on this sound philosophy. But she had not yet applied it to men. She had avoided any entanglement that would encourage regrets. That is, until this week. Until Duncan. Now she felt cut adrift from any philosophy or course of conduct she had ever known. She was not helpless but as they neared the end of the long, intimate closeness of the car, she was no longer comfortable. Nick Orlini remained a stranger yet he had a physical presence, a magnetism of which she was increasingly conscious.

They were crossing a bridge into the city itself. The towers, pinnacles of power that were New York, rose into mauve mist ahead. In the early midafternoon dusk, lights had begun to pinprick their outline. It was a city that beckoned, floated with a dreamlike quality that promised whatever the human heart asked, once the towers had been scaled and the sacrifice made.

The building at which Nick Orlini stopped covered almost a block and soared into the lifting fog. It was the tallest apartment house Ariel had ever seen. She bent her head backward to see the top.

"I'm on the thirty-eighth floor. Not as high as I'd like but the view is good." Nick handed the doorman the keys to the car. Ariel was still wearing her flat-heeled shoes, her country skirt, and her raincoat. Not that she cared, but it was a measure of the overwhelming city that it could occur to her.

A small dimly lit, carpeted elevator with dark paneling carried them with a rush of harnessed power to their floor. Total silence filled the hall. Only the dark doors gave a hint of human habitation. The thick pile muffled their footsteps. One could live here as totally isolated as on a moon mound.

Nick unlocked the door and bowed her in.

There was no sound. Even the door closed almost silently behind them. The room she entered was not large, but it was a corner room and two vast windows to the east and south gave it an airiness that pushed back the walls. She had a quick impression of deep, near-white carpeting, of white walls, and a wide module grouping in coffee-brown velvet. Invitation was implicit in the depth of the chairs, the spaciousness of the lounges. Two dark brown leather chairs balanced the end of the room. A man's room, yet a man with a taste for softness. It gave her no more clue to Nick Orlini than anything else she had seen about him.

But it was the view that caught her breath. Beyond to the south lay the great soaring city, even more veiled and remote than the buildings she had seen from the street. Yet with a magnetism that she felt could draw her through the glass and into space.

"Don't worry, they don't open." He was standing so close that she started. You could hardly hear a footstep in this place, yet outside the city pulsed with noise and motion.

"The windows don't open?"

"That's right. Air conditioning does it all. What would you like—little warmer, little cooler?" He reached behind one of the heavy beige-white drapes. "Just a touch of the button."

"It's all right. But I can't imagine not opening a window."

"Or not putting the top down on a car. A real fresh-air girl, aren't you?"

"I just like to breathe."

"That doesn't always require fresh air."

She was not sure of him in this eerie gray stillness. Or even of her own competence. Her reason for coming on this impulsive, little-understood junket now had all the earmarks of foolishness.

She moved to the south window and looked down. The river flowed almost directly below, neither racing nor sluggish but fluid steel, a working river carrying its burden of barges and tugs, small boats and scows to their destinies. She saw a freighter, inching from a pier, swing her bow toward a silver sheen of wider water in the distance. She wanted to count the bridges that flung grappling-hooks of steel to the solid flat-lands beyond, anchoring this floating city to its world. She had heard that New York City was built on solid rock and the tunnels beneath lay nearly a half mile deep in layers of wires and tubes, subways and sewers. It was rock that gave New York its majesty, possessed by no other city on earth. A city grown out of rock, bedrock that would support any height the fantasy of human mind could evoke. Rock and water, primal elements, frightening in their immensity.

"I'm glad you like it."

She came back to the reality of him. "I do. I never saw anything like it."

"You've never been to New York?"

"I was born here."

"You're full of surprises, Ariel. I thought you were Paris-born and bred."

"My mother preferred to live in Europe but she said there was nothing as reassuring for traveling abroad as

American citizenship. So she came back here to have me."

"And your father?"

She sensed he was not interested. He was talking as if filling time.

"I don't remember my father."

"Oh. Sorry. Now let's put on some lights. This sort of day depresses me."

The room suddenly glowed. He started to close the drapes.

"Oh, please, no."

"No what?"

"Don't shut off the windows."

"Why not? Nervous?"

"That's the second time you've asked me that. If I were nervous I wouldn't be here. I'm really not the nervous type."

"I believe that."

"I want to get used to it out there. It's overpowering. I want to face it and not feel it's out there behind a curtain ready to—to pounce, when I'm not looking."

He laughed and for the first time it sounded genuine to her. "Baby, many people have said many things about this view but nobody came up with that. I assure you the city has no intention of pouncing on you. Nor have I, if that's in that crazy mind of yours. In fact, quite the opposite. Will you have a drink?"

"Not now, thank you." Yet she felt easier. She turned back into the room. And then she saw, glittering in the half twilight of lamp and dusk, something of pure magic, unlike anything she had ever seen before. It was a crystal swan, perhaps two feet in height, mounted on a black ebony stand. It was no dulcet swan drifting on empty waters. The bird had risen, its crystal claws grasping the edge of the stand, its wings flung back in fury, its neck superbly arched, its beak a weapon. Light rippled in pure flame along its feathers, its crystalline throat and the down of its thrusting, infuriated breast. It was a sculpture of violence and the translucent crystal fire only added to its savage, exultant beauty.

"Mein liebe Schwan."

He was watching her with amusement.

"What?"

"My beloved swan. Lohengrin, Act One. If you don't know it, I'll take you to hear it some day. Like it?"

"It's magnificent. Where did it come from?"

"Does it matter? It's unique. Like you, baby." He moved toward her. "Actually it was found in the Kartnerstrasse in Vienna. A long way from Thatcher, baby. You're not the only one who has traveled."

"I didn't suppose so."

He caught her by the arms. His voice was suddenly husky and his strength surprised her. "Ariel, I want you. More than any other girl who has ever walked through those doors. And I'm going to have you, someday. I'm going to marry you. I've never said that to any woman before. But you're what I want and you're what I intend to have. You're not in love with me now, maybe not for some time. I know what's happened. You don't even like me now. You're using me. I know that, too. And I don't mind. Go ahead and use me. Glad to be of service, baby, because I know the day will come when you won't use me, you'll come to me because you want to. I'll wait for that."

He released her so abruptly that she stumbled back against the long couch. He caught her but made no further move to touch her.

"I'm going out for a while. Make yourself at home. Take a shower. Rest. There's some Brie in the kitchen. And fresh bread. I'll be back later. We'll have dinner. And get on back to Thatcher. You don't mind being alone?"

"I like it here." She would match his casualness, but the truth was, she longed to leave, to be on the road again, to escape from the muffled, menacing isolation of this apartment. As for his stilted proposal, she had

239

heard similar words before. Men who would 'wait' until you needed them, counting on their nonexistent fascination. She disliked Nick Orlini, at times was repelled by his slick, thin veneer. She *had* used him. Common decency had given her a sense of guilt. But no longer. She would never come to him, she would never need him. Once away from here she would push the whole episode out of her mind, her memory— Alicia's way. "Men are to be used. Or they will use you. That is common sense. To a clever woman who intends to own her body and her own life, common sense must come first. Even in the bedroom."

He picked up his raincoat.

"If you get panicky and call Thatcher, be sure to tell them where you are. They'd like to know." His laugh was quick and easy. Quick and easy and annoying.

"I shan't bother them. They're all out at a party this evening. I expect to be back before they are. And I don't usually panic, Nick."

"Good."

"If one of those 'other girls' walks in, I'll tell her you'll be back soon."

"Jealous?"

"I don't care enough to be jealous."

She had flicked him. "Then I'll tell you what to do, baby, about those 'other girls' as you call them. Send them on their way. I'm sure you know how to do that. All except one. If she happens to walk in, you decide for yourself."

"Which one is that?" They were needling each other and she enjoyed it. As she would enjoy finding his weaknesses, piercing his arrogance, until they quarreled and the day would be over. "Or doesn't a gentleman tell?"

"Sometimes it's a pleasure." He hesitated and grinned. "Would you believe Lowell?"

She stared at him. "No. That's shabby of you."

He shrugged. "Well, here's something I never did

for the lily maid of Thatcher." He reached into his pocket, opened her hand, and dropped a small object into it. It was a key. "It's yours. Keep it. If you change your mind about leaving Sunday, use this apartment. Stay here as long as you want. I won't bother you. Maybe that will put some understanding into that suspicious little head of yours."

The door closed.

Lowell? Here? A cheap lie to shock her. He was what she first thought of him. Spoiled, self-indulgent, capable of cruelty. Now she had let herself be caught in a trap. Her intuition told her if she did not accept Nick as a lover, which she would never do, she would have him as an enemy and as willing to lie about her as about Lowell. Whatever Lowell was in her small-town way, she had that common sense that Alicia preached. Lowell had seen Nick for what he was. Lowell was marrying the man she loved. Brava Lowell. Bravo common sense.

Somewhere in the silent apartment a buzzer rang once. She had no idea where or what it was. Silence returned. She dropped the key on a table, turned out the lamp, and went to the window. The dusk had deepened. Millions of tiny lights shaped the buildings into paper cutouts, pinpricking the darkness and casting an umbrella of radiance up into the lifting mist. She imagined people behind every one of those lights, meeting, greeting, talking, crying, quarreling, making love, or simply anticipating the new night. The magnetism of the city was stronger than ever. She would like to challenge the raw power of this faceless town. She saw herself becoming part of it. Ariel's imagination could always carry her into new worlds. This man-made splendor stirred her. She imagined herself waiting in the darkness for Duncan, rushing to meet him; they would be swept together into the brilliant quickening tide of living.

Duncan. The pain sprang to the surface. She saw Duncan at this moment, Lowell beside him, the loving faces of a close family to which he would soon belong. A silent cry of pain was so loud within her that she did not hear the opening of the door. But she heard its closing click. She turned but could see nothing in the dimness. "Nick?"

For an instant there was no answer. Then a slight breath. "I beg your pardon." It was a woman's voice. Chilled, cultivated, no longer young. Whoever it was, she had the advantage of invisibility. Ariel saw only shadows. The visitor could see her starkly against the uncurtained window.

"Who is it?"

"I think we'd better have some light."

The room sprang into being. Ariel saw a tall woman with black-streaked hair, a black mink stole wrapped around a black turtleneck sweater and skirt, massive silver at her throat and wrists. Her eyes were large, heavy-lidded, and unreadable.

"I'm Julia Orlini. You must be Ariel."

"Yes . . ." Ariel stopped herself from explanation. In naming her the tall woman seemed to know too much about her.

"I'm very glad to meet you. I don't usually come to my son's apartment. But today—" She dropped the mink on a lounge and sank into the softness of the brown velvet. It became her, as the whole room did. Ariel wondered if she had planned it to become her. "I'm on my way to Washington, and since our own apartment is being repainted . . ." she was scanning Ariel from head to foot. There was neither warmth nor hostility in her appraisal. It was a businesslike evaluation, as cold as the silver she wore. "You're everything Nick said you were."

"He's gone out. He'll be right back, Mrs. Orlini."

"I didn't come to see him. I don't follow my son's activities. But now that we've met I feel well rewarded for my intrusion. Do sit down."

Ariel sat stiffly apart from the tall, compelling

woman. She had met Ben Orlini but she was not prepared for this sensual, commanding woman whose presence, like her musky perfume, pervaded the room. She glimpsed something in Julia Orlini that might have been the source of that mocking flicker of cruelty in Nick. But where Nick's nearly black eyes roved and glittered, Julia's large luminous eyes were veiled, unblinking, disconcerting. She smiled only with her lips. As she smiled at Ariel now.

"You're very beautiful, as you must know."

"I wouldn't know how to answer that, Mrs. Orlini."

"Nonsense. Every woman knows when she's beautiful. And when she isn't. I was a very ugly little girl. I was aware of it every day of my life. But one can overcome even that if one has to."

Julia had a way of making statements to which there were no answers. Ariel searched her mind for the right word, the right tone. Indifference to this suave woman would sound childishly rude. She wished Nick would come back. Yet in another part of her mind she was curious. She sensed a purpose, a calculating focus that belied the languid half explanation. Julia Orlin could not have known she would find Ariel here. It had been only at the last moment that he had swung the car from the Hartford highway sign. Or had it? Ariel had a sharply developed instinct for self-defense. She became wary.

Julia Orlini could be as direct as she could be final. "As you know, I'm sure, my son is in love with you."

"I didn't know it, Mrs. Orlini. And I very much doubt it."

"Julia. As we get to know each other first names will be pleasanter, don't you think?"

"If you want to see Nick, I could go out for a while."

"I want to see you, Ariel. Now that I've been fortunate enough to find you."

Somehow the talk was all out of kilter. Julia Orlini

ignored whatever she was saying while fastening that steady, relentless look on her. The meeting was deliberate. Ariel sensed it now, as surely as she sensed this woman, like her son, would offer possession or enmity. There would be no middle ground.

"Nick tells me you have some notion of leaving Thatcher on Sunday."

"Yes. The man at the local travel agency said I would have no trouble getting on the Paris plane Sunday night."

"Why are you leaving?"

"I came only for the wedding."

"That seems a pity." Julia settled herself with easy grace into the lounge. "Do you often come here from Paris for just a week?"

"No. I haven't been in this country since I was a child."

"Then I think we should make this visit something special. After the wedding, why don't you come to us for a while? If Thatcher bores you, and I'm sure it must by this time, come visit us here in the city. We have a family apartment on Fifth Avenue. Or perhaps at my husband's little retreat on Halcyon Island. He'd be delighted." Her long slender arm reached snakelike to the table behind the lounge. "I can see Nick has already welcomed you." She picked up the key Ariel had left on the table.

"It's very kind of all of you, Mrs. Orlini. But I've made up my mind. I'm going home Sunday night."

Julia Orlini looked at her sharply. "You're not only beautiful. You're clever. And you would be very good for Nick. You think of yourself as a Roundtree, I'm sure."

"I am a Roundtree."

Julia laughed for the first time. "Oh come, Ariel. Outside of Thatcher, what on earth does it mean? In Thatcher it will soon mean even less. The first Isaac Roundtree was a miller. You've been to the Grist Mill.

It was his. The Isaac Roundtree you seem to want to claim relation to was a miller's boy. Whatever happened to him, nobody knows. All that land that the Roundtrees claim doesn't belong to them at all—that's Thatcher's land. It has rightfully belonged to the Thatchers for three hundred years. As Nick has probably told you, I am a Thatcher. And I think now I have the means of getting it." She sat upright in her intensity. "Willard Roundtree is a gentleman and a fool. He could be very comfortable, rich for the rest of his life on the money from that land. Instead he prefers to grovel in a cornfield with an Indian. Well, I can't wait for my husband to make him bigger offers. Especially as I don't have to, now. That's why I'm going to Washington."

"I don't understand any of this but I do know it would be a cruel thing."

"Cruel? To take what belongs to me?" She stood up. Had Ariel known her better she would have recognized the signs of Julia's anger. "Cruel! Cruel! What would you know about cruelty? My father was a high-school teacher in a small New Jersey town. My mother came from Russia. She was a pianist. Times were bad. It was called the Depression. You're too young to know. When my father lost his job, my mother tried to give piano lessons, little concerts, anything. The children would laugh at the way she spoke broken English. There was no money. Only lines at the soup kitchen and men on street corners selling apples and pencils nobody wanted. That's the way I grew up. But my father never forgot who we were. My mother said I must marry a good provider."

She looked beyond Ariel. Her hand stroked the black mink lying across the back of the lounge, the long thin fingers burrowing sensually into the silky fur. "So I did both. I married a good provider. And I never forgot who I am."

Julia reseated herself beside Ariel. She smiled but

not with her eyes. She never let anger, quick as it was with her, spoil an effect. "And now I shall be what I really am. Not a chattel wife but a woman in my own right. Of a proud family. Thanks to you, Ariel."

"To me?" Ariel stared at the strong, dark malevolent face.

"Don't you remember?"

"Remember what? Mrs. Orlini, since the day I arrived in Thatcher I've heard what the Orlinis are doing in the town. What have I ever said or done that would give you the idea—"

"You gave me the clue. Or rather you told it to Nick. My son and I are very close."

"Told Nick what?"

"Don't fret, Ariel. It will all come out some day. Why should you care? You may like to think you are a part of the Roundtrees but, whatever you are, you come from some place further than Thatcher. I want you on my side, Ariel. I want Nick to marry you. You would have everything you ever wanted."

Julia rose and slipped like a graceful animal into the black mink folds. "I'm sure you won't want to take that plane on Sunday, Ariel. Not when there is so much ahead for you here."

If there was a hint of threat, it was as tenuous as smoke. Ariel stood rigid.

"Give Nick my love. Tell him I'm sorry I missed him. But I am grateful for this chance to know you."

Ariel's deepening, horrified resentment exploded into fury. She must scream out at this woman. She must stop her, yet an inner warning bell told her that she could only lose. She was in Nick's apartment. Julia Orlini had cornered her. With Nick's deliberate connivance? Probably. What the Orlinis could want from her, she had no idea. No more, perhaps, than the simple triumph of proving her disloyalty.

"Mrs. Orlini," she managed to steady her voice, even smile. "You don't know me now any better than you did before. There was nothing I could have said about

Uncle Willard's land because I don't know anything. As for being on your side, I don't know what that means. The Roundtrees are my family. I love them."

"Do you think they love you?"

"Yes."

Julia's smile was merciless. "You don't know them, my dear. They love no one outside themselves. If you stayed, they would hate you because you are different. You are a threat."

"I will never believe that."

"Then you will have to find it out for yourself. Goodbye, Ariel. I am grateful to you. Should you change your mind . . ."

"I shan't, Mrs. Orlini. I'm leaving Sunday. Nothing will stop me. I am not in love with Nick. I would never marry him. The fact is, Mrs. Orlini," she drew herself together to fling a last shot but she managed to speak levelly, even softly, "at home, in Paris, I learned contempt for men like him."

Julia turned without speaking and left.

Ariel had made an enemy, yet what did it matter now? She found her way to the bathroom. When she had bathed her face and brushed her hair, she returned to the living room. Nick was stretched out on a davenport quietly smoking one of his long Italian cigarettes.

"Sorry I was away so long."

"Your mother was here."

"Was she?" The remark held neither surprise nor interest.

Ariel felt her indignation swelling to anger. What did these arrogant people take her for? A schoolgirl fresh from behind a convent wall? Alicia used to say: "Patience, Ariel. Be patient. People ultimately reveal themselves."

As Julia Orlini would, as Nick would, she was sure. There was still something unfathomable about him, something she could not or did not want to see. The apartment had already closed in on her. The huge window that could not be opened, the oyster-white carpeting into which she sank heel deep, the heavy folds of pale draperies. No sound penetrated the stifling softness, no sound would escape it.

Nick had not risen. She stood looking down at him.

"If you wanted me to meet your mother why didn't you say so, instead of driving me all the way to the city and then leaving me alone?"

"You were rather willing to come, my pet."

"I am not your pet."

"I think you could get used to it." He grinned and rose. "As a matter of fact, I couldn't care less whether you met my mother. I'm not accountable for what she does, thank God." It was not a denial. Every nerve ending told Ariel it had been prearranged. She would not forget Julia Orlini standing in this room looking her over like a brood mare at auction.

"We didn't part friends, if you're interested."

"I told you, baby, I don't give a damn."

"I do. I felt cheapened and used. You could at least have stayed here and explained."

"Explained? What?"

"Why I was here."

"Why are you here?"

If she lost her temper now, her humiliation would be complete. She had only herself to blame for this predicament. She had run blindly from the hurt of that incredible half hour at the church, wanting only to strike out at them all, especially at Duncan. She had tried to destroy what was indestructible within her.

"As for being used, my pet," Nick seemed taller in the lamplight. Or was it a shadow thrown against the wall behind him? The outstretched swan rising in its violence. "It seems to me I am the one who has been used. I've submitted, I think rather gracefully, to being the means of your escape after you and Duncan had gotten tired of making sheep's eyes at each other. I thought you were worth the price. But I also think I deserve some reward."

He caught her, one hand twisting her arm behind her back, the other hand at her throat, the fingers a vise, the thumb moving caressingly. She could not have guessed his strength. Struggle was useless against her arm bent behind her.

As suddenly as it began, it was over. He released her and she half fell against the divan.

He was straightening his jacket, his cuffs, his dark face no longer boyish but seamed by the fragile light.

"Use, baby, is a word with many definitions. But I have been repaid."

"That was contemptible."

"Agreed. No lady should be completely surprised. I don't think you were. However, I told you I would wait. And I will. But I'm gratified to know that I was right about you the first time I saw you." He took her hand and pulled her to her feet. "We're two of a kind, Ariel. You'll find it out some day. Now where would you like to eat?"

"I can get myself back to Thatcher."

"Don't be a little fool. Are you pretending no man has ever kissed you like that before?"

It was part of the day's unbreakable web that she had spun. He would only believe what he chose to believe. He would never understand that the very ease of her life, the casualness of the people who came and went in her mother's apartment, had driven her into self-denial, self-containment. It was true no man had ever kissed her like that, so bruisingly, so untenderly. She could still feel his hand against her throat, the thumb moving possessively. She knew now why Nick Orlini was dangerous. But deeper than that in her consciousness lay the realization, the horror, that blindly, beyond emotion and sentiment, his violence had stirred her.

She was shivering.

"Come on, let's get out of here. It's been a long time since either of us has had anything to eat."

She did not move.

"All right. Will you accept an apology?"

"Nick, for heaven's sake! Let's be honest."

"With pleasure." He had picked up her raincoat; now he stood with a half smile, waiting. "Although I never met a woman capable of it."

"I've made a mess of the whole day. I came here with you. You had a right to think . . . so had your mother . . ."

"For Christ's sake will you forget my mother?"

"I will when I understand her. I want to forget it all."

"All right. I'll agree to that."

"I won't see you again. I'm leaving Sunday. I accept your apology and I take part of the blame. Now can we drive home?"

He scanned her face, then shrugged. "Sure."

They were at last in the intimate little car again, where it seemed that she had spent half a lifetime. They left the city, crossing a bridge that hung a loop of jewelled lights against the sky, passing a cluster of high-rise buildings, a towering mirage of spangled blocks devoid of meaning or of humanity.

They dined quickly and casually at a roadside restaurant filled with young couples in jeans and families with tired children. They talked little against the insistent beat of five-year-old rock. Experience lay like a wounded bird between them.

Then they were in the car again. "It's clearing. I'll take you back the shortest way. We can cross the river at Oyster Hill and come up through Juno's Landing."

She felt compelled to answer. "All right. What's Oyster Hill?"

"The Indians used oyster shells for wampum. They left a big pile of them along the river when they were driven out of the country."

"How cruel for them."

"The name of the game is progress. Would you like to be hiking home over an Indian trail tonight?"

It was thoughtless talk, empty. Ariel sensed that what had happened had pushed them forever apart, yet, like an unspoken conspiracy, would bind them together.

She would be glad to be going home to Paris.

She felt confused and tired but within her, still, lay that core of integrity that had held her secure. Her inner self. Her own will. Her inviolate strength to command her own life.

Ahead lay the unlit tunnel of the night. The empty miles. And a drying road.

Chapter Ten

The pocked and muddied road through Juno's Landing was clogged with cars. From the gray shingled house with the neon sign over the porch poured a raw, savage beat. Lights flickered behind the ground floor windows of the abandoned factory. In the street, figures jostled and shoved, shouted and cursed in the shadowy crowd pushing into Pete's Rock.

In Big Moon's Diner, Ira Moon put down her counter rag, tossed her golden hoop earrings, and listened.

"They're sure mary janing it down here tonight."

Big Moon gave a final polish to a clean glass.

"Friday night. They got a new band at Pete's. Brings the kids from all over."

"I think there's a gang down in the old factory too."

"I'm watching 'em."

Ira sloshed viciously at a corner. "Sure. And what do you think you can do? They probably got a lot more than grass with 'em."

"If they stay where they are, there's nothing I can do. It's up to the police. If they break out . . ."

Ira looked at her husband with annoyance. "There's nothing you can do anyhow. Nothing at all. You got yourself appointed mayor of this spook hole but it'd be you against everybody."

The big man grinned. "I'll give 'em odds."

"Not only that but Pete's got all your business tonight."

"That's okay. I get 'em Sunday, Monday, and the rest of the week. Don't you fret, Ira."

"I do fret on a night like this. You wouldn't be doing this if it wasn't for Duncan Phelps."

"That's right. I wouldn't even be around if it wasn't for the Deacon."

"He saved your life, maybe, but that doesn't mean he owns it."

"He'd be the first to say you're right, girl. He not only saved it but he gave me a place to use it."

"I know. I heard. You and the Deacon are going to clean this place up some day. Well, if you ask me, it don't clean easy."

"Right again," said Big Moon placidly. "I never did look for an easy job. Anyhow, somebody's got to hang around for kids. Like I said." He nodded toward the door.

The boy who came in was skinny and slight and his ankle-length jeans and cowlick of straw hair showed he still had a lot of growing to do. He had a guarded look.

"Wouldn't you know?" said Ira. "Hi, Billy. How's your mama?"

"She's okay, I guess. Can I have a hamburger, Mrs. Moon?" He settled on a red plastic stool. "Please."

It was an afterthought but he had added it. That was the trouble with Billy Haskell. Hard to get hold of. Billy was just one of a lot of kids drawn down to Juno's Landing after dark by the hot rock, the loud bad mouth, the hint of evil that slid like river mist through the dimly lit streets and past the blind houses. Big Moon rounded them up and sent them home when he caught them. They went.

But Billy was different. Hazel Haskell, widowed

now for four years, used her capable fingers on the organ keys and the library cards to support herself and her son. But Billy had learned early to slip through them, heading like a homing pigeon for Juno's Landing.

Ira pushed the hamburger across the counter. Eyes shining, Billy was jerking around the plastic stool like a puppet on strings to the faint rhythm from up the street.

"Cool, aren't they? Need more stick."

"I wouldn't know, Billy."

"I could give it to 'em." He beat a quick riffle with a pair of spoons. "Like I did last time they came to Pete's. The Slow Freight. Only that's not what they really call themselves." He grinned, his mouth full. "Want to know?"

Ira had an answer but thought better of it.

Big Moon leaned over the counter. "Give him a glass of milk. On the house. When he gets to the bottom of it, I'll take him home. Personally."

"Aw now, wait a minute, Big Moon!"

"You know you're not supposed to be hanging around down here at this hour."

"It's a free country. I got a right."

"And as mayor of Juno's Landing, I got a right."

"That's not for real!"

"It's real enough for you. Now finish up!"

"Aw come on, Moon. They told me the last time they came to Pete's, if I came in late I could take the drums."

"Did you tell them you were twelve?"

"If you tell 'em that, I'll . . . I'll . . ." Billy's eyes skirted the diner.

"I don't tell things, Billy. I just do 'em. And one of the things I'm going to do is what Mr. Duncan wants—keep you out of trouble."

"What's he got to do with me?"

Ira was cutting a piece of cheese cake.

Big Moon sloshed a rag across the counter. "Let's

say he doesn't like to see kids get into trouble." But he said it without conviction. His mind tricked him again into the unspeakable scene, the fetid jungle, the bullet knocking him off balance. He had whirled to see the hidden enemy lunging at him with fixed bayonet. But a sudden shot, Duncan's, pitched the attacker backward. He looked smaller than Billy, browner, but no older. Moon had watched Duncan lift the boy in his arms.

"Christ!" said Big Moon.

Ira shoved the cheese cake at Billy. "You eat this up, Billy. Your mother's got too much on her mind playing for Miss Lowell's wedding tomorrow to feed you up full, so . . ."

"The wedding's off." Billy sat back to enjoy the effect.

"What did you say?" Ira stared at him.

Billy dug into the cheese cake, his eyes glinting. "I said the wedding's off. If you don't believe me, call Mom. Go on, call her, Big Moon."

"And while I do, you'll skip out of here."

Billy shrugged. "If you don't believe me, see if I care."

"If you don't stop telling fibs, you'll come to no good." Ira wanted to wrap her arms around the boy. Billy was a loner. But wrapping your arms around him was like wrapping your arms around water. He'd be gone, leaving a fleeting image of a lopsided grin and eyes that always looked past you.

"Billy honey, don't go around saying things that aren't true. You can hurt people."

"Who's hurting anybody?" Milk had left a mustache on the angry young mouth. "If you mean the ole wedding . . ."

Whatever Billy might have said was lost in a sudden yell, a siren's wail outside the diner.

Big Moon rushed to the door. The street was filled with running figures. A crowd was spilling out of

Pete's Rock, across the porch. Through the din came shouts:

"Fire! Fire! Fire in the factory! Clear the road!"

Before Moon could grab him, Billy had slid past and into the seething street.

"Billy!" Big Moon made a lunge, missed him, and plunged into the rigid back of a policeman. Officer Schiller swung around.

"Oh it's you, Moon. You can't go down that way. The street's jammed. We got to keep them coming up here."

"Billy Haskell's in that crowd, Dutch!"

"I'll go for him. You'll be more use up here. We're trying to move the crowd up this way. They got the fire apparatus coming in below." He blew his whistle. "Keep moving! Keep moving!"

The fire siren shrilled again. Big Moon could see a small funnel of smoke rising from the dark factory, but no flames.

"What the hell is there to burn in the old dump?"

"Nothing much but if it gets into the lathing, it could be bad. The walls are pretty weak now. If they go . . . Every kid in the county must be down at Pete's tonight. We just want to get them out!" His whistle blew again. "Keep moving. Never mind your cars! Keep moving!"

There were some protests, a lot of shouts, but police were lining both sides of the street and pushing the kids along. Big Moon could see no sign of Billy Haskell.

Ira had pushed beside him. He pulled her into the diner and locked the door. "You dim down the lights. We're closed until they clear the street."

"Billy?"

"I'll find him."

"The fire?"

"Nothing much. But they've got to get the crowd out in case the old brick walls go. I'll go out the back way." He went through the kitchen.

But he had a duty first. He picked up the phone. He had no idea where he could reach Duncan on this night. But he'd start at Harlan Phelp's house. To his surprise, Duncan answered the phone.

Big Moon spoke a few short words, hung up and hurried out into the alley blackness behind the diner. The noise was distant from here. The factory rose like a specter. He was pretty sure where he'd find Billy. He half regretted calling Duncan on this night before his wedding. And yet—and yet—dimly the big man understood the young minister's need, as dimly he understood the wordless burden that had changed Duncan's life and would forever lie locked within him.

Faintly he heard an automobile horn. Good. They were beginning to move the cars. The crowd noises were lessening. In another half hour it would be over. As he looked a curl of smoke drifted from an upper window of the stark factory. He began to run. The narrow back alleys were deserted. It was not far. Let the old walls hold, he prayed, let 'em stand until he reached Pete's Rock.

Nick Orlini leaned again on the horn of his car.

"It's not going to do any good, Nick. They're not going to let you through."

For Ariel the long day had deepened into a nightmare. They had been stopped twice on the road into Juno's Landing, and each time, despite the whistle and the warning, Nick had raced the little car past the state trooper. "They'll take the license down and then do their homework. They know the OR licenses— OR–1, that's Dad. OR–2, that's my mother. OR–3, that's me. And so forth."

"And if you get a ticket?"

Nick shrugged. "Dad pays the fine. Later, the cop wonders what happened to his promotion."

The familiar look of sullen arrogance settled on Nick's face again. If Ariel found the words difficult to accept, Nick's spoiled-boy expression made them farcical. He would have his own way. He would bolster his self-indulgence with any tale he could. She quite simply did not believe him, any more than she could relate this sudden petulance with the dark brooding man who had held her in a vise and kissed her as he pleased. He would be a difficult man to escape, an impossible man to reason with, and as she knew now, dangerous to deny. She would not see him again. And in two days she would be gone.

A police whistle blew. An officer stood directly in front of the car. With a smile, Nick slowed but kept the car going.

"Nick! You'll hit him!"

"Not if he gets out of the way."

"You're out of your mind!" She lunged for the brake. He shoved her roughly aside but the car stopped, just short of the patrolman. Officer Schiller walked slowly from the front of the car to the driver's window.

"What's that supposed to mean, Orlini?"

"Good evening, Schiller."

"I asked you a question."

"Would you mind repeating it?"

"Just back that car around and get out of here the way you came." Schiller recognized the girl beside Nick. As he had suspected, Orlini had lost no time. Nonetheless, the officer was disappointed. Somehow he had thought the girl—well, no matter. "Go on, back."

"Sorry, Officer Schiller, I'm taking my girl home and this is the quickest way."

"There are four pieces of fire equipment up ahead and beyond that the street's still filled with kids. Now get out of here, Orlini!"

"Where's the fire?"

"In the old factory. It started in some junk on the ground floor. They got that but they think it's still in the walls. And if that outer wall fell on the street . . ." He was talking to the girl. Her eyes were wide and, he thought, angry. She looked as if she had some sense.

"Nick, back up. Do what he says."

"When I want your advice, baby, I'll ask for it. I've taken enough from you already on this trip. I don't see any fire. And there's plenty of room to pass on the left of those fire engines. Too many petty bosses, as Dad says. Look out, Schiller!"

The officer sprang back as the little car jumped forward. Nick swung the wheel wide to the left, too wide. The car skidded on the muddy surface, went off the shoulder, and was mired in the trampled ooze on the side of the road. The wheels spun futilely and stopped. Nick turned off the ignition.

"Well, that did it, baby. Thanks for nothing."

"Are you blaming this on me?"

"I like my women to keep out of my business."

"I'm not one of your women!"

"You'd have a hard time proving that now." His hand squeezed her knee. Officer Schiller was at her side of the car.

"You'd better get out of here, miss. You too, Orlini. You can't move that car now."

"There's enough equipment over there. . . ."

A sudden shout came from the street. Ariel looked at the huge spectral building, black against the playing spotlights from the fire engines. It seemed to her that the high blackened wall on the street side was bulging. A tide of sound rose. Men were running from the direction of the building. She felt the police officer take her arm and push her toward a lane leading up to the left from the road. "You'll be all right, miss. Keep going up there." He left her.

But Ariel didn't keep going. She stumbled and slid. People were running past her. She felt herself lost in a nightmare of pursuit, not by these faceless runners, not by Nick, wherever he was, but by a towering wall of brick that might come tumbling to engulf her. She struggled to her feet, slipped again, and was suddenly pulled upward and steadied.

"My God—Ariel!"

Where he had come from or how he had found her, she could not guess. But there he was in the darkness. Duncan with his arm around her and his strength holding her to him. She could think of nothing except the rightness of it.

"Did it fall?"

"No, not yet."

"Is everybody clear?"

"Yes. Can you walk three blocks?"

"Certainly I can walk. I simply slipped in the mud and—how did you find me?"

"I saw you get out of Orlini's car." He had released her. "My car's behind Big Moon's diner. I'll drive you home."

"Oh, Duncan."

"Don't talk. Not now." His arm was around her again. He was leading her through somebody's back yard. People were milling around the place and at the back door of a house she could see a table set up with food and coffee.

"Hi, Duncan!" a girl called gaily. Ariel had heard the voice before. In the half light she could see a pale face, long dark hair, a bulky sweater, blue jeans—she had seen the girl somewhere before. But where? The girl lifted a camera, held it, and lowered it with a laugh. "Thanks a bunch, Dunkie. And Ariel!" She was gone.

She remembered. Vivi Vale—the girl at Phyllis's party for Lowell. The newspaper reporter. She had talked a while with her. Why had she taken a picture now?

"Sorry, Ariel. I thought this would be a shortcut. Don't worry about it. We'll take the road."

The narrow back row of small shanties led parallel to the main road, then descended beyond Big Moon's Diner. The crowd had thinned, the streets were nearly cleared.

He had not spoken or touched her again. As she got in the car she wondered about Nick.

"Will the building fall?"

"If you're worried, they strong-armed Orlini out of the area. Though his pretty milk wagon may be damaged."

She did not answer. She would like to remember Duncan in their earlier few moments of closeness. Not as the grim-faced stranger beside her.

To her surprise the house on West Street was fully lighted, Two cars stood at the curb. One she recognized as Willard's pick-up truck. Through the windows of the living room she could see figures.

"I won't take you in. I want to get back to Juno's Landing."

"That's all right. Thank you, Duncan."

"Before you go in, there's something I'm going to tell you. You'll hear it soon enough but since I've driven you home, I think it's only fair that you hear it from me."

"What is it?"

"Lowell has broken our engagement. She wrote a note to me and to her father and left town this afternoon."

If there was anything to say Ariel could not think of it. She could only stare at him and try to sort out the images cutting into her mind.

"Any further details you want, you'll hear inside." He nodded toward the house and swung the car door open for her.

"Duncan!" But the cry was lost in her throat. She heard the car fading into the night behind her.

The front door opened. Claude stood watching as Ariel came up the steps.

She had been crying.

Chapter Eleven

The lights of the *Thatcher Standard* office were burning late and bright.

Franklin P. McQuade, owner, publisher, editor, and sometimes night editor, sat at his desk, the green eyeshade he considered essential to his present function pulled low over his eyes, lending an eerie glow to his unrimmed spectacles. At his right, Craig Simpson, his assistant day editor and son-in-law, shifted impatiently. Opposite, Louise Vale stood watching him sternly, her camera clutched like a security blanket.

The *Thatcher Standard* had not had so much hard news to print since Curtis Plummer shot himself in his forty-eight room mansion up on Eagle Rock.

Frank McQuade should have been a satisfied editor. Two big stories—the cancellation of the Roundtree wedding and the factory fire. Either one would sell the paper out in the morning. He'd do the rewrites himself. Both stories would need new lead-ins. The copy was dull but fairly complete considering Craig had written them.

He could have given the whole front page to the factory fire. He had been writing editorials against the old eyesore for years, condemning it as a fire hazard, a menace, and the cause as well as the symbol of Juno's Landing's decay. And the human interest stories were there. Duncan Phelps had been able to clear the area of the last of the hyped-up kids. Big Moon had found Billy Haskell in Pete's Rock, the solitary occupant of the emptied cafe. Billy was happily playing the drums. Officer Schiller, off duty, had pitched in to head off traffic. A white sports car illegally parked had been crumpled by Bollington Engine #1. The car was later identified as belonging to Nick Orlini. It was towed to Cal's Wrecked Car Lot.

Frank McQuade concealed a smile. That would dismay no one in Thatcher.

The factory could certainly fill the first page and the middle section. His readers liked nothing better than local heroes. As the factory wall had buckled but not collapsed, it continued to pose a threat without tragedy. Now the Town Board would have to vote funds to rebuild or remove it. Frank McQuade would be well supplied for hot editorials for some time.

Craig shifted his thin moccasined feet again.

"Get me another cup of coffee, will you, Craig? There's a little left in the jug."

Frank McQuade pulled the second story toward him. It was a story much closer to Thatcher's hearts. It deserved the front page. In fact, he knew it damn well had to go on the front page. He had to admit Martin Roundtree had done it right. It took guts and it took character and it took something else. A quality, a knowing who you are. The Roundtree family might have run low on money, but they had not run low on anything else. Martin had telephoned the story in himself. "Mr. and Mrs. Martin Isaac Roundtree announce that the engagement of their daughter Lowell to Duncan Phelps has been terminated. Miss Roundtree has left Thatcher for a brief trip . . ."

His eye ran down the rest of the page. By God, it was right. A firm public statement. The gossips would have a thin time of it.

Craig returned with the coffee in a china cup with a matching saucer. It was Frank McQuade's one office indulgence. He disliked mugs and refused to use plastic cups.

"Thanks, Craig. We'll banner the fire story on the three right-hand columns. And give the Roundtree story a left column box."

"What about the picture, Mr. McQuade?" Vivi Vale had waited to pounce.

"All the fire pictures will go in the centerfold. They're very good, Viv."

"What about that one?"

Frank sighed. He knew it was the issue and could be postponed no longer. The print that Louise Vale thrust at him showed Duncan Phelps with his arm around a luscious girl. A stunner, he'd have called her in his day. He guessed who it was. He had not met her but he had heard his women folk talking about the French cousin, Ariel. The picture, under the circumstances, was sheer disaster. Not alone because Duncan's arm was around her or because her coat had swung open on a sweater, hinting at such a figure as was not often seen in Thatcher. What was striking in the print was the girl's expression, lips slightly parted, dark hair tumbled to her shoulders, eyes wide and luminous, a face he had seen somewhere before. The camera had caught Duncan returning that look, enigmatic, poignantly tender.

McQuade dropped the picture on the desk. "You have others just as good, Viv. More relevant."

"More relevant to what?" Vivi Vale did not smile easily. Her voice carried a whiplash.

"More relevant to the fire. That one for instance, at Pete's Rock."

"I didn't take that picture of Duncan and his friend as relevant to the fire. But it certainly is relevant to the big wedding that isn't coming off. We're reporting the news, aren't we? Everybody in this town has been gung ho on the Roundtree wedding. Suddenly, at the last minute, it's called off. No reason except what Martin Roundtree chooses to tell you. Well, you've got the reason right there."

Frank McQuade had known Louise Vale a long time. Through high school, through her long summers of protest marches, her long nights of defiance. He felt responsible for her in a way he could not explain. She was awesomely intelligent but assuming responsibility for her would be like trying to protect a tumbleweed.

He dropped the picture on the desk.

"We're not a gossip sheet, Viv."

"Gossip? Gossip? The big deal wedding is off. Why? There's the groom. And the other woman."

"That's an assumption. It could be libelous."

"A news photograph without a caption is seldom considered libel, Frank."

She was right, as Frank McQuade knew. He sipped his coffee and thought about the situation. Martin Roundtree, difficult as he was at times, stood for something that this town could ill-afford to damage or to lose. As for Edythe, Frank had long ago admitted to himself that if he had met Edythe first he'd have fought Martin to the finish for her. And won. He would not hurt either of them now.

"I'm not running it, Louise."

"To protect the Roundtrees?"

"It's my decision."

Young Louise Vale had buried her natural prettiness and her deepest longings under a mind too bright to bring her peace. A poster hung in her boarding house bedroom read "Love is a cop-out." Now it seemed that her whole being, her life's work was being threatened to protect someone else's happiness. She remembered Ariel Roundtree and her flaunted sexuality. Vivi Vale came back to the present.

"So this is a controlled press, Frank?"

"What the hell does that mean, Louise?"

"It's very clear. The public is entitled to know. The press should be free to inform. But you use this paper to protect the privileged classes. It's an instrument of oppression in the hands of the bourgeoisie to deny the right of the people the free access to truth."

Frank McQuade pushed up his eyeshade. "You read too many books, honey. Let's get to the layout."

But Vivi did not dare to lose. She had one card left. She whirled on Craig. "What do you say Craig? Are you willing to work for a controlled press? Or do you agree with me that the public has the right to see that picture?"

Craig sighed and wished he were home. Vivi could always put him on the spot. On the one hand it was Craig's careful policy to agree with this father-in-law. On the other, he did like to go to bed occasionally with Vivi, whose boney matter-of-factness provided relief from Phyllis's marshmallow softness.

"Well, what do you say, Craig?"

Frank McQuade glanced at them both over his spectacles. He had long recognized the inadequacies of his son-in-law. It sometimes gave him a perverse pleasure to watch Craig wriggle on his hook. He was not blind to Craig's wistful philanderings. But for God-only-knew-what reason, his only daughter loved the guy. Vivi with her starved hang-ups could make things very unpleasant for his child. She could make them even more unpleasant if she chose to show that picture around town.

He leaned back. "I'm willing to hear a majority vote. I admit I never thought of the *Thatcher Standard* as an instrument of oppression but all things are possible today. What do you say, Craig?"

Craig had no desire to say anything. His dilemma was unsolvable. Then a pebble of self-interest tipped the scale. He looked at the picture of the lovely Ariel. He remembered he would have liked to cozy up to her the night she came to Phyllis's party. She was French and willing, he figured. Instead she had turned her back on him for Rick, the fat hardware clerk. It had been a public rebuke. Craig still smarted when he thought of it.

"I think we ought to run it, sir."

Louise flashed him a triumphantly possessive little smile.

". . . but not next to the Roundtree story. I think maybe in the center fold with all the other fire

265

shots." It was rather neat, after all. Wisdom of Solomon sort of thing a man could take pride in.

"Thank you, ladies and gentlemen. Tell Gus we'll have copy and layout for him in thirty minutes."

Frank McQuade swung around to his typewriter. It was the solution he would have had to reach. He wondered how often a man's great dreams narrowed to compromise and the coddling of the young and the insensitive.

He inserted a sheet of paper in the machine. Whatever he had to do, he would match Martin Roundtree's dignity.

It seemed to Ariel she had sat forever in this subdued living room. She had said to them what Duncan had asked her to say. She had explained quite honestly about the fire. They had greeted her vacantly, listened inattentively, and Edythe, at her nervous needlework, had asked her to join them.

There was no discussion. Nothing was said to add to her knowledge. The room had the ordered polish of a house expecting company. On the table in the sunporch she could see the glistening array of wedding presents. She understood that Lowell had gone somewhere. If she expected to read accusation in their eyes, she was denied even that. They were turned from her.

It was as if someone had died, she thought. No, it was not that. They were sitting, waiting. Willard deep and silent in a chair, smoking his pipe. Edythe snipping her fragments of colored wool. Claude, her hands clenched, staring at nothing. Kim upright, the cage in her lap. Only Freddie, in his untroubled security, had relaxed into sleep. Ariel smiled at the child once, but the young eyes were so deep with fathomless emotion, that she dropped her own. Whatever had happened in this house in her absence would become her guilt. If they would only turn on her, if they would condemn her and let her go, if they would just speak.

It was the silence, the waiting. Then she realized that Martin was missing. They were waiting to take their cue from him. It was his voice that would thunder the *j'accuse*. Duncan had no right to let her walk in alone. She began dimly to realize that she was separated from him more widely now than by a dozen wedding vows.

"What *is* Daddy doing in there?" It was a child's cry from Kim.

"He's probably still telephoning, dear." Edythe put down her stitching. "Why don't you go to bed? I'll go up with you."

"I don't want to. Where do you think Lowell is?"

"We know where Lowell is, Kim. You father will tell you everything when he comes out."

So Martin was in his study. He would set things right for them all. Except of course for her, Ariel thought. How this family hung on him. Despite his fragility. Waiting for Martin. Waiting for Martin. All her questions dried in her throat. She felt her heart beating irregularly. Waiting for Martin. Waiting for the study door to open.

"You must be tired, Ariel. If you don't want to sit with us . . ."

"No, I'd rather be here." That was at least honest. She dreaded going upstairs alone, imagining what they would say. "I'm just terribly sorry about it all."

"We all are, Ariel. But it's better that Lowell knew her mind before—"

"I don't think she knew her mind at all." Claude jumped up restlessly. "I think she wanted to do something daring. For once. She'll come back and marry Dunkie, and I can wear my velvet dress up the church aisle." Her voice broke. "It's rotten. Just rotten." She flashed a sudden, lashing glance at Ariel and sat down abruptly.

So it was all there beneath the surface, under that well-bred politeness. If only the study door would open, the climax come, the blame pour out. As she sat in the stiff silence, her mind was running like a small desperate animal in a cage. She would leave this house by morning, she told herself.

Duncan. He was no longer Lowell's, if he had ever been Lowell's. At another level of the cage lay a wonderful, treacherous release. Whatever had happened, Duncan was free. Free to come to her?

The study door opened. Martin walked slowly into the room. Beside him strode a serious young man in lanky tweeds and horn-rimmed glasses. He would be the owner of the other car outside. He would be—she searched her memory. She had no recollection of his face. Then it came to her. He must be John, the second son. She saw the Roundtree resemblance, Martin's high forehead and thin features. Edythe's gentle expression. The irregular beating of her heart steadied. Martin could hardly treat her harshly in front of this newcomer.

If she had expected a broken, embittered man crushed by this sudden family disaster, Ariel found she had something to learn. Martin crossed the room firmly, his back straight, an air of renewed authority like a well-fitting coat on his shoulders.

"Good evening, Ariel." There was neither surprise nor hostility in his tone. But neither was there warmth. The tone of studied control was set. "You may remember Lowell's second brother, John. You met as children."

Ariel nodded and smiled. John said "hi" and held out his hand. At least it was a human touch. Ariel liked the tall, friendly young man with Edythe's smile. She would have liked such a brother beside her now. She wondered if they had told him. Told him *what?* Realistically, she knew the guilt for this broken wedding filled only her own mind. She had no proof yet how far its poison had spread. Kim? Kim avoided her now as she had since the night of Willard's supper. Kim's silence was profound. Claude's emotions were so near the surface that Ariel could not be sure that her occasional furtive tear was for a vanished dream or solid anger. Willard with his stoic pipe had smiled at her once or twice, matter-of-factly.

"Hi," she said to John. And dropped her hand. But a little of the cold tightness inside her lifted. Not a friend yet. Not an ally. But a warmth.

Martin was talking. ". . . so I finally reached Walter at his club. He assured me that Stanton House is a perfectly respectable small hotel on the West Side, for professional and working young women. So we know Lowell's all right. I admit I was surprised that Lowell knew that much about New York. To the best of my knowledge she had only been there twice. With you, Edythe."

"I'm glad she's safe, Martin."

"I was never worried about that. She came to a brave but apparently careful decision. She is very level-headed, and I was sure she would do nothing to worry us. As her telephone call proved. I admit I would have preferred her to go to Boston where Amory and Grace could have looked out for her—"

"Oh, Dad, they're old. *Old.*" It was a wail from Claude.

"I don't see that that has anything to do with it, Claude. Your Uncle Amory was a Supreme Court justice. He might have been governor of this state if he had sided with the Highways Commission instead of with the railroads. But he has his beliefs. Yes, I should have preferred that Lowell went to Boston. We have only Lillian in New York."

"Did you call Lili to tell her, Martin?" Edythe lifted her eyes from her needlework.

"I'm coming to that, Edythe."

"I wonder what Lowell will do in New York?" Claude was swinging between disappointment and drama.

"My hope is that she will take a few days to think things over and then come home where she belongs. It may be that this whole thing has been a little overwhelming. That she is not quite ready for marriage itself. In which case I am sure Duncan will wait. In fact, he has said he would. Or there may be a more profound reason."

The little silence following that remark rose like a tide around Ariel. But no one looked at her.

"I think we'd all better give Lowell a little time to herself," Willard observed dryly. Lighting his pipe spared him any further exchange.

"Of course we shall, Willard. That's the least we can do. Isn't it, Martin? Did you call everybody out of town and tell them?"

"That brings me to point two. I phoned Frank McQuade. He'll carry the story tomorrow. I will read you the complete announcement as I gave it to him. 'Mr. and Mrs. Martin Isaac Roundtree announce that the engagement of their daughter, Lowell, to Duncan Phelps has been terminated. Miss Roundtree has left Thatcher for a brief trip. Mr. Phelps will return to the Episcopal Seminary for graduate study.' "

Ariel caught her breath. Did Duncan agree to that, too? Martin, standing taller than she had ever seen him, was masterminding this farcical drama like a puppeteer. She herself would leave at once, but the image deep within her, the vision, was of Duncan following, of a mist-filled place far from this house, this town, where she and Duncan . . . she came back from her second's lapse to hear Martin's emotionless voice: " '. . . Mr. and Mrs. Roundtree and their family will be honored to receive all their friends as planned at the reception at their home Saturday at four-thirty in the afternoon.' "

"We're going to have the party?" gasped Claude.

"Your father and I have come to that decision," Edythe's head was high.

"But without a bride? Unless Ariel would like to substitute, like she did in church?" Claude's giggle was too high pitched to be genuine.

"I consider that remark unworthy, Claude."

"Dad, if I skipped all the remarks you consider unworthy I'd never open my mouth."

"Now we're getting somewhere, Claudie." It was the first time John had spoken. He was low-keyed and easy.

"You keep out of this, John! If you'd been around here like you should have been, maybe none of this would have happened!"

"Now what on earth do you mean by that, kid?"

"And don't call me kid!"

"That will do!" Martin snapped. "We're facing a crisis. And we're going to face it properly."

"Does that mean I have to go to the party, too?" Kim broke her silence, her face crumpling.

"You'll have a lovely time, Kim."

"I don't want to. Not without Lowell."

Martin looked at his youngest. For an instant, undisguised tenderness crossed his face, then he returned to his generalship.

"It means all of us, Kim. We've invited nearly two hundred friends to our home tomorrow. We shall receive them. We can do no less. As a matter of fact, I may use the occasion to announce a change in John's plans."

This was a surprise.

"What is it, Screwball?" Claude had forgotten her annoyance.

"Will you tell them or shall I, John?"

"You, sir."

"John is transferring to Yale to finish law this year, so he will be near home. And he is announcing for the primaries next year for the State Legislature." There was a flurry of voices. "It's about time we had a Roundtree in politics again."

Willard set down a cold pipe. "Well, that's fine, John. When did you decide that?"

"Dad and I talked about it this evening. With everything else."

So the pieces were all being fitted together again.

Ariel, watching in silence, could only marvel. And wonder. The family front, unbroken to the world. That was their strength. Whatever had happened within this proud circle, the break was seamed over. The name, the Roundtree image, remained. Now Martin was seeing to it again. The secret was sacrifice. Michael had defected and Lowell had been sacrificed. Now Lowell had defected, and John was stepping into the breach. Much as Ariel had longed for the closeness of this family, she knew now that she wanted only to escape, to fly free. She could never sacrifice her own budding identity to this family temple. Resolution came simultaneously with insight. She rose.

"If you'll excuse me . . ."

"In a moment, Ariel." Martin turned full toward her. "I know you must be tired. It's been a long day for all of us. But you are one of us."

Ariel sat down again. The chill of discipline lay in his voice.

"You came to us, Ariel, a week ago. We were deeply happy to have you. And as you wrote, you hoped to stay a little while with us. Edythe, I believe, wrote your mother that we wanted you as long as you would like. Certainly through Thanksgiving. That's the way it was arranged and announced. We expect you to stay at least that long now."

"I'm sorry, but I can't do that." The long day at last broke for Ariel.

"Why not?"

"Because, because. I'd already planned to leave Sunday. The day after the wedding. If there is no wedding I want to leave tomorrow!"

"You do owe us the courtesy of a reason." Martin seemed ten feet tall to her.

"I want to leave. There's no reason for me to be here now." Ariel's glance darted around the room. Six pairs of eyes seemed to be holding her prisoner, impaling her. "I feel very bad about Lowell and her wedding. But there isn't any point in my staying around."

"We all feel bad, my dear." Edythe came to her. "Yet if this marriage was not to be, we can only be glad that Lowell had the wisdom to realize it now. There is very much of a point in your staying around. We are all going to continue to live in Thatcher, to see our friends, to be part of the town. None of us has the right to run away in the face of something that must distress them as much as it does us. Of course you'll stay with us, my dear. We'll need you now, more than ever." She put her arm around Ariel. "Unless you have a reason you haven't told us."

It was Willard who came to Ariel's rescue. He emptied his pipe and rose.

"If you ask me, we're all tired. I'm sure Ariel will stay for the reception. Personally I hate the darned things. Too much noise, too many women, and too much drivel. But I quite agree it should be held. *Noblesse oblige*. And perhaps you'll make an old man happy by paying a visit to the farm. You made quite a hit with Charlie Redwing. He says the sun boy walks with you. And if you like big dogs, Clancy will be delighted to turn on his king-size brand of delirium for you." He patted her hand and turned to Martin. "You've handled things very well, Martin, as you always do. Now, about this factory fire—I'll drop in on Frank McQuade next week. Maybe we can get the old eyesore torn down now. John, my boy, I'm interested to hear of your new plans. Come and talk to me about them. Good night, Edythe, my dear. Difficult day, but as always you've managed with grace. Good night, children."

The old man was gone, his straight back defying time, his warmth taking the last embers of a dying fire with him.

At last Ariel could escape. But only to her room. This circle she had so deeply longed to join had snapped shut around her. They had said nothing.

They had said everything. If she stayed, as she must now, she would exist in a vacuum of silence.

She went numbly up the wide old stairs. She stopped in the dimness outside her room, aware of a small sound. She turned. Kim was standing, staring at her. Whatever light lay in the hall was gathered in the child's glittering eyes. Her arms encircled the little cage like a shield.

"You are a witch, aren't you?" The voice was a whisper. "A real one. You did it, didn't you? I won't tell. If you don't hurt Freddie!" She fled down the hall.

"Kim!" Claude appeared from nowhere. "What are you doing?"

Kim's door closed with a bang. Ariel and Claude stood looking at each other. The same blood flowed in them, the same intensity, the same passionate response to emotions.

In Claude, young, untested, that intensity took the shape of drama, of the present, of which she would not miss one instant. In Ariel, a passionate need to know the truth, to survive. Guilty as she felt, she had a deeper intuitive conviction that she was not to blame for Lowell's defection. That something beyond and outside her had happened to send Lowell flying from everything that was so right, so suitable.

Ariel could not have put it into words. She only knew, blindly, that if she let this moment of confrontation pass, she would have surrendered all that she most wanted.

"Claude, would you come in and talk to me?"

Claude hesitated. She had seen any time she chose to look, the striking resemblance Ariel bore to remote, mystery-shrouded Henrietta. Claude, in her most secret dreams, saw herself an Ariel some day . . . magnetic, glamorous, *different*.

Ariel held open the door to her room. In the darkness, the clearing night cast a bar of pale light across the floor. The old moon fading; the new moon coming. Hunter's moon. Not to kill but to *know*. That would be, for her, survival.

"Will you, Claude?"

"If you like. What do you want to talk about?"

"Lowell," said Ariel firmly. And shut the door.

Chapter Twelve

Duncan Phelps closed the door of the staunch little chapel that had seen so many hours of his private turmoil. He had waited for the last of the student congregation to go. Now, leaving it dark and empty, he crossed the Seminary's venerable campus, bowing his head to the sharp, dry wind.

He was angry with himself, furious at his failure. The student body had been polite. James Scammel had given him a sympathetic pat on the shoulder when it was over. It was that gesture that had finally triggered this blinding self-doubt. He was not, after all, an undergraduate, a novice terrified at the sound of his own voice. He had long ago preached with the uncertain stammering of a first sermon. By this time he should have been in command of himself and his thoughts. That pat on the shoulder bordered on tolerance.

The worst of it was he had thought the sermon good when he wrote it. Not that it would matter in the long run. He was here to fulfill his tacit bargain with Martin and to make things easier for all of them by removing himself from Thatcher.

He nodded to a few passing students in the dusk, first or second year men and women who regarded him with a respect that made Duncan uncomfortable. His story was well known, his war service, his 'call.' Not that it had been that way. He was not even sure what 'call' meant. It had been more like a desperate decision, the only way out of a maze.

He entered his dormitory and closed the door of his room behind him. Without turning on the light, he passed the Spartan iron bedstead and flung open the single window. A cloud of dust settled in the room like homesickness. October in this southern town was a visceral ache. The leaves of the great campus oaks browned until they dropped. And now freshness came with the night. Yet he had been grateful once for the G.I. grant that had sent him here. He would be again. Gratitude, he supposed, was part of godliness.

Duncan Phelps had never felt less godly.

He poured himself a glass of water. At that moment he would have given half his hope of salvation for a scotch. He had decided against keeping a half-pint under his mattress as he had done in undergraduate days. That was kid stuff. What you could get away with, in the eyes of God.

But there was no getting away with what he saw in himself now. He stood naked, beyond even the need of confession. Naked to himself, to his God and naked to his failure. For he knew the reason. He had wrestled with it every dusty hour of these numbing last three weeks.

He wanted her. He had wanted women before. In Vietnam it was what the guys talked about, especially after mail call. Safety-valve stuff. This was different. After the first startling shock of Lowell's letter, he had felt a deep and guilty relief, such light-headedness that he had had to bury it at once within him. When he had found Ariel, later that night, emerging from Nick Orlini's car—God knew where they had been so long—he had felt pain like a bayonet thrust.

All of that had passed. In the solitude of this fading day, with failure like an alter ego and his words like the dust in his nostrils, Duncan faced his demon. He wanted Ariel. Her face was on every page he read or wrote. Her presence was beside him. Her body shared the iron bed. But more than that, he loved her. It had been instant and final and if, in these three weeks, he had learned nothing else, he had discovered his own reluctance for sacrifice. He could not imagine a future without her.

But a future in Thatcher? Where he was committed to stay? His mother had written more than she realized in her first letter. "You will be glad to know, Duncan, that the reception really went off quite well, even without a bride and groom. Martin and Edythe do know how to handle things. Of course there were questions. Everybody managed to get into the dining room to look at Henrietta Roundtree's picture. And I must say Ariel's resemblance is startling. She seems like a nice girl. But of course there were questions. As if Ariel could have had anything to do with it! Everyone knows your deep devotion to Lowell. Whatever possessed poor Lowell I can't imagine, but I am hoping she will come to her senses. And know you are, too. As for the talk, whenever I hear it, I squash it all flat. You see, dear," Emily had written, her neat script scrawling in her concentration, "I'm being perfectly honest with you because I want you to know everything. I am sure it will all blow over soon. Hannah Poole has only so many customers, although it does seem that every woman in town suddenly needs a dress altered." That had brought a first smile to Duncan. His mother's mouselike activity concealed a primal force. With the smallest of needles she could find the jugular. "Martin and Edythe are holding up beautifully but I do think Martin is making a mistake in the solid family front. The sooner Ariel goes home, the better. As long as she is here, poor dear, there is going to be talk. I'm doing my bit. I'm having tea with them this afternoon. I do like the girl and I can guess she isn't happy. Meanwhile," Emily had finished triumphantly, "you are doing exactly the right thing, Duncan. Dr. Wilcox thinks so too. He told me how much he is looking forward to your taking the pulpit in January. You will be so well prepared. He said that your place in this town is secure. Isn't that nice?" Emily had taken another breath. "Don't despair, dear. Girls sometimes do hasty, foolish things on the eve of marriage. I'm sure Lowell regrets it already. Just be patient. But of course the wedding will *have* to be a very quiet one, now."

Emily had crowded a postscript onto the bottom of the page. "You will not believe this, Duncan, but for the first time in my life, I heard the word *witch* mentioned in Thatcher. It was Henrietta, of course. Everything that happens to the Roundtrees is blamed on that poor woman, dead these seventy years. How I'd like to have known her! I *adore* excitement!"

Duncan kept the letter. It was the only word of Ariel he had. Its normalcy served as an early tranquilizer. If the talk had centered around Hannah Poole, he knew most people—most thinking people—would dismiss it. Martin and Edythe had been right to keep Ariel with them. Her own dignity would be her defense.

But God, how he loved her. That damnable newspaper picture had told it all. But as he looked back, every look and every gesture between them must have told it, too. Told Lowell. He had done his duty; he had written to Lowell twice. She refused to see him. Her single reply only repeated what her runaway note had said. She could not marry him, she could not share the life he offered. She hoped he would forgive her.

It was behind him now. He could only hope that his mother was right, that it would blow over. Blow over enough so that he could at least write Ariel. The future would have to wait. He could only think in terms of each day, days marked by the futility of what he was doing and by his need for her.

The knock he was expecting came.

Dr. James Scammel, assistant professor of homiletics, entered. Dr. Scammel was only ten years older than Duncan but already he had the lean face of a Goya ascetic. He wore the clerical collar of the traditionalist. He had obviously made his peace with God, if not with life. Only his eyes showed human compromise. He was Duncan's closest friend.

"Okay, Jay, so it was lousy."

"That's not the word I'd use."

"Oh, come on! Unless you've got a better one, in four letters."

"I have, indeed. It was worse than lousy. It was dull." James seated himself on the bed. "I think on my way out I'll drop a note in the Suggestion Box. I recommend that at the next meeting of the Trustees they be put up overnight in Dormitory C." He bounced on the bed. "In the cause of penance, this mattress is excellent. But as an illusion of comfort! What's in it, small boulders?"

"I never noticed. Can we stick to the point, Jay?"

"If that's what you want."

"So I was dull. What do I do now?"

"I don't think *that* is the point, Duncan. But I'll answer your question. You write a better one. 'I will lift up mine eyes to the hills.' For heaven's sweet sake! Every novice starts with that. It's pretty, it's uplifting, if you'll excuse a pun."

"I won't. But go on."

"But it hasn't a damn thing to do with today. Help doesn't come from a jet stream, my friend. If God has anything to say to you, and I'm not sure he has, He'll say it where you can hear it." Richard stretched his long legs and walked to the window. "We need rain."

"I know we need rain. What else is on your mind?"

"A lot, my friend, a lot. Turn on a light, will you? I never could stand this twilight stuff. If a man's going to make a confession, I like to look him in the face."

Duncan turned on the single lamp. The light jumped at the bare white wall and back. "Will one hundred and fifty watts do?"

"Nicely." James reseated himself. "You're jumpy, Duncan, and that's not going to help anything. Now, I could come in here and tell you what to do next. Write another sermon and another and another, until you're saying something real. Then deliver it. Once, twice, a dozen times until you believe what you're saying. Eventually you'll get the sermon you want. It's hard work, it's tedious, but that's the way it's done. And you can do as well as the next man. Probably a lot better. But I don't think that's the point right now."

"It's what I wanted to hear."

"Sure it is. But it's not what I came in to say. That performance this afternoon tells a lot more about you than a lousy—your word, friend—sermon. And that *is* the point." James Scammel leaned forward with a steely directness that could have taken him into the halls of power, if he had ever recognized their existence.

"Duncan, whatever made you come into the ministry?"

Duncan felt his anger rising. He'd had enough without that.

"I don't think that question is fair. After one bad job."

"Fair? What's that got to do with it? It's the only question you have to ask yourself. If you're wise you'll ask it every day of your life. You'll be surprised how many different answers you'll give yourself."

"Okay. Today's answer is—I don't know."

Scammel surveyed Duncan with satisfaction.

"Good."

"So you think I ought to quit?"

"I think you're at the outset of success. If you'd said 'to give your life to humanity,' who doesn't much want it anyhow, or to serve God, who's got more lip service now than He needs, I'd have worried. But you *don't* know. That's not only hopeful, it's accurate. And you didn't know when you stood up and preached that mush today."

"That's right."

He did know, Duncan told himself, but he was not ready to share that with anybody. Especially not at this moment. Much as he liked Jay, the man had a way of putting him on the defensive. He had earned it but it was beginning to irk.

"What were you thinking about when you wrote all those words for delivery to a Christian congregation?"

Duncan jumped so abruptly from his chair, it tipped noisily to the floor. "Okay, Jay. That's it. I made a fool of myself. I disappointed everybody. But maybe you know too much about sermons and not enough about men. Have you ever wanted a woman?"

James looked at him a long moment.

"Yes," he said mildly. "Quite often."

Duncan replaced the chair and sat.

"But, of course," the older man added quietly, "that was some time ago. I'm the sort of man who has to conquer the lusts in order to believe in my job. Not that I've wholly succeeded."

"Sorry, Jay." He looked at his friend. He wanted to trust this man. "Ever tried it?"

"I can understand it." James touched his collar. "This is supposed to deepen a man's humanity, not diminish it."

"It isn't *a* woman, it's *one* woman."

"I suspected that was the trouble. Broken-off engagement, everything keyed to go. My advice is, either submit or subdue. Just don't live with it. High nuisance value, friend. Very high. You still love the girl."

Duncan hesitated. "I didn't mean just quick sex, quick relief. 'Better than burning,' to misquote Saint Paul. Hell, if I wanted a woman badly enough that way, I'd take a bus to the nearest town. Besides," he paused, "it isn't that girl."

In the silence, a night beetle buzzed outside the screen. A summer sound on this warm October night.

Scammel rose. "Well, I don't think I can help you on this one, Duncan. The usual formula is, sleep with the girl, marry her, or go wrestle the devil in the church tower and see who jumps first." His eyes were warm with understanding. "But keep whatever bargain you have made, for there is left only your honor."

James Scammel left as quickly as he had come. Duncan cursed himself softly. He had put it into words and it had sounded cheap. He had secretly hoped that his friend would tell him flatly he was not suited to his calling. Much as it would have hurt, it would have freed him. He could have returned to Thatcher, swept Ariel away with him, and "copped out." He saw that Jay Scammel had no intention of making that easy decision for him. "Keep the bargain you have made . . ." All Jay had done was to hurl him back on his dilemma and let him hang on its horns.

He pulled a book of selected great sermons from his shelf, then put it back. He walked to the window, looked into the warm darkness, and returned to his desk.

Because he wanted every link that would bring her near to him, he opened that morning's edition of the *Thatcher Standard*. Willard Roundtree had sent it. That shrewd old gentleman, Duncan reflected, always saw farther through a millstone than most.

An editorial on page 5 was marked. It was entitled "Tell It Not in Gath." Second book of Samuel, Duncan noted automatically. The article carried the subtitle; "Historical Note from the General Courts Record."

" 'Three hundred and two years ago this month, in the hamlet of Thatchers Corners, goodwife Mercy Witcomb was strapped to a dunking stool and dipped three times in the Birch River, as true and just punishment for her sin of gossip. In the opinion of her judges, her serpent's tongue had so enflamed the baser elements of the village that they had set fire to the house of Mistress Anne Barlowe, in the false belief that she was a witch. Mistress Barlowe thereupon suffered burns on face and body. It is hoped that the icy water of her accuser's chastisement will soothe her spirit if not heal her scars. Goodwife Witcomb has been forbidden to talk or hold converse in public for twelve months.' "

"The *Thatcher Standard* reprints this reminder of the evils of gossip because, in the opinion of the Editor, it is time that the malicious gossip running through our streets be stopped. It is a direct reflection on the family of one of our most respected citizens and on a visitor in our town. It serves no purpose but mischief making and can only add to the pain of a family which has already had its share of disappointment.

"We hope the vandals who splashed red paint on a prominent headstone in Thatcher Cemetery will be brought to justice."

Duncan drew a long breath. His agony was increased but his dilemma solved. He folded the paper under his arm and crossed the campus at a long lope.

The Reverend Scammel was holding an informal study hour in his rooms. Duncan brushed through the seated students.

"I have to see you, Dr. Scammel."

"I'll be free in thirty minutes."

"No. Now, please."

Scammel glanced at the younger man. Duncan's shoes were covered with dust, his hair tumbled, his face pale. He murmured an excuse and ushered Duncan into his study. "What's up?"

Duncan steadied his voice. "Jay, I'm leaving for Thatcher tonight."

"I'm sorry to hear it," the Reverend Scammel remarked gently. "Why?"

"Look." Duncan thrust the crumpled newspaper at him. "You told me an hour ago to fight the devil in the church tower. I don't have to. He's loose in the streets of my town. You won't believe it. I don't either. But I'm not letting that girl face that town's meanness." He stopped for breath. James finished the article and slowly folded the newspaper.

"How convenient."

"What? What the hell does that mean?"

"God moves in mysterious ways. So does the Devil."

"Get off it, Jay, will you? Maybe you've been holed up in this dead end so long you've lost your perspective. I mean, look, I'm sorry. But there's a girl in Thatcher taking a lot of flak over—over what my fiancée did—breaking off the marriage. But this!"

"Is there any truth in it?"

Duncan hesitated. The cluttered study stifled him. James's clerical collar irritated him almost as much as the gently patient voice. He would not bring Ariel's name into this place. "What difference does that make? It's nobody's business."

"Quite right. So you intend to return to Thatcher as you've been wanting to do, take the girl in your arms, and defend her from all evil. That's why I said 'how convenient.' "

"I don't get it, Jay"

"Temptation is almost impossible to resist when it makes us a hero."

"Don't preach to me now, for Christ's sake. I've got to see her."

"I think you do, Duncan. But that's another problem. The girl seems to have plenty of defenders. But if you're determined to go back to add coals to the fire, then you must go."

James was right. Duncan could only compromise Ariel and his own future,—*their* future, he liked to imagine—by returning to Thatcher now.

"What in hell should I do?"

"I've found that three days' thought is usually adequate to find a solution."

"Yes. Well, thanks, Jay."

By the time he reached his room, Duncan knew that neither three weeks nor three hundred would solve his dilemma. God answered those who sought His help. Maybe. But as he had learned in the dark loneliness of battle, God more often helps those who help themselves.

He stopped to make a telephone call. Then he returned to his room, packed his bag, and tried not to think.

Ariel walked rapidly along Main Street. Darkness came earlier now and added a dimension of excitement to the small-town stores. In another two weeks it would be Halloween. Shop windows already sparkled with orange and black bunting, grotesqueries of masks and false faces, cats and witches, and plastic jack o'lanterns. Ariel had never known an American halloween. The fantasy of it all delighted her. There would be trick or treat first, whatever that was. And a bonfire on the green afterwards with storytelling for the children. The town had found that it was the best way to keep mischief at a minimum.

The pungent October air, the passing of time, had lifted Ariel's spirits. And a certain steely resiliency had set in. It was three weeks now since Lowell's flight had shaken the town. Ariel had done what she was asked to do, had held her head high against what seemed at times a wall of hostility. Now the wall was beginning to lower, the furtive talk, the sly glances, the uncertainty as to what she would do next.

She was doing nothing, actually. She remained in the Roundtree house, with the family. But not part of it; never part of it, now. For beneath the everyday politenesses, the flow of restored routine, there was the unspoken censure. Ariel felt it. Why else would Lowell have done what she did? The wedding had passed into a determined, eloquent silence.

As the days passed, she found a curious fortitude in her isolation. She woke each morning to a sense of pitched battle. Let them say what they would. Let them talk—and not always behind her back. Let them fling a mesh of Henrietta's scandals around her, whatever they were. She no longer had any wish to know, for they were all outside herself. She stayed for the simple reason that she could not leave. Not until she could see Duncan, not until he would take her once in

285

his arms and all the world would dim to nothingness.

Every day was a test, a test for them both. She was thankful that he had the wisdom to stay away. She would not let herself think of a future. Only of one meeting, sometime, somewhere.

A horn blew close at the curb.

"Well, it's about time!" Nick Orlini stopped his new white sports car and jumped out. "Where in hell have you been, Ariel?"

"Oh, hello, Nick." She started on.

He grabbed her arm roughly. She remembered his strength. "Now wait a minute, baby. I don't deserve this!"

A passing woman gave her a curious glance and hurried along. Ariel shook her arm free.

"Nick, I can't stop to talk now."

"Oh, yes, you can. I've called you at least half a dozen times. Didn't they tell you?"

"I talked to you once, Nick. I said I couldn't see you."

"I remember. We've been closer than that, Ariel. I'm the kind of guy who wants a reason."

"Let's just say I didn't enjoy my last evening with you."

"At the apartment? Funny thing, I think you did. Still carrying the torch for the Deacon? He's all yours now, honey, but you have better sense. Let's have dinner tonight."

"Thank you, Nick." Her voice was gentle. She did not like discourtesy. "But I don't want to go out with you."

Nick smiled, slowly, with his teeth. His eyes had a narrow cunning. "That's frank enough. But not good enough. We'll leave it at that for now, though." He released her. "But in case you're worried about me, don't be. There's somebody else I can count on. Any time. See you, baby."

It was not in the words he used. It was in the tone.

Something knowing, tantalizing, cruel, that lingered with her. She went quickly into the stationery store.

"Evening, Miss Ariel." Bent, balding Mr. Slater, the proprieter, had been a friend ever since that rain-swept day she had met Duncan and they had held hands for a brief, hurting moment alone in the little store. So long ago, now. She had come back and back, always to relive that moment, always as if Duncan were there waiting. Now, after her encounter with Nick, it seemed a refuge.

"I got two of those French magazines you asked me for."

"You're wonderful, Mr. Slater," she glowed at him.

"Just let me take care of these customers and we'll see about that." A sheepish half smile wreathed his lined face.

His customers proved to be a lanky boy who looked familiar—he was busy fingering rubber false faces—and two women who were also familiar.

"Ariel Roundtree! How delightful to see you!" It was Hannah Poole descending upon her. "How chic you look. I always say that's Paris for you. I can always tell."

"Thank you, Mrs. Poole." Ariel moved toward the magazines.

Hannah Poole followed. "I haven't seen you since the—well, I guess we can't call it a wedding reception, can we? Such a charming afternoon, though. How is dear Lowell?"

"Very well, I believe."

"You hear from her?"

"Oh, yes."

"You personally?" Hannah Poole's black eyebrows rose.

"Hannah," a stocky, strong-featured woman approached. "Mr. Slater wants to know if he should wrap the book for you?"

"Oh, mercy, no. I was just looking at it, dear. Mr. Slater," she called, "I'm just taking a paper." She moved closer to Ariel. Not for anything would Hannah Poole have lost this moment of moving in for the kill. "I was just talking to dear Emily Phelps last week. Such a fine person. She tells me they've hardly a word from Duncan. Of course, it's not surprising but I wondered if you'd heard. I'm so devoted to that young man. I've watched him grow up. And I do worry."

"Hannah, for heaven's sake. Why would Miss Ariel hear from him when his own mother hasn't?"

Ariel remembered. This broad-framed, broad-faced woman had helped serve Willard Roundtree's dinner for Lowell and Duncan. She felt her face flush. That night so long ago, that tremulous, moon-shot night. She wondered if this woman, too, had guessed. She had been somewhere in the back of the room when she and Duncan had returned.

The woman was looking at her with a surprising kindness. "You don't remember me, do you, Miss Ariel? I'm Gladys Beemer. I was. . . ."

"Of course I remember you. You were at Uncle Willard's with us."

Gladys Beemer liked that. Ariel hadn't put on airs and said she was *serving*.

"Were you, Gladys? At the engagement dinner? You didn't tell me!"

"In the first place, Hannah, it wasn't the engagement dinner. It was just a party. And in the second place, I didn't tell you because you never listen. You're so busy telling what you know."

"At least I don't get it backstairs." Hannah withered her and turned a smile on Ariel. "Such happiness as there must have been that night. Those two beautiful young people. I will never get over it. I was absolutely dumbfounded when Lowell—"

Gladys Beemer settled her knit wool hat. "I wasn't."

"Whatever do you mean by that, Gladys?"

"What I said, Hannah. I was not dumbfounded or even surprised when Lowell Roundtree broke off that wedding."

"Mrs. Poole," Mr. Slater's voice rose from the counter. "You want this magazine here?"

"No, Mr. Slater!" Hannah shouted back. "I was only looking at it. I just want a paper, for heaven's sake. I'll pay you now. My goodness, Gladys, I don't think you have any feelings at all."

Hannah sailed over to the counter.

Gladys Beemer looked around furtively. Then she turned to Ariel. "I meant what I said, Miss Ariel. I've seen Miss Lowell when she was—well, different. And she didn't look at Duncan Phelps the way I've seen her look. And I say when your true feelings aren't in it, a girl's got no business getting married. Right?"

Ariel loathed gossip. She had heard too much of it in her mother's drawing room. And it had hurt her beyond repair in this town she had come to so hopefully. Nor would she descend even to an exchange with these two women who had trapped her with their chatter. Yet Gladys Beemer had no malice in her plain face, only an air of troubled compassion.

"Right, Miss Ariel?" she repeated.

"I don't know, Mrs. Beemer."

"I think you do, dearie. I wouldn't say this to everyone, certainly not her." She nodded her annoyance at Hannah Poole, searching her change purse at the counter. "But I've seen Miss Lowell when she was shining like a candle."

"She will again, Mrs. Beemer." Ariel took a tentative step toward the door.

"Maybe. But I remember it like yesterday. I was helping out at one of those fancy parties at the Country Club. All of a sudden I saw Miss Lowell there, dancing by, all in yellow and sparkling and looking up with all the stars of heaven shining in her eyes. A prettier sight I . . ." Gladys Beemer drew a sigh deep from her ample bosom. "Never saw her look like that before or since."

Ariel sensed there was more. She also sensed something she could not define in Mrs. Beemer's earnestness.

The bosom heaved again. "Like yesterday. How time flies! But it was a year ago last summer. June 16. I never forget dates. Mrs. Orlini gives one of them parties every year. You know. The ones who are building that ugly house on the Ridge. Then Mr. Duncan came back from Seminary and there was the engagement party at the Roundtrees'. But I said to myself. . . ."

"Gladys!" Hannah Poole had reluctantly edged to the door. She had lost the advantage but there was no point in letting Gladys have it any longer. "Are you coming or are you going to stand there gabbing all night? So charming to see you, Ariel." She flapped a long hand. "Love at home."

Ariel was barely aware that they had left. Something that had been formless was taking shape in her mind, something she would not name.

She warmed Mr. Slater again with a smile and paid for her two French magazines.

"Gotcha!"

She felt her arms clutched, turned and screamed. A monstrous head, bulbous green and purpled, fangs bared in a nightmare of savagery, was grinning at her.

"I know who you are. Betcha don't know me!" The voice was hollow but very young.

Mr. Slater leaned across the counter. "Billy Haskell, you take off that mask before you scare people to death."

"Aw, you spoiled the whole thing."

Ariel leaned weakly against the counter. She had never seen anything like it and her heart was beating like a jackhammer. She pulled herself together. The boy had not yet taken off his mask, and she forced herself to look at it again. It wasn't any worse, maybe, than what one saw at Le Grand Guignol or even the Children's Guignol in the Luxembourg. But someone had fashioned into that pliant rubber face all the evil, all the ghoulish savagery that could lurk in the depths of human nature.

"Take that thing off, Billy."

Billy yanked it off and flung it on the counter. "There are going to be a lot worse on Halloween. You'll see!"

"Halloween is one thing. Scaring innocent people is another."

She felt sorry for the boy. There was something lonely in his thin, defiant face. He had only played a joke.

"So you're Billy Haskell. How did you know who I am?"

The defiance lingered. "I know."

"Then tell me."

His fingers clawed the air in a mock voodoo ritual. "You're Duncan's girl friend." The young voice turned hollow. "You're the witch woman who came out of the gravestones to take him away!"

Mr. Slater made a dive for him but like quicksilver he slid to the door and laughed.

"That's what Kim says."

Mr. Slater shook his head and picked up the mask. There was a rip at the back of the head.

"Don't pay any mind, Miss Ariel. The kids today . . . I don't know what's in 'em. Used to be a time I could sell Pluto masks and the Three Little Pigs and Buck Rogers and Flash Gordon. Even the Green Dragon, a hot seller in those days, was baby stuff compared to this. All horror and violence. Seems they can't get enough. The worse stories they can make up the better they like it. Especially at this time of year. You just forget it." He tossed the mask aside. "A two-fifty item. Now it's good for nothing."

"I'd like to pay for it, Mr. Slater."

"Now that's not necessary. No, no."

"I mean I'd like to buy it. Really."

"What would you do with a thing like that?"

"I might wear it on Halloween."

She smiled and the single dimple flashed. What had his wife called it when she regaled him with all that talk after the wedding hadn't come off? The Devil's Kiss. It was all rot and he was ashamed he had ever listened. He liked this girl. She was prettier and had nicer manners than any he'd seen for quite a spell. And if Duncan had looked at her twice, well, what man would blame him?

"Miss Ariel, if you want a mask for Halloween I'm not going to sell you damaged goods. I've got some real pretty ones."

"I want this one."

"Look at the rip."

"I don't mind. Two-fifty? There. Good night, Mr. Slater, and thank you for getting me the magazines."

She was gone, taking with her the brightness from Mr. Slater's little store.

The rambling old house was sparingly lighted, as usual, when Ariel let herself in. The hall was dim, the dining room dark. Through it she could see the light from the kitchen and hear voices. Edythe. Claude. And yes, Kim. Kim, her darling and innocent enemy. She did not believe what the boy Billy said. Whatever fantasy Kim had spun must have filtered through a dozen horror-loving, narrow minds. Hadn't she filled her own lonely childhood with fantasies that had carried her from the back of the winds to the dark side of the moon? In the end, she had bought the wretched rubber mask to confront her own silly terror and demolish it. She would drop it in the refuse bin tomorrow.

She had another purpose now, and Billy Haskell's antics had delayed her. She listened. The voices blended busily in the kitchen. Martin's study door was closed. She ran quickly, quietly, up the stairs. She was troubled by what she intended to do. "Compromise with one's principles means weakness," Mam'selle had taught her. It could also mean life itself, Mam'selle, her future, the very air she would breathe.

She passed her own darkened room and pushed the door open into Lowell's empty one. She had been in it only two or three times. She realized how far apart she and Lowell had been, their separate worlds touching at only one anguished point. She found the small desk lamp and turned it on, hoping it was not visible from the kitchen. The weeks in this centuries-old house had not yet taught her all its twists and angles.

The room already had an unlived-in look. Neat, dusted, and everything in its place as if someone—no, something had died. The heirloom wooden doll spread with even folds of its calico skirts against the bed pillow. The patchwork quilt lay precisely triangled at the foot. The cherrywood dresser and desk showed recent polish. And the souvenirs, a girlhood forever past. Beneath the gold-and-blue pennant of Thatcher High hung a picture of Lowell's graduating class, already dated. The closet door, half open, revealed a few clothes on wooden hangers. The wedding dress in its cellophane shroud was gone, a white chrysalis from which Lowell had escaped.

There was no full-length mirror in the room. Ariel had a fleeting image of her own bedroom at home. Had Lowell never stood looking at her own budding body, imagining a lover's hands touching, caressing until she fell weakly on the bed in a first ecstasy of young, unexplored desire? Had she never felt . . . ?

Ariel remembered her purpose. The desk was clear except for a very small, silver trophy cup, "Runner up—Senior Tennis Doubles." She opened the drawer. In it lay a dark brown imitation-leather date book.

Ariel drew a quick breath. There was no other way. She riffled the pages; June 16. There was one entry. Dentist 1:30.

Ariel shut the book. So much for gossip. So much for her own evil intentions. She put the book back in the drawer, then glanced at it again. It was this year's datebook. Mrs. Beemer had said a year ago. Last year.

Last year's date book. Did she dare look through all the drawers? Girls often kept their old date books.

"Ariel!" Ariel whirled. Edythe Roundtree was standing in the doorway, her face a study in surprise.

"Oh, Aunt Edythe."

"Whatever are you doing, dear?"

Ariel suddenly wanted to throw herself into the arms of this warm, sweet-faced woman, and talk and talk until she had poured out her love, her hopelessness, her anguish. Instead, she stood rigid. Even if she had found what she had come for, she would never tell. What would be solace for her would be agony for Edythe Roundtree.

"I love this room, Aunt Edythe. I wish—" Emotion shook her voice. "I wish everything could be turned back to the day I came." She meant it.

Edythe looked at her closely. "I'm not sure that would be for the best, dear. I was afraid when I saw the lamplight up here that something was wrong."

"No, nothing, Aunt Edythe."

"Will you do me a favor? I'm running late. Willard will be here in twenty minutes. He hates to sit downstairs alone. Will you dress and take over?"

Edythe vanished as abruptly as she had appeared.

Ariel hesitated. There was no time now to search. Nor did she want to, now. She had seen the question in Edythe's eyes. She had missed her chance. On an impulse she scooped up all she had found with the innocent date book, turned out the lamp, and hurried to her own room.

She would dress quickly but first . . . she sat on the bed, slowly turning the sparsely filled pages. There were few entries after June 16. It was as if Lowell had put the date book away. As if her life had been so full, so ordered, or so empty that there was no need to remind herself of anything again.

Except on June 17. In the blankness of that week, Lowell had written this poem. In her neat, square penmanship, she had penned: "So forever do we pass on the stairway of Life, proffering each our flowers to some figure with averted eyes."

In the next month, on July 12, she had written only: "Duncan arrives tomorrow."

The final entry, July 15, read "Dad wants a formal wedding."

Ariel closed the book gently, ashamed of having looked into its spare intimacy.

But she thought she knew at last whose eyes had been averted from Lowell's outstretched gift.

Despite Edythe's cherished notion, Willard Round-tree had no objection to sitting alone anytime, anywhere. He not only enjoyed solitude, he had learned to prize it. A gift of the years, perhaps. But he had always believed that man was more than a herd animal. Men clung to the group because they felt threatened. Had always felt threatened. Only a man who had outgrown this immaturity could discover his inner wealth, his true humanity.

A pity, Willard thought, that the young could not be taught this.

A faint pulse of strident music from somewhere upstairs mocked him.

Willard smiled. He was out of step. Where would any youngster today find the solitude to look into his own unique world? The whole system was a conspiracy against solitude. Yet, he thought, fundamentals do not change nor does human nature. Some must find solitude to grow outside the herd . . . or where was progress for any of them? He suspected Ariel was one who had found it. She had an inner firmness. She had had to look to her own resources.

He was anxious to see her. It was the reason for his inviting himself to dinner.

"I got that damnable music turned off." Martin walked into the room. "Good evening, Willard."

Willard rose.

"Don't get up, Will. No need to do that."

"My need, Martin. Not yours. Good evening." Martin had a new briskness these days, a new air of authority. Good for him, of course. Very good, yet somehow, at this moment, Willard found it irritating.

"You're looking well, Martin."

"Feeling better. A lot better. One adjusts, doesn't one?"

"I've always found one has to," said Willard, dryly.

Martin took his own deep chair, which Willard had been careful to avoid.

"I talked to Lowell last night."

"How is she?" Willard sought refuge in his pipe. It was the only shield he permitted himself.

"She's taken a job. I can't say I like that."

"Why not?"

"Because, damn it, that sounds too permanent. She tells me it's with one of those secretarial service offices, filling in where an office needs extra help or temporary replacement. You know the kind of thing."

"Lowell was always good at her work. Expert secretary."

"She had a good job here in Thatcher."

"You can't expect her to come home yet."

"I don't, of course. Not yet." Martin tried to sound convincing and failed. He scratched his knee, a signal of impatience.

Willard sat back easily. "Well, Martin, I don't think you have anything to worry about. Lowell had the grace to call you."

"She didn't have the grace to call me. She hasn't shown any grace in this whole affair, or she wouldn't have walked out the way she did. I don't blame the girl if she didn't want marriage. A lot of girls don't. But there's a way to do these things. A proper way, within the family. Lowell has shown damn little grace about any of it. As a matter of fact, I had to call her last night."

Willard forbore to ask why. It was plain in Martin's

face. Beside, Willard's chief business in this house was a kind of disloyalty in itself. He puffed on his pipe.

"It's all too bad but these young people have to work out their own destinies. Not much we can do."

"I believe there's a great deal we can do—we must do—if we're to preserve a family. Oh, I know. I can hear it every time we talk, Will. You think I'm on my children's backs. I should let them fly away wherever they want. Well, I've lost one son. Four years ago he walked out of this house. God knows where he is tonight, but where he ought to be is right here in this room. If a family means anything, it means ties, ties of blood and upbringing, a place where you belong and will come back to, whatever you do with your life. That's what I believe in, Will. That's what I live for." He drew a long breath. In the hall the great clock measured a few more relentless seconds.

Willard heard it. Martin sat silenced by his own thoughts.

"This family will come back. My father told me that. He never got over what he called his failure. He held the family's trust. He managed the funds. He lost it all."

"Very few men saw the crash coming in 1929."

"Some did. Father felt he should have. But he believed until the day he died that we'd come back. 'We're Roundtrees,' he used to say to me. 'Never forget that. Roundtrees have a place and they'll hold it if they hold together.' "

Martin stood up abruptly.

"My God, Will, you must believe that or you wouldn't have hung onto that land against the biggest offer you'll ever get for it!"

Martin seemed to need an answer.

"I believe it, Martin. Even if I didn't, I wouldn't do business with Orlini."

They were on safer ground now. Martin retired behind his screen of objectivity. "Well, you can forget Orlini, Will. I heard from Harlan today that Orlini has withdrawn all offers for the land. I'll send you a copy of his letter."

"Good," said Willard easily.

But beneath his ease, his mind had turned terrier-alert. Orlini giving up? Not little Ben. And, more assuredly, not Julia, not that demonic and devious priestess of the dark soul.

But he had no time to think of Julia Orlini.

"Good evening, Uncle Willard." Ariel came toward him with the grace of a blown leaf. He kissed her hand with old-fashioned courtesy, patted her cheek, and sighed himself back into ease. She had a way of brightening a moment. And a room. And a man's life.

Claude followed, then Edythe. Kim was missing. She had gone to Mrs. Haskell's story-reading hour at the Library.

The table was small but complete. Ariel had made a place for herself in this family, thought Willard, awkward as it was.

He waited restlessly until dinner was over. Then, with a coffee cup, he sat beside her on the divan.

"How are you, my dear?"

"I'm very well, thank you, Uncle Willard." Her love, her pain, sat between them like an open secret.

"You look as if you could use some country air."

"Country air!" She laughed, aware of the wisdom in his eyes. "I've been breathing it ever since I came here."

"You can't breathe country air in a town house. Let me tell you about this house. The man who once owned my farm, old Nathaniel Thatcher, got tired of rural life. Felt he needed a little more society, culture, and high living. So he bought this house for what he called his town house, spruced it up, added to it, and spent his winters here. When spring came around he'd move out to the farm—for the country air.

Her laugh was a tonic. "But that's only five miles away."

"Five miles in those days was a far piece. Still is, in

some ways." He glanced at her sharply. "Yes, indeed. I recommend country air. When are you coming to pay me that visit?"

"I—I don't know yet."

"I do. I'm driving into town tomorrow morning with a load of pumpkins for the Boy Scouts. They sell 'em for Halloween in the lot behind the school. I'll pick you up on my way back. Two-thirty. Will you be ready?"

She hesitated, trying to find her way between the lightness of his words and the seriousness behind them.

"Yes," she said quietly. "I'll be ready."

Ten minutes later, Willard made his troubled way home.

Willard arrived the next afternoon ahead of time. Ariel was ready and alone. He took her one bag and asked no questions. Now, under a sky of clouds that billowed darkly from the horizon, he drove steadily, purposefully along the winding country road. Ariel, beside him in the pick-up truck, welcomed the silence.

No one had minded her leaving. She sensed something near relief even in Edythe's durable kindness. Had she outstayed their need of her? If so, she would know it when she returned. Yet the thought of leaving Thatcher was still intolerable. Uncomfortable as she was in that house, it was her only link to Duncan.

Duncan. That was the core of it. She had heard nothing from him, of course, or even about him since he had gone back to the Seminary. She had endured the glances, the whispers, the open gossip, and even the newspaper editorial whose innuendoes had only made things worse for her. If it had stopped the gossip, it had not erased the momentary silences when she appeared, silences quickly covered with artificial greetings. She had borne it all because there was Duncan, somewhere, and now he was free. Or was he?

For the unadorned fact remained: if she had not come to Thatcher, Lowell and Duncan would now be married, as the town wanted, as the Roundtrees expected. If, as she discovered, Lowell had a secret, deeper love, hadn't Alicia told her that the Roundtree women give their hearts once? If they lose, they go on. As Lowell might have gone on.

Whatever Lowell's secret impulses before that abrupt flight, there was no doubt in Ariel's mind that she was part of it. She thought hotly of the bizarre role she had played in the wedding rehearsal, when her face must have betrayed her. Then her escape from the church with Nick as the only way out.

However tangled the threads, Ariel knew there was no way to lessen her guilt in the town's eyes. As long as she remained in Thatcher, she would be branded.

But Thatcher was Duncan's world.

She shifted restlessly as the truck jolted.

Willard gave her a sharp glance, then smiled. "No way to escort a lady, I guess. There was a time I'd have called for you in a carriage and pair."

She found she could laugh. That was more of Alicia's teaching. "Never thrust your troubles on a man, my dear. They simply bore him."

"You're not that old, Uncle Willard."

"No. But my sentiments are. Best way in the world to travel. Behind a fine, high-stepping pair of sensible horses. That's what your great-great-grandmother thought, too."

"Henrietta?"

"Yes. Nothing she liked better than driving her spanking matched bays around town. My Uncle Amos used to tell me that!" He laughed, glad to see the brightness returning to her face. He would go on talking to keep that stricken look from her eyes. They hadn't much further to drive.

"Yes, indeed. She cut quite a figure. She'd ride a horse like the wind over these hills. Or else she'd put on her latest Paris hat and sashay out, driving those bays. It annoyed the townsfolk plenty. Connecticut Puritans to the last shoe button. And God-fearing old

Isaac, her husband—he saw the Devil in everything she did. But he couldn't resist her. No more than anyone else could."

"Was she really beautiful?"

"You've seen her picture every day you've been here. All that wild lovely hair, that Mona Lisa smile, that one dimple. The Devil's Kiss, they called it. Look in the mirror, my dear."

Willard, she realized, had the heart of a gallant. Or else he was teasing her into good humor.

Willard steered deftly around a narrow curve and winked at her. "There's another portrait of Henrietta in the Roundtree Room in the library. Put it up there myself. I figured if old Isaac was up there for his benefactions, she ought to be there, too. Bonnet and shawl, hair tight, and no sign of the Devil. The way he wanted her. But that wasn't what he married her for. Not by a country mile."

The wind had risen, bending the trees, spinning the last, faded leaves earthward.

"More rain coming," said Willard. "We've had too much already. Used to mean bad flooding in the town. We've got a dam now but I never thought they put it in the right place."

But Ariel was looking out to the valley where a woman so much like herself, yet so different, had come, a stranger, because she loved a man.

"But what did she do? Henrietta, I mean. I've heard so many awful hints. Even witchcraft."

"It isn't what she did, my dear. It was her flair, her style. In a town as set as Thatcher, without much to look forward to, they get to raising a regular crop of gossip over anything that's different."

"I know, Uncle Willard."

He grinned and patted her hand. "They called her a witch because they were a little short on vocabulary, outside of the Bible. You know the story about Colin Thatcher, who tried to prove Isaac Roundtree had no right to the land Nathaniel Thatcher had willed him.

Well, he never proved it, but his eye fell on Henrietta and the Devil was loose. I don't believe she looked at him twice. Why, Henrietta could have been a duchess if she'd ever wanted to pull up stakes. But Isaac let go with fire and brimstone and Colin left town. Some said Isaac bought him off. But nobody knew the facts or ever learned them. Within a year, Henrietta was dead."

"Dead?"

"No one knows how. The records of that year went out with the flood."

"She died young, didn't she?"

"Henrietta? Forty-seven wasn't so young in those days. Not for a woman who'd had ten children. But from her pictures, I'd guess she never looked more than thirty. Isaac raised up that monument in the cemetery, closed the house in Thatcher, and sat out on the farm for twenty-three more years. Read his Bible and said nothing. Nobody even dared show him sympathy. They buried him up there with her and took their curiosity out in gossip." He glanced at her. "Still do."

He turned the truck into the narrow dirt road that led to the farm.

"I never should have come here, Uncle Willard."

"Think not?"

"Yes, I do. I had no idea about Henrietta. Or that I looked like her. Or how people could talk. I shouldn't stay any longer."

"If you're anything like her, you'd never use that word."

"What word?"

"Should, shouldn't. She lived boldly and honestly. My mother once told me she kept a diary. But if she did it must have been lost in the flood, too."

The farmhouse was in sight now. She looked down the long valley. What had been so riotous, so splendid in September brilliance, now stretched mute and lonely to the hills. How quickly it had all changed. Yet it would remain forever the same.

The wind whipped a dead branch across the dirt road and sent a flurry of unresisting leaves against the windshield. She sensed the waiting sadness of autumn. Yet something deeper stirred within her, a kinship to these empty, enduring hills that rolled to the sky, as if the land were waiting for her. As if, as if, she thought wildly, against hell-fire and brimstone, against all that happened, she would someday belong. With Duncan.

Ariel lost herself in her own emotions, so new, so intense that she wondered whether any woman in the world had ever known them. Even Henrietta.

Willard glanced at her, satisfied. The truck jolted to a stop. Clancy, the huge red setter, his mouth wide and drooling in joy, bounded down the steps of the farmhouse.

"You go on in," said Willard. "I'll drive down to the barn and let that scalawag Indian unload the three bad pumpkins he put at the bottom of the pile. The scoutmaster once tried to talk Tarzan language to Charlie and he's been avenging his dignity ever since." He swung the truck door open. "Make yourself at home, Ariel. I have a morning's work to do. Come on, Clance. You get to ride."

The big dog leaped into the front seat. Ariel waved and turned toward the house. How many eons had passed since that first evening when she had walked uncertainly, with Duncan, up those steps. The days had lost their perspective. Quickly, with the first drops of rain at her back, she opened the front door.

He was standing in the center of the room, wearing a worn windbreaker, his blond hair rumpled, his eyes hungry.

"Duncan!" It was a choked whisper.

His arms closed around her in a completeness that banished time and place and all awareness except of each other.

* * *

They walked in the rain. They clung to each other. They walked on, heedless of their damp clothes, their water-soaked shoes, their rain-splashed faces. It was as if they wanted to savor each of the small steps of love, surprised by its reality into silence.

They stopped at last in the shelter of dark pines. He caught her in his arms, felt again the softness of her body beneath the clinging dampness of her clothes. Yielding, giving, as it would be for the rest of their lives. But because it would be for the rest of their lives, he would hold to this unspent sweetness for just a little longer. Something had to be said first. Something he could guess that, in her sensitivity, she would want to hear.

"Ariel . . ."

But she put her hand across his mouth. "Don't talk. No words, Duncan. Not yet."

Clinging together, their private world was walled by the tattoo of rain on pine needles.

He released her and found her hands. "Ariel, will you marry me?"

Because it was their private world and all the uncertainties lay far outside, it was easy.

"Yes," she said, as simply as the drop of a flower.

He leaned back against the trunk of an aging pine tree. "Do you know how long I've wanted to ask you that?"

She answered his grin with mischievous eyes. They had reached a new plateau of confidence. But the weeks of denial had taken their toll. A certain strangeness, a shyness, lingered in this sudden dazzling freedom.

"How long?" She asked lightly.

"Since . . ." he stopped. "That's all past. It's us now. Isn't it?" His grin was gone. His voice roughened. "Isn't it? Isn't that what's it all about? We're going to be married."

Now it was here, that outside world. It had come too soon.

"We still have to talk about it, Duncan."

"Talk about what? The past? All right." A half grin returned. "The winter nights are long here, my darling. We can sit in front of the fire and talk until hell won't hold it, if that's what you want. I have better ideas."

"You make it sound so easy, Duncan." She shivered.

"We're going to make it easy. Look, you're getting wet and cold. Let's go."

"No, not yet. Duncan, I said I'd marry you. It's all I want. But do you think I could live here as your wife and—and be a help to you? After what's happened?"

He sighed. Then he took off his windbreaker and wrapped it around her.

"Duncan!" she protested.

"This sweater would keep out a fall of buzz bombs. You want to talk now? Okay. I suppose it's about Lowell?"

It wasn't but she let him go on.

"I wrote Lowell twice. I tried to call her. She finally wrote me one note. I can show it to you. It's over. She calls it a mistake. She blames no one."

"Duncan, I'm not talking about Lowell. I know what she did. I know . . ." There was no use going into that. She caught her breath and began again. "It's this town. It's Thatcher. They blame me. You don't know how it's been."

"I can guess. Don't you think I've thought about that? They won't dare when we're married."

Did he really believe that? Did he know so little about human nature, its jealousies, its meannesses, the petty scheming she had grown up with in her mother's drawing room? She realized how little she and Duncan really knew each other. She longed for him so that her body, like her mind, ached. But the enemy was there, just beyond the warmth.

"Duncan, I love you. I've said I would marry you because I—I didn't know how to say anything else. But your work is here, your church is here. If they wouldn't accept me, if they don't want me—"

"Who is 'they' ?"

"This town, the people in your church. Don't you see, Duncan, how hard it would be for you?"

"I see only one thing. I'm an idiot to ask a girl brought up as you've been to share my life. But I have asked you because I love you. I love you in a way that I never believed possible for any man. My mind, my body, whatever I am as a man. I want you with me as long as I live. I know this."

The rain had let up. The last pattering drops sounded like drum beats to her in the silence.

"But your work, Duncan. Your church."

He whirled on her, his face taut. "Don't you think I've thought of that, too? Do you want to tear me to pieces? Because I can do that for myself. I made my commitment. I thought it was forever. Then I met you. I'm not a saint. I know, God help me, what it is to kill a man. I know what it is to take a woman without any thought for her. I went away from this town a spoiled kid. I came back . . ." He stopped and looked at her, so slight and so proud, and realized again his desperate need for her.

"What the hell does it matter? I came back and met you. If that makes me human, if that means I'm not fitted, not called, whatever the words are, I'll find it out. Maybe I'm finding it out now. It won't be easy for us. But I don't have to stay here."

"You mean, you'd go to some other church?"

"If I don't make it here, I wouldn't want another church."

"Duncan, you will make it here!"

"There are other ways to make a living." The harshness drained from his face, leaving his eyes warm and a half grin twisting his mouth, boyish, vulnerable. "You see, I'm not offering you much, Ariel. You can think it over as long as you want."

"Well?" He was looking at her with a tenderness she had never seen in any man's face.

"There's nothing to think over. I love you, Duncan."

She was in his arms a moment more, so close that she felt his body hardening against her own.

Abruptly he let her go and they walked out of the pine woods, hand in hand.

"When will I see you again, Duncan?"

"I'll pick you up at six o'clock for dinner. By that time you should have figured out a date."

"A date?" It was still unreal to her.

"Like next week or the day after tomorrow or whatever the law allows. It can't be too soon for me. I'd like to tell my mother. She's stood by me through an awful lot. And Dr. Wilcox."

"Not yet!" It burst from her.

They walked through a small silence. "Okay," he said. "Okay. It's up to you. Not quite sure, are you?"

"Yes, I am sure, Duncan. You know that. But it's so new. We have so many things to settle." Even as she spoke she knew that doubts now could only damage them. Nor could she have put them into words. They were as ephemeral as the glances that slid past her in the streets.

Without being aware of it, they had stopped walking.

"Ariel, has anything happened while I've been away?"

"Like what?"

"I'll be blunt. Because we'll have to talk about it someday. Like Nick Orlini."

"I haven't seen Nick."

"Has he called you? Tried to date you?"

She had forgotten Nick in her tumultuous happiness. He was at a distant, past perimeter of her life. Yet she was honest with herself, as she wanted to be with Duncan. She had used Nick Orlini to screen out the anguish of that wedding, to conceal her own awakened feelings. She had been foolish and, as Alicia had warned her, there was always a price.

"He called me twice, Duncan. I told him both times I wouldn't see him. I never want to again. I only—"

"I'm not censoring you!" he interrupted. "Where the hell would I get off doing that? But he did pick you up at the church—and the night of the fire . . ."

There it was—an open, angry wound.

Ariel turned with a helpless shrug. "I have a lot of faults that you don't know anything about yet. I don't think twice. I often just let things happen because they look exciting. And because I really don't care. Nick was there. Like somebody I'd met a hundred times in Paris. He meant nothing. He never really had a face. No man ever had until I met you."

"Did he make love to you?"

"He wanted to. The answer is no."

"Okay. I'll live with that. Because I have to, Ariel, I want to say something to you. I want you to try to understand it. We fell in love against all odds. I never believed anything like this could happen but it did. We're free now to have each other." He paused, and for an instant he was like a stranger, taller than she had realized and bigger against the open hills.

"You don't know me. I don't know you. And we won't for a long time. That's part of marriage. It's no wonder you have doubts. So do I! I'll do the best I can with my life. But I can't offer you what a man like Orlini can. I can't offer you anything like the life you know."

"I don't want it!"

"But I love you, Ariel. I'll love you as long as I live. If I fail you or you fail me, if you should reject me or leave me, it wouldn't change my loving you. It would only change how we live."

"I couldn't leave you, Duncan. I couldn't go on living . . ."

"Yes, you could. So could I. But what happened between us—you can never change that."

She had never heard such words. It was a kind of vow; it frightened her a little. Standing there against the angry sky, his shoulders braced against the wind that bore down from the empty hills, he had the strength of the land itself. A strength she had never known, much less tested. Whatever happened, she was bound to it.

He pointed to the barn. "There's my old green puddle-hopper. Shall we drive up to the farmhouse?"

"I'd rather walk." She put her hand in his. "For good, Duncan?"

His strong fingers tightened. "For very good, darling."

Pumpkins had their uses, Willard reflected. They had brought Ariel to where she belonged, given Charlie his little revenge. He himself would have liked to walk out to his harvested acres and thank Charlie's corn gods for their plenty.

Instead, he had turned his truck around and driven back to Thatcher in the rain. Harlan Phelps was waiting in Martin's office. His promptness could mean confidence or frustration. You couldn't tell much about Harlan these days. His dissipations were beginning to show in flushed skin and sagging jowls. Willard closed the door on the smell of bay rum and shoe resin on the stairs, nodded, dismissed Betty Muller, Martin's secretary, and sank comfortably into one of the fine old leather chairs. It still shaped to him, he noted wryly.

Harlan showed his large teeth in what passed for a smile, drew on an expensive cigar, and flapped his hand. His eyes glittered. He did not rise.

Confidence, thought Willard. He was glad he had persuaded Martin to leave the meeting to him. Harlan was a man moving in for the kill. After very brief amenities, it came.

"She's making her last offer, Will. It's as generous as she could make it. She'll meet any price you name for the land."

Willard waited. Julia Orlini knew damn well there was no price on the land. He would let Harlan trip over his own rope. But Harlan did not trip.

"If you still refuse, she'll go to court."

Willard smiled. "It will give her something to do. My guess is that a woman like Mrs. Orlini needs something to do. She's smart and that, in an idle woman, breeds mischief."

Harlan's flush deepened. He'd like to take this old has-been down a notch or two but he had not come to quarrel. He had no need to.

"If she goes to court she'll win. There it is." Harlan held out a folded sheet of paper. The old lawyer opened it, read it, and handed it back.

"Where did she get that?"

"She hasn't been going back and forth from Hartford to Washington for nothing. As you say, she's a smart woman. Damn it, Will, sell that land to her before you lose your shirt. Old Isaac Roundtree or whoever he was had no right to the Thatcher land. The whole thing was a fraud. You let that come out in court and you'll make fools of the whole clan, as well as ruin 'em."

Willard rose. "Maybe."

"But she's still willing to buy."

Willard put on his lumber jacket and picked up his work cap. "I'll think about it."

"Damn it, Will. Julia's not going to wait forever!"

Willard opened the office door. "I haven't got forever," he said dryly.

Harlan heard his steps go firmly down the long straight stairs.

The sky was clearing as the pick-up truck turned onto the dirt road. Shafts of silver light slid through the heavy clouds in the west, fingering the valley with cold brightness. Ten acres under cultivation now. There had once been hundreds. Except for a few ancient oaks and a grove of soaring pines here and there, the woods were second, even third growth, threaded by the crumbling, dry, stone walls that had once marked off farms and pastures.

In places old springs had yielded to swamp, sumac, and cattails. Somewhere the brake held the remnant of a saltpeter marsh that had once supplied colonial guns.

Why would she want it? Willard glanced up at the ridge to the place of slaughtered trees. He had lately heard construction trucks rolling. Now that the leaves had gone, he could see the beginning of a shape. Of what, he did not know. Change. Assault. The wave of the future. Possession was as transitory as life. Julia Orlini would find that out someday. But, like it or not, she was the present. He was the past.

It would be easier to sell out, to admit his day was gone. He thought of them all. Martin and Edythe had no use for his valley. Lowell? He did not know Lowell as he had once thought he did. Claude? He smiled. She would be airborne as thistledown too soon. John? His young eyes were already somber with sacrifice. He would hate the valley. And Michael? Who was Michael now! And where?

He came in sight of the farmhouse. A light showed. His steady heart did an unaccustomed flip. Time slid away. His Anne. She had loved the valley. He had brought her there, young, tremulous on a spring day before their wedding. In a cluster of shimmering birches, with the sunlight dappling her body, she had come to him, so sweetly, so willingly that her response held the rapture of a bee's flight.

The next week in the church, her eyes downcast, demure beneath the wedding veil, she had flashed him a smile so mischievous he had thought his chest would crack. How often they had returned in their two short springtimes to the vaulted shimmer of those birches.

October was a cold month for love.

Cold for Ariel and Duncan. No one had made it any warmer. He could not forget the strain that shadowed her eyes, the pinched look beneath her smile in the Roundtree living room last night. He had gotten her away and to his immense satisfaction, he had seen a quiet release in her face as they drove into the valley. For all her chaotic, veneered upbringing, she responded to the land and its creatures in some kind of distant throwback. Clancy, his wise dog, had sensed it. So had an Indian of greater profundity than his own. Ariel living in this valley? Ariel and Duncan. And the land safe.

He was a meddling old man. Worse, he was a spinner of hopes. But what else did a man fight for if not his dreams?

The telephone was ringing as he entered the house.

It was Edythe and she was excited. The message was important and where had they been? Obediently, Willard wrote it down on a pad. And hung up with a sigh.

He turned to see Ariel coming into the house. She had changed her clothes, but was dressed simply. Tweed something. Perhaps it was the scarf at her throat or the way her hair fell or the lamplight. How long was it since he had seen a woman's face glow like that?

"Duncan's coming at six to take me to dinner." Her voice caught. Her arms went around his neck, her scent as heady as a memory.

"You knew all the time, didn't you?"

"I guessed." His eyes twinkled. "The way a man guesses that water runs downhill. And the grass comes up in the spring."

"We're going to be married!"

He nodded. "It's better that way." She laughed, freely, lightly. Vulnerable, he thought.

"Uncle Willard, I adore you! You make it all sound so—so easy and right."

"It is, Ariel. Hang on to that."

"Could I stay here at the farmhouse until then?"

"It's already claimed you."

He felt the telephone message like a stone in his pocket.

"I heard the telephone ringing while I was outside." She looked quizzically at him and the paper in his hand.

"It was for you, Ariel. A telegram came this afternoon. Edythe was relaying it."

She unfolded the paper. In Willard's handsome angular writing, the words looked strange. She read them twice. "Come at once. Urgent. Mother."

She handed the paper back, mechanically. It did not surprise her. She might even have expected it. But she had forgotten reality. Alicia never did.

Part Three

Paris, October 1970

Chapter One

The blue twilight of Paris drifted into the streets, blurring the crassness of neon and glass, misting the beehive lights of small shops and cafes, and wrapping the ancient glories in a timeless pallor.

Recent rain had stripped bare the trees in the Tuileries. The nursemaids and children had long since departed the walks and benches for lamplight and warmth. Couples were beginning to appear, arms entwined, strolling in the wet leaves plastered underfoot as if they were fragments of clouds. An occasional man of affairs hurried across the gardens, his umbrella furled, his attaché case glistening with success, his lips moving with the unfinished details of the day.

Alicia Roundtree walked along briskly. She loved this hour of dusk suspended between daytime and night. Her Yankee blood, which she took such pains to conceal, responded to the excitement of change, whether in hours, seasons, or faces. She had chosen the long walk home because it would give a glow to her skin for the evening and because it might drain her of the irritation which always showed if one let it.

But it was indeed a long walk through the Gardens, across the Pont Solferino to the Boulevard St. Germain. She had shopped too extravagantly. Now, unless she hurried, she would be late. Both haste and tardiness in Alicia's carefully planned life were social disasters.

It was Ariel's fault. After Lili had written the calamitous news of the canceled Thatcher wedding and sent a copy of the *Thatcher Standard* with the story, Alicia had written Ariel at once. It was perfectly apparent what had happened. If one picture was worth, as they said, a thousand words, that picture was to Alicia's practiced eye a life story. Ariel in her stubborn innocence had flirted too openly with the groom. There she was in the centerfold of a ridiculous small-town newspaper looking at whatever-his-name-was—Duncan—like a bitch in heat. In private turmoil, Alicia's careful elegance was inclined to fray.

And what was the man? A small-town minister. When Ariel had not answered, Alicia had written again and minced no words. How could Ariel have been so foolish as to involve herself in a tawdry rustic little affair like this? Not that Alicia had any private qualms about how a woman acquired a new man. She believed wholly in free enterprise. Any man one met was assuredly claimed by some other woman. *Ce ne fait rien.* If she could not hold him *tant pis!* But this Duncan. Without prospects. A completely unrelieved, dreary future. Poor little Lowell was probably crying her sweet little unmascaraed eyes out. Alicia saw no use for the Roundtree attachment in the predictable future. Still, one never knew. They were all the family she and Ariel had. Ariel couldn't have done worse.

In any event, Alicia had at last taken action. She had sent the cable that would reel in Ariel at once. Alicia had threaded Ariel's adolescence with slight, brave hints of a heart flutter. If Ariel was old enough now to recognize its convenience, she would still not dare to ignore it.

But to herself, Alicia faced a deeper truth. She wanted Ariel back. Ariel was youth. She brought youth to the apartment. She was the *raison d'être,* the reason for inviting young men with bright talk and long futures, who made Alicia feel a part of them. Robbed of this heady current Alicia would dissolve like a figure in sand.

All of which brought her to the Boulevard St. Germain and home. She nodded to the watchful, aging concierge, entered the rickety little elevator of iron grillwork, wondering again how much longer it would convey her safely to the fourth floor. One had to make compromises at every step of life. It was a pity Ariel could not have learned that.

She let herself into the apartment. Dusk had become night and Jeanette, her young, pert *bonne*, had drawn the curtains and lit the foyer lamp before leaving. Alicia no longer permitted herself the luxury of a live-in maid. But she made the pleasant discovery that sacrifice had its own rewards. She had the apartment completely to herself at night. Except for Ariel. Ariel.

She glanced into the little salon with its gilded chinoiserie, its Louis Quinze chairs and its pillow-deep, white-velvet divan. Henri, le Baron de Bonnerville, was sitting in the corner of it, his thinning hair ruffled, his neatly waxed mustache in need of smoothing, his lowest vest button open on a small round belly. He was asleep.

"Henri!"

He opened his eyes and jumped to his feet, reaching for hair, mustache, and vest in one sweeping gesture.

"My darling!"

"I am not your darling, cheri, when you sit unannounced in my drawing room. Have you forgotten that I'm dining with the American consul tonight?" She would have liked to say 'ambassador' but she was on the fringe list at the Embassy. So it was important to keep her standing at the Consulate. "A dinner for some American businessmen and their wives." She made a pretty little pout. "Phillip asked me to come as a favor, to save it from utter dullness."

Henri, his sartorial pride restored, regarded her with fond amusement. "I have not forgotten, Alicia. I'll wait for you to dress and drop you off there."

That would mean he would want to watch her dress and she knew from the strain around her eyes she would need a quick mudpack.

"Please, darling. I'm late now. Phillip is sending a car."

"Very well."

"But Henri, I do need you. It's about Ariel. She's still over there in that dismal little town. I've cabled her to come home. Isn't there some young man you know? We could all take a weekend over All Saints Day. Zurich, perhaps, or London?"

Henri had always found her blond prettiness appealing, irresistible when she opened her china-blue eyes so helplessly. He was not a tall man but in moments like this his inch or two above her gave him in his own mind a male dominance. "My advice to you, little one, is to let Ariel work out her own destiny."

"And let her ruin her whole life by staying in Thatcher?"

"If that's what she wants."

"It's not what I want. I've dedicated my life to giving Ariel the upbringing she should have."

Henri's little smile held sympathy. He knew that whenever Alicia said this, she believed it.

"And I don't intend to see her throw it away. Why, do you know what her last letter said? She was thinking of going to stay on her Uncle Willard's farm if he asked her. A farm, Henri! She's probably there now, milking goats or making soap or whatever Willard does. You wouldn't think that he had once been one of the most brilliant lawyers in the state. That was when the Roundtree name stood for something. Now I must dress. I'll look a hundred tonight if I think of this any more!"

She caught her breath. She had forgotten the most important matter. "Anyhow I've cabled her. She'll come home. She's a good girl."

She kissed him lightly, standing on tiptoe not because it was necessary but because long ago she had found it was a beguiling gesture. "I'll call you tomorrow, darling. Do find someone rich and interesting and young for Ariel."

Henri knew Alicia in this mood. He kissed her on the brow, walked to the door, and let himself out.

She felt the sudden emptiness of the fragile, pretty world she had so carefully constructed in this room. For an instant she saw invisible cracks, felt an invisible chill. "Rabbit running on your grave," they would have said in Thatcher. Well, she had banished Thatcher once. She would again.

She lifted her chin and her face muscles with a forced smile. She could still pass for thirty—thirty-two—with care.

Care meant never showing worry. Ariel would have to wait. Alicia's first duty was to her public.

Most of the guests had already gathered in a smaller drawing room of the Consulate. Alicia arrived a permissible twelve minutes late, shimmering in sea-foam green shot with silver that sheathed her from throat to ankle to wrist. The silk clung so close to her slight, fine-boned figure that there was no need to reveal anything more. Her only jewel was a large, square-cut emerald on her left hand. No one questioned Madame Roundtree's jewels. They were so simple, so superb that they must either be genuine or remarkable copies of those she most prudently kept in a vault.

Alicia was adept at entering a room. She gave her most charming smile to her hostess, lingered for a moment while her eyes swept the room, and allowed the group to see her. When she had discovered where the most interesting, the most celebrated, the most expensive had gathered, she made her way gracefully, unobtrusively toward them. It took skill, and those who knew her best would watch with admiration and not a little envy. With malice, in the case of some of the women. But Alicia did not concern herself overly much with women. One made women friends, one entertained them. They were one's social passport. But otherwise . . .

The party consisted of five American couples, the

men emanating the kind of coarse, confident, new success that marked Americans anywhere in the world. The women? She recognized the familiar cabbagelike wigs, the expensive non-chic. She dismissed them with a glance. Phillip, the Consul's young-old assistant who dedicated himself so earnestly to his job that he would never advance above him, was useful but a few flirtatious moments were enough to bestow upon him.

The last guest to arrive had upstaged her. He was a small, dark-skinned man in midnight-blue tuxedo with a discreetly lace-ruffled dinner shirt. His face had the smooth agelessness of the Italian male, and the heavy diamond on his small finger was as genuine as the lace on his shirt-front.

She watched him move through the group, his near-black eyes missing nothing, his small hands slicing the air. One false note was his short, absurdly pointed shoes. Still, thought Alicia, how often must one look at a man's feet? The guests parted for him. He seemed to know most of them.

"Mrs. Roundtree . . ." The Consul's angular frame was at her side. ". . . may I present Mr. Benjamin Orlini?"

He bowed, looked sharply at her for an instant, then was swept along into the shifting knots of people.

Cocktails, a variety of sticky canapés, and heightened chatter punctuated by brittle female laughter told Alicia what the evening would hold. Another *pro forma* dinner for visiting American businessmen. They all knew each other. They had simply shifted their ambience to another place. The Consul was already wearing his tired gray smile.

Finally, long after the announced dinner hour, they drifted into the dining room where, as Alicia knew, conversation would abruptly collapse in the presence of hot food.

She was not, somewhat to her annoyance, the ranking lady present. The chair on the Consul's right was occupied by a woman with black dyed hair, a brisk manner, and a black, long-sleeved dinner dress. She promptly engaged the Consul with penetrating questions that left the redhead on his left with her giggles unspent. The formidable lady was a business executive. Alicia dismissed her at once. She might know how many barrels of something or other meant something or other but she did not know that no one, absolutely no one, was wearing black to small dinners in Paris this season.

Alicia found herself seated near the other end of the table. (She must be more careful in accepting invitations to the Consulate in the future.) On her right was Phillip, the dreary assistant consul, who had no doubt arranged the table with a view to inflicting another evening of heavy-handed flirtation on her. On her left sat Mr. Benjamin Orlini, the ranking male guest. Alicia promptly turned a slender and eloquent shoulder on Phillip.

Conversation revived sporadically after the Consomme aux Printemps. (The Consul was clearly not extending himself tonight. At the Embassy it would be Bisque Homard at the least.) But the table was too wide, the carnations too tall, and the candles too near eye level for general conversation. Alicia had long ago learned to make the best of circumstances, though.

She turned her full charm on the dynamic, if ordinary, man on her left. Ben Orlini seemed to be waiting for her. He talked easily, said little, and revealed nothing about himself.

He had come to Paris with the group on a project involving new sources of energy. Tides, to be specific. There was to be a meeting in Zurich. Energy was the world's vital problem. He paused flatteringly for her opinion. True, without energy there would be no war, but there would also be no progress. Nations had to choose, he smiled. Yes, the superjets had indeed made the world small. The Concorde would squeeze it further. Personally, he was not entirely comfortable with today's speeds. He would like more time to think, to plan—he looked into her blue eyes—to savor life. He would like time to go to Perugia, to sit idling in the square as his grandfather had done. And his great-grandfather.

Alicia listened with the raptness that was so large a part of her charm. She knew when to sit quiet, when to inject the small, attentive question. If she had heard it all before, she gave no indication, following with her smile, letting her mind dart. What puzzled her now was the oddly penetrating way this man looked at her. Curious, appraising, unfathomable. It began to make her uncomfortable.

With the Poire Helene (it would have been Mousse Framboise at the Embassy, she thought) it came. He pushed the dessert aside, lit a pencil-thin cigar, unaware of his error, and studied her.

"Mrs. Roundtree, your name interests me."

"Only my name?" She gave him her best parrying smile.

"On the contrary. But we can begin with your name. It is unusual, and yet I know it very well. Have you always lived in Paris?"

"Ever since I had a free choice."

"Well said. My wife and I live in New York City . . ." So he was married. She could imagine his wife, a fussy little woman adept at keeping his socks neat and his shirt buttons in place, whom he kept reassuringly at home. ". . . but we have a summer place in Connecticut."

"How nice," she murmured.

". . . near a town called Thatcher."

Coincidence. She had heard it defined as two events occupying the same space. More than once coincidence had disrupted the uneasy tenor of her life. But this was not coincidence, this was the malevolence of fate. She had struggled to keep Thatcher, with all its implied and overt criticism, out of her life. Now it had turned on her.

There was no use denying anything. He would hear

all about her when he got back, probably from the fussy little wife, who probably thrived on scandal like a fat beetle. Alicia always saw women as natural enemies.

She let a light laugh float between them. "Thatcher! So you know them, the Roundtrees in Thatcher. I'm related to all of them, unfortunately."

"They are very prominent people. In Thatcher."

"In Thatcher. Yes." Her blue eyes sparkled into his. "They might have amounted to something if they had ever uprooted themselves."

"As you did?"

"As I did. I'm Alicia, Martin's sister. The maverick one."

"You make it sound challenging. Actually, I was not thinking of the settled Roundtrees in Thatcher. But of a very charming young woman who recently arrived."

She sighed inwardly. The admission would add a decade to her carefully radiant face but she could not avoid it now. "My daughter Ariel. She went over for a family wedding."

"Of course. I see it now. The resemblance—"

"She's dark. I'm not, Mr. Orlini."

"True. But anyone can see where she gets her beauty. And she is very beautiful."

The remark irritated her. It hinted at a life Ariel was leading beyond the one she shared with her mother. Even worse, it implied the passage of time, of a background role for Alicia herself, perhaps of replacement.

"She is becoming a pretty girl. But she is still very young. She has been brought up in the French tradition. Quite unspoiled. An *innocente*. I worried about letting her go alone."

"I can understand," Ben Orlini said dryly.

"I'm expecting her home any day now."

"That will disappoint my son."

His son? Had she guessed wrong? Was it the son of this rich little nouveau, and not an impoverished church minister who was keeping Ariel from everything that was right for her? But there was the picture in the Thatcher newspaper, the passionate upturned face. How little Alicia knew about her. Ariel had no sense of what money or lack of it could mean. With her beauty, she might have a title if Alicia managed things properly. A title to assure her of position all her life and put a plank over the quicksand of Alicia's own days and nights. They were terribly rich these days, she had heard, these new Americans. Almost as rich as the Arabs. She looked at Ben Orlini with quickened interest.

"You have a family, Mr. Orlini?"

"Twin sons and a daughter. My wife did very well."

It was not what she intended to discuss. "And one of your sons has met Ariel?"

"Nicholas. He's in business with me. He thinks her captivating. As I do."

"How nice. But perhaps I should tell you, Mr. Orlini, there is a young man, a count, of very old French family, who is waiting for Ariel to return in the hope of an engagement."

"My congratulations. In that case I'll have to tell Nick he's out of bounds."

"Out of bounds? How old-fashioned! I have always understood that a man's interest is—shall we say— sharpened by a little competition."

Ben Orlini leaned back in his chair, blew a stream of cigar smoke ceilingward, and smiled. If she knew him better she would have recognized the look of shrewd appraisal beneath that smile. His enemies knew it as a warning.

"My son doesn't compete. He doesn't need to. As Ariel discovered."

Ariel? This confident little man must know Ariel better than she could guess. She felt she was losing control of the conversation.

"You intrigue me, Mr. Orlini. Whatever do you mean by that?"

He leaned toward her familiarly, waited for the table conversation to rise again before continuing.

"Oh, come, Alicia. That's a very nice name, by the way. You can't send a girl like Ariel into a town like Thatcher without stirring things up. She was rather foolish, I take it, about the minister boy but I must say she had the guts to face it out. Sure, Nick liked her. Any man would. But all that small-town talk? Nick doesn't go for that kind of thing any more than I do. Even for a little lady as delectable as your daughter."

Alicia was furious. At herself, at Ariel, at this crude little potentate with his earthiness, his presumptions. But one of the penalties of her lifestyle was that she could not afford anger.

She lowered her eyes and sighed. "You're quite right. Ariel has been foolish. She's so young. But once she's home, she'll be herself. She has absolutely no interest in that—whatever he is—minister. She's assured me of that. Just a country boy who lost his head. And she was innocently flattered. That's all it amounted to." She widened her blue eyes. "It isn't easy to bring up a child alone, Mr. Orlini. Especially a girl. Not in these free and easy days, when all manners, all restraints have gone with the wind, as they say. I've wanted so much for Ariel but most of all to keep her the sweet, lovely girl she is. I blame myself for letting her go so far away alone, but it was impossible for me."

"Sure, I understand that. It isn't easy to raise kids anytime."

The guests were rising from the table. As Ben Orlini held the chair for her, his eyes slid down her slight figure. Her breasts were small and round. They would still be firm. If he were interested.

"May I drive you home?"

She felt rather than saw his glance. So she was still in control, as she always could be when she put her mind to it. But another hour of this dull party still lay ahead. She would take her time.

"They always have a car to drive me back."

"I'll take care of that," said Ben Orlini abruptly, and he moved out among the guests.

Phillip, the consul's young assistant, was demanding her attention. She smiled distantly, patted his hand, and crossed the room to where her bored and isolated hostess stood. And from where she could watch Ben Orlini. A little Napoleon, she guessed. All compressed power. He would make his way. She had no idea what it was yet. But he could be useful if Henri ever—dear Henri. He had grown as settled in his ways as if they had been married twenty years. But Orlini—she wondered if he had Corsican blood. They were the wildest. As lovers, too. She would be very careful about that. She watched him walk daintily on his small feet, talking rapidly, gesturing, his white teeth glinting with a smile that never reached his eyes. Yes, she thought again. Compressed power. Raw, even ruthless. Ben Orlini could be a dangerous man.

In the end Alicia agreed, as if conferring a favor, to let him drive her home. She sat wrapped in furs, remote and small, in the dark corner of the limousine. When he suggested a nightcap in the bar of his hotel, she refused.

When they arrived at the tall house on the Boulevard St. Germain, he accompanied her to the gate. As the concierge unlocked it, Alicia held out her gloved hand. He hesitated a fraction of a second, then bobbed his head to kiss it.

"You're quite a woman, Alicia."

"Good night, Mr. Orlini," she said softly.

She entered her apartment as the telephone was ringing. She disliked unexpected late calls. They interrupted her mood. The evening had been invigorating, challenging. A new game lay ahead and she had won the first move. She would like to savor her triumph.

But for the fact that a call might come from Ariel, she would shut the telephone off.

"Hello? Henri!"

"I'm sorry to disturb you, my dear."

He sounded sleepy. There was no denying that Henri was beginning to age.

"I just came in. Whatever is the matter?"

"I had a call from Ariel."

"Ariel? Where is she?"

"She's still in—that place, Thatcher."

"Why on earth would she call you?"

"Because she couldn't reach you. She's tried all evening. Your cable rather frightened her. She thought you might be ill."

"I'm never—" Alicia caught herself. Wasn't that exactly what she wanted Ariel to think? The euphoria of the evening was beginning to fade. "What did you tell her, Henri?"

"I told her you were never better."

"Oh, good heavens! Did she say when she is arriving in Paris?"

"She told me she was going to be married."

"*What?* Henri, she couldn't have said that. This is madness! Who in the world could she marry in that town? Not—" Alicia's sables slid to the floor as she sank on a settee. "Did she tell you who it is?"

"Certainly."

She heard that twinkle in his voice that had captivated her so long ago.

"She said, the most wonderful man in the world."

"Henri, I can't possibly go to Thatcher now. You must go. She'll listen to you."

"She sounded very happy, Alicia. I told her—"

"She doesn't know what she's doing!" Alicia interrupted wildly. "She must come home! What did you say to her?"

Henri's voice grew less sleepy. "I wished her great happiness, Alicia, as I'm sure you do. But I told her

329

that I thought she should come home first. She owed you that."

Cautious relief trickled through Alicia's breath. There was still time. Perhaps.

"What did she say? Henri, you're driving me crazy!"

"I'm sorry, my dear." His voice was mild and amused. "I had thought I was bringing you pleasure. Ariel agreed. She'll be here in a couple of days. I told her not to worry about the airfare, I would attend to all that."

"Will you meet her?"

"Have you forgotten? I must be away on business for the next two weeks. Munich, Geneva, then on to Milan."

"Of course I haven't forgotten, darling." Alicia pushed back a moment of panic. She must show strength, control. "How could I forget? Ariel and I will be delighted to see you when you get back. Then we shall all have a little vacation together."

"Charming, my dear." She heard the dry chuckle. "But I think it will be à deux. Your daughter, my sweet, is in love."

An hour later Alicia lay across her bed, wrapped in a blue velvet dressing gown, reading again the clippings from the Thatcher newspaper that Cousin Lily had faithfully sent, marked in her usual purple ink. The wedding reception without bride and groom. The photo of Ariel and the young minister, escaping from a fire. The editorial on gossip "Tell It Not in Gath." Whatever that meant. So it had all been true.

At least Ariel was coming home. But there was very little time. And no Henri to help. No new young man. No titled prospect in the wings.

There was, however, Ben Orlini.

Alicia slept soundly the remainder of the night. As she always did when she had made a plan.

Chapter Two

Ben Orlini was not surprised by Alicia's phone call. He had half expected it. Nor was he displeased. He had returned to his hotel after a disappointing day to find the neat little message under his door. Mme. Roundtree. She clung to that name. They all did. In Thatcher it was a weapon. But in Thatcher he would never have received a message like this. Mme. Roundtree looks forward to the pleasure of his company tomorrow for cocktails at six. Clever of her not to ask him to call back. She must be quite sure that on reflection he would accept. To Ben Orlini, conquest in any form was the reason for living. This one had a peculiar bitter-almond satisfaction he would savor.

He sent his regrets with nineteen long-stemmed roses. Alicia was a lady who would probably count. Then he undressed, showered, and threw himself on the bed, a small rounding figure with absurbly short blunt feet, on a uselessly wide expanse of mauve silk. Stripped, Ben Orlini had no choice but to face the truth about himself. He needed every prop, from the monogrammed silk shirts and silk shorts to the elongated, pointed shoes that he liked to look down on. Otherwise he was the round little punchinello of his distant, bruising childhood.

He reached for a heavy black-and-gold brocade dressing gown, made two telephone calls, and felt better. But he had to admit that so far this Paris trip had been disappointing. Ego-building perhaps, but it had not yet accomplished his real purpose. For Ben Orlini was now thinking in the new dimensions of the spreading international conglomerates. There lay the power tomorrow. He saw himself moving swiftly, dexterously through its mazes, above politics, protected by the very laws he could ignore. Ben Orlini, touching a button to command presidents, or to change the destiny of a nation. Invisible to all except those he chose to see. No more mocking laughter at little punchinello in the streets. No more lofty, amused tolerance from Julia. She had for him the fascination of a swaying cobra yet he could not break with her. Power, that was the only language a woman like Julia understood. Or any woman.

He picked up the phone once more. There was only one man he wanted to meet in Paris, the elusive, invisible head of Umex Corporation. He had anticipated an encounter at an Embassy dinner. Then something had gone wrong. The dinner had been a third-rate affair at the Consulate. Then silence. Remembering that, Ben put back the phone. No eagerness. He had plenty on his side to offer. Know-how, that was the word. Meanwhile he would remain a little longer in Paris.

Two days later he invited Alicia to dinner. She accepted at once.

"So Ariel is coming home?"

"She hasn't cabled yet but I expect her any day."

They were sitting, late, in Alicia's elegant off-white, paneled salon, its pale gold curtains drawn against the Paris night. Ben Orlini had to admit he liked this little enclave of refined living, with its aura of assured feminity that made a man aware of his success and his masculinity. He would not fall in love with Alicia. He had outgrown that schoolboy fantasy. He was not even sure a sexual adventure with her would be satisfying. But he liked her beside him, her chic, careful beauty, her bright, deferring mind. Her smallness.

He tipped his cigar ash into a Sèvres bowl.

"You're quite a mother, Alicia."

"I don't think of myself as Ariel's mother," said Alicia rather quickly. "We're more like sisters. Close friends."

"I'm sure of that," he smiled.

"Oh, yes, she's very happy to be coming home. I

don't know what possessed her. She must have been bored to death to indulge in a flirtation with a minister. Well, I'm sure all the talk has taught her a lesson. I'm also sure that as soon as she leaves, Lowell will be back for her pathetic little marriage. It's probably her only chance."

Ben stirred. He disliked gossip. He began to realize that Alicia had a dangerous talent for twisting facts into whatever shape she could use.

"Perhaps I'll get to see Ariel before I go." He rose.

"You're not leaving Paris yet, Ben?" Alicia knew she had made a mistake. Things never went well when she dwelt on Ariel. If the girl would only come home. Ben Orlini had surprised her. He spent as lavishly as an Arab. His tips alone . . . that's how you could really judge a man. Alicia had not even broached her plan yet. Besides, she liked Ben Orlini; he had an earthiness, yet he conveyed power. And he had not asked her for anything. He seemed to like her just for being herself. It made her feel young.

"Don't leave Paris yet!" She meant it.

"I'm a working man."

"But I thought you said your son was taking care of things at home."

"I'm not as confident of my children as you are, Alicia." He twisted his cigar into the bowl. One end was frayed. He had some habits that a clever woman would have corrected, she thought.

"Is your son like you, Ben?"

"Nick? He's six feet tall, if that's what you mean."

"I didn't mean that."

"Takes after his mother. He hasn't much respect for me, but he'll do the job well enough. If I'm not away too long."

Alicia's mind was darting into *cul-de-sacs*. The only way left was the direct one. "I don't believe that. I know he has *all* your distinction *and* your cleverness. I'd like to meet him." She clapped her delicate hands together. "I have a wonderful idea! You said Ariel knows him. Why not bring him to Paris for a week or so? We four could have such a good time!"

She was like a child. Ben Orlini smiled. One of the things he enjoyed about Alicia was watching her mind twist and turn—and the predictability of the outcome. She was matchmaking. His money had made its mark. But she was a Roundtree. By God, she'd have to come on her knees for it.

"The last thing that young man needs is a trip to Paris. Good night, Alicia. Thank you for coming out with me."

"I loved it, Ben. The ballet was marvelous!" She held out her hand. Ben kissed it and heard at the back of his mind Julia's amused laugh. He picked up the Paris-bought gray homburg that gave him height.

Alicia's smile was tender. "I'll see you again, Ben?"

"Why not?"

It was totally unsatisfying. Alicia drifted back into the empty living room, annoyed with herself and with Ben. She had broken two of her own rules with men. She had become personal, gossipy. And worse, she had been obvious. She had seen it in Ben's shrewd eyes. She would have to mend fences. What was the son's name? Nick. Nicholas. Nicholas Orlini. It had a certain distinction. He was tall, like his mother. Alicia preferred to think of him as motherless. Probably dark, like his father. Possibly handsome. Not that it mattered. Anymore than a faded title mattered. Nick Orlini belonged to a new breed—the unpolished, the untitled, who would inherit the earth.

With a sigh, Alicia turned out the last drawing-room lamp. If Ariel did what she should, she would be here in forty-eight hours.

By that time Alicia would, in her own favorite phrase, be in control again.

Ben Orlini walked briskly along the Boulevard St. Germain. He did not know the semidark of the Left Bank streets and ultimately he would have to find a cab. But now he wanted fresh air. The overrich dinner sat as heavily as its $113 check. He had fought drowsiness through the endless ballet. Alicia's tantalizing scene had grown cloying. He dreaded the lonely reality of his hotel room.

Mist lent halos to the street lamps. The gauzelike air drew a flow of people to the sidewalks, walking arm-in-arm, as unaware of him as of some night-scratching pigeon. The city lay remote and veiled around him.

He quickened his pace and came to the crossing of a garishly lighted avenue, strident with commonplace cafes and jostling, noisy groups of young people, the long-haired and blue-jeaned, flamboyant night prowlers of the Boulevard St. Michel. They were, had he known the name, the Boul' Mich itself, its raucous student soul uninhibited at this hour with *vin ordinaire* and sleepless vitality.

He entered a café at random, took a vacant table along one wall. Aware of glances, he slid the gray homburg under his chair, loosened his tie, and ran his short fingers through the black slickness of his hair.

Suddenly Ben Orlini felt better. He ordered a *cassis.*
"*Bon soir, m'sieur.*"

She could not have been more than sixteen, full lips open and slightly pink, eyes soot dark. Beneath a low-cut, gray, slinging sweater her pale breasts swelled temptingly; below her absurdly brief skirt, her nyloned legs were shapely.

He wanted her. He wanted to go wherever she would lead him. He wanted to shed his tight, expensive tailoring, pursue her through the streets, up dark narrow stairs, into a hidden room under the eaves where, with the stars shining through a musty window, she would let him catch her, take her. It had been that way the first time for him. With this child-girl he would put away time and fears.

But Ben Orlini had coupled ambition with caution too long. He shook his head.

She shrugged and walked away.

He ordered another glass. And began to think about Ariel Roundtree.

He had seen Ariel Roundtree twice. He remembered her air of sophistication, like a filmy scarf around her. She had said little, yet her quiet appraisal had left him uncomfortably aware of himself. Nick was less sensitive. He would like to see his son master this coolly exciting girl. Marry her, if that's what it took. Suppose he played Alicia's little game and sent for Nick? It would be a pleasant, even amusing week, and would give him another excuse for remaining in Paris.

There was more to it than that, though. Ben thought how it might be with his son and without Julia. Nick was her favorite and she had damned near ruined him. Alternately indulging him and dominating him, she had made the boy her personal province. In Ben's childhood world, a man headed his family and his sons learned from him. No woman was fit to bring up a man-child. Julia had proved that. He would enjoy Nick's company as he would enjoy infuriating Julia.

She deserved it. She had virtually brushed him aside in her senseless ambition for the Roundtree land. She had no use for it. She would tire of it as she had tired of so many other things. Yet she was possessed by a demon to have it. She had gone to Washington despite his objections. She had come home with evidence that it was really hers. She would make a public spectacle of them all, whereas his way was to burrow quietly, finally forcing old Willard to sell. All Julia asked of Ben now was to stay out of her way. She had said so clearly, contemptuously, before he left on his trip.

It would satisfy something deep and masculine to hurt her now. Sending for Nick without her would do it.

By the time Ben Orlini entered his hotel room he had reached his decision. He glanced at his watch. There was a chance Nick would be at his apartment. Probably not alone but that couldn't be helped.

The telephone rang once, as promptly as if he had merely called the lobby.

Nick's voice was guarded. He was not alone.

"Nick . . ."

"Yeah, Dad."

"I want you to come to Paris."

"You're kidding."

"I'll be here another week or ten days. I want you with me. Where's your mother?"

"How the hell do I know? Probably Thatcher."

"Call her just before you leave and tell her. Call the *Thatcher Standard* and tell them you're joining me on a business trip. They'll run it. Take an early plane. The office will arrange it."

"Sure." Nick's voice lightened. "I like it. But why?"

"Because that's the way I want it."

"Okay!"

"See you tomorrow, son."

Ben hung up. His voice had suddenly choked.

Chapter Three

Ariel sat in the waiting lounge at Kennedy Airport, looking out at the brilliantly lit night, her hand tight in Duncan's. She had postponed leaving as long as she could. Now that she was on her way, she longed for the trip to be over and done with. Her real life would begin when she returned.

Yet already that life had taken on an ephemeral distance. She had been delighted that Duncan would drive her all the way from Thatcher to the New York airport. Yet now that he was here, he sat stolid in his old tweed coat and as detached from the impersonal airport scene as she was part of it. The tide of lights, of chatter, of faces seemed to flow not around them but between them. He had hardly spoken in the last ten minutes. Her hand tightened in his.

He smiled at her. "It's becoming."

"What is?"

"People, excitement. All this."

"I've had too much of it."

"I wouldn't say so. You look the part."

It was almost boarding time. She would have to listen for her flight number through the tangle of announcements. Tokyo, Cairo, Athens, London, Delhi, names like threads that unraveled their leave-taking.

He caught her glance. "Want to start for the gate?"

"No. Not yet. Duncan, you will write, won't you?"

"I thought we settled that, my darling. I will be here in this airport the day you come back. But I will not write."

"But why not?" In her own ears she sounded like a child.

"Because I'm going down to the Seminary for a couple of weeks of study." He managed a grin. "I'm still weak in homiletics."

"What's that mean?"

"I'm a lousy preacher."

"I don't care, Duncan. Besides, you can't practice all the time."

"It involves a little more than practice."

"And you don't want to be distracted writing letters? Is that it?"

"Something like that." His smile faded, his eyes grew somber. "Ariel, I've asked you to share a life you know nothing about. It will never be glamorous. Or even easy. It can be tougher than a girl like you would have any idea of. I'm not sure yet it's possible for us in Thatcher."

"We'll make it possible! We said we would."

"Maybe."

"Duncan, why are you talking like this, now? All the drive down, you've been so quiet. As if we weren't going to see each other again. I don't want to go back to Paris. But I should see my mother before we're married. Alicia would never come to Thatcher. I'll be back before you've finished with your, your—whatever it takes to become a good preacher."

He laughed because he loved her and because inside it hurt even to look at her.

"It takes a lot, my darling. I want you to go back to Paris. Not for your mother but for us. I ask only one thing. If you change your mind—"

"Duncan!"

"Listen to me, Ariel. This matters to me!"

His voice rose. The heavy woman with packages, sitting on the other side of Ariel, looked at them with interest. So young, such beautiful people, quarreling at a time like this. What was the matter with young people today? Duncan met her glance and lowered his voice.

"Ariel, I love you. I always will. But I can't give you the life another man might. The life you were brought up for. If you decide that's what you want, write me. Just one letter but I beg you, let it be the truth. Don't insult me with anything less."

"Flight 612, for Paris. Boarding at Gate 9."

His tone stunned her. She rose mechanically; he picked up her totebag. The heavy woman watched them, his set, unsmiling face, her wide staring eyes that looked as if they might fill up with tears. What was wrong when they so obviously belonged together?

At the departure gate Ariel spun around and went into his arms. "I'll be back, Duncan. As fast as I can!"

He crushed her to him, his cheek against her hair, as if no other human being were on earth. Then he let her go and walked rapidly away.

"Goodbye, Duncan!" But her voice was thin. He did not look back. She showed her boarding pass, went through the gate, and began her lonely walk down the long corridor that led to her own world.

Duncan stopped once in his rapid stride. He took a newspaper from his pocket, the *Thatcher Standard* he had bought for Ariel. He had looked at it while waiting for her and hastily crammed it into his pocket.

Now he opened it and read the announcement once more. "Mr. Nick Orlini is joining his father for a week's stay in Paris."

Duncan twisted the paper savagely and dropped it into the waste can. He found his shabby green car and, in a light rain, headed it into the lighted flow of traffic.

Homiletics. He wondered what made a man a good Minister of God.

Alicia sat propped up in bed, the blinds drawn against the sharpness of the October sunlight. She stretched out her arms as Ariel walked in.

"*Mon Dieu*, chérie, I'm glad you're home!" She smelled deliciously fresh and her champagne hair was swept back in careful disarray. She looked young and vulnerable, and Ariel had the long-familiar pang of not wanting to hurt her. The whole scene had an air of inevitability, the invisible filaments of a trap opening at her feet.

"I'm glad to see you, Alicia." For the moment she was. The cord was not easily broken. "Uncle Henri said you were fine. Are you? One doesn't tell a man one's little fatigues."

"You've been overdoing!" Ariel would keep the conversation on her mother. Time enough to talk when Alicia was on her feet.

"Of course I've been overdoing! What else does one live for? But I am a little tired. And with such a busy week ahead. Let me look at you, Ariel."

Ariel always hated that scrutiny. It seemed to transfer Alicia's own powdery lines and calculated efforts to her own face.

"A little thin. And you do need new clothes. This season, darling, it's glamor. Women are to be women." She laughed. "As if we've ever been anything else! I have no patience with these silly ideas they call modern. I hope you haven't picked up any of them in the States. Any woman who prefers to be called a person

340

rather than a woman simply gives up her identity. And her charm! Oh Ariel, it's good to have you back. I need you to talk to. To be here. I've been lonely. And when I'm not well . . ."

"Have you seen Dr. Sachs?"

This was a new, detached Ariel. Alicia bridled.

"Of course I haven't seen Dr. Sachs. Why would I? I know what's wrong with me. A little rest always helps. And now that you're home at last . . . !"

Ariel patted her mother's hand. This was definitely not the time to talk about Duncan. "Alicia, why don't you ask Mam'selle to come back? I'm sure she'd like something to do."

"I'm sure she would, too. And I'll be very happy to help her in any way I can if she wants to come out of her retirement. But not here."

"Why not? She adores you."

"She adores you, cherie. She's never quite approved of me. I'm not among her angels or even her tiresome saints. As if it mattered." Alicia's laugh faded. "I wouldn't mind even that. But she's . . . darling, she's old. And I'm sorry. But I don't want—well, I just don't want to think about that. To live with that around me." She smiled faintly. "I know it's selfish of me. But I don't like age and I fight it every day of my life."

"You do *very* well, Alicia."

"I don't want to do well, cherie. I want to win."

It had lasted long enough. It was like sparring with feathers. "I'll go unpack, Alicia. We can talk after lunch."

"About what, darling?"

"A great many things, Alicia. My life primarily."

"Oh, my darling, it hasn't begun. This afternoon I advise you to rest. We have a perfectly enchanting evening ahead."

Ariel stopped at the door. "Alicia, you haven't made plans for me?"

Alicia laughed and her cheeks turned pink with excitement. "Oh, but I have . . . for the most delightful week, beginning with dinner tonight."

"With Uncle Henri?"

"Oh no. He's out of town on one of his dull business trips. I don't know what on earth he's doing these days but he certainly does not consider my schedule."

"Who is it tonight?"

"A little surprise, darling. I know you'll have a good time!"

Ariel left the cloying room with the words unsaid. She should have expected this. The sooner she explained the facts to Alicia, the sooner she would be on her way back to Duncan. She almost cried his name aloud as she entered the mauve-and-white bedroom. This was her private world. Here she could think of him, talk to him, see him. Yet as she closed the door behind her, the very familiarity of silk and pillows, white-framed Renoir prints, the deep pile under her feet, the flounced dressing table, the oversized Marie Antoinette doll, the childhood closeness of it all dimmed his image. Here was everything she had never shared with him . . . could never share with him. In silence, not in communication, their love had happened.

Tomorrow she would talk frankly and bluntly to Alicia. She would remain only as long as kindness demanded. Then Ariel drew a deep breath as if a range of hills had unrolled beyond her window.

She let herself quietly out of the apartment. The sunshine was warm, the fine old Boulevard splashed with yellow leaves. Nostalgia flooded through her, nostalgia and new happiness.

Mam'selle would understand.

But Mam'selle was not at her small apartment. A neighbor told Ariel that she had gone, nearly a month ago, to a convent where the nuns were taking care of her. She was not well. She needed care.

Nearly a month ago? A month in which Ariel's own

life had turned upside down. But why had Alicia not told her? To be fair, perhaps Alicia did not know. Mam'selle was as proud as she was competent. She would scorn any outward sign of merely human weakness.

Ariel stopped long enough to buy a pot of sun-yellow chrysanthemums, then hailed a cab.

The convent stood in an old section of Paris, an *arrondissement* of narrow streets, leaning gray houses, decaying eighteenth-century mansions, now tenements. Among them crowded a small cemetery, a harsh place of crusted soil and darkened stones. Ariel had come here often on Mam'selle's visits to her sister's grave.

She dismissed the cab. She wanted to walk the last two squares, into the past.

The dingy shop windows were brightened with pink and red and purple immortelles, the dried little flowers that splash the poorer cemeteries of Paris with color on *le Jour Des Morts*. All Saints Day was not two weeks away. It would please Mam'selle that Ariel remembered those visits. She bought a pink and red wreath. She would drop it on that long-forgotten grave on the way home.

A plain-faced nun with a wraith of a smile opened the convent door, nodded, and led Ariel down a dim corridor. She whispered not to stay too long.

Mam'selle was sitting in a low chair, her black skirt spread neatly, a rosary between her thin fingers. Ariel caught her breath. Mam'selle had always been wiry. Now she was a transparency, a cobweb of a woman clinging for a moment to this bare room before a kindly gust of wind blew her beyond it.

"Ariel!"

Ariel, unable to speak, set the yellow plant on the floor and dropped to her knees, burying her face in that familiar lap. Mam'selle!"

"Child! Child! I knew you would come!" Her thin face lighted as she saw the flowers. "And bring sunshine! Oh, *ma petite! Ma petite chère!*" She lifted Ariel's face. "You are well? So! We will light the lamp and you will sit on that chair I bullied from Sister Agathe and you will tell me everything. You have been to America!"

"How did you know?"

"Your Maman told me when you left. It upset her very much."

"It still does." A weight slid from Ariel. She sat on the hard chair and her eyes searched the tired face. "You are not well."

"I am very well. I am in the hands of *le bon Dieu.* Now tell me about America."

"I'm going back, Mam'selle!"

"You are in love."

"How could you guess?"

Mam'selle's laugh was merry. "*Ma petite!* I am from Provence. We know these things. Tell me about him."

Ariel was suddenly a child telling her secret. Her face glowed. She talked, as she had longed to talk since the first night she had met Duncan. What he looked like, how he laughed, how much he knew, how intelligent he was, how much people respected him, loved him.

"I am so glad for you. No such man has ever walked the earth before, yes?" Her eyes twinkled. "And what does he do?"

"He is a minister." ──

"Good. Good. He is very important in the government?"

"No, Mam'selle. In the church. You would call him a priest."

There was a small silence. The thin fingers worked their beads. "*Mon Dieu,* Ariel!"

"It isn't the way you think. In Duncan's church he is allowed to marry. He was engaged to be married when I met him."

The beads clicked nervously. "My poor child." Her

344

face seemed to have sunk even more; a shadow had settled on it. A death mask.

"Please, Mam'selle. Don't be upset. We're happy."

"Listen to me, child. You do not know what happiness is yet. You are living in a delusion. You have trapped yourself. No man can dedicate himself to God and to a woman. If he does, he is committing a sin. He has vowed himself to God. Can he stand at an altar and vow himself to you? If he puts you first, he has failed God. If he puts God first, you have no right to take him from that service. Think what you're doing, Ariel!"

"I love him. He loves me."

"Then he has already renounced his vow. Is that what you want? To take a man from his life's work? How will you live with him, day in and day out, when you have done that? If this man has truly pledged himself to God, can he break that pledge and live with himself?"

Ariel had grown up dependent on Mam'selle's sternness; that unyielding sense of right and wrong had been her ballast in the shifting patterns of her childhood. She answered unsteadily.

"I don't know. I only know I love him."

"Of course you love him. I loved once, too. It's splendid and exciting. But that is not all of it. You are young. You have become very lovely. You are good. The love that comes to you must be from the world you know. Where you belong. Where you have the most to give. And therefore where you will be happiest."

Mam'selle lay back, spent by her intensity. Ariel rose and rested her cheek against the older woman's. "Dear Mam'selle, I will think about what you have said. May I come back to see you?"

"Yes! Yes! I know you will do what is right, child, when the time comes."

Ariel was halfway home when she remembered the

paper bag containing the immortelles. She had left it beside Mam'selle's chair, like part of her youth.

Alicia was seated, in delicate perfection, in the living room when Ariel entered. Only the drumming of her fingers showed her impatience. And the glitter in her eyes.

"You're late, Ariel. Where on earth have you been?"

"To see Mam'selle. She's in the convent. She's ill."

"I didn't know. Why didn't she call me?"

"Don't worry, Alicia, I'll look after her until I leave."

"Leave?"

Alicia thought better of finishing. It was like Ariel to be difficult when she should be dressing to look her best. If she could just get the girl suitably married, then Ariel could do as she liked. In France, they did these things so sensibly. A girl found her freedom after marriage, not before. All these new ideas of liberation, a single girl living with this man or that, contributing to his support, enduring all the tedious domesticity of marriage with none of its practical benefits. To Alicia, this was simply bad management. Why would any woman want to support herself when a man—that is, a successful man—could do it so much better? Alicia picked up her discarded volume of Colette. One could always find an adroit jest to quote on man versus woman, sex versus marriage. Ben Orlini would not have heard it. His son, Nick, was an unknown quantity.

Ariel dressed quickly, indifferently. Her visit to Mam'selle had thrown her life out of focus. She felt as if she were looking at it from far away. She missed Duncan with a physical hunger. Her old life had become impossible. Yet the future lay ahead like a question on a road that came to a vanishing point. A surrealist landscape with Duncan on the distant edge of a shoreless sea.

She would lose this detachment once she had firmly

told Alicia what she intended to do. Once she had said it aloud, set the hour, and bought the ticket for her return to him.

"If he has made a vow to serve God, child, would you come between . . ."

Mam'selle's faith was encrusted with centuries. She had no tolerance, no awareness of change. Ariel would cherish that beloved figure with its rock-ribbed sureness like a fading daguerrotype. Yet her own detachment persisted.

She returned to the living to meet Alicia's chill appraisal.

"Ariel, we must get you some clothes. That simply will not do."

Ben Orlini ordered second scotches for himself and his son and glanced again at the entrance of the chic bistro he had chosen for the evening. He disliked women being late. Nick had already begun a flirtation with a girl across the room, a lush, metallic girl with platinum hair, platinum dress, and furry eyes. Her escort, wizened and white-fringed, sat nodding beside her. The spectacle made Ben uncomfortable. Worse, the camaraderie he had anticipated with his son had not developed. He followed Nick's suggestive glances.

"You may find yourself in trouble, Nick."

"The old man's in a coma. She's bored to death. And, if you should ask me, Dad, so am I. You haven't yet told me who the dates are. But knowing your taste, I don't think anything's going to walk in handier that that blond."

"The trouble with your generation, Nick—"

"Oh, come on, Dad!"

"—is that you don't know how to savor anticipation."

"Not when it's thirty-five minutes late. Since you've busted up my little fantasy across the room, you might level with me."

"Sure, what do you want to know?"

"What's the real reason behind this big gesture? Inviting me to Paris."

"Do I need a reason to want to see my son?"

"You've always had one. Usually a tough one."

Ben sighed. In a real family, feelings should flow. In his, they chipped off like fragments of flint.

"Okay. I've got a tough one this time. I want you to know more about the business. Get your feet off the desk and your tail off the chair and work with me."

Nick laughed. "That's more like it. Dear old Dad. It'll be a pleasure, as long as the pay is good and the hours short. But you know, I guessed wrong."

"You usually do, Nick."

Nick drained his glass and signaled the waiter. His father's hand chopped the air. "I do the ordering tonight, son. Two's enough until the ladies arrive."

"Yes, *sir*!" Nick grinned. He sensed his father was trying to reach him and he liked the feeling of power. "Or maybe I didn't guess wrong. I figured that you invited me over to annoy the hell out of Mother."

"Just maybe you're right." Ben wanted this son's love, yet he suspected that if ever he dared look beneath conventional emotions, he might discover how much he disliked the man his son had become. "When you're married, Nick, you'll discover that a woman needs . . ."

"Stow it, Dad. You're never going to touch gentle Julia. She came home from Washington with the goods. She's got everything you couldn't get. She's got a hammerlock on that Roundtree property nobody's going to break. Would you like to know what it is?"

Ben's eyes narrowed. The syllable came like a bullet. "Yes."

Nick laughed. "Gotcha, Dad! You see . . ." Ben Orlini was rising.

Beside a mink-wrapped, enameled little woman, Ariel Roundtree had entered the restaurant.

❈　❈　❈

The evening was a disaster. Alicia chattered with an increasingly brittle laugh. Nick kept sipping from his glass, his mocking eyes on Ariel. Ben Orlini's mind returned to the thrust-parry-and-kill of the business world. He propped his eyes open and wished he were home in bed.

Ariel's smile had frozen when she saw Nick. It had not defrosted. She sat cool and quiet, answering Ben Orlini's occasional polite remarks. She could not have explained why she felt a little sorry for this small slayer of giants. And of trees. He was so transparently a ploy in her mother's delicate, groomed hands. But she guessed it was only because he had chosen to be. Ben Orlini was rough but he was shrewd. She despised Alicia's bubbling obviousness.

But mostly Ariel spent the evening trying to draw her knee away from the relentless pressure of Nick's.

At last it was over. Ben Orlini was riffling through his credit cards. Small lines were showing at the corners of Alicia's tired smile. Nick put his hand over Ariel's.

"When do I see you again?"

"I'm going back very soon to Thatcher, Nick." She ignored Alicia's signals.

"So am I, honey. But don't knock fate. I'll pick you up tomorrow at eleven."

"I'm sorry, Nick."

"It's going to be a lovely day tomorrow, Ariel." It was a command from Alicia, not a comment. "Don't think about me, darling. I've a frightfully busy day." She smiled at Ben.

"Good. Eleven, Ariel?"

"That would be lovely, wouldn't it, chérie? Then we'll all meet together in the evening. Ben has all kinds of plans."

Ben had found his credit card. "Sure. Anything you want."

"I'm sorry." Ariel sat stiffly, her hands in her lap.

"I'm visiting someone who's very dear to me and who's very ill."

"I'll wait."

Ariel took a little breath. "I'm sure your father wanted to arrange a very pleasant evening and I do thank him. But I want to be very clear. I haven't time to see you, Nick, while I'm in Paris. And I don't want to. I really don't."

Nick's eyes hardened with the dangerous glint she had come to know. But his laugh was easy. "What did you say about women, Dad? Unpredictable? This was the girl who picked me up at the Bollington station for a ride into Thatcher. She was willing to see me then. Oh, yes. And she was crazy to see me while the preacher boy was busy. Oh, I understood it all. And I can be very patient." His fingers gripped her wrist. "You'll be crazy to see me again, baby. I promise you. So let's cut through all the crap. I'll pick you up around eleven."

Ben had found his credit card. Alicia's age was showing. Ariel's face had gone white with anger. Then she laughed.

"Why not, Nick? Alicia adores company at a late breakfast. Don't you, dear?"

The door of their apartment had barely closed when Alicia whirled on her daughter.

"Ariel, that was contemptible! I've never known you to be so rude. If what that young man said was true, you deserve every word he said!"

"I went out with him. Until I found out what kind of man he is."

"You picked him up. You accepted his invitations. Then you tossed him aside for a—for a . . ."

"For a man I fell in love with. Yes." Ariel would not, if she could, explain the desperation of those days in Thatcher. Her willingness to go anywhere, do anything to conceal her real feelings for Duncan.

"You used him."

"If you want to put it that way." Mockery crept into her voice yet not without a remnant of pity for her mother's disappointment. "Isn't that what you've always taught me, Alicia? Use a man or he will use you? I went out with Nick for my reasons. Until I discovered what kind of man he is. He's despicable. I also think he could be dangerous. I don't want ever to see him again!" She regarded Alicia for a long searching moment, feeling a pang at the shadows under the wide eyes, the fatigue that showed through the careful veneer. Her mother had a gallantry beneath her fluttering foolishness. Ariel put her arm around Alicia's shoulder. "Alicia, don't make any more plans for me. I don't need them any more."

Alicia might have let the tears come. Stay in control, she told herself.

"Very well, chérie. I would not think of planning your life. But I will do everything I can to guide it. You don't understand the world as I do. Life can be very hard for a woman. You don't think so now. But there are certain things a girl like you should have, a certain background, comfort, nice things around you."

"Alicia . . ."

"I don't ask you to see Nick Orlini. Although I found him most attractive. I had no idea how you felt or how well you knew him. It's a long time since you confided in me. But I ask you to think about your own future. Apparently you have something in mind."

"I have a great deal in mind. I've come back to see you. I'll stay here for a few days then I'm going back to Thatcher. I'm engaged to be married, Alicia."

Alicia stiffened. "Who is it?"

"Duncan Phelps."

Alicia sank into a chair. "So it was true? All that hideous gossip?"

"It was all lies! We did nothing wrong. Lowell never loved him. She walked out on the wedding. He's the most marvelous man I've ever known. We're going to be married as soon as I go back. I hope you'll be there. I hope you'll like Duncan. But if you don't, it won't change anything."

The words dropped as evenly, as flatly, as pebbles. Alicia stared at her daughter, turned without a word, and went to her room.

The walls of the old building were too thick for Ariel to hear Alicia put through a telephone call.

Halfway across Europe, Henri awakened from a deep sleep, sat up in his nightshirt to tell Alicia that no man yet, or woman had found a successful way to change the course of love.

Chapter Four

Mam'selle worsened. Ariel visited her daily. The four or five days she had hoped to stay lengthened. She wrote a letter to Duncan explaining her delay. And realized how hopeless it was to explain anything about her life in Paris. She had told him so little about herself. And knew so little about him. It had been enough to be together. From this distance, they were almost strangers. She did not even know where his Seminary was. He had told her not to write unless she was not coming back. But this was different. She needed the anchor of his presence. She addressed the letter care of Willard and then began to count the days until she would hear from him.

Nick regarded her refusal to see him as a challenge. Confidently and with some malice he telephoned every day. Alicia was happy to report his calls.

"Ariel, you do not look well. Mam'selle is depressing you. She wants to die yet she takes so long about it. God forbid I do. I sent roses today. I've invited Nick to tea."

"Then you entertain him, Alicia. I won't be here."

"What is wrong, chérie? If you are so happy about this—this Duncan of yours, why do you not behave like it? If you ask me, you're suffering from a bad conscience."

"You *will* not understand, will you Alicia?"

"Very well, chérie! You do not hear from him. You look sad. It is a very old story. A young man on the way to his wedding. The flower outside the fence looks sweeter." Alicia laughed. "Darling, it is such an old story. But I do not think in the end you will marry this man. I think you are coming to your senses!"

Ariel fled the apartment. She would walk until it was time to go to the convent. Through the winding paths and gardens of the Luxembourg, around the boat basin where as a child she had played primly within Mam'selle's sharp sight, loading her young visions on someone else's toy boat. Alicia had not liked her to return looking messy. She even lingered at the Punch and Judy show and heard again Mam'selle's careful, "Enough foolishness for today, *ma petite!*"

Long-ago spring afternoons. The Luxembourg was sere now and cold. On one of her walks, Ariel thought she caught a glimpse of Nick. She had taken a cab quickly and not returned to the gardens.

She wondered if she had lived deeply. Or not at all. Still Duncan did not answer her letter.

Then came the day when the plain-faced nurse opened the convent door with tears in her eyes. Ariel had never seen anyone die. She was not prepared.

Mam'selle was still breathing when Ariel knelt beside the narrow bed and took the thin hand in her own. The heavy-lidded eyes were open, unseeing, the strong face bones so fined down, beneath the drawn bleached skin, that Ariel hardly knew her.

She remained motionless. She was not afraid. It was not death that seemed so awful. It was the finality of living, the end of all one had to give and to love. There must have been some point, some hour in Mam'selle's rigid days when she could have stepped out of them, laughed into the morning, flung her arms to the sun, and changed her destiny. Ariel, kneeling in silence, so aware of her own youthful vitality, longed to unwind the spool, to know Mam'selle as she had once been, to thrust into those dry-veined hands the fullness of living.

Mam'selle's eyes closed. Peace, like a greeting, suffused her face. She's beautiful, Ariel thought. She must have been—she started, so violently that she let go of the still hand.

No one had told her of the last hoarse cry, the breath's protesting release.

The nun came from her corner and bound Mam'selle's face, serene in its new wisdom, unutterably satisfied.

Ariel went slowly down the steps of the ancient building. A dark twilight had fallen into the gloomy street. She was aware of nothing but an emptiness deeper than grief.

He was standing at the curb.

"I have a cab," said Nick Orlini.

She shook her head.

"Don't be a fool, Ariel. Alicia told me. Come on, get in." He took her elbow. "You can't fight the whole world, baby. You can't even find a cab around here at this hour." He half led, half pushed her into the cab, gave the driver an order, and got in beside her.

She sank numbly back. The shabby buildings began to slide by.

A silent quarter of an hour later, Paris began to show its brillance. Nick glanced at her.

"That wasn't so bad, was it?"

"It's no use, Nick."

"Right. You're going back to Thatcher and marry the preacher boy."

Alicia must have told him. She could hear the bright intolerance as Alicia tried to salvage her plans.

"You'll find a few things changed."

"Will I?"

"For one, being a Roundtree isn't going to make a damn bit of difference any more."

"I'm not going back as a Roundtree."

"Oh, come on, you can't help it. Thatcher's first family. Has been for a hundred years in that tight little, right little town. Don't think the preacher boy doesn't know it. He couldn't make it with Lowell, so he's going to try with you."

He was goading her but the offensive words glanced off. Her rigid childhood lay dead in a virginal white bed beside a praying nun. She was beginning to sense an odd, if anguished, release. She was too young to recognize it was one of death's lingering footprints.

"I'd rather not talk, Nick."

"You don't have to." He looked at her searchingly. "I'm sorry for what's happened. Your mother said the old lady meant a lot to you. So okay. I'm sorry. But you've got to come out of it, Ariel. There's a big world out there and I have an idea you've slid over it on some kind of moth wings. Thatcher! You think it's some kind of Christmas card. It's a dead-end town that hasn't taken a step forward in fifty years."

"I like it."

"Good. Then you'll like it better when we get through with it."

"Who's we?"

"You'll hear it soon enough when you get there. The Roundtrees don't own that big hunk of land that old Willard sits on. They never did. The real Isaac Roundtree never inherited it. He was a Civil War soldier, a kind of bum who went West after the war. He was hanged as a horse thief in Missouri."

The streets were brighter now, the traffic heavier. She stared at him. "Where did you hear that?"

He sat back in the cab, pleased with the effect. "You met Julia. My esteemed mother. She gets what she wants. Ultimately." He grinned. "I take after her. She also happens to be a Thatcher, the family the town was named for. The original landowners. Which now makes Willard Roundtree's whole valley hers."

Ariel was emotionally drained. She saw again the peaceful selflessness of Mam'selle's quiet face.

"Nick, I don't believe all this. I don't know why you're telling me now."

"If you don't believe it, go argue with the War Department records. Why am I telling you? To get it through that beautiful, hard head of yours that there's nothing for you in Thatcher now. Oh, the Roundtrees will go on scratching for a living. And the preacher boy will have his poor little church. As long as it's there."

"What does that mean?"

"Julia has plans. So have I. There's money to be made up there. But you and I will spend it somewhere else. The good life, baby. That's where you belong. That's what I'm going to give you."

The cab had crossed the neon-bright Boulevard St. Michel and entered the tree-lined elegance of St. Germain. She hardly saw it. She was icy with anger and worry. Somehow his words had the ring of truth.

"Do they know all this in Thatcher?"

"They will. When Julia's ready to tell 'em. Don't fight it, Ariel, because you can only lose. You and the preacher boy."

The cab jolted to a stop. He looked at her for an instant, his eyes hard, demanding, possessive.

"I'm not giving up on you, Ariel. You're what I want, and the more you push me off the more I want you. I'm that kind of guy. I found you today. I'll find you anywhere you go. Even Thatcher. If you're crazy enough to go back. It's going to be you and me, baby. And I think you know it."

He held the cab door open but made no move to follow her. "Good night, Miss Roundtree."

Ariel let herself into the dim apartment. She was relieved to find it empty. She stopped in the foyer to look through the mail. There was nothing. Nothing at all.

She went quickly to the telephone. The funeral would be held on the third day. She would see Alicia through that.

She dialed quickly. "I wish to make a reservation. Single seat. Economy. The first flight you can get me on after Thursday. To New York. And a connection to Hartford, Connecticut."

Then she went into her dark room, threw herself on the bed, and let the aching emptiness within her fill with dry sobs.

Ben Orlini stood at the window of his hotel suite, rocking on his small feet. His mind flowed with the stream of lighted traffic below. Impatient, hurrying, full of purpose. His trip had in the end gone better than he had foreseen. They had finally begun to listen to him, these shrewd foreigners with the world-shifting schemes. They recognized in him a man like themselves, indifferent to politics, immune to history, the new patriots of power and profit who operated outside of outmoded boundaries and ideologies. Ben saw himself already in those coveted circles, playing global games of corporate manipulation for huge, invisible stakes. Better still, he had uncovered the name of the elusive man behind Umex, the newest, most rapidly expanding cartel. With that connection . . .

Ben clasped his hands behind his back, realized as he always did his arms were too short for ease and unlocked them He had made one mistake. Despite his intentions, he had been unable to resist calling Julia to report his success. She had listened silently, then curtly reported her own triumph. She now had proof that the Roundtree land was hers. She would begin legal action at once. Julia never hung up on him. Any more than she ever really quarreled. She merely diminished him. She had done it again this afternoon in four words.

"How nice for you." She had not forgiven him for taking Nick away. But she had brought him back to Thatcher with a jolt.

Thatcher, his one defeat. He would make them pay for that. Thatcher was no more than the head of a pin in his future. But to Julia, Thatcher had become an obsession. He would never be free of it as long as he wanted her. Deny it as he would, Ben still wanted his disturbing wife more than any other woman he had ever known. Her lean elegance still fired his possessiveness, her indifference still drove him to excesses.

He heard a step and turned to see his son enter. Julia's languid grace. Julia's height. But that petulant, overconfident grin. God knows where the boy got that.

"Party's over, Nick."

Nick moved to the side table with its array of bottles, poured himself a drink.

"What party?"

"This one. You've just got time to pack."

Nick sat down in a deep-pillowed chair.

"What for?"

"We're taking the nine o'clock plane. Home."

Nick took a long swallow of whiskey. He smiled. Even sitting, he seemed able to look down on his father.

"Why did you get me over here, Dad? To irritate Mother?"

"I said a week. The week's up. Get moving. Unless you want to pay your own bill. Rate is $240 a day."

Nick unfolded his long legs. Julia's legs.

"At those prices I could run up quite a bill. I could say you owe me that, Dad. You had some idea that you and Alicia—sweet Jesus, isn't she incredible—and Ariel and I . . ."

"If I did, I don't any more. I thought no girl ever turned you down. But this one put you where you belong, all right. No doubt good for you. Come on. Get moving."

Nick rose. He had to respect the source of wealth.

"You're an old lecher, Dad. You've looked her over yourself. You'd like her in the family. Ariel hasn't turned me down. If I get around to marrying, she might be the one. As a matter of fact, I saw her this afternoon." Nick yawned and stretched.

Ben stifled any surprise. Even a sense of disappointment. He had liked the steel he had sensed in Ariel. A challenge was what Nick needed.

"She's headstrong but she can be managed." Nick glanced at the telephone table. "What did Mother have to say?"

"How the hell did you know I called her?"

"You doodle, Dad. Circles. Lots of circles. Whenever you talk to her. Old family joke among up kids. She drives you up the wall, doesn't she?"

"Keep a civil tongue in your head, Nick!"

"Did she tell you how she got the Roundtree land?"

"She hasn't got it yet."

"You think there's any doubt?"

"I haven't seen the evidence. But I'm going to make damn sure it holds up before I begin developing the land."

Nick sloughed toward the bottles on the table. Not that he gave a damn about the land himself. But his father had the Midas touch. Whereas if Julia had her way . . .

"You've had enough to drink, Nick. I told you to get packing."

"Yes, Daddy." Nick finished refilling his glass. "If Julia gets the land, and if she lets you into the action, what did you have in mind?"

Ben stifled his anger. There was no use quarreling with Nick. The boy would do as he pleased. Like his mother he had a dozen ways of flicking him on the raw. Besides, Nick was no longer a boy. He was a grown man. The tall, handsome son he had wanted, who would work beside him, carry on his business, be his confidant, even his friend.

"I'll tell you exactly what I'm going to do." It was a relief to rechannel his anger. "Your mother has some notion that she is just going to sit and look at that land. It's a gold mine if you know what to do with it. I'd like to build a hunting lodge at the far end of the valley. The area's full of deer, upland birds, any game a man wants to hunt. Rich man's place. Very exclusive. Private landing field. Private cottages. All strictly luxury. High-stakes gambling. Oh, I'll have protection. Tucked away up in that valley, a man'll be able to get anything he wants, provided he can pay for it. I'll run a decent road out of that town."

"Do away with a few churches, maybe?"

"What?"

"I like your ideas, Dad. I like 'em real good. I want to be around when Julia gets a load of 'em."

"You'll learn, if you haven't already, son, that women like to fuss. It's built-in with 'em. But in the end they'll go for anything that keeps the money coming."

"That's what I'm counting on, Dad."

Ben laughed, Nick joined him. For an instant a spark of warmth flickered between them. Then it went out. Ben returned to the window and reality. He was a loner. He would remain one. Thanks to his scarred childhood, the runt of the streets, he was tough enough to make money. He was also tough enough to keep his loneliness to himself.

The face of the pink-lipped prostitute on the Boulevard St. Michel took shape for an instant in his mind. To be young. To be able to taste surprise and delight. To be driven by no other voice but your own. To love and be loved and to believe. He could not even buy all that again. But he would come back to Paris. Soon. And alone.

He set his bags neatly beside the door, folded his coat across them, deliberately leaving the absurd gray Rue St. Honoré homberg where it lay, at the back of the closet shelf.

"Nick! Get your butt moving, will you? Or you can pay this hotel bill yourself!"

For three brief days, Mam'selle's death had come, like Mam'selle herself, as a healing presence in the apartment on the Boulevard St. Germain.

"I'll make the arrangements," Ariel had said.

"The nuns will do it all," said Alicia. She seemed vulnerable, clinging. A prop had gone that she could ill afford to lose. She has so few, thought Ariel, and stifled her own sense of guilt that lay with the airline reservation in her purse. It would not be easy (as if it ever were) to talk with Alicia after the funeral.

With a long line of nuns, a handful of strangers from Mam'selle's private life, of which they knew so little, Alicia and Ariel accompanied Mam'selle to her long-reserved grave above her sister and to the rest in which she had so fervently trusted. In a gray day of restless clouds, sprinkling rain, and a moist wind that tugged at full skirts and plucked at white coifs, the nuns saw God's will. When pale sunlight at last fell scantily on the bare new grave, they lifted their faces like whitened flowers and saw a benediction.

Alicia entered the apartment and turned up every lamp in the drawing room.

"How do they do it, those women? Poor Mam'selle! If it hadn't been for our lilies and chrysanthemums!"

Ariel forebore to point out that flowers had no part in the convent's ritual. Rain had splattered the blossoms with city dirt. Wind had shredded and broken the petals. But the stern metal crucifix the sisters had laid on the black coffin would last Mam'selle into her eternity.

They had lunched afterward, at Alicia's insistence, at a fashionable restaurant, which somewhat restored her. Now, at home, there was nothing to do but pick up the pieces of the day. Ariel saw in her mother's nervous hands and shifting eyes, danger signals.

Alicia lit a cigarette, puffed, fiercely tamped it out.

"I really mustn't. It dulls the hair and yellows the eyes."

"I thought that was coffee." Ariel put a pillow behind her mother's back.

"It's everything. It's all such an effort. Do's and don'ts. Always the struggle, simply to keep yourself up to minimum."

"You do a lot better than that, Alicia. You could have passed for thirty-five today."

"Until the sun came out. I think I should live in one of those places where the sun shines three days a year and on those days I could always take the cure. Wasn't it depressing?"

"I think Mam'selle would have been satisfied. All the nuns were there. And a Monsignor."

"Did I tell you Ben Orlini called me from the airport?"

"Yes."

"You're a very foolish girl, Ariel."

"I expect so. Would you like a drink? That won't yellow your eyes."

But Alicia was in no mood for poor jokes. Something she would not name was stalking her from the corners of the room.

"When is Uncle Henri coming back, Mother?"

"I haven't any idea. He called me from Athens last night. Athens! What in the world is he doing in Athens? Ripe olives give him indigestion and he can't stand the wine. He says I don't understand business. I tell him it's part of my charm. You know, Ariel, this is your fault."

"What is?"

"This completely desolating time we're having."

"I think we owed it to Mam'selle."

"I'm not talking about Mam'selle. If you don't think I miss her, I do. But life goes on. The point is, what life? If you hadn't been so absolutely hideous to young Nick Orlini, I'm sure Ben would have stayed on."

"Did you really like him, Alicia?"

"What has that to do with it? You're so simple-minded about things, Ariel. Black or white. Hot or cold. Aren't you ever going to learn that one lives life by what's in between? Now, let's plan our little trip. Sardinia is very chic now. We'd have no trouble getting into that fabulous new resort. Henri owns part of it."

It had come. Ariel sat down quietly and wondered if the beating of her heart could be heard over the glass of water she had poured for herself.

"Alicia, I'm not going on a trip with you."

"Perhaps you're right. We'll stay in Paris. I'll give a few parties. Intimate little dinners. Where everybody becomes bosom friends before the first entrée. You should meet new people, darling. We can't wait forever for Henri."

"Mother, I'm going back to Thatcher."

As Ariel feared, Alicia met this with silence.

"Nothing has changed, Alicia. I told you I loved Duncan. I'm going back to him. We're going to be married."

Alicia lay back on the divan, her hand on her heart. "You don't care what you do to me."

Ariel's voice was soft with patience. "But I do. And I know I do give you the flutters. But I don't know how else to tell you. You'll have the flutters no matter how I say it. I'll never change about Duncan."

Alicia turned with the fury of a small cat. "You won't change! Do you think you're different from any other woman ever born? You're in love, the great love of your life, you think. If it is, which I doubt, do you think the world will stand still and let you have it as you want it? Forever? Oh, no doubt you've sworn that. You won't change, not you. But he will. And love will. And the world will!"

The fury faded. Alicia had spent her anger but not her desperation. "Ariel, my darling, darling child. If you do love this man, then remember that love. Keep it. Cherish it. But don't go back. Think what this marriage would be. A minister's wife in a town where you've already created a scandal. Never mind the fact that you'd have no money. But day by day, what would it be, for you? If he is the man you say, he will be tolerated but he will be pitied. But you, the woman who took him from his bride, will be hated. You will never be accepted or at ease anywhere. I know women. Once they turn on you, there is no place to go. Thatcher has already turned on you."

"But I didn't . . ."

"They think you did. That is enough. In a year you'd want to be out of it. Would you make this man you love ridiculous by asking for a divorce then? What would you do?"

"Duncan said he'd leave Thatcher."

"Oh. And that is to be the solution. If he stays in the church, don't you think the story will follow you wherever you go?"

The light, insistent voice penetrated like a needle. Ariel felt numbed yet compelled to make a crumbling defense.

"Duncan may leave the Church."

With a little smile, Alicia sat back. She let a few seconds of silence pass.

"And you, my poor dear darling, you plan to sit every morning at breakfast opposite a man whose career you have ruined?"

Ariel stared at her, turned, and fled the room.

Alicia had shut herself in her bedroom and locked the door. There was no sound by the time Ariel was ready to leave. She wrote a careful note, left it on the foyer table.

She saw her departure as abrupt and cruel. If she had not already bought her ticket, she could never have left so soon after Mam'selle's funeral. Yet she knew, when she could clear her mind of Alicia's stinging words, that if she did not go now, she might never. She had sunk too often, too helplessly into the cloying morass of Alicia's demands.

Yet she knew also, as she stepped into the freshening air of the dark street, that her mother's words would live with her, perhaps forever. Duncan had not written. She had no idea what lay ahead. Or what had happened. Would it all be as she remembered? Or had Julia Orlini made good her threat? Perhaps already Willard had left his farm. And Duncan—where under these same stars was he tonight?

She slung her tote bag over her shoulder and picked up her suitcase. Inside Ariel lay something deeper than all the unanswerable questions, all Alicia's angry recriminations.

For the first time in her life, Ariel truly felt she was going home.

Part Four

Thatcher: The Legacy

Chapter One

As soon as Ariel left Thatcher, the talk died. Not entirely. Flickers of it still ran like a deep grass fire, close to the soil, to feed and flare where the roots were dry and the moisture of tolerance gone. Some said Lowell had been foolish to run away and leave the field to that French girl, cousin or not. A few said Duncan Phelps had no business looking over the fence and he, a clergyman. But most agreed that he had behaved with dignity, that he had met temptation, which only showed that he was young and very human but, then, he had resisted it, hadn't he? In his return to the Seminary, Thatcher saw expiation and was prepared to forgive him. Duncan was theirs beyond the seduction of "that girl."

Lowell returned for a weekend and tongues wagged again. Hannah Poole said if you asked *her*, which no one did, she wouldn't be surprised if Lowell and Duncan got married, quietly of course, before the year was out. Hadn't she herself seen Ariel—what an outlandish name that was—flirt openly with Duncan in Slater's Stationery Store, throw herself at him, you could say. She, Hannah, for one couldn't find it in her heart to blame the boy. Mark her words, it would all come out right.

In the rambling white house on West Street, gossip was forbidden. Martin went to his office every morning with the untouchable assumption that he had handled the matter properly. He missed Lowell but now that the currents flowed smoothly again, he was inclined to share Hannah Poole's anticipation (vehemently as he would deny sharing anything with that female) that Lowell would return. The two young people would come to their senses. Ariel should never have come into the house. She had the wild strain, fortunately bred out of his own children. Yes, they had only to wait. Lowell would come back.

If Edythe saw deeper into this too-quiet daughter, she said nothing. As for Ariel, she had brought a lightness into this home, like forgotten music. Edythe remembered her own youth, returned the wedding presents with charming little notes, and wondered aloud if they could afford to paint the house in the spring.

Claude, to everyone's surprise, lapsed into silence. At the dinner table she snatched glances at Henrietta's knowing portrait and saw herself as beautiful and magnetic, in distant lands, hopelessly adored by handsome if faceless men, while spurning their offers of diesel yachts and marble villas. The Roundtree destiny was surely hers. But she kept her real secret. For one brief evening, she and Ariel had become confidants, when Ariel had hinted at a hidden romance in Lowell's life. Not that Claude could believe that. But if her subdued sister was capable of buried passion, what lay ahead for Claude? The world, Claude told herself, and Ariel was the way to it. That was the most titillating part of her secret. Claude had watched Ariel closely every time Duncan's name was mentioned. She was as sure as she was of stardust that Ariel would come back. Just as Claude herself would come back, would do anything, for an all-consuming passion. For that she would sacrifice everything, even if it meant dying too young, too beautiful. She wondered if Ariel would come back to die too young and too beautiful, or to marry Duncan and make pies for the church fair. Claude said nothing, for the simple reason that there was too much to say.

It was left to Kim to express herself. Not in the

house, of course. But to her wide-eyed, eager-eared peers. Ariel was a real witch, Kim whispered. The real ones were always beautiful. She had risen out of the graveyard. Anyone brave enough could see her there at midnight when the cock crowed. As there were no cocks to crow within five miles of Thatcher, and none known ever to keep a midnight tryst. Kim enjoyed considerable prestige without challenge to her veracity. Besides, Kim had striking evidence. She had found in Ariel's wastebasket the most hideous mask, all green and purple and fanged. She'd wear it to the Halloween bonfire. To prove it was magic, she might even fly over the monument. Kim's honest little soul had no way to express the depth of her pain that Dunkie was never to be her brother. Never to walk in the door as Michael used to long ago and swing her to the ceiling in his arms.

But all the talk died away one day, smothered by a new piece of gossip. Thatcher learned to its astonishment that Julia Orlini—cool, gaunt wife of that odious little man intent on cutting down trees—was not an outsider like her husband. She was a Thatcher. As everyone knew, the Thatchers had come with the original King's Grant to found the town in 1632. Thatcher's Corners, it was first called. That would explain why the Orlinis were building a house on the Ridge. It would certainly not explain the kind of bat-winged monstrosity they had chosen to build. It would also explain the rumors that Ben Orlini had often tried to buy Willard Roundtree's valley. Willard had held firm. The town knew it could trust him. But the idea was unsettling.

Julia Thatcher Orlini was obviously of a branch that did not care what it did with its name. She had cold-shouldered the town and here she was on its doorstep with a husband who was circling it like a hungry jackal.

Willard Roundtree avoided questions, reassured

them when he had to and sought seclusion, tidying his acres for winter. Julia's ultimatum, in a five-line letter, lay in his desk drawer. Isaac Roundtree had been an imposter, she wrote. His descendants had no legal claim to the land. If he had any evidence to disprove this, she would see him at her home on the last day of this month. Otherwise she would begin legal action on the first of the next.

Willard was not yet willing to admit failure. He had not revealed the letter. Julia would not act publicly until she was sure. But time was running out. Stacking his corn shucks by day, sitting with Clancy in the evening, stroking the big dog's silky head, Willard felt the loneliness of his burden. He would like to hear Ariel's light step, her lovely, oddly different voice. But as the days passed, he had begun to mistrust that glimpse of young love and his part in it. He had forwarded her letter to Duncan and it had failed to bring the boy back. Whenever was the course of love anything but unpredictable?

But he was thankful, now that he was so near the point of being forced to surrender to Julia, that Ariel had not come back. How many of the gilded peaks of his own youth had been flattened by time.

Willard rose stiffly and turned on a lamp. Tomorrow was the first of November. "Then if ever come dreary days." He must be getting on to let the old words surface in his mind. Foolish to ask schoolchildren to learn 'em. Gave 'em an entirely false notion of what was good. He glanced at the mantel clock. His appointment was at six. Odd time but then everything had turned suddenly odd. Odd and unbelievable.

He had a little time left. He had searched every nook and cranny of the old house. He had gone through every paper in the safe deposit vault and all the old Thatcher records. Without telling Martin why, he had asked for any documents relating to the Roundtree inheritance and old Nathaniel Thatcher's bequest to Isaac Roundtree. Martin reminded him rather testily that Willard had kept all family documents in his own hands.

In the full light of the lamp, he knelt again at the brass-handled chest Henrietta had brought to Thatcher so long ago. He knew, of course, all it contained. Still, he was goaded by the thought that if there were any way to prove Isaac Roundtree's identity, and to disprove Julia Orlini's monstrous assumption, the clue would lie in Henrietta's ghostly hands.

It was futile. Only the ivory lace gown in its tissue paper folds. The little volumes of Shakespeare in their crumbling, cinnamon suede bindings. Mathilda Boler's letters, a neatly tied bundle of faded sensible advice. One of Mathilda's letters had been thrust into the volume of Shakespeare's "Tempest," Act III, scene 1. Henrietta had underscored four lines: "Beyond all limit of what else i' th' world, do love, prize, honor you." And then the next line, ". . . I am a fool to weep at what I am glad of."

Willard read it again. A passionate filly, Henrietta. Her blood in all their veins. Seventeen when she married Isaac—if he was Isaac. He'd like to have known her then.

He read the letter she had slipped between the pages. Mathilda had written: "Joseph and I have decided you should have the brooch no matter how unlawfully Isaac came by it. I am sending it separately. I am also forwarding a letter for Isaac that was delivered to the tavern. The woman who runs the place brought it over herself. I'm glad you weren't here, dear child. She was so very curious. I'm afraid she is quite common. I don't know how primitive Connecticut is, but we are shipping you the wool wheel that you enjoyed so much. And a very good recipe for homemade soap. Be sure you keep the fat and caustic boiling, not simmering. . . ."

Willard smiled again. If he indulged a youthful image of Henrietta, he also savored a kinship with this warm strong presence of Mathilda Boler. There was a woman a man could bed with comfortably each night, knowing that the next day he would be capably, tenderly reassured.

He sighed and closed the chest. Nothing, nothing. The wool wheel stood in the corner, mute evidence of the riddle of time. But whatever brooch, whatever letter, the good Mathilda had sent on had vanished. As had any proof of the identity of Isaac Roundtree, if it ever existed.

It was time to go.

The night was moonless, starless, and without wind. At least, thought Willard, as he climbed into the pickup truck, the youngsters would have their Halloween bonfire on the Green. He would drop by if he got back in time.

He would keep this imminent disaster to himself, as long as he could.

Julia Orlini stretched languidly into the divan and regarded her guest. Her long body was outlined in clinging dove-gray. Heavy silver hung from her ears and wrapped her throat and wrists. Her hair was tied at the back of her neck with something silver. The only excitement lay in her large mascaraed eyes, intense and restless. She liked the old man. He had a quality she missed in her life. Call it principle or direction or perhaps simple gallantry. She would like him for a friend. She was not above looking her best for him, as a victim.

She had offered him, rather self-consciously, madeira. He had accepted bourbon, neat, and seated himself facing the fireplace. He had to turn his head to look at her.

"I believe in justice, Mr. Roundtree, don't you?"

"I believe it's one of life's pleasanter fantasies."

"Nor do I want to hurt anyone."

He sipped the bourbon and watched the flames. Applewood. The best. "No one ever does, after the fact, Mrs. Orlini."

"The name's Julia." She sat upright. "Don't you believe in looking at a lady when you talk to her?"

Willard smiled and swung his chair toward her. "It's been a lifetime enjoyment of mine. I might say you give me no reason for dropping it."

She laughed. She had been lonely, furious with Ben for inviting Nick to Paris and deliberately excluding her. She had remained in this silent house until the business was finished.

"You're really wonderful, Mr. Roundtree."

"So they tell me, so they tell me."

This was more the kind of banter she liked. "Who tells you?"

"Women of all kinds. My grandniece, for instance, as recently as yesterday when I managed to mend a Halloween mask she had set her ghoulish little heart on."

Julia Orlini had no interest in children. "She sounds charming."

"Some day I hope she will be, if it isn't too old fashioned by then."

Julia leaned forward.

"I want to be fair, Mr. Roundtree."

"Of course you do."

"But you must see the justice of my claim. The War Department keeps accurate records. They must. My lawyers say there is no possibility of an error. And if you haven't found any proof that your ancestor was in fact Isaac Roundtree, then the land comes to me, naturally."

"Naturally."

"And there's really no argument."

"I didn't come here to argue, my dear lady. I came here because you asked me."

It was not going the way she had intended. She wanted to humble this man and all his breed. Then she would bestow her generosity. But his courtesy held no meekness, merely self-assurance.

"Mr. Roundtree, I don't wish to put you or your

family in uncomfortable circumstances. Or even to take away your name. The land is mine, But I'm prepared to pay you any sum you think is fair. If you refuse, then I'm prepared to take it through the courts. I hope I won't be driven to that."

"It would be a pity. A woman like you should be protected from that kind of scruffy business. No place for you."

He rose.

"You won't name a price?"

"My dear lady, I cannot sell what you have told me I don't own." He bowed and moved toward the door. "It's been a pleasure to find you looking so well. By the way, you must tell me where you get that excellent-burning applewood. Just the right dryness. Good night, my dear."

She listened to his truck rattle into the silence, the deadly, numbing silence. So he would not let her be generous, to keep her dignity, as she had wanted.

She poured herself another glass and wondered at her own obsession. But she could not turn back now if she wished. The land was proven to be hers, legally, therefore justly. It was all in the world that was hers by her own inherited right.

Halfway through her drink, she sank back into the cushions and watched the flames. She had once, in girlhood, told herself that if she ever found a man she could not manage she would follow him to the ends of the earth.

Ben Orlini had been too easy.

Willard parked his truck on a side street and walked to Thatcher's Green. Two hundred years ago it had been the village common, a grazing ground for village sheep and goats. Prosperous farmers like the Thatchers brought their grain to the Roundtree grist mill. Willard shook his head to clear his mind. The past was over. He would have to think now of the future. And time was a shortening lance.

He came out of the dark side street to the Green. They were building the bonfire. Small figures whooped and danced around it, while adults lined the sidewalks.

Willard made his way to the monument and to the Reverend Samuel Wilcox standing near it.

"Fine evening, Sam."

"Glad you're here, Will. More trick-or-treaters out tonight than I ever thought lived in Thatcher. Duncan should be here to keep 'em in order."

"We two will do our best. Have you heard from him?"

"Duncan? No. And I hope I won't for a while. I advised him to think things out."

The old man looked pale and tired. His weight hung on him in folds. Sam Wilcox had counted on Duncan. He would die content, Willard knew, with his beloved church in Duncan's hands. As he, Willard, would have died content to pass the land on, whole and sweet, to his own. The dreams of old men for young men to destroy. Change, the lifeblood of humanity, the root of hope. Maybe. God certainly fulfilled Himself in strange ways.

"Do you think he'll come back, Sam?"

"Duncan? I hope he'll want to come back. He thought a lot about the ministry before he entered it. He learned the awful loneliness a man can know when he has nothing higher than himself to look to. I told him then that he'd better be sure of his motives. If he was going into it to serve God or man, he'd better think again. If he was going into it because he could not think of doing anything else, then God wanted him." Sam Wilcox chuckled. "I don't expect an old reprobate like you, Will, to go along with all that."

"I could surprise you. At my age, I like to think that eternity is something more than eternity." He sighed. "Duncan's got something on his mind besides motives, Sam. He's young."

"Well, it would be easier for him if he were forbidden to marry. Then he could sit back comfortably with his sacrifice. In any case, the decision is his." The old man took a deep, rasping breath. "I'm sure of one thing. If Duncan Phelps gives up the ministry, he will live as only half a man the rest of his life. He doesn't know himself yet."

"Who does, at his age?"

A train whistle moaned faintly in the distance.

Willard held his vest-pocket watch close in the dim light. "She's late by twenty minutes."

Sam Wilcox grunted, "When you hear her that clearly it means rain. More rain."

"We don't need it, Sam. River's too high now."

He caught sight of Martin rounding the corner with Edythe. Claude was not with them, nor was Lowell. Maybe that meant Lowell had gone back to the city. He hoped so.

He thought fleetingly of Ariel, so passionate, so vulnerable, so helpless against the mischief of this town. She was where she belonged. Time would do the rest.

Time. He nodded to the Reverend Wilcox and walked thoughtfully toward Martin and Edythe. Time was a healer but it was also a weapon. He would use it to the fullest against that unhappy, sexless woman, Julia Orlini.

The conductor leaned across the seat toward the girl beside the window.

"Next stop is Bollington, Miss."

"Thank you."

"We're running about twenty minutes late."

She flashed him a smile. "I don't mind. No one's meeting me."

The conductor moved along the aisle. His feet hurt, he was tired, and he was retiring next year. But if all his passengers smiled at him like that, the job would be a lot easier. He wondered how a girl like her could arrive in a town like Bollington and have no one to meet her. He'd see that she got off safely.

Ariel looked out the window but the black pane only reflected her own face. Too drawn. She hoped she would look better than that when she met Duncan. She was as confident of seeing him as of the turning wheels of the train. She was relieved that she had not cabled him in advance. The plane had been late, there had been a delay in finding her baggage, and she had barely managed to catch the afternoon train to Bollington. She would call Willard from the station. Maybe Duncan would be at the farmhouse as he had been before, waiting for her. Duncan might even answer the phone. She'd hear that warm voice first. He had not answered her letter but then he had told her he would not write her. He had wanted her to be so sure.

She was sure now. And for another, an intuitive reason, she could not have framed in words. The blood had run true. She had a family, a place of belonging in Thatcher. If Nick Orlini had not lied in what he had told her, her family was in trouble. The land, the Roundtree land, was threatened.

"I am a lemming," she told her reflection wryly. "I have to follow them over the cliff if that's where they're going." But Ariel had little real fear that anything bad would ever happen again. She had reduced the future to one simplistic formula. Duncan.

The Bollington station was dim and deserted. From an outside phone booth she made her call, her fingers trembling, her heart pounding. In another moment she would hear his voice, or Willard's telling her that he was there. But in the full flight of her imagination, Ariel had overlooked a practical contingency. There was no answer, either at Willard's farmhouse or at the Roundtree house which she reluctantly phoned next. She had come all this way unannounced. She would have to finish the journey thus. For the first time she began to wonder what her welcome would be. What if Duncan were not there? If Lowell had returned? Where could they all be on this black, starless night?

To her relief, a taxi rolled up to the platform.

"Thatcher," she told the taxi driver.

"Where in Thatcher?" The driver was a woman.

"The—the . . ." Ariel hesitated. "The stationery store—Slater's—on Main Street." She could call again from there.

The woman gave her a curious glance. The cab rattled into the night. Ariel tried to remember the winding road, the wood and hills, the river that lay out there in the darkness. And then she shut her mind to it all. She had made her first mistake in Thatcher. Heedlessly confident of herself and the superficialities she had grown up to accept, she had stepped into a stranger's car and met Nick Orlini. That was behind her now. She would never be alone with him again. She would never see him again if she could avoid it.

The drive seemed twice as long on this night. At last the cab emerged from the darkness and into a street bordering Thatcher's Green. Ariel gasped. It was thronged with people, silhouetted against a bright leaping bonfire.

"Halloween," said the woman driver. "I can't get through."

Ariel felt a surge of relief. This was where they all were. Somewhere in that shifting shadowy crowd was Duncan.

"You don't want to get out here?"

What she wanted most was to jump from the cab and slip among those moving figures until she found him. But there was her luggage.

"Can you get to Slater's store another way?"

"I can go around the rear, I guess."

The store had a curious opaqueness when she entered. It came from the blues and greens and mustards of the children's paintings that covered the front windows. Mr. Slater, on his stool behind the counter, looked sallow. He stood up when he saw her. "Miss Roundtree! Miss Ariel!"

"You remember me?"

"Indeed I do!"

"Mr. Slater, could I leave my bags here for a little while?"

"Long as you like."

"I want to go out on the Green for a few minutes. I want to find someone."

"Sure."

"My Uncle Willard. He's expecting me." Why did she always lapse into little unnecessary fibs when she was nervous? "I mean, I couldn't get him on the phone."

"Miss Ariel, you go out and enjoy yourself. Your bags will be safe. Here, I'll put 'em under the counter. You'll find things pretty quiet here after Paree. Nothing much happens." He looked at her closely. "Didn't figure we'd be seeing you again so soon. But you're always welcome in my store."

It was not exactly what Ariel had hoped to hear, but the old man meant well. She walked quickly down the street to the edge of the Green. The flames of the bonfire were blazing higher. Adults clustered in the background. Around the flames danced small masked figures—goblins, witches, ghosts with monstrous faces made more horrible by the slight bodies that bore them. Small, wild demons cavorting in unconscious mimicry of some savage orgiastic rite that lingered, if at all, in the dimness of tribal memory.

Ariel, her eyes dazzled by the flames, moved through the shadowy knots of people. Somewhere among them would be Willard, Edythe, Martin, and others she might know. But she was not looking for them. Twice she caught a glimpse of broad, tweed-coated shoulders and a tousled head. Twice she confronted a stranger. She circled the Green again. The crowd had grown denser. She felt suddenly caged by the darkness and the unfamiliarity and the ring of dim, uncaring figures. She stepped closer to the fire and heard a sudden cry.

"Ariel!" The huge, fanged face slavered purple and green, the little hands clawed toward her, but the voice was one she knew. "Ariel! The witch! The witch is here! Dunkie's witch!"

Her own voice was lost in the childish shouts. She was surrounded by gibbering figures, plucking at her, touching her, screeching. Other small, demonic figures leaped out of the darkness toward the group. Suddenly the night, the flames, the jumping, dancing circle of evil blended into terror. Ariel broke free and began to run. With delighted yells, they pursued her. "The witch! The witch!"

She felt a sharp sting on the side of her head. Someone had thrown a stone. She ran toward the monument and stumbled against the base. A hand reached out to her.

"This way! Come!" Sam Wilcox took her firmly by the arm and hurried her, heavily, across the street to the safety of the library steps.

"Are you hurt, my dear?"

"No. I don't think so. Just a scratch. Thank you." She felt the warm blood above her temple.

"Here, take this." He held out a large handkerchief. She saw him sway toward her. He caught his breath and grunted sharply. With a gasp of surprise, Sam Wilcox toppled over on the steps and lay still.

An hour later the rain began, dampening the flames and hysteria on Thatcher Green. At eighteen minutes past ten, in the Bollington Hospital, Dr. Samuel Wilcox was pronounced dead.

Duncan stopped his car by the side of the road and listened. Then he got out and started to walk through the sodden woods. He was only eighteen miles northwest of Thatcher but he was still reluctant to return. He had not gone south to the Seminary. In his new torment after Ariel had gone, he saw only frustration in those vined walls, those too-familiar books, those homilies muffled against time and change.

He loved one woman and hated one man with an intensity that had brought him a searing knowledge of his human limits. It left his mind possessed by a poison he could not release. Ariel. Ariel and Nick Orlini. They had been together in Paris now for how long? What did it matter? One day would have been too much.

He had stopped at the Seminary only to pick up his things. He had seen no one. He headed his car west. He needed to breathe and to know whether he could exorcise the flesh of its demons. More profound was whether that was what he wanted.

"Let's go, Duncan! God isn't going to help us on this one!"

Those were the words his close friend, the company chaplain, had shouted across that long-ago rice paddy. Minutes later, the man of God had stepped on the mine that blew him to pieces.

The truth of the matter, Duncan told himself, was that God wasn't ever there until you worked it out for yourself. That was hardly Christian faith. Sooner or later he'd have to expose his human limitations to the fine old man who listened to him, encouraged him, and now looked on him as a son and spiritual heir. God wasn't going to help him on that one either.

So he had wrestled with his doubts during the long, empty miles. As they fell behind him Duncan found a kind of direction. He stopped at one Veterans Hospital where a former buddy sat in a wheelchair—and would for the rest of his life.

"Watta you doin' now, Dunk?"

"Would you believe the ministry?"

There had been a slight pause. "Why not? There must be some way to tell 'em what hell was like."

He had gone on to his old training camp. A new sergeant—young, untried—sat at the desk.

"Just want to see the old place," Duncan had said.

"Where did you serve?"

"Mekong, Khesanh, Hill 381."

"Not thinking of reenlisting?"

"I don't know."

The young sergeant shook his head. "Not after where you've been. We find it doesn't work. Too many hang-ups. If you need a job, go to a Vets Bureau."

He turned the car north. He had touched the hard reality of his experience and it was now behind him. Sam Wilcox had known that. "There are other places than Thatcher, Duncan. I guess you know the toughest job for you will be right here." He had bought that. If he couldn't make it in Thatcher, he wouldn't make it anywhere.

A few strides carried him through the woods to the dam site and the sound that had caused him to stop his car. Water was pouring over the dam in muddy, roiling torrents. Orlini's dam. He had used town funds to create a large and useless lake that would some day make him a bundle in some development. The dam should have been built twenty miles downstream, to turn dynamos for a new factory and lift the perpetual threat of flood from Juno's Landing.

He looked across the lake. There were houses under that spread of useless water. A summer boarding house. An old dance pavilion. He thought of the summer night he had gone there and the skinny little waitress he met. He was fourteen, tall for his age. She had led him out into a now vanished grove of pines, filtered by moonlight, and with a knowing, overcharged body and skilled fingers had led him into mysteries he had only half guessed. He would always be grateful.

The covering slate-gray water had the desolation of a tomb in the dying afternoon. But as it slid over the dam, it was alive with menace.

Orlini's handiwork. Orlini. He felt the twist in his gut.

He climbed up the embankment to his car. Two boys walking on the edge of the road hailed him for a lift.

"Where to?"

"Pinesville."

Eleven miles north. He swung the car around. He was in no hurry to reach Thatcher. He had exorcised nothing.

Brady's Pub, a roadside tavern a mile out of Thatcher, was bright with lights. Duncan parked his car in the empty drive with relief. It had been closed for some weeks while Tom Brady took his ailing wife for a stay in the old country. Now the lights were back on, and Bantam Brady was where he belonged.

Duncan pushed open the door and felt a surge of deep nostalgia. It was part of his headier days—the long, dimly lit bar polished to an ersatz mahogany. The ancient black-and-white TV that flickered and blinked above the bottles shelved behind the bar. It was still flanked by an enormous horseshoe bearing a faded "Success" and on the other side by a candy-box poster of a girl in pink flounces.

Bantam was bent over, washing bar glasses, a stance that took him almost out of sight. He was five feet tall and thin as a wafer. Not that it troubled him. He would still remind his customers, as if they hadn't heard it for thrity years, that he had been bantam-weight champion of Castlebar, County Mayo.

"Hi, Bantam!"

The wraith of a man shot upward, his wizened face slit in a smile. "Duncan!" He pronounced it Dooncan. "Duncan, me boy, yer Reverence. If it isn't a sight for the angels. Hester! Look who's here!"

The red-haired girl at the far end of the bar swung her hips toward him. She was Bantam's daughter, auburn-haired, deep of shoulders and broad of breasts, with a white, soft skin that any customer would like to touch. It was said that she had been Michael Round-tree's girl before he disappeared. Whatever the truth of the rumor, Hester kept her own business and her lush beauty to herself.

"Duncan!" She leaned toward him across the bar as

if to kiss him. "Your Reverence, that is!" Her eyes gleamed.

"Cut it out, will you, the two of you! And Bantam, don't ask me if I'm twenty-one, the way you used to!"

"Ah, you were a pack of hoodlums then, the lot of you." He surveyed Duncan's muddy windbreaker, rumpled hair. "And from the looks of ye, I'd say you still are. No, there's a difference. Too much, I'd say. No need for a man to grow old doin' God's work." Bantam produced a bottle and two glasses. "On the house, m'boy, and a celebration for seein' you."

Duncan knew better than to refuse.

"And don't be turnin' good Irish whiskey into holy water. I get no calls for that!" He pushed a glass toward Duncan and set the bottle on the bar. "I heard about yer trouble, boy. You'd rather not be talking about it?"

"Right!"

The whiskey warmed him. It also reminded him that he needed food.

"How was the trip to Ireland, Bantam?"

"The beat of me heart, lad. And the song in me soul." Duncan didn't smile. Bantam had flights of oratory that impoverished the speech of most men.

"And Mary?"

Bantam's wrinkled face shadowed. Then he smiled. "The better for breathing the wild and holy air of County Mayo, God help us. She's up sleepin' now but she'd be that glad to set her darlin' eyes on ye, Duncan."

He nodded. "Bantam, have you got any of those tired sandwiches you keep around to make this place legitimate?"

"The very same ones. Ham or cheese. Cheese or ham."

Hester was still leaning across the bar. "How would you like a steak sandwich, Duncan?"

"Steak! God Almighty, the man's already passed a miracle. Now where would we be getting a steak?"

"From our freezer, Pop. And French fries and onions, Dunk?"

"And coffee maybe?" He looked at her and grinned. The tension was beginning to slide from him. A warm girl, a great girl. The image of Ariel suddenly took her place. His throat closed.

"And apple pie?"

"You got pie, Hester?" Bantam breathed heavily.

"The piece I was saving for your supper, Pop. But would you deny a starving man?"

Duncan found a laugh. "She's your daughter, all right, Bantam."

"Sure. She'd give ye the shirt off me back!"

The door opened. Hester looked up, then turned away and busied herself. Duncan heard Bantam's mutter. "One of me regulars, wouldn't ye know!"

Nick Orlini sauntered to the bar and took a seat with careful deliberation next to Duncan.

"Well, well, the Deacon. 'Pon my word. Boozing in a saloon like any of us commoners. Evening, Bantam. Hester, sweetheart."

She turned her head. "I'll get your steak right away, Duncan."

"Steak? What do you do for the lady to get steak, Deacon?"

"If you want a steak, Mr. Orlini—" Bantam began.

"I don't want it. I just want to know how he does it. But then the Deacon gets everything he wants. Almost."

The whiskey warmth had gone. Something ice cold flowed through Duncan.

"What'll it be, Mr. Orlini?"

"The usual. And if his Reverence will join me . . ."

"No, thanks." Duncan knew he should leave. Yet there was something inevitable, something primitively satisfying in this murky encounter. They were already invisibly circling like knife fighters.

"Why not? Come on, Deacon. Loosen up. I just got back from Paris yesterday." He winked at Bantam.

"Saw your girl friend. Matter of fact, I had dinner with her."

"Come now, Mr. Orlini. Don't be after making trouble." Bantam had his eyes on Duncan.

"I buy your liquor, Brady. But I don't take your orders." He lifted a glass. "Not much fun being a Christer, is it Deacon? You don't know that girl until you take her out in Paris. Real class. But she's expensive. Too expensive for a country parson, I'd say."

Duncan took out his wallet to pay his check: his knuckles showed white. He'd make no trouble for Tom Brady.

Nick saw the gesture and misread it. "Very expensive. Dad said he'd like her in the family. I told him I thought it wouldn't be hard to arrange. That little dish is hot as—"

"Cut it!" Duncan whirled from the stool and yanked Nick to his feet. "You're too yellow to hit, Nick!"

"Let go!"

"But you'll listen!" He pushed Nick back against the bar. He saw Bantam dancing around from behind it, Hester with wide eyes at the far end. "You're everything rotten that's ever come into this town! You don't belong here. Nobody wants you or your big money. Or your bigger mouth. You and your tin-horn father have spoiled everything you've touched here. Ask anybody in this town what they think of you. They despise you! You came out of the woodwork, Orlini. I'm telling you to crawl back before I step on you!"

He hadn't said all he wanted to but he felt better. He saw something satisfying in Nick Orlini's sallow fear.

"If you've got the guts, come outside."

But Nick was bent over the bar, his hand shaking as he drank. He didn't look up.

Duncan laid a bill on the bar and zipped up his windbreaker. "Hold the steak, Hester. And thanks."

Bantam went with him to the door. "It's grateful I am, Duncan. For not starting trouble."

"Okay." As he opened the door, Nick turned.

"I don't fight lace petticoats, Duncan. You better get into yours now the old man is dead."

Duncan stopped, frozen. "What was that?"

"Didn't you know?" Nick's mockery had returned. He felt safe now. "I heard it on the local radio, driving up. Old man Wilcox, your boss." His mouth twisted. "No more boozing and bedding for you—your Reverence!"

Duncan drove too fast into Thatcher. The rain was falling heavily on the darkened town. There was nothing he could do tonight, perhaps ever, except the duty that lay ahead. But he was pursued by a self-image, that of a jungle fighter, wanting to kill. For a few moments in that dim pub he had been that killer.

But now the old man's steadying voice was gone.

The rain continued to fall.

The *Thatcher Standard* carried a three-column, front-page obituary on the death of Dr. Samuel Wilcox after forty-two years of service as the beloved rector of St. Mark's Episcopal. The cause of death was a massive coronary thrombosis. No mention was made of the ancient evil that had welled out of the darkness on Thatcher Green. And no mention was made of Ariel.

Ariel was waiting behind the curtain of rain in Willard's old-fashioned parlor, waiting for him to bring her word of Duncan. She had learned he had not gone back to the Seminary after her departure for Paris. Willard had forwarded her letter, only to have it returned by the Post Office. She was beset by a sense that something hurtful, perhaps final, had happened. Already this trip looked like a foolhardy impulse, ending in unbelievable disaster. Was this to be her role in Thatcher? Had she held out her arms to this place that never forgot and could not forgive? She was an outsider, a foreigner, the 'French' cousin. An alien, perhaps even to Duncan. Whatever had made her so sure of him when the entire experience of her young life had been of men who came and went, indifferent and fleeting, through her mother's drawing room?

Even Edythe, who called in the morning to ask how she was and send her love, whatever that could mean now, had released her quickly. They were all too consumed by the suddenness of the tragedy to consider her part in it. It was simpler to ignore her.

She wondered what she would do next, not with her time but with her life, if Duncan did not come back to her. But Ariel could not live with inaction nor could she let hours slip by in little vacuums, each one emptier than the last. She searched for dust cloths and a mop, discovered where the sweeper was kept, and found enough food to fix Willard lunch when he came in and dinner that night. The frantic purpose of her return to Thatcher dwindled to agonizing self-blame. But she could be useful here.

When she finished, she put on old boots, took a worn slicker from a peg in the closet, and called to Clancy, finding warmth in the big dog's delight. Together they went out and down the path.

Charlie Redwing sat in the barn mending a scythe handle when she entered. The Indian rose to his feet.

"Charlie, is there anything I can do around here? I mean, to help you?"

He regarded her silently, then handed her a second scythe, a hammer, and pointed to the box of nails beside him. Then he made a place for her on the bench, sat down, and resumed his work. Ariel looked helplessly at the scythe, picked up a nail and met Charlie Redwing's smoky eyes. She heard herself giggle. The uncontrolled laughter held a hint of hysteria before she could stop it.

"Oh, Charlie, I'm just useless!"

Charlie's own dry cackle of laughter had embarrassed him. He bent over his work.

"No. But you must know the steel and the wood before they will answer you."

"Like a kitchen pot?"

The moment had left Ariel with an odd and hollow peace. As long as there were things to be done, plain, homely things that stood for living, she could manage.

"Do you know where Uncle Willard has gone?"

"To the river."

"All this time?"

"It must be watched. It is angry. When it is angry it brings sadness to the land."

How easy it would be, she thought, to blame it all on the river. Yet she suspected that this silent strong man knew more truths than she could guess at. She returned to the house, Clancy beside her.

Willard came in midafternoon. He hung up his wet oilskins and went to the fire she had built.

"Good girl. How are you, Ariel?" He looked at her sharply.

"I'm all right."

"And the cut on your head?"

"I'd forgotten about it."

"Little savages. Violence. It's the age. There's something pagan about bonfires. Maybe we'll have to think of something else next year."

He seemed to be talking to fill space.

"Have you had lunch?"

"Oh, yes. Don't worry about that. The outer man can't do much, if the inner man isn't with him." He stretched out his legs to the fire.

"Anybody call?" The question was so casual she suspected it.

"Aunt Edythe. It was very kind of her. They're all quite upset."

"I'm sure. Sam Wilcox was a good man. I've known him all of forty years." He would not reveal to this slight girl his own sense of loss, this reminder of his own mortality. "The funeral is tomorrow at two. The Bishop will preside, so it should be lugubrious enough.

I like Charlie Redwing's way better. Death is a friend from the instant you're born. He walks slightly behind you all your life until it's time to take your hand."

"I like that."

"I don't think it's unique with Charlie. He reads a lot." He straightened. "Ariel, Duncan is back."

She caught her breath. She had not dared to ask, yet she had been aware there was something he was not saying to her. She steadied her voice.

"When did he get back?"

"Last night."

Last night. Nearly a day ago. And he had not called. But maybe he had; maybe she had missed him on her walk to the barn. Maybe . . .

"Where is he?"

"With Cora Wilcox, now. Where he should be."

"Yes. Yes, of course." She would not press. He would call her when he had time. When he had time, dear God!

She rose. "Uncle Willard, I'm going to make you an apricot brandy soufflé for dinner."

"Good heavens, girl!"

"No?"

"Yes!" He saw her strained face, the violet shadows under her eyes. She was badly wounded, and he felt helpless. He knew what had gone wrong. Duncan had been explicit. He had no way of knowing whether it was true or false. He silently wished all the Orlinis in hell.

"He blames me, doesn't he?" It burst from her in a cry.

"For what?"

"They all do! If I hadn't come back, hadn't gone down to the Green last night, Dr. Wilcox would still be alive."

"No!" Willard jumped up from his chair. "Don't ever say that, Ariel. Don't even think it! Sam Wilcox knew he had a heart condition. By rights he never should have been down there last night. But he wouldn't change his habits. Why should he? They become an old man's backbone. We'll have no more of that kind of talk!"

But she wasn't listening. "I'm glad Duncan's here for the funeral," she said at last.

He nodded. He had one thing more to say and he was not happy about it. In fact he would rather postpone it. But that would mean presuming her frailty and indulging his own. If Willard had learned one thing about this troubled young Roundtree, it was that she not only had Henrietta's good looks, she had that indomitable lady's tenacity. Ariel would not be easy to cross.

He drew a long breath. "You're not thinking about going to the funeral tomorrow?"

"Of course."

"Why?"

"I must!" To Mam'selle, the funeral of even the most remote acquaintance was a duty. She and Mam'selle would cross Paris endlessly on the Metro on those sad journeys. Mam'selle kept a black band always ready to pin on Ariel's little-girl coat. "Of course I'll go with you." Ariel glanced at him. "Is there any reason I shouldn't?"

He hesitated. "No. Not exactly. I don't think it's necessary for you to go. I don't think it would be a very happy time."

"Are funerals ever happy?"

He had used the wrong word. He might have found the right one except that she broke into his thoughts.

"Why did you say that? What are you trying to tell me? That I wouldn't be wanted?"

"Of course you'd be wanted, my dear. What an idea!" He was retreating, he knew, before her wide direct glance and the anger replacing the hurt in her voice.

"Uncle Willard, please be honest with me. I can take it. Just as I could take it from Duncan if he'd come and tell me *what's happened*. What I hate so much is not *knowing*! There's still talk, isn't there? About me and what I did to Lowell? Or what they think I did. That's what would embarrass you tomorrow!"

He rose and went to her. Was he getting senile to have made such a botch of things? "Ariel, nothing you did or ever could do would embarrass me. I have only the deepest respect for you. And affection. I only thought you might be upset."

It was more of an admission than he realized. She understood. But he did not know her. Nor did any of them. She did not upset easily or she would never have come back. It was they who would be embarrassed. Perhaps even Duncan, after their long separation. But he would have to come and tell her. Willard's concern for her, his solicitude had irked her. It had also stiffened her.

She loved Duncan as she would never love another man. But he had suddenly become a rippled image in water that was somehow sliding from her. She had not come back to beg from him or any of them.

Willard saw her small pointed chin lift as she went into the kitchen. She had not answered him.

By dinnertime, Duncan still had not called. As if defying her need, Ariel had gone for a long, wet walk with Clancy. She did not ask about Duncan when she came in. Willard was more than willing to let the subject pass. He had been listening to an unnerving drip of water below the house.

Ariel brought her soufflé to the table. "You have no apricot brandy, Uncle Willard. But I found some applejack."

He tasted it. He would have tasted iron filings if she had served them. She warmed his table, his very bones. Duncan was a fool but he could not blame a young man for his pride. When did the course of love ever run smooth? Not a love as disparate and unpredictable as this. She was watching him.

He let the golden froth slide down his throat. "Ariel, my dear . . ."

"You don't like it?"

"I can only say that if Lafayette had brought this with him, the American Revolution would have been won the day he landed."

She laughed and he joined her. It was as if another lamp had been lighted in the pine-paneled old dining room.

"Uncle Willard, what have the Orlinis done to you?"

The question came with the suddenness of a hornet sting.

"Where did you hear about that?"

"In Paris. Nick Orlini boasted about it. He said his mother had a claim to your land."

So she had seen Nick, and Duncan's torment was real. Willard looked into the innocence of her face and saw the hint of Henrietta's left-cheek dimple. The Devil's Kiss. What kind of women had his unconquerable family produced? He felt a kinship to young Duncan's bewilderment. Ariel with the light of a spring morning in her face? She was waiting for an answer.

He had finished his soufflé. "Mrs. Orlini is a Thatcher. She thinks she has proof from the War Department that the real Isaac Roundtree was hanged as a horse thief. Away in Missouri. And that whoever the man was who inherited this land from Nathaniel Thatcher, he was an imposter." He gave an uneasy chuckle. "I have no doubt that Isaac Roundtree should have been hanged for something, sometime, but I am equally sure that he managed to elude his just desserts and now rests in some kind of peace under that monument up in the cemetery. The claim is poppycock."

"Did you tell her that?"

"In several ways. Unfortunately, our legal system does not take a gentleman's word. It demands proof. So far, the lady has it."

"But you've lived here so long."

"Possession in this case, my dear, is not nine points of the law. It's merely nine-tenths of the crime. In all the relics of ancestry cluttering this family, we have not found one shred identifying our venerable ancestor. Not a piece of paper, not a line. They took things casually in those days."

"What are you going to do? Just give it up?"

"One never 'just gives up' anything. You should know." His words trailed. He rose abruptly and went to the kitchen door, listening. "Do you hear that?"

She had heard it while she was getting dinner. A thin flow of water like an open faucet. It was heavier now.

"Yes, what is it? A pipe?"

"I think I'll have a look."

"Let me come with you."

"It's a little rough." He snapped on a switch beside the cellar door, and she followed him down a flight of open steps to a dry basement with a concrete floor. She had not seen it before and she took French delight in its neatness. A hook for every household tool, bushel baskets stacked with precision, orderly shelves of preserve jars filled and labeled, by whose hand she could not guess.

On the opposite side of the basement was an old-fashioned, wide-planked door with an electric lantern hanging against it.

Lantern in hand, Willard pushed open the heavy door. It led down four steps to a large dank area, a dark subcellar with an earthen floor. Dampness streaked the earth walls. The floor sloped upward to two flat doors. She had not noticed any doors outside the house. Perhaps they were overgrown by grass.

The flow of water had become a sullen stream on the other side of the left wall.

Willard listened. "Do you know what this place is?"

"I can't imagine. It's so big."

"Big enough to hold a team of horses and a wagon. That's what they built it for. When the Indians attacked, and later when the British came, they'd drive the team and wagon down here to hide 'em. Since the dam was built, there's an underground stream running through here. Water has to go somewhere." He tapped the left wall. "But it's holding."

Something ran across the earth floor. Ariel gave a little squeal.

"The field rats get in here. Nothing much to feed on, but they come in when it gets cold."

He flashed the lantern toward the steps. The door was barred on the inside with a two-by-four beam. It creaked protestingly.

"If it floods it can't do too much harm. Just pour through the cellar and out under the hill. But I'll keep an eye on it."

They were back in the warm fire-lit living room.

The rain continued to lash at the windows.

"Does it often rain like this?"

"We've had spells like it before. There's an old saying that we get almost any kind of weather here in Thatcher and the rest is twenty miles north."

Willard tapped out his dead pipe and set his magazine aside. "You might amuse yourself with Henrietta's old chest there. She knew this country when it was a lot wilder than it is now."

He let Clancy out and waited for the dog's returning whine, which came almost immediately.

"Clancy thinks even less of this weather than we do. Good night, my dear."

She watched the old man go slowly upstairs. Then she patted the wet dog, turned out the lamp, and made her own way up the narrow stairs to her room. She was beginning to feel this house like a warm cloak around her.

* * *

The mortal remains of Dr. Sam Wilcox were laid in the sodden earth at two o'clock the next afternoon. Under dripping skies a file of umbrellas bobbed down the cemetery path; some to waiting cars, others carried on foot back to town. The bearers of the umbrellas stood aside to let a shiny black limousine pass. In it sat the Bishop and Cora Wilcox. Beside them, stiffly somber in a black suit, eyes straight ahead, his face without expression, sat Duncan.

A white sports car stopped at the intersection. Nick Orlini watched with interest as the limousine disappeared down the hill.

Willard returned to the farmhouse immediately after the funeral and changed into his work clothes and boots.

"The dam's holding," he told Ariel. "But the river's flooding further down. Juno's Landing. We're evacuating."

"Let me come with you. I can help. I'm strong."

He was tempted. She could soothe nervous women and frightened children. But he had heard it today, as he had feared he would, a rustle, a whispering. She had come back, the French cousin. She had brought trouble again. He saw also the glances of sympathy, and pity directed toward Lowell as she sat in the church.

Where it would end he had no idea but there was a greater threat to this town than anything they could see in this slight girl with her dark, somber eyes.

"You can be more help here, Ariel. Charlie's coming with me. If there's any danger up at the dam they'll phone here. Take the message and relay it to this number." He wrote hastily on a pad.

"I will." Then the question shored up by pride broke from her. "Did Duncan conduct the service?"

"The Bishop presided. Duncan sat with Cora Wilcox. He has a lot to do, my dear."

Willard hoped he sounded convincing.

"You'll be all right, Ariel. Clancy will see to that."

　　　　✳　✳　✳

Now she was alone. Clancy went outside and had
not returned. But she hardly missed the big dog. The
mention of Duncan had sealed her loneliness. The
hurt became a physical pain. He had been back more
than twenty-four hours. He might have telephoned.
Just once. To reassure her. To let her hear his voice.
As he might have written to her in Paris. Willard's
explanation had been too careful.

She reached toward the phone as if it had rung. And
let her hand fall. Silence. Except for the relentless beat
of the rain and the steady flow of the underground
stream beneath the house.

Outside the fields were covered by a muddy slime.
But this house, on its sloping hillside, would be safe
and dry. It had weathered more than this. So had two
centuries of its inhabitants. Henrietta, who had come
here, a 'foreigner' like herself. But a bride. A bride at
seventeen. Ariel wondered if she had been lucky
enough to marry the man she loved. "Few do," Alicia
had said. "Even if they do, the fire won't burn forever."

But Ariel was light-years from that now. She wondered how she could ever go back.

She dropped on her knees beside the chest and noticed the carved initials. H.B.R. That *B* gave Henrietta an added dimension, a part of her life no one
knew.

She forgot the rain as she opened the chest. She
lifted the ivory lace dress from its tissue paper with
delight. She found the bundle of letters addressed
neatly to Mrs. Henrietta Roundtree. And at the bottom the layers of small suede volumes. She opened one
at random and found it heavily underscored.

". . . come gentle night, give me my Romeo and
when he shall die, take him and cut him out in
little stars that all the world will be in love with
night."

She shut the book abruptly as if she were trespassing

into another woman's secret. There was no diary, only the impassioned underscorings in these fragile books.

She held up the lacy dress, smoothing it against her body, its delicate flutings, its intricate hand-made lace. She saw herself a bride.

Suddenly she was aware that the lamplight was dimming. It flickered for an instant. She heard a choked tinkle from the telephone. She went to it. But it went dead, as the light went out.

The solitary hours of her childhood had taught Ariel not to panic. Willard had explained the workings of the oil lamp in the kitchen. It was not yet dusk.

She had just returned with the lighted oil lamp, when she heard a car stop and almost immediately strong steps on the porch. She ran to the door with relief.

But the door was already opened.

Nick Orlini was pushing his way in.

"Hi," He smiled. His eyes were bloodshot. "My lucky day. Thought I'd find you. Terrible weather."

"Nick, I don't want to see you now."

"But I want to see you, baby." He took off his wet raincoat and threw it on a chair. "I very much want to see you. Well, well. Nice and cozy here. Oil lamp and everything. I suppose you know the lights have gone. So has the phone. Aren't you going to ask me to sit down?"

"No, I'm not, Nick. You shouldn't have come here. You can't stay. Now please go."

He didn't answer at once. He walked to the fire. Then very deliberately sat down on the sofa. "Who, my pet, is going to make me?"

"All right. If you won't go, I will."

"Where? Look outside. Come on, baby. We were pretty good friends once. You liked going out with me. You made a mistake turning me down in Paris. I didn't like that. But I'm willing to forgive and forget. We can start all over again, right?"

"No, Nick." If she could keep him talking until she

400

could get her own coat and boots. Maybe get to the barn.

"Don't try it, Ariel. You wouldn't get very far in that mud. I've had a hell of a drive out here."

"How did you know where I was?"

"How did I know? Ask anyone in Thatcher where Ariel Roundtree is. The French cousin. You're famous, baby. Very, very famous." He got up and walked unsteadily toward her.

"Let's have a drink first, just you and me. Then I have something important to tell you. Very, very important. Where's the whiskey?"

"There is none."

"You're the prettiest little liar I ever knew. Old man Willard knows good whiskey better than any man in this God-forsaken town. Ought to be somewhere."

"Nick, will you get out! I told you in Paris I didn't want to see you! Why would you come here?"

"Let's say, a little something I owe the Deacon. I had a few words with him the other night. He said some things I didn't like."

"I'm expecting him later."

"That's another lie, baby. You're not expecting him or anybody else. All able-bodied men are down at Juno's Landing. If he qualifies." He grinned. "So it's you and me, baby. Just the way it ought to be. And I'm going to prove it to you."

She was afraid, now. She looked out the window. Water and mud.

He walked to the fireplace, poked at the ashes. "Needs shaking up. But the wood's too damp. Well, we don't need a fire. We can always make our own. Right?"

"I'll get dry wood in the kitchen."

"I can get it. When we need it. If we need it."

She moved from his path. "What were you going to tell me, Nick?"

"Oh-oh. Curious now? You should be. It involves us both. God, I wish I had a drink. My old man's come through. Said if and when I married you, he'd make me a junior partner. And let me tell you, baby, nobody but nobody is any kind of partner to Dad. But it means a big salary and a lot of time to ourselves. The whole world our clam shell. You and me, baby. Just you and me."

"But, Nick, I'm not going to marry you. I don't want to see you."

"That's what I gathered that last night in Paris. Not that I minded. I'm like Dad. I like plenty of pepper."

The fear that Ariel had kept at bay rose in her throat. He was beyond reason. And he was strong. She had used all her charm, her little tricks of coquetry, that last evening with him. They would only inflame him now. Talk was useless. She moved toward the door.

He was beside her, his hand on her wrist.

"Wait a minute, honey. Where you going?"

"Out to call Clancy."

"Who's Clancy?"

"The dog. He's been out in the rain too long."

"Then let him stay out." He led her back into the room. "You're shaking. What are you afraid of?"

"I'm not afraid of anything. I don't know why you came all the way out here this afternoon."

"You know why I came."

He shoved her down on the sofa and released her hand. He was still standing.

"And I'll tell you what you're afraid of. Your own bad conscience, my girl. You thought you could go out with me and pump me dry about Thatcher and the Deacon and anything else that might be in your devious little mind. Having done that, you'd wave me good-bye." He leaned over her and tipped up her face. "I told you I wanted you, Ariel. I'd marry you to have you. Why should I wait?"

She slid from him and was on her feet, her eyes blazing.

"Get out of here, Nick. There's nothing I'll ever want from you. I'm not afraid of you."

He strode past her, picked up the ivory lace gown, looked at it for an instant. "What's this?"

"It's a dress."

"Put it on!"

"What!"

"Put it on. I like it." He came toward her, tripped on the dress, and steadied himself. He was more drunk than she thought.

"All right." She took the dress and backed away.

"Here. Now. Where I can watch you." He reached toward her, clutched the throat of her blouse. With a powerful sweep he ripped it to the waist.

Once before she had seen this primal violence in Nick Orlini. Now her only weapon was a mass of filmy lace. She smothered it against his face, his eyes, and broke away. Through the dim kitchen she found her way down the cellar steps. She heard Nick stumbling after her. She snatched the electric lantern from the heavy planked door, pushing it open. Below was the darkness of the earthen subcellar and the sound of flowing water. She barred the door behind her with the great rusty bolt.

From above, she heard Nick calling her name. But there was no way he could reach her here. She listened to his tread—heavy, uncertain. He stumbled once. She heard a crash, a curse, then silence.

The beam of her lantern only deepened the black emptiness beyond her. The floor was under water but she could not tell how much. The underground stream had become a torrent. On the left wall her flashlight found a pipe-sized stream of water. As the light probed it, something scuttled down the wall, as large as her hand.

She stifled a cry and huddled on the top step. Willard must come home soon, long before the subcellar could deepen with water. Her flashlight would keep any creature of the darkness at bay. She would be safe.

She leaned her head against the damp planking of the door and listened for the sound of a departing car. She could hear nothing above the rushing sound of water. But Nick would not stay long. He was not a man to wait out his frustrations. Even loathing him as she did, she understood the tragedy of Nick Orlini. She could feel a ghost of pity for this man who could not give love without violence, who would forever be denied its sweetness.

She listened again at the heavy door. There was no sound beyond it. Now she was shivering with cold. Setting her lantern on the step she pushed cautiously at the heavy, rusted bolt. It did not yield. In fright, she pushed with all her strength. But the old metal bar would not budge in its corroded bar-way. It was gripped as if the parts had fused.

Ariel sank back on the step, clutched her lantern, and wondered how long its beam would last. To the dark sound of flowing water, she lost track of time.

By dusk the river had crested and begun to drop. The lights of Thatcher went on. At Juno's Landing battered and twisted waterfront houses gave evidence of the water's rampage.

Thatcher's doors opened. As they had for nearly three centuries, Thatcher and Juno's Landing met disaster as one identity. Later and less gallantly, each would return to its separate cross-purposes.

Duncan made his way through the mud of Juno Street carrying a child's tricycle and a portable TV set. Billy Haskell plowed along beside him carrying a wet cat.

"This about does it, Billy."

"Yep."

"You didn't see any looting?"

"We saw a guy going into the back of Al's store but we drove him out."

"The police have taken over. You can send your gang home. Good job, Billy."

"I'd like to keep this cat."

"Sure. Until we find the owner."

Billy stroked the sodden little creature. "Mom says you're going to take the service at the church next week now that Dr. Wilcox is dead."

"Who told her I'd take it?"

"I dunno. Aren't you?" There was a pause. "Say, you're not going away again, Duncan, are you?"

They had reached a parked truck. Duncan added the tricycle and TV to the assorted salvage in the back.

"Are you, Duncan? Going away?"

"I don't know." He looked at the boy. Tired, Billy showed none of the mocking mischief that ran one's patience thin. "You'd better get home and dried, Billy. And thanks."

"Sure. Sure, Duncan." He started then half turned, embarrassed. "I—I mean . . . the gang sure hopes you stay."

Duncan went on to Big Moon's Diner where four or five people sat huddled.

"Moon's still down at the waterfront," said Ira. "The power's back on but I can't get the stove working. These folks need hot food."

A woman was sobbing. "I told Jed we oughta get out of that lousy house. He said wait until times were better. This is better? If he tries to take me and the kids back down there I'll kill him."

Duncan moved toward the group.

The sobbing woman lifted her head. "You gonna help us, Mr. Duncan, aren't you?"

He patted the woman's shoulder. "We're going to get you something to eat first."

The Roundtree house showed lights in every window. As it had before, thought Duncan as he stopped the car. But the wedding, the sudden inexplicable reversal, seemed as distant now as a passing comet.

Inside, the old house pulsed with people, stunned women, elderly men. Edythe, in the kitchen, her sleeves rolled up, was presiding over three huge, steaming pots. Through the crowded rooms, Claude and Lowell were passing soup and coffee, baked beans and sandwiches. In the sunporch, Kim had marshaled a cluster of suspicious children to whom she explained the endearing charms of Freddie.

Martin Roundtree, an overcoat over his thin shoulders, was standing on the porch. The welcoming host, Duncan told himself. The reassuring town elder. Duncan helped the carload of evacuees up the path. Martin held out his hand.

"That's the last of them, sir."

"Will you come in too, Duncan?"

"I don't think so, sir, thank you."

Martin hesitated. He had his pride and knew Duncan had his.

"I wish you would. I have something I want to talk about."

Duncan did not know how to refuse. He had thought of nothing but Ariel these past days, the agonizing decision which had kept him from her. He had no heart now to enter this house, much less to meet Lowell's studied matter-of-factness. But he followed Martin into the hall—just as Lowell emerged from the living room with an empty tray.

"Hi, Duncan!" She smiled, flushed, and shifted her eyes.

"Hello, Lowell," he answered gently.

"Like some coffee?"

"Not now, dear," Martin interrupted. "I want to talk to him. I still look on Duncan as a member of the family."

"So do I, Dad." She had regained her poise. "They tell me you've done marvelous things today down at the Landing. You were everywhere, helping everybody."

"I did what every other man did."

"You were the one they talked about." She met his eyes, and went on. The encounter was over. Regret, perhaps. But no passion. In time, Duncan thought, they might become friends. At least this house he loved would hold no awkwardness. Yet he was anxious to escape it.

"Sit down, Duncan." Martin let his overcoat slip to his study chair and opened the desk drawer. "This came today from your father. It concerns Julia Orlini."

The door burst open. Whatever the letter contained Duncan was not to know. Edythe stood at the threshold.

"Willard just phoned. He's at the Town Hall and terribly worried about Ariel. He called the farm and when he couldn't get her he thought she might be here. Of course she isn't. So he's gone right out there. But heaven knows what the road is."

Duncan was at the door. "I'm on my way. I'll catch up with him or get there before he does."

The rains had washed out the dirt road into the farm. Duncan struggled over it, hardly aware whether he was on road or field. He had a premonition, an ugly fear born of his own knowledge of the unpredictability of the waters in this valley. More than that, the helplessness of guilt. His own introspective indecision had brought Ariel to this place.

In the clearing he saw red tail lights ahead. Willard was nearing the house. In a burst of reckless speed, Duncan caught up with him.

Willard was mounting the steps as Duncan joined him. The front door was open.

"Ariel!" Duncan called. "Ariel!" There was no answer.

In the lighted living room, the oil lamp was still burning. Duncan picked up a fallen mass of ivory lace. Willard shook his head. "It's from the chest." He had already noted a pewter ashtray overturned on the floor. His rocking chair faced crazily into a corner.

"Ariel!" Duncan called again. From far below came a sharp anguished bark followed by a whine.

In the kitchen, a three-legged stool lay on its side.

"Willard! What's happened?"

The door to the concrete-floored cellar was open. Through it they could hear splashing water. They raced down the stairs. Against the heavy planked door, Clancy was crouching, his nose at the crack; his deep, frantic scratches had ripped into the wood. His great paws were bloodied from clawing also at the cement floor. He was whining but he did not lift his head.

The electric lantern was missing.

"She's down there, Duncan!" He pushed at the door and stepped back. His face had gone gray. "It's bolted!"

"Ariel!" Duncan shouted again. He cupped his hands to his mouth. "Ariel!"

The big dog whimpered. Above the reverberating roar of the rushing water, they could hear nothing.

He shouted once more and listened. Then they heard her, a weak cry from somewhere on the other side of the door.

"Ariel!" Willard called. "Push the bolt back, so we can open the door."

They heard her more clearly now.

"I can't. It's stuck."

"Listen to me! We'll break through. Go to the bottom step and wait. Can you hear me?"

There was a faint, "Yes."

Duncan raced up the stairs to the kitchen shed and brought back a wood axe.

"Get down the steps, Ariel! Away from the door," he shouted.

He swung at the heavy door until his blows had shattered the rusted bolt and forced the heavy door open.

Once inside, he saw her in a shaft of dim light, huddled on the bottom step, the black water up to her thighs, her eyes wide with terror. She clutched her sweater across her breasts. He did not see that her blouse had been torn open.

He lifted her to her feet, held her close as the broken phrases came. "Duncan! Oh, Duncan! The flashlight burned out! It was so dark!"

He helped her up the slime-covered steps and through the shattered door. "Got some whiskey, Willard. And we'd better call Dr. Cartwright."

"No, no. I'm all right. Honestly!" She was walking firmly but clinging to him. "Oh, Duncan, it was so cold. And the hole—I watched it until the light went out. I thought the water would come through and fill the place."

She was shaking again. In the living room, she took the drink Willard offered, gratefully. As the warmth went through her, she managed a rueful smile. "I'm a mess but I don't need a doctor. I just need to change my clothes."

"What you need is to get into bed, young lady. At once." Willard spoke harshly in his relief but his face was gentle. "I'm a pretty good cook. I'll get some hot food for you."

But she did not go. She watched Duncan as he picked up the ivory lace dress. "What's this?" he asked. She saw his eyes searching the room.

"It belonged to Henrietta Roundtree. I took it out of the chest, Uncle Willard. I hope you don't . . ." She stopped. Duncan was staring at her, his face a frozen mask. He let the dress fall.

"Ariel, what happened here?"

She glanced down. Her cardigan sweater, its buttons gone, had slipped open. Both men could see her ripped blouse. Ariel felt her face burn. She wrapped the sweater around her.

"Who was here, Ariel? Who did that?"

She looked helplessly from one to the other. It was almost as if the silence spoke for her.

"Nick Orlini . . ."

"Orlini!" Duncan's voice was savage.

"He pushed his way in, Duncan! I didn't ask him in!" The words spilled from her in a rush. "He had been drinking. He was still angry at me because I refused to go out with him in Paris. Then he said he owed you something! You, Duncan! I didn't know what that meant. I got away from him and ran down the kitchen steps into the basement. Then I got that old door open to the earth cellar and bolted it behind me. It stuck and that's why I couldn't get out."

"I'll kill the son of a bitch." Duncan spoke so quietly that Willard knew he meant it.

But Ariel wasn't finished. Passion, hurt, loneliness, outrage, too long pent-up, blazed from her. "And what about you, Duncan! What do you think I thought about all that time in the dark and the cold? You, Duncan! What happened to you—to us? If you'd called me just once or let me know where you were . . . if you'd written just one little letter to me in Paris! Don't you think I would have come back to you sooner if I could have? Instead, you let me go on wondering and worrying! What happened that you didn't even get the letter I wrote you?"

"What letter did you write me?" He broke in. He was at the edge of a truth sharper than the night's ordeal.

"It was sent back here. You have it, Uncle Willard. Give it to him! I don't care whether he reads it or not!" She ran from him to the stairs. "Nick Orlini is a—a viper!" She flung the words. "He tried to hurt me but he didn't succeed! But you! You, Duncan! You tore my life to pieces and you don't care!"

She turned and ran up the stairs.

In the silence, Willard busied himself with the fire he had lit. "I'd better go down and look at that hole she talked about."

"Where's the letter, Willard?"

The older man went to the desk and silently handed him the letter.

Duncan read it, thrust it into his pocket. Willard watched his face. Age wasn't easy, he thought, but sometimes it was a lot harder to be young.

"I've got to get back to Juno's Landing." Duncan moved to the door. "I'll phone tomorrow."

"She'll be all right, son." Willard picked up the lace dress and folded it. "She's fire and steel. Henrietta, all over again."

He listened as Duncan's car rattled into the night.

An hour later, when he had made sure that Ariel was comfortable and asleep, he returned to the subcellar beneath the house. Pushing the shattered door wide, he waded into the water, now nearly three feet deep. It would drain off through the earthen floor when the flooding stopped.

With the beam of his flashlight, he scanned the walls. Then he saw it, the hole Ariel had watched, a jagged rent a couple of feet wide. He waded to it and probed it with his light. At the rear, the water was flowing in a full stream, to a depth he could not estimate. But the beam glanced off something else, a round white object, satin-smooth, that lay partly concealed beside what looked like a piece of flat, rusted tin. He reached into the opening and tugged. A metal box came away in his hand and with it a new release of water.

Willard could only glimpse the white, smooth skull before it was swept away. Clutching the box, he sloshed his way to the steps and turned. His flashlight told him the earthen wall was holding, the rent was not widening; indeed, the gush of water seemed to be abating. It had found some deeper subterranean course that would conceal its skeletal burden forever.

Willard lay awake long that night. If he had thought his family task was over, he knew better now. The skull was small, the bones beside it fine. Whatever grim secret of the Roundtree past had lain so long behind that earthen wall was his now.

The metal box had finally told him.

Chapter Two

Ariel lay in the wide, old-fashioned sleigh bed, still possessed by the languor of warmth and sleep. It was pleasant to drift in this nothingness and let the kaleidoscope of images shift, blend, and finally disappear. There was yesterday, there would be tomorrow. But this hour was a bubble floating in space.

She gazed at the sharp November light that slid under the blind and listened to a murmur of voices downstairs. Men's voices. She could not identify them. She wondered if Duncan had returned. Duncan. He had come to her last night in the sodden, icy darkness. He had held her in his arms. She had clung to him.

In the depths of sleep, a deeper, subconscious layer of herself *clung* to him as it would forever. But when she awoke, her decision was made. Clear and correct.

It had not been so difficult, after all.

She heard a light knock.

"Come in."

To her astonishment Lowell entered.

"Lowell!" Ariel slid from the bed and put on her robe. "Lowell, how nice of you!"

"I drove out with Dad this morning. He's downstairs talking with Uncle Martin. Very serious, I should say." She was quiet and poised, her smile friendly. "I wanted to see how you were, Ariel. I heard about—"

"About what?"

"That you'd gone down to the cellar to see if it was flooding. Nobody goes down to that old place, Ariel. Not even to store things any more. It floods all the time and then drains out. How are you?"

So it was to be light and pleasant. Ariel found herself warming again to this cool, quiet girl, as if the past had never happened. But it had happened.

"Would you like some coffee?" Lowell raised the blind. The room brightened.

"I'll get it later, Lowell. I'd like to talk to you."

Lowell faced her directly.

"You don't have to, Ariel. I saw Duncan's face last night when he thought you were in danger." She hesitated. "He's in love with you."

"Lowell, I never wanted . . ."

"No, let me finish. I don't mind it, Ariel. Honestly. I couldn't marry Duncan. I don't love him. Not the way I'd want to."

Lowell was staring out the window, twisting her hands.

"That's what I've wanted to say to you. It's all right. I never blamed you. None of that horrid gossip is true. I just couldn't marry him. And I knew that finally. The day before the wedding. At the rehearsal."

Ariel closed her eyes against the memory. She had made a fool of herself that day, coming down the aisle on Duncan's arm, the mock bride, in Lowell's place. She had revealed her feelings to anyone who saw her.

"You must have hated me for being so silly."

"Silly? Ariel, you did it beautifully. I thought then that you were the one who should be marrying Duncan. But you're too sophisticated. When I saw you drive away later with . . ." She caught herself. Lowell would never reveal herself to that extent, Ariel thought.

"When I saw you drive off, I thought about your life. So exciting. So glamorous." She gave a shy laugh. "That's a word Father hates. But it's real to me. Ariel, do you know what it is to live in this town all your life, with people you've always known, doing what they expect? And that's what marrying Duncan would have been. The same thing, over and over—until I just rotted away. I know there's a different world out there—I saw you and Nick going into it." She had spoken his name. Her face flushed. She sank into a chair.

Ariel went to her, put her arm around her shoulders, and laid her cheek against Lowell's hair.

"Lowell, dear. I have no interest in Nick. Or his world. I went with him that day because I had to get away. I made a mistake. But I learned one thing. He's not worth a second thought. He's . . ." she groped for a word. Not to hurt Lowell but to tell her. "He's selfish. He can be . . . unkind."

To her surprise, Lowell rose calmly, distantly, "That's because you don't know him, Ariel. How could you? You were only here a few weeks. I went out with him. A long time ago. I never wanted my father to find out. He doesn't like the Orlinis. But I'd go out with him again. If he ever asked me." She glanced shyly away. "Not that he ever would, I suppose. He's like that. But he's not what you say."

She went to the door and listened. The men's voices downstairs were clearer. "Dad's getting ready to leave. I'll go too. I'm glad you're all right, Ariel." She wore the same friendly smile that she had when she entered. "Please forgive me for talking about myself."

Ariel had underestimated this quiet, controlled girl. She had forgotten that Lowell, like herself, was a Roundtree.

"Don't knock it, Duncan. That's what people are saying."

Duncan looked hard at the editor of the *Thatcher Standard*, rose restlessly and walked to the window. He liked Frank McQuade. That was why he had come when McQuade's message reached him. He was bone-tired. He had worked through the night at Juno's Landing. His clothes were coated with mud. He had stubble on his face. And he did not like the turn the conversation had taken. It was not the only reason he was anxious to get away.

"If you're looking for heroes, leave me out," he snapped.

"I intend to." The short stocky editor understood a few things about Duncan Phelps. Better than most people in Thatcher. "But I'll run a piece on young Billy Haskell. Might do the kid some good."

"He could use it." Duncan returned from the window. "Big Moon and his wife have been handing out food to the workers all night. Their own. And Charlie Redwing, you know him?"

McQuade nodded. "He doesn't like being a hero, either."

"Yeah. But he's still down there, shoveling mud."

The door opened. Vivi Vale, her eyes on Duncan, put her head through the opening. It was her third interruption.

"Anybody for coffee?"

"Duncan?"

Duncan shook his head without looking at the girl. He heard the door close. He suspected that McQuade had not asked him to the office just to discuss the flood. His reporters must have been down there all night. He picked up his windbreaker.

"If that's all, Frank?"

"I've heard a rumor that you're leaving Thatcher."

So that was it.

"I'm taking the service at church next Sunday. Mrs. Wilcox asked me to."

"That doesn't quite answer me. I'd want to print the story if it's true. Or kill it, if it isn't."

"I've told you my plans. Through Sunday. What's on your mind, Frank?"

The editor looked at him closely. "Off the record, Duncan, are you quitting?"

Duncan sat down. There was no reason for surliness. If he could talk to any man in Thatcher, it was Frank McQuade. McQuade had been through it all. World War II. Pfc. Purple Heart. Ramagen Bridge. The Bulge. Places Duncan's generation never heard of. He still carried a silver plate in his head. He had called at the house the day before Duncan had left for Vietnam. No cheers. No flag-waving. Just a handshake, his face somber. *You won't change anything, Duncan, but it will change you. Hang loose, boy. And get back, somehow.*

"Am I quitting? I don't know, Frank."

"Is it the girl?"

"You know better than that!" He'd keep Ariel out of this at any cost.

"Yes, I think I do." He doodled on his desk pad. "When I got out of the service I went into the newspaper business. For a simple reason. I wanted to find out what in hell made people tick that they could get into such useless insanity as war." He paused. "I figured maybe you went into the ministry for the same reason."

Duncan watched the pad grow crowded with images.

"I knew guys who made bargains. A tight place. Bad pain. Or a bayonet coming at you. Get me out of this, God. And I'll . . . The kid either dies or he forgets. Maybe you didn't."

"Does it matter?"

"I think it does. When you're about to quit, you ought to know why."

"You don't approve of quitting?" The question came despite his will. Anxious as he was to escape, he sat half mesmerized by this glimpse of understanding.

"The hell I don't." McQuade dropped his pencil. "Any man who finds he's a round peg in a square hole ought to get out."

"That's it! That's the bloody hell of it." Duncan felt something breaking inside him. "Sure I made a bargain, like every other guy who got trapped in it. Sure, when I got out I was different. Also like every other guy who went through it. But back home nothing was different. Nobody had changed. Nobody but me. I couldn't understand that. I was a round peg in every god-damned square hole I could think of. Everything I thought of doing. Everything but this. The ministry. That's a laugh, isn't it? I wasn't out to serve God or make the big scene for mankind. I didn't even feel called. I was doing a job I felt good doing. That's a hell of a basis for your life's work, isn't it?"

McQuade sensed Duncan didn't want answers.

"There's nothing much else I want to do. But I'm not ready for this. I've found that out. I've got to preach next Sunday. I'm not good at it. But I'll get through it. Then . . . I don't know." He gave a helpless, boyish grin, surprising under the seams of fatigue on his face. "I just don't know. You print anything you want. I don't care."

"I can wait."

"Up to you. I'm going home and clean up."

McQuade rose. "Thanks for coming in, Duncan. Before you go, you might like to see this." He picked up a sheet of paper from the clutter on his desk.

Duncan had already put on his windbreaker.

"Do you know Julia Orlini?"

"I know who she is. But I never met her. I'm not much concerned with the Orlinis."

"They're a little hard to avoid. Read this."

Duncan glanced at it, read it, then reread it slowly.

"She brought it in this morning. She wants it run on the front page."

"Is she crazy?"

"Like a fox. She's a Thatcher. Or didn't you know? She's wanted Willard Roundtree's property for a long time. She thinks it's hers. She may just fasten her hands on it now."

"By claiming old Isaac Roundtree was an imposter? That was a hundred years ago."

"That's just it. Nobody's around to remember. Isaac Roundtree went off to the Civil War and then he went on to Tennessee. He didn't get back here to Thatcher for nearly ten years.

"He had with him a letter from Thatcher's lawyers notifying him that he had inherited the land. Nobody asked him for identification, I suppose. Now Julia's dug up records of a man named Isaac Roundtree, a discharged private from Thatcher, hanged in 1871 in

Missouri. Unless the Roundtrees have some kind of record, who's to deny it?"

The final Orlini outrage. Duncan felt a resurgence of his fury of last night. Ariel, her torn clothes, the terror she had known. Nick Orlini's hands on her, although she had denied that. He loved her with a tenderness he could not express even to himself. But Nick was still between them. He would settle his own account with Nick privately. He had said he would kill him. Men often said that idly. He was capable of it.

Frank was looking at him curiously. He came back to the present. "Bad business, Frank. When does Mrs. Orlini intend to take over?"

"She didn't say. Nick's supposed to run the operation. If he ever stays around."

"He's around."

"Is he? Julia Orlini said he went back to New York last night. Came in drunk and she can't stand that. But she has only herself to blame. Strong women, Duncan, the old silver cord—it's strangled more than one son. But I only print the news. I don't try to understand it."

"Are you going to print that story about Willard Roundtree's land?"

"Not until Willard confirms it. This morning he had only one word for it."

"What was that?"

"Poppycock. I wish I were as sure."

Duncan returned to the Wilcox house, learned that Cora Wilcox was resting, and, grateful that he could escape talk, changed and went out.

So for the time being he was to be deprived of the bare-knuckled punishment he ached to serve on Nick Orlini. But he would catch up with Orlini someday. A man needed one enemy to make him whole. Duncan felt nearer whole this morning than he had for many weeks.

And he knew, as he knew last night when he held

her chilled clinging body in his arms, that whatever the past, however she may have failed them both, she was what he wanted. He would never give her up. The coils of this town, its grudges, its gossip, its loyalties, and its hatreds stretched like an octopus toward him now. But without her? She was the completion of life, the fullness of it, beyond flesh, beyond the tightening of the clerical collar.

Did she still want him, need him, love him? There was no way of knowing. But she had come back. For him?

Ariel was standing in the doorway when he jumped from the car.

In three long strides, he was bounding up the steps and across the porch. She went into his arms as if she had never left them. He kicked the door closed behind them and buried his face in the dark masses of her hair. They stood, their bodies and minds locked beyond the measurement of time, aware only of the sweet, insistent pulsing within them. He searched her face.

"There's no one here," she said.

They went arm and arm up the narrow stairs. There was no furtive hurry, no stealthy madness. Only the rich oneness, the inevitability of what they had known from the beginning.

He closed the door to her bedroom and undressed her slowly, lovingly, as if afraid each touch would shatter their happiness. At last they lay together in the white-covered sleigh bed. With a groan his arms went around her, his lips moved over her.

The light of the short day faded. The young twilight slipped gently over the symmetry of their union.

It was nearly dark when they sat down together at the hand-hewn table in Willard Roundtree's kitchen. Ariel had made coffee, heated soup, and scrambled eggs.

"I don't want to leave until Uncle Willard gets here," she explained.

"Neither do I." Duncan ate with a hunger born of deep, masculine joy.

"I suppose we should talk."

"Why?" He laid down his fork and reached for her hand.

"Because we haven't, yet."

"I didn't miss it. Did you?" He grinned and she felt that nowhere else in the world would she find the happiness of this moment, in this old-fashioned, starkly bright kitchen.

"Besides," he continued, "I thought you'd said about everything you had to say last night. Or is it my turn?" He said it lightly but his face had lost its boyishness. "Ariel, I want you to try to understand one thing. These past weeks while you were in Paris—you and Orlini—I was eaten away with jealousy. All right, it's over. It's past. But I can be jealous, I will be—anytime there's a reason. If that's a confession of weakness, I stand guilty. But a man's jealousy is as strong, as powerful as his love. I don't think a woman understands that but I want you to." His eyes were warm on her. "Shall we talk any more or shall we . . . ?"

She slid from her chair, kissed him, and then faced him solemnly. "Duncan, this morning I came to a decision."

"Good. Always a sign you'll change your mind."

"Male ego!"

"I'm full of it."

"Duncan, please, I want to talk seriously. If we're married . . ."

"If? We're married already, my darling. There are a few essential public steps. Is that what's worrying you?"

She shook her head. "No. It's after that. Where are we going to live?"

"We'll have to work it out."

"I want to stay here with you in Thatcher."

He looked at her intently. "I don't think so."

"I mean it. Your work is here, your church. You belong here, Duncan."

"I don't belong any place where I can't make you happy. You've seen what this town can be like. It's hurt you cruelly. I've heard what happened on Halloween."

"Those were children!"

"Before that there was the gossip. Maybe all small towns gossip. But they've had too much to gossip about in Thatcher. No matter what the truth is, the seeds are planted. You don't think I'd ask you to endure that?"

"I'm not afraid of it." She moved to the window. Outside a half-moon outlined the hills. She turned to him fiercely. "If we don't live here, what would we be doing? Running away! That's what it would be! Running away! Somewhere. Anywhere. You'd work at something you don't believe in and I'd watch you . . . dwindling. And know it was my fault. Duncan, I want to stay here. You belong here. So do I!"

He loved her achingly, but she was not yielding. She would not be easy to sway. He loved her for that, too. She would need it all, if they were to stay in Thatcher. Yet he knew there was an elemental truth in what she said.

He heard a car in the distance. Willard, Thatcher, reality coming nearer. He had only a few moments to make sure of this happiness.

"We'll be married, Ariel. Where and when, you'll say. But as for where we'll live . . . will you come to church for my service next Sunday? Sit there among them all? Then tell me."

Chapter Three

Julia Orlini was giving a final house party in the lake-side house she would soon be leaving. She had stayed later than usual this year. Now that the Roundtree matter was settled, as she thought, it had amused her to fill the house once more with the chic, glittery, chattering people that were her life. She would meet them again soon enough in New York or Washington or London or wherever Ben expected her to be. Some were useful, some hangers-on, some merely entertaining. They were almost faceless to her, now. But they warmed the rooms. They would witness her triumph.

For Willard Roundtree had telephoned that morning. Would she see him? She had deliberately set the hour for six, when cocktails and curiosity would pique her party to its liveliest. She would be generous with Willard Roundtree but she was not above humiliating him, in his farmer's clothes and old truck. She had carefully not included Harlan Phelps. He was a fool. She always regretted her brief infidelities with inferior men.

She moved among her guests in clinging flame chiffon dinner pyjamas. She knew only one woman in a hundred could wear them. Turquoises and diamonds set in heavy silver hung from her ears, encircled her throat and wrists.

"Darling, you look divine!"

"I adore the new house. It's a fortress."

"It's a barony!"

"Why not, she'll soon own half the town!"

"We'll come and spend weeks, darling!"

Julia met each of them with the little laugh, the arch response she had long perfected. She glanced at the clock, heard it chime. A maid appeared at her elbow.

"A Mr. Roundtree to see you, madam."

It was exactly six.

"Show him into the den."

Willard elected not to sit. She would keep him waiting, he was sure. He looked at the matched sets of leather-bound books lining the shelves. He opened one; the pages were uncut. He listened to the brittle voices, the light tinkle of artificial laughter, and felt an inexplicable twinge of futility.

The excellent fit and tailoring of a dark gray business suit, the smooth silver of his hair, gave him the distinction that had been notable not so long ago in the superior courts of the state.

"I'm so sorry, Mr. Roundtree! My guests . . ." Julia stopped, looked at him. "My maid misunderstood me. I asked that you be shown right in!"

"I would rather say what I have to privately."

"I do understand. Won't you sit down?"

Instead he drew an envelope from his inner pocket.

"Mr. Roundtree." The long slender hand lifted graciously. "I don't want to bargain. I want to be generous. The land will come to me, of course. But I want to pay for it so there can be no more questions. Whatever you think is fair and equitable."

He opened the envelope and handed her its contents. She studied them. He saw again that Julia Roundtree was not stupid.

He explained gently: "Isaac Roundtree's discharge papers from the old Fourth Hartford Company, Connecticut Infantry, in the Civil War. And, as you see, his certificate of birth, August 8, 1843, Thatcher's Corners. I have spent two days in Hartford. I am assured they establish the identity of my esteemed ancestor."

Except for an added pallor, Julia showed no emotion.

"They had been stolen from Isaac Roundtree in a tavern in Maryland. The man who stole them was later hanged. But he had apparently some decency of heart and conscience, because he asked one of the witnesses to return Isaac's papers to him."

"And the War Department records?"

Willard smiled in his best court manner.

"Oh, come, Mrs. Orlini. The government is not always careful of these niceties. Nor is it infallible. It's easier to close a case with a wrong name than without any."

Julia's tone was the same as she used among her guests.

"How did you happen to come on all this?"

"In a box I had overlooked. The kind of metal box that holds family secrets."

Her laugh tinkled.

"Were there other secrets?"

He had to admit she was game.

"A few."

"You must tell them to me someday."

He smiled.

"I think they should stay with the land."

"Will you come in and have a drink?"

"I think not. Thank you."

She handed him back the papers and walked with him to the door, her head high and with that catlike grace that was her shield.

"I hear the French girl. . . ."

"Ariel?"

"Ariel. Yes. She is with you?"

"For a little while."

"I met her once. At my son's apartment."

If it was a threat, he was ready for it.

"So she told me."

"Did she?"

As abruptly as it had flashed, Julia Orlini's hint of venom died. She would have liked this substantial man, with his quality, his quiet sureness, for a friend. If that was not possible she did not want to part on a shabby innuendo.

A half smile revealed for an instant her vanished girlhood, her unfulfillment.

"I had arranged it. I would have liked Ariel for a daughter-in-law. My son, like his father, is—" she groped for the word, "restless."

She held out her hand.

"Goodbye, Mr. Roundtree."

His bow was courtly.

"Good night, Mrs. Orlini."

He knew as he went to his car why he had felt earlier a twinge of futility, of sadness. It was the waste which passed for living when, as he knew too well, the years were so brief. He had won but he had no sense of victory. He must be getting old.

The stone church was crowded.

The side windows with their simple, stained-glass figures filtered the morning light. Memorial windows, the largest, center right: To the memory of Henrietta and Isaac Roundtree from their children."

Two bowls of white chrysanthemums were the altar's only adornment. From the Bible on the lectern hung a wide, black ribbon.

Duncan faced the congregation in a plain black robe without surplice or trappings. His face was pale and serious as his glance slid over the full pews. Cora Wilcox in the first pew, shriveled into herself in grief. Martin and Edythe, Claude and Kim, in the traditional Roundtree pew, third left. He was grateful for Lowell's tactful absence.

He saw others. Hannah Poole, a large hat firmly set on gray curls; Gladys Beemer, her eyes in the hymnal, whether from embarrassment or Christian humility, he could not tell. His mother, proud and alone. Behind her, Frank McQuade, that humane skeptic; his wife; his daughter Phyllis with husband Craig, reluctant but present. Near the back, he could see Billy Haskell, uneasy in a tie. Next to the boy, Big Moon, self-conscious in a business suit, and Ira dangling her golden hoops.

In the last pew, beside Willard Roundtree, sat Ariel.

Duncan tried once to meet her eyes but she held her head high looking beyond him.

The hymn ended. Duncan walked to the first raised step, bowed his head to the altar, and turned to his congregation.

Ariel felt her heart pounding. It had to be this way; she had made that decision herself. Yet it seemed to her that the Duncan she knew had become someone else, separated from her by the very words he was there to speak. She thought back to the night when he had pleaded with her to run away, to put everything they had known behind them and start together somewhere, anywhere. She thought of the wild sweetness of their union at the farmhouse. But was anything worth this, even their passionate love?

Duncan began to speak.

"I will not take the pulpit this morning. I am not ready to fill the place of the man who spoke to you from it for so many years and with so much love. So the few things I have to say, I will say here, closer to whatever friends I may have today in this House.

"My text is taken from the Old Testament, Second Book of Samuel, chapter 1, verse 20.

'Tell it not in Gath, publish it not in the streets of Askelon.' "

A murmur rustled through the church. Duncan waited.

"My second text is taken from the New Testament, the Gospel according to St. John, chapter 2, verse 20. 'Everyone who doeth evil hateth the light!' "

Ariel clasped her hands together. The palms were damp and she was trembling. He would spare them nothing, not himself, not even her.

He began unsteadily. Then the caution, the uncertainty drained away. His voice soared. It was a deep voice, she realized, filled with the music of its conviction. She seemed to hear it, not from where he stood, but from the walls of the church, from the very stones themselves.

"An ancient evil rose from this town, flowed through the streets on a wind of gossip. And at last, in the darkness of the night, flung a deadly stone. I would rather see this lovely town of ours razed to rubble, if I thought this evil could ever return. I am here because I think we, all of us, can do better. If I am wanted here then you must know what I will do. I will meet with you here in this House. Or in any other house of God or man. There will no longer be walls here in Thatcher, neither walls of stone or brick, nor walls of old prejudice and cruel words. Where two or three of us are gathered, there any man, woman, or child will be welcome, whatever he believes. For if we are looking for a light, our search will be easier as we share it. I cannot talk to you of God today. Because I think at this moment no one in this town knows Him. I don't. Not yet. But I hope together we may find a way to the love and the goodness of His word."

Duncan stopped so abruptly that Ariel caught her breath. She was afraid to look at him through the silence, afraid to see a look of failure in his eyes. Then he spoke again, quietly, boyishly.

"I thank you for coming today."

Mrs. Haskell let the organ thunder. It would cover any stony silence, any embarrassing whispers.

When it died away, Duncan faced his listeners.

"There will be no public collection in this church. There is a closed collection box in the vestibule. However you may wish to use it," he smiled, "will not be told in Gath."

A ripple of warm near-laughter swept the pews. He has won, Ariel thought. On his terms.

Duncan took the single step down. He stood now at the level of the congregation.

"This church has stood in Thatcher two hundred and fifty-four years. The three other churches are nearly as old. I would like now to borrow a custom in

427

use among them all when the first settlers brought their foot warmers to these benches. It is called Publication of the Banns of Marriage."

Ariel felt herself go cold. He had not warned her. He was looking at her now, his hand outstretched, his face strong and so tender she thought she would not get to her feet. Willard helped her and she walked slowly past countless pairs of staring eyes up the aisle to where he stood.

Duncan nodded to the third pew. "Will the Senior Vestryman of the Church, Mr. Martin Roundtree . . ."

There was a second's pause. Martin rose, the old words returning to his mind. Standing between Duncan and Ariel, he uttered them.

"I hereby make known for the wisdom and approval of this congregation the intention of marriage between Duncan Phelps and my niece, Ariel Roundtree. If anyone knows just cause why this marriage should not take place, let him rise and speak now."

A silence met him like a held breath. "The ceremony will take place in this church on Wednesday next at three o'clock. It will be in the privacy of the two families but at the request of the young couple the doors of the church will remain open. May we have the blessing of God and this town on this marriage."

The wedding was so brief, so quiet that hardly anyone in the hushed crowds inside and outside the little church heard it. The Reverend James Scammel performed the ceremony, his voice as low and intimate as a professor of sermonizing could make it. Ariel wore a beige dress newly bought in Thatcher and held a small cluster of tea roses. Lowell stood beside her. Claude's eyes shone with tears. Kim slipped her hand into her mother's.

It was over.

An hour later, the newly washed green car slid from the white Roundtree house on West Street. Edythe put away the last remnant of a homemade wedding cake.

The starkness of the November hills lay open ahead when Ariel laid her head on Duncan's shoulder. He put a hand over hers.

"Forever," he said.

"Forever," she answered.

He stopped the car on the lonely road and took her in his arms.

Late that evening, after the wedding, Willard Roundtree sat alone, as he would always now, in the fire-lit room, and removed all the contents of the rusted metal box. The crumbling paper wrapping that had held Isaac Roundtree's returned wallet. An old-fashioned, diamond-and-pearl brooch of remarkable beauty. And Henreitta's unfinished diary.

He read again the final page of her delicate, schooled penmanship. The date, November 6, 1900.

"I loved him with all the passion I knew. I married him in my best sprigged gown to follow him anywhere on earth. But I know now that with all I had to give him, wanted to give him, my love was not enough. Is love ever enough for the long journey a woman takes with a man? Whatever destiny lies ahead for me . . ."

In a sudden splattering of ink, the sentence broke and hung like a torn cobweb.

With a sigh, Willard drew from the bottom of the box a single sheet of yellowed paper. It bore the faded bluntness of Isaac Roundtree's writing.

"The Devil came to me on a night when I was a stranger in a strange place. He tempted me and I succumbed. I hereby confess that, for my soul's salvation, I have at last conquered my base hunger and consigned this woman, whom I falsely wed, to the lower darkness from which she came. And with her, all records of myself and my sin. May God give me peace."

Willard reread the confession. He saw for an instant the satin-smooth skull in the earth cellar, carried now, no doubt with Henrietta's small bones, to the lowest darkness. He slowly shredded the yellowed paper and cast the fragments into the fire. They blazed, spiralled upward, and were gone.

He would think often of that long-ago anguish. And the progeny it had borne. Ariel, in her new, untested happiness. Lowell and her troubled depths. Claude and her unchanneled eagerness. And the others of this dark and passionate legacy, the Roundtree blood that ran wild and deep.

But the future, like the flames, kept its secrets.

The Roundtree Women

This saga offers unparalleled reading pleasure both in its entirety and in each individual volume.

Each novel depicts the compelling story of one of four Roundtree Women, descendants by blood and marriage of Henrietta Roundtree, whose story is contained in volume one but whose spirit is reborn in *The Roundtree Women.*

In addition to this volume,
in 1979 be sure to look for

Claude

Hester

Lili

Three brilliant novels—
to be savored separately or together.